Books in the Watervalley Series

More Things in Heaven and Earth

Each Shining Hour

The Splendor of Ordinary Days

For short stories and news about the illusory little town of

Watervalley,

visit us at

watervalleybooks.com

THE FULLNESS OF TIME

A Novel of Watervalley

-Jeff High

This one is for Dawn,

my best love story.

There was a time when meadow, grove, and stream,

The earth, and every common sight,

To me did seem

Appareled in celestial light.

...The things which I have seen I now can see no more.

...Whither is fled the visionary gleam?

Where is it now, the glory and the dream?

-William Wordsworth, *Intimations of Immortality*

He has made everything beautiful in its time. He has also set eternity in the human heart; yet no one can fathom what God has done from beginning to end.

-Ecclesiastes 3: 11

PRELUDE

Watervalley, Tennessee

Can you hear her? Close your eyes and listen...she's singing again.

The doors, the walls, the stones...they all hear her. They were slumbering, resting their ancient bones through the cold, unkind hours; the long, dormant halls of winter. But she is sleepless. Far above, she murmurs.

Her song is old and melancholy. Downward it floats, haunting the air of the old mansion. It is crackled, nostalgic, pushed through a funnel. You hear her, don't you? At first, it is a quaking, dreadful thing. And yet slowly, she calms you, pulls you in. You stay and listen because her voice is smoky and melodic. The tune is sultry, distantly familiar. It weaves around you, teases you, bewitches you. Soon, you are lost into it. Then languidly it fades and drifts away, leaving you drugged, breathless, wildly tormented with feelings both dark and jubilant.

Now you are addicted. You want more.

Fearfully, you wait. But there is nothing. All that remains are the doors, the walls, and the stones. They know her secret. For years, she has perfected her silence. But something has awakened her, and they know. They know the woman in the shadows is still there, still restless, still waiting...waiting for the fullness of time.

Chapter 1

ARRIVAL

It is a widely-accepted practice in Watervalley never to let tangible facts burden a good rumor. In my year and a half as the town doctor, I had learned that in the absence of valid information, the people of this remote community simply created their own. Such was the case regarding Matthew House.

As the new owner of Society Hill Manor, the local bed and breakfast, Matthew's imminent arrival to town had been a matter of great anticipation. But much to the dismay of the locals, in the first week of December, his car had oddly appeared in the small hours of the night and ever since he had been virtually invisible. Knocks on the door by welcoming neighbors had gone unanswered, mail was left in the box for days, and fallen leaves and limbs accumulated on the once stately grounds of the old estate. Quickly, the whispers grew.

As the days past, Matthew became the talk of street and store. Whenever a chance gathering of two or more occurred, the new B&B owner was the default topic of conversation, fueling a hunger for details that simply didn't exist. Ominous rumors began to permeate the village, seemingly floating on the menace of the air. Grand theories materialized daily, each more sinister than the last. Over time, repeated opinions became accepted reality, hardening yesterday's speculation into today's fact. Yet, despite the huddled debates, no narrative proved sufficient. Their words exhausted, the conversations invariably ended with silent, uneasy stares toward the ghostly mansion rising distantly above the pale, misty heights of Society Hill.

Converted to a bed and breakfast years ago, the old estate overlooked the entire town. A surviving icon of a wealthier time, the home was made of smooth-cut limestone and built in the style of a grand French Chateau. The surrounding trees and extensive grounds were enclosed by a tall wrought iron fence, placing it in a class of its own among the majestic houses on the Society Hill Historic Register. From this high vantage point, the imposing stone structure had stood sentinel for decades; quietly, secretly watching the ebb and flow of Watervalley life. Now, despite its new occupants, the ancient mansion seemed long in slumber. Veiled in the thin, bleak light of December, it sat lifeless, grey, mysterious.

In the second week after Matthew's arrival, three large moving trucks arrived under the cover of darkness along with a van full of workmen. There was a fury of lights and activity that went well into the night. But by morning, all was quiet. Days later, during the deep evening hours, other large trucks were seen pulling into the long-cobbled drive. Yet once again, when daylight arrived, the old estate sat in distant silence.

Further scandal arose from events that occurred in the third week after Matthew's arrival. Well after midnight one evening, neighbors noticed lights fluctuating on and off in the far corners of the house. Delivered packages and neighborly gifts continued to remain on the front porch, undisturbed. And the fact that Matthew had bought the B&B practically sight unseen and, now as a single parent, had abruptly moved his small family from South Carolina to Tennessee, only fueled further conjecture. By Christmas Eve the town was in a fervor. Speculation had grown to epic levels.

But I knew better.

Despite the hearsay that shadowed him, the first time I saw Matthew, there was little to suggest that he was a man of many secrets. In truth, his unkempt, almost comical clothing conveyed quite the opposite. Wearing a frayed sports coat, a wrinkled shirt, and a look of painful uncertainty, he was standing in the back of the Episcopal church, protectively holding the small hands of his two children. He seemed lost. The only note of pretentiousness in his otherwise ruffled appearance was a pair of black-trim designer glasses that framed a rather sophisticated and handsome face.

They were late, and the Community Christmas Eve Service had already started. While the thunderous pipe organ bellowed the opening prelude, he stood there for an uncomfortable, indecisive minute, surveying the packed house. He was searching, outwardly deliberating on whether to stay or depart. And as I watched him in those wavering moments, there was something transparent in the expressions on his face. He seemed to have a cautious, curiously vulnerable nature; the quiet, friendly manner of one who was, by all observations, entirely and authentically shy.

Despite his obvious hesitation, he finally assumed an air of resolve and shuffled his small troupe forward toward a partially open pew near the front of the sanctuary. But somewhere mid-journey the opening music stopped, abruptly. And, so did Matthew.

Moments before, the blaring peal of the organ had provided a kind of cover for his exposed passage. In the ensuing silence, heads turned, and all eyes fell to him and his son and daughter, stranded in the center aisle. Retreat was out of the question. Noticeably embarrassed, he lowered his gaze and gently ushered his children forward.

But his arrival was not well met.

The open space was at the far end of the pew, and the aisle seat was sternly guarded by Danforth K. Stanwell, a retired lawyer, and a notably pious old stiff who wore his haughty Episcopal devoutness like a Merit Badge. Cruel chance had delivered Matthew into the hands of one of Watervalley's most insufferable self-proclaimed blue-bloods.

Danforth was an old goat who prided himself as a WFF, a descendant of Watervalley's First Families whose ancestors had been Episcopalian since the crucifixion. He openly disdained the annual joint community service because the Baptists and Methodists tended to clap during the hymns and the Pentecostals held up their hand like they had a question. These reckless displays of emotion were a little too free-spirited for Danforth, who preferred the smells and bells decorum of the more rigid Episcopalians. With him, even the Baptist's choice of music was a little too frisky. A song like "Go Tell It on the Mountain," and its attendant clapping during the service was unthinkable to Danforth, but a perennial top ten for his Christian cousins. And while the people of Watervalley generally had a tradition of infinite courtesy, such was not the case with him. From my vantage point near the choir, I caught every nuance of the small drama between him and Matthew.

At first, Danforth coldly stared forward in a ploy to ignore Matthew's presence. Realizing the futility of this tactic, he slowly rotated his gaze toward the straggling threesome, clearly assessing them to be low-bred and shabby. Matthew offered a fleeting, acquiescent smile and made a gesture toward the open space at the end of the pew. Begrudgingly, Danforth turned and looked. Then, he again faced forward, crossed his arms, and offered a sullen nod of acknowledgment.

While Matthew whispered small apologies, he and his children awkwardly climbed across Danforth and the rest of his related ilk before squeezing into the available space at the far end. The small opening could only accommodate them by Matthew placing his daughter in his lap while her twin brother sat snuggly beside. As the service finally resumed, Matthew exhaled so deeply it made me think that for the previous ten minutes, he had been holding his breath underwater. From the very beginning, it was impossible to regard him with anything less than a melted empathy.

From what I had heard and by his presentation, Matthew House was in his late thirties, making him six or seven years older than me. He was of average height and modest build but with firm, straight shoulders. His hair was dark, thick, and floppy, falling lazily away from his forehead.

Conversely, his children were blonde with fair blue eyes and by appearance were about six years of age. Both were beautiful, especially the daughter, whose face had a sensitive, almost luminous delicacy. They sat silently, carefully absorbing the world around them with tender, watchful expressions. But in the balance, their appearance bordered on whimsical. Apparently, the two sibling's efforts at getting dressed had been halted at various levels of completion. Socks didn't match, hair was uncombed, and the little boy's untucked shirt looked conspicuously like pajamas. They were poster children for sponsorship on the Angel Tree. Matthew seemed unaware.

Even still, the glow of the twin's near-angelic faces against the soft candlelight brought a sense of fullness and warmth to the moment. Despite their mismatched clothing, there was about them a delightful, compelling aura of enchantment and sweetness; a sort of uncanny illumination of something beyond the veil. I was both amused and fascinated. For the longest time, I was powerless to draw my attention away.

As everyone rose for the opening carol, the two of them stood in the pew to be shoulder height with their father. Oblivious to the words, they slowly gazed around the sanctuary.

That's when I noticed the oddest thing.

They were searching the room and occasionally casting small, discrete, yet knowing glances between themselves. This curious endeavor was augmented by a guarded show of fingers indicating that something was being counted and then confirmed by the faintest of nods. The entire enterprise occupied them for only a brief minute or two. Afterward, as demonstrated by the daughter's small tug on Matthew's sleeve, the activity appeared to involve some need to report their findings. But Matthew was lost to another world and paid her no attention. The children, who apparently were accustomed to this absent reaction, exchanged a subtle shrug.

As the hour passed, Matthew bowed his head when appropriate, stood when instructed, and sang when required. On more than one occasion, he lifted his head slightly as if he were listening for some far-off voice. The balance of the time he seemed elsewhere. He had the soft, reflective manner of one whose days were occupied with the thought of loss. There was about him a kind of patient sadness, a tender melancholy that, mixed with his unassuming appearance, easily tugged at the hearts of those around him.

At one point in the service, as the choir sang "O Come, O Come Emanuel," a trace of unintended tears welled upon his face. Having quickly steeled himself, he carefully gathered up his son in his lap as well and, for the longest time, gently held both of his children as close as possible.

While the evening progressed, the largely unadorned and ordinary people of Watervalley discretely stole short glimpses of this quiet newcomer and his endearing twins. And with that, it seemed that one by one there was a softening of the eyes and a gathering warmth expanding toward the three of them, a swell of unspoken affection and understanding.

As the service closed and the melodious words of "Silent Night" echoed in the high rafters, the packed sanctuary overflowed with a reflective joy; a heartfelt reminder of the richness of the season and of shared lives. Matthew's entrance into the life of Watervalley could not have been more perfectly timed. Filled with spontaneous holiday cheer, the entire town now looked upon him and his children with a yielding, tender regard. The gossip and hearsay had been nonsense, for there was nothing in Matthew House's nature that spoke of calculation or pretense. Thankfully, that evening, the ruinous myths surrounding his reclusive behavior largely vanished.

But on reflection, all that was actually known about Matthew at the time was that his wife had passed away earlier in the year, leaving him a widower with six-year-old fraternal twins. He had taught classical languages at the College of Charleston. And, for some still unknown reason, he had bought the old Society Hill Bed and Breakfast although he had no previous experience as an innkeeper.

Nevertheless, there at the Christmas Eve Service, he was seen for what he was…a kind and intelligent soul doing his best to start a new life, care for his precious children, and bravely suffer the loss of a beloved wife. After observing his rather unceremonious arrival, his disheveled appearance, and his endearing albeit, slightly distracted regard for his darling twins, the people of Watervalley filled in the blanks of Matthew's life with a more charitable, gentler narrative.

For me, as I watched him that evening, beyond any doubt, Matthew House presented as one whose story and personality were readily on the surface. This was not a man who harbored any great surprises or was fueled by any manner of cloaked agenda.

I couldn't have been more wrong.

Chapter 2

CONNIE

I had resolved to introduce myself to Matthew as soon as the service ended, hoping to shield him from what I feared was a certain inevitability. While most of the people of this rural farming community had a careful friendliness and politeness, there were also those who saw the new B&B owner as social currency. These snobbish few were forever vigilant to the clarion call of upward mobility. To their thinking, association with a newcomer of the right breeding and education could prove highly advantageous. As might be expected, in the previous weeks, these same society butterflies were the most maliciously vocal regarding his earlier seclusion. But now that he had made an appearance, all was forgiven. Matthew was fair game.

Unfortunately for me, and maybe for Matthew as well, I had a job to do. I was responsible for pumping the pipe organ.

Years ago, the Episcopal church had retrofitted the massive old organ with an electric motor that filled the pipes with air. But it had gone out during the rehearsal earlier that afternoon. I knew this because I was there, leaning against the rear wall, waiting while my fiancé, Christine, practiced with the choir. The original pump handle was the only back up left. The second the organ motor went out, I should have backed up and left also.

Suddenly, all eyes were upon me for help. In truth, I wanted to say no, to make up some excuse, to devise an outright fib if need be. But then I would be telling a lie in church, which –I'm quite certain – doubled the fines. So, even though I held the esteemed position as the town doctor, was a Summa Cum Laude graduate from Vanderbilt University Medical School, and privately thought of myself as a reasonably important guy, the whole choir and apparently, the Holy Ghost as well, thought otherwise. The lowly, laborious, sweaty task of pumping the pipe organ had fallen to me.

But the real problem that evening was Sadie Jean Armstrong, the Episcopal Church organist, who insisted on playing a closing anthem while everyone departed. A lovely idea except for the fact that no one was leaving. The Watervalley locals, who inherently possessed a certain carefree attitude to time, even on Christmas Eve, were all standing in the aisles; laughing and chatting and enjoying a bit of gossip about relatives, or the weather, or "how's your back." So, there I was, trapped, pumping away at the long wooden handle like a galley slave.

And for some reason, Sadie Jean wouldn't quit playing; impulsively pounding out one Christmas Carol after another. My attempts to get her attention proved useless, receiving only the occasional indifferent glance. A slow, dreadful realization washed over me. This was payback for recent events.

Sadie Jean was an accomplished organist and knew all the hymns by heart. But she was old enough to have gone to the prom with Eisenhower. Until recently, she had been driving an ancient Buick that was about the size of a river barge, a car that was easily recognized around town by the permanently flashing left turn signal. After the third rear-end collision in as many months, I had performed an eye exam on Sadie Jean, determining that she was so blind she couldn't tell whether the car in front of her was using its brake lights or perhaps was on fire.

At my recommendation, the family had taken her car keys. So as sweat rolled down my face, Sadie Jean played away, occasionally grinning at me under a thin veneer of smug politeness.

Simultaneously, I had to bear witness to Matthew's desperate plight. As soon as the final "Amen" was said, Polly Shropshire, who was a WFF snob by marriage, approached him at Socialite warp speed. Within seconds she had him cornered with the deft skill of a seasoned sheepdog. Polly was a rotund, difficult, and meddlesome old bird who wore heavy face powder and colorful but ridiculous hats. With her rather high-brow, haughty voice she had the uncanny ability to talk without ever moving her jaw or lips. Under different circumstances, a wooden dummy was the only thing separating Polly from a life in show business.

Others milled around, hoping for a chance to politely welcome the new innkeeper. But Polly, with her probing inquiries, was undeterred. Being the first to have the skinny on Matthew would be a grand coup, and she felt it her calling to vet this newcomer properly. The little people could just wait.

Under Polly's incessant questioning, Matthew's face looked like he was passing a kidney stone. His entire body language spoke of naked discomfort, as he did his best to edge away graciously. I began to feel a collective embarrassment for Polly's brashness and the impression she was making. Some of the crowd had cleared out, but there was still a considerable group seeking an opportunity to speak to him.

These were the everyday people of Watervalley. People who were not too good or fine or proud and who, unfortunately, unlike

Polly, shied away from any hint of rudeness. Painfully, she remained insolent to everyone else, and her imprudent inquisition continued. The situation was getting out of hand. I searched for Christine to possibly intervene, but she was nowhere to be found.

Then a miraculous parting of the "imminent-social-disaster" waters occurred. Emerging from the crowd was the one person in all of Watervalley who had the panache, the harmony of exchange, and the natural elegance needed to properly handle this awkward situation with delicacy, ease and grace; the one person of refined etiquette who could gently and judiciously find just the right words to intercede on Matthew's behalf...my housekeeper, Connie Thompson.

Connie was a lively, robust black woman with a brilliant mind, a no-nonsense demeanor, and a heart of gold. She was also surprisingly and decidedly wealthy. In this small town, she was beloved by most and feared by many. She was a force to be reckoned with.

Still in her choir robe, Connie walked up to Polly, quietly took her by the arm, and spoke in a soft, instructional voice. "Polly, sweetie. I don't know if you heard that little buzzer go off, but your time is up."

Polly was aghast. "And what are you saying?"

Connie tightened her grip, remaining calm and firm. "I'm saying we'd all like to have the opportunity to meet this nice gentleman. Come along, dear and let some of the other folks introduce themselves."

This choice bit of guidance served to finally unhinge Polly's padlocked jaw, which dropped so hard her pearls rattled. "Why, I'm simply trying to make Dr. House feel welcome!"

With quiet authority, Connie led her away. But I could see that she had grown weary of Polly's resistance. "Umm hmm, I'm sure you are, honey. But I'm thinking you look a little hungry. Might be a good idea for you to go swallow a great big bite of 'hush.'" Then, for added emphasis, Connie dipped her chin and peered over the top of her gold inlay glasses, making missile-lock eye contact.

Polly's mouth quivered indignantly. She stiffened her neck, trying to regain her fortitude. But ultimately, she withered under Connie's stern glare. Incensed, she spoke defensively. "I was just asking him a few questions. I don't see the harm in that."

As they moved out of earshot, Connie released her and spoke in a kindly and engaging voice. "Why Polly, darling. There's no harm in that at all. But if you truly want to know so much about him, invite him over to dinner so you can get to know him on your own time." Having said this, she de-glossed into a breezy monotone: "Knives and forks will be on hand, and you can dissect him properly." Connie's eyes tightened, accentuating her point. Polly bristled but kept her silence, further wilting under the scrutiny. Satisfied, Connie nodded and turned away, but not before energetically remarking, "By the way, sweetie. Love your hat."

Meanwhile, Sadie Jean had played her way through a fourth Christmas Carol and seemed to be gleefully itching for more. She was canvassing the room like she might start taking request from the crowd. Enough was enough. Before she could start a fifth, I stepped away from the handle, waved, and spoke quickly. "Well, it's been fun. Have a Merry Christmas!"

She was caught off guard with a gape-jawed face that quickly hardened into a baleful and disgusted stare. Indignantly, she snorted and played on. Within seconds the notes faded. The pressure in the bellows was exhausted. It didn't matter. So was I.

Grinning complacently, I kept walking. But Sadie Jean was not to be outdone. Coolly, she reached over and pushed a button on the electronic console beside the organ, filling the church with music...something she could have done a hundred and fifty organ pumps ago. While the sound system played "The First Noel," Sadie Jean was having the last laugh. The little Christmas witch.

By now the remaining crowd had loosely formed an ad hoc column leading up to Matthew. While one by one the kind people of Watervalley greeted him with polite courtesy, his two children clung closely behind him. The exchanges were brief and affable, driven by a sincere desire to welcome him to the community. Curiously, however, Matthew handled it well. He managed to put on a face of appropriate cheer and, despite his previously reserved nature, it was clear that he was practiced in social exchange. There was about him a kind of pleasant warmth that easily received the widely varying train of well-wishers. I stood at a distance and waited.

But a moment later I was surprised by someone embracing my right elbow. It was Connie. Staring straight ahead, she held my arm and spoke in a voice rife with mirth. "My, my. You were awfully cute up there pumping on that handle. Reminded me of a monkey grinding an organ. Would it be okay if I called you 'Monkey Boy' for the rest of the holiday season?"

"Funny. Would it be okay if I made a Piñata in your likeness?"

"Humph," Connie giggled, delighted with herself. "Cool your heels, doctor. I'm only teasing. Estelle doesn't have a patent on having a little fun sometimes."

Estelle was Connie's flamboyant and colorful younger sister. Normally Connie was quite starched and serious, making the two of them polar opposites.

"Yeah, well… sometimes I have a hard time remembering if you're the good sister or the evil one."

Unaffected, Connie responded casually. "Careful, doctor. Don't make me have to smack you in the Lord's house."

"Hey, by the way, nice save earlier with Polly Shropshire."

She shook her head. "Poor, poor, Polly. She's got more issues than Reader's Digest. I remember when she first moved to town after marrying Clayton, God rest his soul. Despite his family name she's never felt like she belonged. First thing she did was claw her way into the High Society Book Club. Over the years she's been President of the Junior Auxiliary and Chairman of the Benefit Ball. But none of that's ever made her happy. Now she just hands out misery like they were complimentary breath mints."

I grinned and folded my arms. We fell silent, content to observe Matthew until the crowd thinned. I felt for him. Being new to Watervalley could be daunting. I knew from experience.

"I guess I was lucky, Connie. I had you to hold my hand those first few months."

"Humph," she replied. "Say what you will about the hand holding, doctor. But you and I both know it had more to do with you being all ogle-eyed with a pretty brunette. In fact, as I remember, she cast her little spell on you exactly one year ago tonight, out on the front steps of this church." Connie snickered, proudly content in the unquestioned truth that I had been thoroughly love-struck by Christine Chambers.

I responded coolly. "Eh, maybe." But who's to say it wasn't that world-famous Connie Thompson cooking. If you hadn't been around my diet would probably consist of peanut butter and Milk Duds."

Connie nodded, regarding me with a sullen, sideways glance. "Might be more truth to that than should probably be told. Which, by the way, reminds me. Given your upcoming nuptials, you and I need to have 'The Talk.'"

I turned toward her, searching. "The Talk?"

Connie was aloof, staring straight ahead. "Umm-hmm. The Talk."

"What do you mean, 'The Talk?'"

She crossed her arms. "I mean just what I said, 'The Talk.'"

I rubbed my chin for a moment. "Okay, Connie. I'm not sure whether I've mentioned this in passing but, I'm actually a licensed physician. So, I think I've already got a pretty good handle on the whole 'The Talk' subject matter."

"Oh, good heavens! What is it about men that automatically reduces every conversation to the topic of sex?"

"Are you allowed to say that word in church?"

"Knock it off, doctor. 'The Talk' is not about sex."

"Okay. Gee. Ceasefire."

I exhaled slowly, thinking. I had no idea. "Well, if that's the case, then what is it about?"

Connie turned and lifted her chin, appraising me stiffly through her glasses. Her only response was a curt, "You'll see."

I shrugged. "I think I'd rather not. This is starting to sound like the mother of all teachable moments?"

Connie's stiff demeanor melted. She smiled and spoke instructively. "Well, my, my, my. Nothing gets past you. And here I thought your IQ was barely room temperature."

We again stood silently, taking in Watervalley's grand welcome to Matthew House. "So, what's your opinion of the new B&B owner?" I inquired.

"Too soon to tell. Seems to be a little introverted for the hospitality business. Something's not right there."

"Oh, good grief. Not you, too?"

"What?"

"The poor fellow likes to keep to himself, so that translates to there being something wrong with him."

"No. That's not it."

"What then?"

"Not sure. But I'll figure it out."

I let the conversation stand at that, unconvinced of Connie's assertion. My attention was drawn to Matthew's children. "Beautiful little boy and girl, don't you think?"

Connie nodded. "They certainly are, even if they are dressed like they come from the land of misfit toys."

"So noted."

With growing curiosity Connie began to watch the two children who once more were buried in a private conversation, quietly pointing to distant corners of the choir loft and sanctuary before whispering behind a cupped hand. Something in their actions was mesmerizing. Connie was being drawn in.

Following the gestures of their small fingers, she began searching the high rafters for the object of their secretive exchange. But there was nothing to be seen. It was all just an endearing game of imagination typical of young children. Connie, however, seemed to have other ideas. Her gaze tightened, and she smiled sweetly and cleverly, lightly nodding her head in a manner that I would be hard pressed to explain.

The line had finally dwindled, and I started to migrate toward the end. But something in Connie had changed. She hesitated and spoke abruptly. "Luke, I'll make my introductions later. Why don't you stay and speak to Matthew? I'll go on over to your house and start getting everything ready for the Christmas gathering."

"You sure? I'm guessing Christine, and her mom have already headed that way. They've probably got things under control."

"No. I'll visit him later. But I think it's important that the two of you meet."

I deliberated. She was stonewalling her true thoughts. Her behavior was odd, off balance. But I knew it was useless to press her and gave her an easy out. "Oh, I get it. I know what you're up to. You haven't wrapped my Christmas gift yet."

Immediately, her prior uneasiness vanished into a breezy indifference. "What makes you think I got you a gift at all?"

I took her arm in escort fashion, and we ambled up the aisle. "Because, Constance Grace Thompson, it's common knowledge to everyone in the valley that you completely and absolutely adore me."

She was unaffected, offering only a dispassionate "humph."

"I know, I know...sometimes you get a little mushy, and it's embarrassing, but I realize you simply can't help yourself. It's just your bubbly nature."

Connie rolled her eyes. "I'll give you a gift of fifty dollars right now if you'll just shut yourself up."

I ignored her, continuing with great ceremony. "And, even though that tough exterior of yours could probably deflect a small caliber bullet, we both know that you're a caring, considerate person; the kind who takes gift giving seriously...selecting something that is unique, tasteful, and, in my case, absurdly expensive."

Connie remained unaffected. "I see. Any other details I should consider?"

"Hmm, age-appropriate, too, I guess."

We had reached the narthex doors. Connie spoke dryly. "Then I'll be sure to get you some crayons and a coloring book."

"Okay. Good talk."

She stepped away, smothering a cunning grin. "Let me know what you think of our newcomer."

Chapter 3
INTRODUCTIONS

By the time I returned to the front of the church, the last well-wisher had bid goodbye. A few volunteers were working their way through the pews, re-shelving the hymnals and collecting the random programs that were left behind. Matthew was down on one knee preparing to button his daughter's coat but rose as I approached.

"Hi. I'm…"

"Luke Bradford," he said, finishing my introduction for me.

I stopped abruptly and smiled, slightly surprised. "Yes, that's right."

He held out his hand. "Matthew House."

We shook. "I believe it's Dr. Matthew House, is it not?"

He shrugged in a gesture of deflection. "Technically, yes. But that's not too important here. I um, I was a language professor."

I nodded my understanding. "Welcome to Watervalley."

"Thank you. It's good to be here finally."

"Getting settled in, I hope?"

He hesitated. "Um, yes. Yes, we are." There was a noted brevity in his response, leaving a void in the exchange. I filled in the silence.

"Well, Watervalley's not exactly Charleston, but it grows on you."

He responded with an amiable nod but offered nothing else. I leaned to the side to catch a glimpse of the twins. Instinctively,

Matthew understood my inquiry and brought them around in front. "These are my children, Adelyn and Andrew." He rested his hands on the back of their heads and spoke in a voice that was patient and undemanding. "Guys, this is Dr. Bradford."

I bent down, resting my elbows on my knees. "Hi, I'm delighted to meet both of you."

They responded with a cautious "Hi."

Up close, the twins were even more enchanting. Despite their tempered reserve, both had faces of radiant life. I smiled, and as I stood, the daughter tugged on her father's sleeve. Her voice was soft and lilting, with music in it. "Daddy, can we go walk through the benches?"

"Sure sweetheart. Just stay where I can see you."

They scampered off like limber little elves.

"They're quite beautiful."

Matthew looked down, clearly warmed by my comment. "Thanks. They're good kids, but very independent. They can be a handful."

I nodded. Another awkward pause followed. The topic of Matthew's children seemed the natural prelude to a proper mention of his departed wife.

"I uh, I understand you're a recent widower. I'm sorry for your loss."

Matthew said nothing but rather cleared his throat, tightly pressing his lips together with a slight nod of acknowledgment. I realized that this was his first Christmas without her and I sensed that he would rather avoid the topic. To his credit, he had the presence of mind to change the subject.

"So, tell me about Watervalley."

I scratched the back of my head. "Not a lot to tell, really. You'll fit right in, you know, so long as you realize that the use of chewing tobacco is a cherished way of life."

His mood lightened, and we talked on, exchanging the usual small discourse of new acquaintances. And as we spoke, there rose between us the first faint validations of a fair camaraderie; an unspoken, deeper layer of understanding shared by those of broadly similar geographic and academic backgrounds. I sensed that with me, Matthew was less guarded; desiring to cautiously explore some matters of confidence. Nevertheless, the conversation was framed by sensitive boundaries that neither of us wanted to cross. He seemed to be choosing his words carefully.

"The people here are a lot more diverse than I expected. Some of them are rather proper."

"Yeah, and some of the rather proper ones are rather improper."

He smiled and tilted his head appraisingly to one side, noting his understanding. I gestured toward the narthex, and we headed in that direction.

As we walked, Matthew absently rubbed his chin, his eyes cast reflectively toward the floor. He seemed preoccupied, musing pensively, his words tinged with unease. "I was a little caught off guard by the reception at the end. I doubt I'll remember half of their names."

"I wouldn't sweat it. It's mostly a farming community. The people here are pretty much salt of the earth with a few notable personalities sprinkled in the mix."

He glanced up at me briefly, absorbing my assertion before returning his ponderous gaze downward. "Yeah, there was one fellow. Seemed nice enough but boy was he peculiar. Said he was with the local radio station."

"That's Gene Alley, and yeah, peculiar is an understatement. He's got a metal plate in his head; an old Vietnam injury. But, somehow, that doesn't quite seem to explain it."

"Recreational pharmaceuticals?"

"Hmm, I almost wish. That would make for an easy answer. But there is no evidence to that end. Gene's unusual brand of weirdness comes from deep within his DNA. Still, all in all, he's a good guy. His radio show is actually syndicated."

"Really?"

"Yeah, he's gets e-mails from little towns all over the country and, given Gene's ethereal strangeness, probably even from a few parallel universes."

In keeping with his quiet manner, Matthew politely grinned at my comment. But while doing so, there was also a moment's hesitation; a quick tightening of the eyes at something I had said.

As we arrived at the narthex door, Matthew turned and surveyed the empty room. "Hey Luke, one other thing. The fellow they honored tonight, Luther Whitmore was his name, I believe. What was that all about?"

"It's kind of a nice tradition. Every year at the Christmas Eve service, the town honors one of their own. Luther's a long-time native. But it came out recently that he was a big-time war hero. He's the most highly decorated soldier in the town's history. Never said a word about it for forty years. So, rightfully, the town has a tremendous reverence for him. The honor was well deserved."

"Interesting. So, who received the honor last year?"

I chuckled. "Well, funny you should ask. Actually, I did."

"Well, that's impressive."

"Eh, not really. In the fall of last year, the town got hit by a strange flu epidemic. I managed to figure out the cause. It was just a timing thing."

"Must have been a big deal to them."

I was evasive and looked away. "Hmm, hard to say. The truth of the matter is this. Every year, when picking the person that has touched their lives the most, the people of Watervalley are told to vote from their heart. That being said, the real winner for the last three years running has been Peyton Manning. But the rules say that you must physically reside in the county. So, I kind of lucked out."

Matthew smiled. "Luther Whitmore's been trying to get in touch with me the last couple of weeks." He paused, again choosing his words carefully. "I've been uh, pretty busy and haven't had a chance to get back with him. Any idea what he wants?"

"Sure, an interview. Luther is editor of the local paper. You're the new owner of Watervalley's only bed and breakfast. That's big news for this little community. The stuff that normally hits the front page includes things like 'Someone saw a squirrel.'"

"So, I take it Watervalley is not a hotbed of tourist activity either?"

"Matthew, I don't want to burst your bubble, but most Tennessee Travel Guides describe us like this: 'Watervalley: Don't bother.'"

"That bad, huh?"

"Well, typically, over the course of the summer, at least ten or eleven visitors will flock to Watervalley. Of course, they're usually lost and just asking for directions to Lynchburg and the Jack Daniel's Distillery."

Matthew nodded in what was now becoming a notably consistent dry manner, seemingly unaffected by this observation. I thought this strange but let it pass. "So, what are your plans? Think you'll be opening up Society Hill after the New Year?"

For the first time in our conversation, his well-moderated demeanor eluded him, and an uneasy look was cast upon Matthew's face. He made a gesture of feigned uncertainty, and his eventual response seemed to mask his deeper thoughts. "There are a lot of renovations that I'd like to do first. So, it's hard to say. Might be a while."

This was only a modest surprise. The previous owner, Lida Wilkens, had left the old mansion in generally good order. But even she had admitted that upkeep was a cash hemorrhage and that many repairs were needed. She had gladly sold the bed and breakfast so she could focus her efforts on the Depot Diner, Watervalley's local restaurant. I had no idea of Matthew's financial status, but the near-term profitability of the inn looked rather slim. He seemed unconcerned.

"Well, okay then. Hey, just out of curiosity, how did you happen to know my name?"

"I, uh…I've been spending a lot of time online lately researching the B and B. One thing led to another, and I came across the newspaper article from last year announcing your arrival to town. So, is Watervalley home for you now?"

My response was not immediate. Unknowingly, Matthew had asked a painfully troublesome question. My life in Watervalley was rich with love and purpose. But the imprint of earlier ambitions, long consigned to the far reaches of my mind, still plagued me. He had chanced upon a small but deeply buried regret.

I dreamed of doing medical research.

Despite the daily rewards of being a small-town doctor, sometimes I pondered this different calling and wondered if I was employing my talents to their highest use. But the turns in my life had brought me here and, regardless of my aspirations, being the town doctor was the only future available to me. So, I had pushed these thoughts aside and did not speak of them, even to my fiancée, Christine.

"Did I ask the wrong question?"

I surfaced from the temporary fog.

"Oh, sorry. It's a bit of a complicated question. I'm about halfway through a three-year commitment to the town wherein I agree to be a doctor, and they agree to bail me out of debtor's prison. They're paying off my college loans, two hundred grand worth. I originally thought I'd do my time and then return to Vandy to do medical research. But, Watervalley has grown on me and, turns out, I'm now engaged to one of the locals. So, right now, looks like I'm here for the duration."

"Congratulations. Was she here tonight?"

"Yeah, in the choir. She sang the advent solo."

"I remember. Pretty girl."

"Thanks." Under different circumstances, I could have spoken at length about Christine. But all conversations, even ones of endearment, invoke comparisons. And I was sensitive not to once again trespass near the subject of his deceased wife and what was surely a boneyard of tragic memories.

By now the last of the volunteers were ready to leave. Matthew called out to his children, and as they came scampering toward him, an idea struck me.

"Listen, I don't know if you have plans or some Christmas Eve tradition, but a sizeable group of friends is gathering at my house. I'd be delighted for you and the twins to join us. I'm sure they'd all love to see you."

Matthew's response was quick and decisive. "Thank you. But, no. I uh, I probably need to get the children to bed soon." As he spoke, he reached down and tenderly clutched their hands. His daughter immediately tugged on his sleeve and spoke in a whispered voice.

"Daddy?"

"Good to meet you, Luke. Hopefully, we can catch up again soon."

On impulse, he released his daughter's hand and shook mine.

"Same here. Hope you guys have a Merry Christmas."

When once again Matthew clasped his daughter's hand, she tugged on his sleeve a second time.

"Daddy?"

I was turning to leave when Adelyn implored her father for a third time.

"Daddy?"

Just as before, Matthew regarded her with caring patience. "Yes, sweetheart."

"Guess how many?"

"I have no idea?"

"Guess."

"Five hundred."

She wrinkled her perfect nose. "No, silly."

"Seven hundred."

"Stop."

"I give up. How many?"

"Seven," replied Adelyn.

But upon hearing this, her brother, Andrew, spoke in an expressive whisper. "No there wasn't, Adelyn. There were eight. One was in the choir."

Adelyn paused a moment and counted on her fingers. Then she nodded in confirmation. "Andrew's right, Daddy. There were eight."

"Okay. Eight. That's very good."

I had stood silently and listened to this curious exchange, quite certain I was missing something.

Matthew read my face. "Oh, it's a little game they play where they count the angels." He shrugged, clearly wanting to make light of the matter. "Kind of a kid's thing, I guess."

The two children nodded in confirmation. It took me a moment to process this before lifting my eyebrows and speaking in an animated voice. "I see. That's very good. Very good, indeed. I guess a church is probably an excellent place to look around and take an angel inventory." My response had been okay up until the last comment which likely was about as dumb as it sounded. The children cast confused looks toward their father, who stood quietly, offering nothing further.

For an embarrassing moment, I froze; my open mouth swallowing air like a fish. Finally, pursed my lips together, smiled, and spoke with an emphatic nod. "Right. Okay. Merry Christmas."

With that, I turned and departed into the narthex as Matthew bent down to button his daughter's coat. I was about to push my way out the large entrance doors when I distinctly heard Adelyn speak in the loud whisper that children often use. No doubt, she thought I was out of earshot and unable to hear her confidential message. I was on the third step down when her exact words registered. I stopped.

Oblivious to the December cold, I cautiously looked back over my shoulder at the massive, solemn entry doors to the Episcopal Church, replaying her words in my head and reassuring myself that I had heard them correctly. Her comment was profoundly odd. I endeavored to understand, to assign meaning. But no clear answer prevailed.

Adelyn had whispered, "This time, Mommy wasn't one of them."

Chapter 4

THE LETTER

Adelyn's whispered declaration was curious, but after giving it a moment's reflection, I resumed my steps toward the car, thinking no more of it. Despite the chill of the air, I was wrapped in a mild euphoria, warmly anticipating my arrival to Fleming Street and a house filled with the laughter and cheer of good friends.

Yet, the past rode along with me during that short drive home. Christmas Eve always stirred memories of my lost parents. I was an only child, and from the age of twelve, I had been forever tainted by their sudden and tragic death. Over the years there was always some part of me that was fragmented and reluctant; an outsider who insulated himself, least I once again be vulnerable to such a devastating wound.

But during my time in Watervalley, I had come to realize another hard truth. A totally isolated heart is not only unattainable, but it is also inherently self-destructive. Something in our design programs us to seek out at least one intimate with which to entrust our thoughts, our concerns, our longings. Our sanity demands it. I had come to think of it as "the need for one."

As the car eased slowly from streetlight to streetlight, my mind was lost in reflection.

On the occasions when I made house calls to the remote corners of the valley, I would sometimes chance upon those whose circumstances availed to them a perfect seclusion; some by choice, others not. Yet upon closer observation, the lack of that one confidant came at a price; it left all of them with gaps that needed to be filled and even sometimes, a kind of small madness. Often the imbalance would be subtle, surfacing as an odd eccentricity or a peculiar outlier in their personality. But it was a hidden torment that forever robbed them of contentment. For most of my life, I had been a loner. I knew the symptoms well.

Adrift in this netherworld of introspection, I suddenly realized that I was sitting in my driveway, unaware of my arrival. Full reality set in when I noticed that someone was standing alone in the faint reaches of the front porch light, waiting. It was John Harris... the man, who, for better or for worse had become my best friend in Watervalley.

Wealthy, retired, and in his late fifties, John was a native of the area. He was a tall, ruggedly handsome fellow with penetrating eyes and a devilishly sharp wit. He was the most intimidating man I had ever met. He held a doctorate in chemical engineering and for many years had worked for DuPont as well as teach at the college level. He listened more than he talked and knew more than he said. With his imposing stature and hard demeanor, he radiated sheer presence.

In decades past, he had been a quiet, selfless leader in the community. But that had changed two years earlier with the tragic loss of his wife to cancer. By the time I arrived in Watervalley he was a brooding and reclusive alcoholic. Nevertheless, we had forged a strong friendship.

He had a magnificent modern house of wood and glass situated among the high hills that rimmed the valley. From the vantage of his Adirondack chairs, we had enjoyed many evenings of shrewd exchange and friendly banter. As the months passed, John had largely turned his drinking around and modestly re-engaged in the life of the town.

My fiancée, Christine, was John's niece. Even though my long talks with John had become less frequent, he remained my closest friend. Perhaps more than anyone in Watervalley, John knew me. He also knew about the letter, a matter that I had permanently dismissed and, as well, a subject that I had never mentioned to Christine. As I excited my car, I had no idea that that decision was about to hauntingly come home to roost.

I breathed in a large draft of the cold December air and walked toward him. Inside, my normally quiet cottage home was a riot of conversation, music, and celebration. The presence of so much merriment washed away my reflective mood, consuming me with a light-hearted air.

The magic would be short-lived.

"Evening, Professor Harris. Not sure you got the memo, but I think the party is actually inside the house."

"Merry Christmas to you too, smartass."

I laughed. We shook hands.

He was holding a heavy tumbler half full of eggnog. The unmistakable smell of bourbon wafted in the air. "Gee, John. Looks like your holiday glow has been enhanced by an accelerant. How many of those have you had?"

He took a healthy swallow, emptying his glass and offering little more than a patronizing sneer. "More than a little and less than enough."

"Nice. Good answer. Well, when vertical gives way to horizontal, you're welcome to the couch. Just make sure no one is sitting on it. The lumpy feeling will be your clue."

33

"Oh, relax, Sawbones. I'm fine. Even I know it's not kosher to get holly-jolly hammered on Christmas Eve."

"Okay, odd choice of words, given the holiday. But, glad to hear it."

"You're late to your own party."

"Doesn't sound like it's holding anyone back."

John looked over his shoulder at the cacophonous roar from the inside. "True enough. What was the holdup?"

"I hung around to meet the new innkeeper. Nice guy. A little quiet."

"So, you two exchanged pedigrees, huh? How'd that go?"

"Fine. In some respects, I sympathize with him. When you're new to a place, it's easy to feel like you're being observed by unfriendly eyes and mocking tongues."

"Eh," John sneered dismissively. "Matthew House was a college professor. He's probably used to being regarded that way." He turned and placed his hands on the porch rail, gazing into the night sky. I filled in the void.

"A shrewd insight, I'm sure. But not everyone handles it as well as you do, John."

"What do you mean?" he grunted.

"I mean you're not bothered by other people or what they think. Face it, Professor Harris, you never seem to like anybody."

He was unaffected. "That's true. But in my defense, they usually don't like me first."

"Mmm, I don't know, John. Over the years you've run rough-shod over a lot of folks. I'm guessing every therapist in a three-county

34

radius feels like they know you personally."

"Yeah, whatever. Listen. I was waiting out here because I want to ask you something."

"Ask away."

"Have you told Christine about the letter?"

"Well, to clarify. Which letter are we talking about? The research offer from Vanderbilt or the one I wrote to Santa?"

"Cut the crap, sawbones. I'm talking about the one from Vanderbilt, the job you turned down."

I folded my arms and studied him for a moment. The letter had arrived over a month ago and was now a forgotten matter. Something was compelling John to bring it up again.

"No. I haven't told her. What would be the point? My life is here."

"Did you throw the letter away?"

"No."

"I see. So, what's that telling you?"

"It's telling me I haven't thrown it away. Why are we having this conversation?"

John stared out above the lights of Fleming Street and exhaled into the frozen air. "I may have screwed up."

"Screwed up how?"

"I may have said something to Madeline about the letter."

"You may have, or you did?"

"Fine. I did."

I was speechless. Instantly, a dozen panicked voices screamed for center stage. I gathered myself, speaking firmly, deliberately. "Hold it. You're telling me that you told Madeline Chambers, Christine's mother, that I had a job offer from Vanderbilt to do research. Something I chose not to tell Christine for reasons you fully understood."

John nodded gravely, breathing out his swallowed response. "Yeah."

I could feel the blood rush to my face. "Holy crap, John! Do you have any idea what kind of mess this puts me in?"

He glanced at me briefly before looking away. "I know. I know. I'm sorry. I screwed up."

"I received that letter right after Christine was diagnosed. She was devastated. Did you forget that little detail?"

John held up his hands in surrender, shaking his head. "I know. I know. I remember all of it."

My rant was quick and bitter. "Well, apparently you don't remember the part where I told you why. I love Christine, and she loves this town. After learning she had premature ovarian failure she was an emotional wreck. I wasn't about to burden her with the thought of leaving Watervalley, not on top of the torment that she may never be able to have kids. Between the heartbreak of going and the guilt for not going, the whole business would have been an emotional can of worms for her. I didn't want to put her through that. Now it's all going to come out anyway, and you just layered that happy cesspool of feelings with a healthy dose of 'by the way honey, I don't trust you with the truth, either.'"

John pressed his lips together tightly, saying nothing more. He despondently looked at me, accepting the full brunt of my admonishment. I knew he was a proud man who rarely miss-stepped. His clear remorse served to diffuse my angry state. The damage had been done. Further berating him would serve no purpose. I spoke strategically.

"Okay, when did this happen?"

"Right before the service tonight. I mean look, Madeline may not have said anything to Christine yet."

"Well, seeing how they stood right next to each other in the choir, I'd say Madeline had both motive and opportunity. Don't you, professor?"

John shrugged. "Yeah. Good point."

Utterly bewildered, I took a step back and pressed my hands to my head, still trying to assimilate all the pieces. John filled in the silence.

"Look, just tell Christine that it was my idea and that I told you it would be best not to say anything."

"Oh. There's a great plan. Let's cover the whole thing up with a lie."

He frowned, offering an acknowledging shrug. "Well, gee. When you put it that way, it doesn't sound like such a great idea."

"No, John. Not telling her was my call. I'll just have to work it out."

"Hey listen. It may not even be a problem. When I saw the look on Madeline's face, I realized what I had done. So, I came up with a pretty quick response that may have diffused the whole thing."

This was a glimmer of hope. "Really? What did you say?"

"I um, I gave her a confused look and said, 'Or you know, maybe I just dreamed Luke got a letter.'"

"Maybe I just dreamed Luke got a letter? Seriously? That's the best you got?"

"Look. It was tough to be creative on the spur of the moment. Madeline's known me forever. She can see right through me just like her sister did."

"You're not helping here, John." I bent and looked through the front window, searching. "Have you been inside? Is Christine even here?"

"Yeah, she's here."

"Have you spoken to her?"

"Yeah."

"And?"

"She seemed fine."

I was deliberating, chasing my options, already rehearsing the words I would need to repair the wounded feelings. But it was all a cloud of uncertainty. I grasped for signs of what to expect. "Hmm, I don't know. I don't like it. She left the service without even speaking to me. That doesn't bode well."

John pursed his lips. "Hard to say."

"So, what do you think?"

"I think your guess is as good as mine," John smirked and looked away, returning to his derisive self. "Probably even better…considering, you know, you're sober and I'm not.

"That's comforting."

Having served his penance, John had regained some of his imposing stride. He slapped an authoritative hand on my shoulder, gripping me firmly.

"Oh, come on, sport. Let's go face the music. This was my screw up. I'll go with you and draw fire, so maybe you won't get shot up too badly."

"Thanks for the sentiment, John. But this conversation won't involve a wingman. I'll have to do it on my own."

My stomach churned. I had no way of foretelling Christine's response. Perhaps she would see it as no big deal. Perhaps she would understand my reasons. But even if that were the case, the past would shadow the future. I feared that my previous silence would haunt her. The knowledge of the offer would linger at the edges of every conversation, every plan, every decision. There were many reasons for not taking the position. But now Christine would justifiably believe that she was standing between me and my dream job. This wasn't the end of the world, and I knew that any damage would eventually mend. Yet in the moment, I was consumed with a dreadful, sickening feeling, one that I wanted to put behind me as soon as possible.

We were about to head inside when suddenly, the front door flew open and out stepped a very unhappy Connie Thompson. Penance would have to wait.

Chapter 5

SPARKS FLY

"Why are you two hiding out here? And look at you, Luke Bradford. Who are you trying to be... not showing up to your own party and all, The Great Gatsby?"

John responded casually. "Merry Christmas to you too, Constance. Looks like you've already made your choice between naughty and nice."

Connie's neck stiffened. She closed the door behind her and spoke in a breezy monotone. "My, my, John. I can see that you've entered full clown mode just for the occasion. Can I get you anything...a slice of cake, a glass of punch, a likable personality?"

These two had known each other for decades, even graduating high school together where Connie had edged him out for Valedictorian. And while there was between them a long-standing one-ups-manship, beneath the surface, there was also a deep and abiding friendship, a lifetime of privately shared regard and respect.

"Play nice, Constance. Tell you what. Meet me under the mistletoe, and you can demonstrate some of that Christmas goodwill towards men."

"Umm hmm," responded Connie. "Personally, I favor the death penalty for whoever came up with that holiday tradition."

"Gee, no kiss? I'm heartbroken," John replied teasingly. "Tell me what will change your mind?"

"Probably a ransom note for one of my children."

John winked at me. "I've lost my touch, Luke. I'm going to need some more grog in my nog."

Connie crossed her arms. "John Harris, I should have known that given your lack of maturity, you'd be getting a little pie-eyed."

"Now, now, Connie. Why should I solve my problems with maturity when alcohol is so readily available?"

"John, the inherent lack of intelligence in that statement could be plumbed for decades. I'd love to deliberate this deranged logic of yours further, but I'd hate for you to burn up that thimble full of testosterone you carry so proudly."

Even John was hard pressed to hide his amusement. "Constance, don't you need to go somewhere dark and hang upside down for a while?"

Connie raised her chin, doing her best to feign indignation. "John Horatio Harris, it's a good thing I've got the love of Jesus in me. Because otherwise, I would have already slapped your nose around to the back of your hairy head. You'd go to your grave looking like 'Cousin It' from the Adam's Family."

John responded innocently. "Constance, why are you being so nice to me this evening?"

"I'm just stalling while my cattle prod recharges."

"You know what I think, Connie?"

"No telling, John. A penny for your thoughts seems a bit pricey."

"All this sauciness of yours just makes you all the sexier."

Connie shook her head, regarding her old friend with an odd mix of compassion and reprimand. She spoke bluntly. "John, you've got your beer goggles on, and you're just being foolish. There's plenty of sweets inside if you want some granulated sugar. But know this, as far as any lipulated sugar goes, if teasing turns to trying you'll be spending Christmas Eve with the paramedics."

John grinned and turned to me. "I just love a girl who plays hard to get."

Connie ignored him. "I have a better idea. Why don't you two get inside before I start to whap both of you on the head like a whack-a-mole game."

I finally intervened. "We're just wrapping up, Connie. We'll be in shortly."

She scrutinized us for a moment, apparently not satisfied with my response. "Well, hurry along, Moe, and bring Curly here with you. Christine's been looking for you."

With that she stepped back inside, shutting the front door with an accentuated whump.

"Well, you just walked right into that butt whooping, didn't you?"

John was undaunted. "Eh, it's nothing. She adores me. Women love it when I give them a hard time. It just endears me to them all the more."

"Remind me never to hire you as a life coach."

The evening had become surreal, taking on more drama than a Greek tragedy. Between all the theater with Matthew House, John's slip up, Connie's angst, and my looming chastisement from Christine, the night had turned into a blur. Furthermore, Connie's last words about Christine sent a menacing spike into my already convulsive stomach.

I breathed a long, airy sigh. "Well, John. I think it's time to head in." He penitently nodded his agreement. With his empty tumbler in tow, John led the way; his expression wooden, detached. He knew my encounter with Christine was imminent and the impending dread in my manner was likely contagious.

I followed him, my heart sick with apprehension. I had so looked forward to this evening, to a warm, cluttered house bursting at the seams with laughter and celebration. Yet now I crossed the threshold of my own home, anxiously scanning the faces before me and brooding uneasily over what was about to happen.

Chapter 6

EXPECTATIONS

My entrance sparked a spontaneous chorus of shouts and greetings that surged from room to room as word passed that the host had finally arrived. In truth, it was both odd and embarrassing to be so warmly greeted to my own party. Ironically, there was an unreserved acceptance of my ill-timed entrance. The erratic nature of a doctor's work bred a tolerance for such delinquency, even when my tardiness had nothing to do with anything medical.

Every inch of my crowded cottage home was bursting with high spirits; a festive roar of noise, chatter, and the occasional explosion of howling laughter. Voices fought to be heard above the rumbling thump and beat of the music. Children spilled into the hallway, gleefully dodging and chasing. The air was electric, filled with a pungent brew of baked goods, mulled cider, and the resinous, woody smell of pine wreaths.

It seemed that the gathering had achieved a status of blissful chaos. In every direction was an ocean of smiles, a grand pageant of eager celebration. I responded warmly to the many handshakes and hellos, but all the while I was feverishly searching for Christine.

After not seeing her in the entry hall, living, or dining room, I began to edge my way toward the oversized kitchen in the back. The path was crowded and the conversations were many, delaying my progress and intensifying the spastic knot in my stomach. I had to practically shout to be heard above the den. When I finally shouldered my way into the packed kitchen, Christine was not to be seen. My spirits sunk even lower. "Surely, she wouldn't just leave," I thought. I moved to the rear entry to see if she might be part of a small gathering on the back porch. There was no sign of her.

I was about to work my way toward the front of the house when there she was, across the room descending the back stairs into the kitchen. Her mother, Madeline was with her. They were thick in conversation and had slipped upstairs for a private discussion. I felt confirmed in my darkest forebodings. But when Christine spotted me across the room, her expression was completely unexpected.

Her eyes softened, and her yielding smile conveyed a sense of complete and total affection, full of secret warmth and joy. Her momentary gaze held the affirming intimacy shared by two in love, an understanding that went past words or spoken vows. Unfortunately, she was immediately engaged by one of the guests, drawing her attention away. But she seemed flushed with a happy energy. This was not someone fresh with the disappointment of upsetting news.

I began to breath new air. As the strangling anxiety of the previous minutes vanished, the pendulum of my emotions swung decidedly, leaving me euphorically floating on a wave of relief and deliverance. But I sobered quickly and resolved to tell Christine about the letter at the earliest possible moment.

I began to move in her direction when a broad, pudgy hand grabbed me on the shoulder.

"Hey doc, got a minute?"

It was Walt Hickman, the mayor of Watervalley. While everyone else at the party was dressed in casual holiday style, Walt was wearing his suit, as if he had no other life to change into. In his early fifties, he had a bald spot and more than a suggestion of a paunch around his waist. But he seemed to be cheerfully unconcerned with either. Collectively, I liked Walt. He had an all-embracing affection for the town and approached his job with the zeal of a missionary.

"I heard tell you had a conversation this evening with the new innkeeper, Dr. House?"

"Wow. That news travelled fast. But yeah. We spoke for a few minutes after the service tonight. I saw you there. Did you not meet him?"

"Only long enough to make introductions. I told Matthew I would love to have lunch with him sometime, but I didn't get a really good vibe in return. Seemed evasive. What do you think of him?"

"Not much to tell. It was a short conversation. But, he's a likeable fellow. Kind of quiet."

"You think he's up to something?"

I was slightly taken aback. "What do you mean?"

Walt shrugged and scratched the back of his head. "Honestly, doc, I'm not sure what I mean. I can't quite figure him out."

"Walt, I think you're looking for answers to questions that don't exist."

He nodded, perplexed. "Yeah, you may be right. But then again, there's been a lot of rumors floating around about him. I'm willing to give the guy the benefit of the doubt, but it seems awfully strange for him not to be out and meeting people…you know, engage with the community."

"It also seems unfair to put him on trial by innuendo. You do know he lost his wife earlier this year?"

"Yeah. That's gotta be tough. They say it was cancer."

I caught a faint hint of skepticism in his tone. "Have you heard otherwise?"

Walt held up his hands in a gesture of innocence. "Hey, again. It's just a rumor. But when a guy comes to town to be in the hospitality business and all he does is keep to himself...people start to wonder."

"Wonder what?"

"He's a smart guy. Maybe he knows how to poison somebody and make it cause cancer. I'm just saying."

"Oh, good grief, Walt! Are you serious? You saw him tonight. He was Mr. Vanilla from Vanilla Land. There wasn't the first thing cold or calculated about him. He's a widower with two kids to raise. Cut him some slack. Besides, he's been busy settling in. He said there were a lot of renovations he needed to do to the place."

"Oh, really? Did he say when?"

"Well. Not exactly. He was a little vague on the point."

Walt fell silent. He tucked one arm under the other and rubbed his chin, thinking. He grunted a low "hmm."

"What?" I inquired. "Seems to me that adds yet another layer of pressure on the guy. He's probably going to be in hock up to his ears before he makes the first dollar."

Walt's face tightened into a doubting wince. "Eh, I don't think that's going to be the case, doc."

"How so?"

Walt looked from side to side before shouldering next to me, signaling that his next words were confidential. "I heard tell Lida sold the place for a chunk of change. Your boy paid cash. I don't think he's too worried about money."

"So, what does that prove?"

"Not a thing. But, his wife was a doctor, like you. The rumor is that she came from a lot of money to boot. And I imagine she was covered with a ton of life insurance."

I understood Walt's insinuation, but candidly, I was mildly indignant to it. I knew he meant no harm and that to him this was idle chatter. But it embodied one of the failings of small-town life, the presumptive need to assume the worst of those who didn't fit the norm. I responded with a notable level of sternness. "Well, for Matthew's sake, I hope she did."

I nodded and tried to edge away. But Walt grabbed my arm. He was either oblivious to my angst or chose to ignore it.

"Hey, doc. I want to come by and talk with you sometime. You're an intelligent guy, and I'd like to get your input on something."

"What might that be?"

"Business growth has more or less been flat the last couple of years. I'd like to get some folks together to come up with ideas for attracting new companies to the valley. The availability of medical care is a fundamental asset. So, your input about upgrades to the clinic would really be helpful."

I wasn't particularly enthusiastic about Walt's request, but I was open to anything that helped the clinic. I would have to play a role, but hopefully, a small one. "Sure, give me a call. We'll set something up."

By the time I escaped Walt's inquisition, Christine was once again nowhere to be seen. But despite the annoyance of the mayor's careless insinuations, I had fallen into a relaxed, happy state. Christine's bewitching smile had changed everything. Hungry, I budged my way to the dining room and began to gaze at the endless spread of food. As the host, I probably should have been working the crowd. But I found myself content to remain on the periphery, amazed and gratified at the uninhibited joy of those around me.

Soon afterward, Connie shouldered up beside me. In contrast to her usual critical demeanor, her mood was light and cheerful.

"Having a good time?"

"Sure," I said absently. "But you know me. I always feel a little awkward at these things."

"Oh, that's just silly. Be yourself." She took a sip of punch and surveyed the crowd. "Unless you're a jerk, like John. Then you should be someone else."

I cut my eyes at her, smiling.

"Anyway, doctor. You put on quite a lively shin-dig."

"Hardly. You and the other little Christmas elves did all the work...all the food and trimmings. I just provided the venue."

"Well, that's true. But you can probably redeem yourself by chairing the clean-up committee."

I grimaced. "Yeah, I guess that's only fair. Who's all on it?"

"Just you."

I frowned at her. She ignored me and gazed about the room with a notable air of satisfaction. "Umm hmm," she continued in a rare moment of self-praise, "we did a pretty fabulous job of getting this little place all decked out."

"Yes. I had no idea that magnolia leaves had so many decorating variables."

Connie's happy mood tempered. "Careful, Luke. Life's full of disappointments. Don't make me add you to the list."

"Pretty sure that ship has sailed."

Connie grunted a short laugh. "Fine, fine, doctor. Speaking of lists, I've thought of a few other things we need to discuss when we have 'The Talk.'"

I spoke with pronounced indifference. "Forget it, Connie. You're just trying to have a little fun at my expense." All this fervor about "The Talk," doesn't scare me one bit.

She answered with a smug, "Humph."

"Hey, I'm serious here."

"Really? And here I was thinking you were practicing your audition for clown school."

There was no getting the upper hand on Connie, and she knew it. Mercifully, she changed the subject. "I saw you talking to Walt earlier. What's the good mayor have on his mind?"

"What else? Matthew House. Somehow Walt knew that I talked to him after the service tonight. He was pumping me with questions, and when I didn't have the answers, Walt just filled in the blanks with his own rumors."

Connie chuckled. "I'd think you'd know by now that the people of Watervalley are more than willing to talk about somebody else's business just for the sheer pleasure of it."

"Yeah, but Walt's the mayor. You'd think he wouldn't be so short witted and long-winded."

"Sweetie, Walt didn't get the job by being the smartest. He got the job by attending the most picnics. And remember, he's a politician, which means he has a God-given talent for laying it on with a trowel."

"I just wish he'd make some effort to keep the rumors in check."

Connie nodded. "I guess it's simply Walt's nature. Besides, there have been rumors about Society Hill Manor long before Matthew House arrived. You do know everyone thinks of it as spook central?"

"Lida once said something about that, but I thought she was joking. Don't' tell me you're buying into those old stories?"

"I'm a God-fearing woman, Luke Bradford. And the only spirit I believe in is the Holy one." She accentuated her declaration with an ardent nod of her head. But a moment later, she nudged my shoulder and whispered confidentially.

"But just in case, I'm keeping an open mind about Society Hill. Ever since I was a little girl there's been some pretty ookey-spooky stuff told about that place…things that would make your hair frizz up."

I was about to ask her to tell me more when John Harris approached. Connie spoke first.

"Why hello, John. How's your evening of 'raise it high and drain it dry' going?

John put his arm around Connie's shoulder and lightly rotated her around to face the wall mirror behind them. "Well, would you look at that? I've always wondered if you really cast a reflection."

Connie responded by playfully elbowing John in the ribs. He grabbed his side and the two of them regarded each other with sportive grins.

"You know, John," Connie reflected. "Sometimes when I look at you, I often wonder; why has no one hit this man's head with a shovel."

"Just what are you saying, Connie?"

"I'm saying you need to have better people skills."

"Humph," John retorted as he surveyed the room. "I'd have better people skills if I was around better people."

"Don't you have a pretty little nurse girlfriend?" inquired Connie. "Where is she?"

Connie was referring to Ann Patterson, my nurse at the clinic. She and John had sparked a growing romance in the last several months.

"Gone," replied John.

"What happened? She finally get a good look at you in full sunlight?"

"Pennsylvania. Visiting her relatives for the holidays. Doc there signed off on it."

"Don't blame the doctor because you don't know how to behave without your steady."

John had alcoholic gravity and wavered a little. He studied his glass reflectively. "Yeah, it's been a rough evening. On two occasions, I almost had to socialize."

"Sooner or later, John," replied Connie. "We all have to be adults. Isn't it time you took a turn?"

John straightened himself and spoke with great ceremony. "Constance, I think we need to kiss and make nice." He turned to me. "Luke, grab some mistletoe and hold it over us."

"Not unless you can guarantee me a new identity in Federal Witness Protection."

John winked at Connie, bumping his shoulder against hers. "Come on, CT. You're not fooling anybody."

"John Harris, you're more toasted than a marshmallow. I don't know what fantasy world you think you're on, but you need to book a ticket back to reality." She pretended to ignore him sternly. But the subtle upturned corners of her mouth betrayed her. In truth, there was an endearment between them that even I didn't fully realize.

John fell silent, and somehow, despite the previous exchange, Connie seemed to understand completely. John was lonely. It had been almost three years since his wife, Molly had died. And even though in the past months, John had largely come out of his reclusive shell, the persona still defined him. I now realized his vulnerability to Ann Patterson. But Ann wasn't here. She was the reason John had largely curbed his drinking and had re-engaged with the town. She had become his one person. Probably due to his abiding love for his departed wife, he had likely not even admitted this to himself. But his return to the bottle during the evening told volumes.

John stood in a fog, brooding. Even though she disguised it well, I could read the empathy in Connie's face. "What's wrong John? Nothing in your arsenal of snappy comebacks?"

He took a healthy sip of his eggnog and responded with a smile of resignation, saying nothing further. Connie shook her head. Then slowly, her face compressed into a puckish grin. She winked at me and then ran her arm underneath John's elbow, easing in close to him.

"Come on, John. Let's find that mistletoe. Your whiskey breath will probably make me gag, but I sure will enjoy giving everybody something to talk about."

John was doing his best to stifle his surprise, but he went along with Connie's bidding. As she led him away, she added, "Let me grab my cell phone. I want to take a selfie."

It should have come as no surprise that Connie Thompson understood John more than I could have imagined. A minute later, the cheering roar from the hallway confirmed the fait accompli. I could only stand, and smile, and shake my head. Just when I thought I knew Connie Thompson, she managed to baffle me completely. It had been quite the evening.

Once again, I set my mind to finding Christine; to be near her, to hear her voice, to find a moment to penitently tell her the things I needed to say.

But first, I stopped by the dining room table and grabbed a few more pigs in a blanket. Contrition didn't require an empty stomach.

Chapter 7

CHRISTINE

The next hours melted into a blur of holiday greetings, continuous laughter, and hearty exchanges. I never caught up with Christine. It seemed that both of us were in high demand that evening and somehow, the crowd managed to keep us apart for the duration.

But every so often I would see her, still not believing my good fortune regarding John's blunder and the letter. I wanted to confirm my earlier assumption that she, as yet, knew nothing. To my delight, she was always animated, laughing, radiant. Meanwhile, I was drowning in an ocean of spontaneous conversations; encounters often made awkward by my own failings at small talk.

Christine, however, suffered no such shortcoming. Her response to everyone was warm and natural; engaging all she talked to with an air of delighted surprise and genuine interest. I marveled at her. In those stolen moments when I watched her from across the room, time slowed, conversations faded, and all the holiday colors blended together, leaving me to see only her above the crush and noise. She occasionally noticed my errant stares and would respond with a warm, seductive smile.

The explosive laughter and merriment continued until almost midnight. The evening had been exhilarating, but exhausting. As the party closed, Christine was on the front porch in an extended goodbye with a couple of old friends from high school. I retreated to the kitchen to help with clean-up but was politely and quickly dismissed by the women to "go outside and look for Santa's sleigh," which was code for "get lost." I was glad to oblige.

I wandered into the enveloping darkness of the backyard, breathing in the crisp, moist air of the night. Far, far above, the evening sky was lightly glittered with distant, delicate stars made faint by a brilliant and luminous moon. Its serene, phantasmal radiance cast the world into a monochromatic dreamscape; an ethereal, comforting presence that was silent, intense, beautiful.

I breathed in deeply. The frozen air was magical and penetrating, a lulling potion that whispered of slumber. In the distance, the glow of a few porch lights remained, standing sentinel over a Watervalley that had joyfully and deliriously gone to bed.

Moving further toward the deep center of the yard, my breath plumed out in the soft, pristine air. The cacophonous voices of the past hours had faded, but I was warmed with the rich, buoyant afterglow of their memory. We had all been a little drunk, I believe, with unspeakable joy that evening. It had been a grand gathering, and I couldn't help but reflect on what an unbelievable difference a year had made.

I had spent the previous Christmas Eve alone in my small cottage on Fleming Street. Alone, but not lonely. The events of that evening, the incredible, delightful surprise of being so grandly recognized at the service by the entire town was a moment I would keep for a lifetime. I had not seen myself as one of them. But they had seen me as one of theirs. Over the past year, I had grown to care deeply for the unsophisticated people of Watervalley. They were men and women of the soil who rarely pretended to be what they were not. They enjoyed a richness of love and relationships, of shared lives…despite the hard reality that many of them likely lived barely ahead of their circumstances. They had become my people. Nonetheless, my old unrest and dream of doing medical research stirred within me.

But it was Christmas Eve, and I was happy. I was gazing into the vast bowl of sky above when I heard Christine call my name from the kitchen door.

"Out here. Come join me."

Against the backdrop of the porch light, I saw her silhouette move toward me. My eyes had adjusted to the dark, and I could easily discern the flowing rhythm of her long, deliberate strides. As she drew close, she immediately took my hand and with a warm, momentary pressure, pulled me towards her, boldly yielding the full measure of herself in an all-embracing kiss.

"Merry Christmas, Dr. Bradford." Her voice was lovely, sweet, and delightful; her radiant eyes were filled with liquid stealth.

"Merry Christmas to you as well, Ms. Chambers."

She kissed me again then draped her extended arms loosely on my shoulders; lifting her chin and appraising me with an impish smile that was touched with both tenderness and humor. There was between us a natural and casual intimacy.

"By the way, if you want to, you know, you can just call me Luke. Why all the 'Dr. Bradford' formality?"

Her words were full of teasing playfulness. "Welllllll, it's probably because for the last several hours all I've heard is 'Dr. Bradford is so wonderful this, and Dr. Bradford has been so good to us that, and blah, blah, blah, blah, Dr. Bradford is our hero.' They just went on and on."

"Oh, they did, did they? So, what was your response to all these accolades about your fiancée?"

"Oh, you know…I just smiled and said, 'Are we talking about the same person?'"

"I expected nothing less."

"Anyway, everyone seemed to have a wonderful time. I don't think we could have squeezed another person in."

"Yeah, about that. I realize that all I contributed to the effort was just the idea of having a Christmas Eve party, but I thought it was going to be a group of about twenty or so."

"It started out that way but then word began to get around, and people kept calling wanting to know what they could bring, which was code for 'I want to come.' We had a least a hundred or more over the course of the evening."

I nodded thoughtfully. "Well, there you go. No doubt, the people of the valley love a party."

"No, Luke Bradford. No doubt, the people of the valley love you. Everyone was so excited to be here, to be included. Have you not seen the stack of gifts that have mounded up in the living room?"

"Yes, I did. However, I also noticed that none of the packages are in the shape of a jet-ski."

"Stop. You should be grateful."

"Au contraire. I am, in fact, very grateful. I probably have enough homemade preserves and canned goods under the tree to last until the second coming...which, you know, could come in handy if someone turns out to be a lousy cook."

"Easy, big boy. You might want to pump the brakes on that line of thinking. I haven't given you your Christmas present yet."

"The naughty or the nice one? For what it's worth, I'm okay with naughty?"

"Careful what you wish for."

"By the way, I saw you and your mom coming down from the upstairs. What that was all about?"

"We were checking out your bedroom."

"My bedroom? Your mother was in my bedroom? I feel violated."

"Why on earth would you feel like that?"

"Because that's where I have my most private, intimate thoughts."

"About what?"

"You, of course."

"Oh, good grief!"

"Anyway, what's to check out in my bedroom?"

"Oh, you know. The wall color, the furniture, the closets."

"Are you telling me you and your mother went rifling through my closet? I hope she didn't see my onesie Superman pj's."

"Nope. Completely missed that."

"Well, that's a relief," I said dryly. "But... seriously. I've got a king size bed. What else is needed?"

Christine gently placed her finger on my lips, something she always did before morphing into her instructional, school teacher voice. "Luke, sweetheart. I truly do love you. But that doesn't mean I also love your man-cave, fraternity house decorating vibe."

"Oh. Fraternity house, huh? So, what do you have in mind?"

"We'll get to that."

Her response meant trouble. But I had come to realize that any decisions pertaining to my upcoming nuptials should be treated like an iPhone user update in which I simply clicked, "I agree."

Still, the subject matter had other potentials.

"Okay, fair enough. But here's an idea." I pulled her snuggly close and spoke barely above a whisper. "I think everybody's gone by now. So, why don't we go back up to my bedroom and talk over the decorating possibilities."

Christine's whispered response was deliciously slow and deliberate. "I see. And then?"

"And then, gee. I don't know. Maybe smooch it around when the lights go down."

"Oh, I think you do know, Luke Bradford. I think there's more than visions of sugar plums dancing around in your head."

"It's not my fault your kisses are a gateway drug."

Christine looked up at me with mirthful, luminous eyes before once again placing her index finger on my lips. She spoke in a voice that was soft and sensuous. "Well, that sounds kind of nice. But there's one little problem."

"What's that?"

"My uncle has gone to sleep in your bed."

"What?" My blurted response was almost a yell.

Christine shrugged. "Yup, I'm afraid Uncle Whisky Breath had a little too much medicine tonight. Mom took John's keys, and we helped him up to your bedroom. He's out for the count."

I stared at her in disbelief. "Wow, this is doubly upsetting."

"I don't understand."

"Well, it's bad enough that John's in my bed...given the possibilities of the moment. But now I've got not one, but two images of your mother in my bedroom. That sort of thing puts a real damper on a guy's imagination."

Christine rolled her eyes. "Bradford, you are so predictable."

I gathered her in even tighter. "Completely bewitched."

She responded with a taunting grin. "Tell you what. Why don't you follow me out to the farmhouse and you can sleep in the guest bedroom? And if you're lucky, maybe one of Santa's elves will come and tuck you in."

"Hmm, I think I like this plan. You sure your mother's okay with me staying?"

She took my hand, and we began to walk toward the house. "Quite sure. It was her idea. She's already left to get the bed ready."

Christine continued walking, but I stood frozen. After another step, she stopped and looked back at me. "What's wrong?"

"Your mother's idea, huh?"

"Yeah."

"Which part?"

"I don't understand."

"Using the guest room part or the tucking me in part?"

Christine shook her head and turned toward the house. "Wait and see, Bradford. Wait and see."

She left, and I crept upstairs to grab a few things to throw in a duffle bag. My stealth probably didn't matter. John was making snoring noises that only an exorcist could cure.

As I walked downstairs, I realized that I had completely neglected to talk with Christine about the letter. After a moment's reflection, I shrugged it off. Our conversation in the moonlight had been too delightful, too perfect. There would be a time to talk through the matter with her. But tonight was not it.

I unplugged the tree, turned off all the lights, and walked out the front door. From downtown, I heard the clock tower on the courthouse faintly chime the midnight hour. The excitement and adrenaline of the evening were finally expended, and I was consumed with a complete and total exhaustion. Sleep at Christine's farmhouse couldn't come soon enough.

Nevertheless, it was Christmas Eve and the night was filled with a solemn, inspiring presence. Before walking to my car, I once again stared toward the lonely stars and into the vast and enchanted universe. All the world seemed peaceful, expectant, listening. In the distance, random lights from the houses on the encircling hills formed a twinkling wreath around the town.

Yet even through my weariness, something odd drew my attention; a strange and obsessive flickering in the distance. Somewhere from the recesses of boyhood, a memory clicked. I recognized what I was seeing.

The peculiar, flashing light was coming from the high tower of the old mansion on Society Hill…the home of Matthew House.

Chapter 8

SOS

The blinking light was whispering through my drowsy stupor, triggering an ancient lesson from the past. It was Morse Code.

There were three dots then three dashes followed by three dots again...the international distress sign for SOS. Decades before, during a brief tenure with the scouts, I had attained a handful of merit badges. One of them was in Signaling. Over and over the light beamed into the night, broken by an occasional and irregular pause.

Reality finally registered.

"Oh, crap!" The words were spontaneous and involuntary.

On impulse, I rushed toward my car, jumped in, and swiftly closed the door behind me. But just before turning the key, I stopped.

"What was I about to do?" I thought.

My first instinct was to call the sheriff's office. Then I quickly realized that I was reacting to a rather thin observation...a supposed SOS flickering at quite a distance. There were consequences. Once the sheriff was involved, if my observation turned out to be false, the story would roar across the whole of Watervalley, providing fodder for yet another toxic rumor about Matthew. I had no clue as to his cell phone number, and after a quick directory check, I dialed the landline to the inn. It was no longer in service. My choices were few.

Urgency had now been replaced with apprehension. I sat frozen, staring vacantly ahead. The moment was rich with irony.

My entire evening had been crowded with people and conversation, well-meaning souls who had exhausted my normal preference for polite detachment. Now, I desperately wished for company, for someone with whom to decide what should be done. Christine was probably home by now, and rousing John was highly unlikely. I would have to go it alone.

Reluctantly, I started the engine and turned on to Fleming Street, moving more from reflex and instinct than from a definitive plan. Somewhere in those moments, the air of the evening elusively changed.

A light fog had rolled in, cloaking the street before me. I drove slowly, cautiously, and all the while deliberating on what to do. The car passed under the street lamps one by one; small islands of illumination in a landscape that now felt obscure and lonely. This strange, distant signal had altered the mood of the night. The warm, festive spirit of the previous hours had been swept away, and all that remained was a stagnant, brooding intensity.

Watervalley after midnight was frozen and lifeless. The shadowed lawns were covered with heavy frost, petrified; thinly illuminated by the frail luster of the moon. All the houses were darkened and asleep, napping in the oblivion of a snug winter night. Weary, I returned my attention to the lane before me, questioning my own actions.

Downtown was quiet and deserted, a barren world of closed shops and empty pavements. Life and sound seemed held in abeyance. The unpeopled desolation gave the streets an odd, haunting stillness as if the entirety of Watervalley were mystically locked in a cataleptic trance. A drained, sleepy voice in the back of my head whispered that I should turn around and go to Christine's. Immersed in a foreboding uncertainty, I exhaled and accelerated.

The car rounded the Courthouse square. Three blocks further I turned and began the long ascent up Society Hill, straining to catch a glimpse of the tower section of the old mansion. I ardently wanted to confirm the reality of the distress signal. But the angle of approach offered no such vantage point. I continued up the winding lane, my headlights tunneling through the black cavern formed by the canopy of trees that lined the road.

Upon arriving at the mansion's entrance, I stopped and cut my lights. The heavy iron gates were wide apart but the trees surrounding them obscured a view of the house. My trepidation grew. I didn't want my presence known. At least, not yet. With my headlights still off, I pulled quietly on to the long, cobbled drive, creeping so as not to be heard. After easing the car to a stop beside the broad stone steps of the front entry, I quietly cut the engine, gently turning the key as if it was fragile and might break.

Nagging doubt had accompanied me the entire way. Now that I was here, I openly felt like an intruder whose presence would be difficult to explain. Yet, I had come this far. There was no choice but to settle the matter. The car was too close to the house to see the signal up above, and I had to walk into the yard to attain a better view. High overhead a thin layering of wispy clouds had moved in, veiling the moon and giving the once familiar night a peculiar, disturbing presence. But upon opening the car door, I was thrust into a different world.

A savage burst of colder, frozen air hit me, hard. Its effect was immediate, fierce, and jagged, shocking my body into full wakefulness. Briskly, I excited, shut the door behind me, and impulsively blew into my hands. My movements were fearful and erratic. My eyes went everywhere, skittishly canvasing everything around me. I stood for a moment, adjusting, struggling to gather my senses. Then, another bitter, scoffing wind gusted by me, scattering the last remnants of leaves and sending a hardened shiver down my neck. Tugging nauseatingly at my throat, an involuntary wave of dread and indecision was swiftly consuming me.

I grimaced, pulled my coat collar tight, and tramped stubbornly on to the front lawn. Once there, I turned to view the high tower and was thoroughly baffled. The flashing light had stopped. The distress beacon was no more. There was nothing, nothing but the low dim of a single lamp from a window on the third floor. Cold, anxious, and clouded with doubt, I shivered in the frozen grass, watching, waiting. Still, there was nothing. Except for the lone, solitary light, the vast estate was dark and asleep.

Then slowly, something primal within me became aware of a larger attendance; an overpowering, eerie feeling that I was not alone. Its presence was overwhelming and unmistakable. I shook uncontrollably. A hard trembling, monstrous and uncontrolled, bristled over me. My eyes pierced sharply into the gloom of the enormous mansion. It seemed that something secret and immense waited inside; a larger authority, a breathing reality that was watching my intrusion from within the shadows, regarding my movements with a vicious curiosity.

I wanted to ignore it, to detach myself from such a foolish notion. But doing so proved impossible. Another tingling chill ran across my skin; an unexplained, instinctive warning.

Then it began; a kind of ghastly whispering on the surface of the air, pleading words that were ancient and muffled. There was only a single voice at first, but it quickly thickened into a discordant blend, an earnest and cacophonous imploring. Initially, I doubted what I was hearing. But that was to change quickly. Faster, louder, harder, the deep, gurgling words came, swirling around me, encircling me, escalating into a raucous harmony of singing voices. There was no processing this, no instant means of grasping what was happening. A galling panic convulsed through me. I was stunned, paralyzed, waiting for my mind to catch up. Then, just as quickly, the murmuring tones cooled and receded into a low hum, ending in a somber, spectral moaning of wind. And then, it was gone.

Words exploded from me. "What in hell was that?"

I was heaving for breath, and after one hyper-vigilant second of scanning the darkness around me, I bolted in a terrified run back to the car.

That had done it. I no longer searched for any rational definitions or clung to any sense of noble cause. Escape from whatever creepy heebie-jeebies I had just witnessed was now my new life priority. The curiosity that had previously prompted me to go on this hero's errand was long gone and had now been replaced with a healthy dose of spineless fear.

Yet just before reaching the car I caught a glimpse of another damnable flicker from the high tower window. It was only three dashes and three dots…not a full signal. I ignored it and moved quickly. But before opening my car door, once more, I stopped. Feverishly, I deliberated. Perhaps I had simply missed the first part, having lowered my gaze in my haste to depart.

Reluctantly, I stepped back into the yard and waited. The signal didn't repeat. I again pulled my coat tightly around me, bracing against the strange, piercing cold of this high hill. Admittedly, for the first time in my adulthood, I was scared to death; plagued with a consuming fear that everything about my presence here was wrong. But I knew what I had seen. With quaking determination, I climbed the stone steps and moved into the shadows of the massive porch. Under my breath, I whispered, "Bradford, you're a total idiot."

Peering through the side glass, I saw nothing within but swallowing darkness. I couldn't find a doorbell, so I proceeded to give the door a solid knock. But after the first rap, it gave way, swaying open with an unsettling groan. Cautiously, I stepped inside, shutting it behind me. The massive estate was permeated with the smells of accumulated time, the pungent and quiet sternness of many decades.

"Hello?"

Admittedly, my volume was modest. It was a fool's task; attempting to make my presence known without making my presence alarming.

"Hello? Matthew? It's Luke Bradford."

My inquiries were met with complete silence.

I stood and waited to see if my eyes might adjust to the darkness. But after what seemed an eternity, little had changed. I retrieved my cell phone and used it for a light. Again, I called out.

"Hello? Matthew?"

Nothing. I was in a sizable entry hall with thick stone walls and a towering ceiling that was vaulted like the nave of a cathedral. Tall gothic windows were to either side and before me was a broad cased opening that gathered to a high, pointed arch. I walked toward it, my footfalls echoing rudely across the marble floor. Beyond the opening was a grand space that perhaps had been a ballroom in the estate's former years.

"Hello? Matthew? It's Luke Bradford. I saw the distress signal! Is everything okay?"

Still, there was nothing. Cautiously I eased around the furniture, endeavoring to find a light switch. I found several antiquated brass wall plates with large black buttons labeled with faded letters for "on" and "off." None of them worked. I pressed them repeatedly, but there were only meaningless clicks in the darkness.

My uneasiness grew. I had the haunting feeling that my small phone light was in truth, my enemy, serving only to expose me and illuminating little else. Choking panic began to re-emerge. I felt vulnerable and shut it off, desperately trying to keep my wits. But in my apprehension, my mind raced.

In the face of so many ominous uncertainties, the human brain has a dreadful capacity for fabricating horror, for imagining all manner of grisly fictions, especially when such ill-omened circumstances convince the mind that something sinister and supernatural may genuinely be near. And that was the problem.

I truly thought something was near, watching me. Illogical fear was taking over, overwhelming me, knotting every muscle. I felt an unexplainable, menacing presence as if at any moment, the singing voices would break the tense silence, wildly reaching at me from some dark corner. I was convinced of it. But still, there was nothing; no voice, no movement, no sound.

"What am I doing?" I thought to myself. I was in another man's house, in the dark, uninvited. What absurdity had brought me to this? The SOS signal had stopped, and, in my flustered state, I began to doubt it had ever been genuine at all. What if I was mistaken and had only seen the errant flickering of holiday lights?

All the uncertainties had finally overcome me. I was dreadfully fearing what I could not see and desperately afraid of being discovered. All that mattered now was to leave, to escape, to move quickly to my car and speed away.

I was halfway to the entrance hall when the voice called out.

But this time, it was full-throated, clear, completely audible. It had come distantly, echoing down from the labyrinthine darkness of the upper floors. Using my phone light, I crossed the room and stopped on the second step of a grand, looping stairway.

"Hello? It's Luke Bradford. I'm down here. Is everything okay?"

The response was more pronounced. "I'm on the third floor. Can you hear me?"

"Yes, I hear you. I'm coming up."

I practically sprinted up the stairs, covering two steps with each stride. But when I arrived at the wide hallway at the top, I stopped abruptly and listened. Here the previous silence of the house was broken by the nocturnal creaks and groans of the night, as if ghosts were sliding along the walls; watching, waiting, listening. I called out.

"Hello? Matthew? It's Luke Bradford. Are you up here?"

I heard a brisk rapping on the second door to my right. "Yes. Down this way." His voice was now clear, filled with urgency. I stepped quickly.

The knocking continued, and as I approached, I could discern a thin line of light glowing at the door's bottom edge. My heart was thumping. "Matthew, are you alright? I saw an SOS signal."

"Yes. I'm fine. Somehow, the door bolted behind me, and I can't get out."

I held my small light near the lock. It was a relic of decades past; a raised brass box mounted to the door with a rounded knob and a key slot below. A more modern deadbolt had been installed above it. I tried to turn the handle but to no avail. "It's not working from this side either. What should I do?"

"Look in one of the other rooms. There will be a skeleton key on the inside of the lock. They're universal. Try it on this one."

I understood. Using my phone light, I stepped to a door across the hallway and found a key on the room side of the lock. I returned and inserted it into the slot. After a moments' fidgeting, the key rotated and clicked. I turned the knob and swung the door open. Standing before me was an extremely embarrassed and eternally grateful Matthew House.

Chapter 9

GHOSTS

Matthew grabbed my hand and held it firmly. His words drenched in relief.

`"Thank you! Thank you so much for coming. I got locked in, and there was no way to get out."

I blurted something in response to assure him. But in truth, I was still catching my breath. We both were in a staggered state, wide-eyed, breathless, shaking our heads in an amused exhilaration. And while the adrenaline of the moment seemed to demand a lengthy exchange of accounts and explanations, nothing was said. Instead, there fell between us a wordless and automatic understanding, much the same as a bond formed by two strangers who had just narrowly missed being hit by a passing train.

Then, in an instant, Matthew's elation was replaced with a labored urgency, and I could sense from his movements that he was straining to get past me.

"I need to go check on the twins. Do you mind waiting here? I'll be right back."

"Sure. I'll come with you?"

"No!" Matthew immediately realized that his answer was oddly abrupt. He stopped and held up his hand while gathering his response. "It's…it's just that if they're awake, your presence might frighten them. Look, I…I'm sorry. I'm not wanting to be rude. I just need to go check on them."

"Sure. No problem. I'll hang tight."

He turned toward the stairs, clicking on a large flashlight. It had likely been the one that he had used to signal the SOS. For some reason, though, I hadn't noticed it before. Then it occurred to me that he had been stiffly holding his left hand close to his trousers, almost as if he had wanted to keep the flashlight hidden. It was all rather odd.

I stood for a moment, gathering my wits. Then, I used my phone to find the hall light switches; more of the brass plates with the black on and off buttons. They didn't work either. Perhaps that explained the flashlight. Then again, how was it that the lights were working in the room where Matthew was trapped? There were no immediate answers. From the hallway, I made a passing glimpse into the other rooms and then returned to the one of Matthew's entrapment. Along the way, I realized something that my previous trepidation had not allowed.

The interior of the old mansion was a work of splendor. All the walls and high ceilings were of dark, raised wood paneling. Heavy moldings, polished brass hardware, and brilliant light fixtures of cascading crystal. Matthew's room appeared to have been a library or study originally. Given the mahogany desk and the accompanying laptop, it appeared that he now used it for an office.

I stood in the room's center, absorbing all the rich details. The outer wall had three massive and ornately trimmed windows that during the day probably afforded a commanding view of the town below. His desk was to the left and centered on the wall to my right was a grand fireplace bordered in granite and surrounded by an enormous and intricately carved wooden mantel. Fascinated, I drew closer. Left of the fireplace were floor to ceiling bookshelves that extended to the outer

73

wall. Oddly, the wall to the right of the fireplace was wood paneled and flush with the front of the firebox, making for a peculiar offset to the otherwise square chamber. That aside, the furnishings were magnificent and yet strangely, the desk and bookshelves as well as the entire room, were straight and orderly; quite the contrast from the disheveled appearance of Matthew.

At that moment, I noticed a message on my phone that had been there for some time. I had silenced it during the Christmas service and not changed it back. It was from Christine. "Where are you?"

I quickly texted her back. "Small emergency. I'm fine. Explain later. Be there soon." Christine knew that the life of a doctor had its interruptions. I hoped that for now, this would suffice.

Seconds later I heard Matthew's footfalls echoing up the broad marble stairs followed by a hardened click of an electric switch. The chandeliers of the wide hallway came to life, replacing the previous shadows with a warm, pleasing light. As he entered the study, he thanked me again. His manner was now more of light-hearted relief tempered with mild embarrassment.

"Your children okay?"

"Yes, fine. Thanks. Our bedrooms are on a wing of the first floor. They're sound asleep. Apparently, they missed all the excitement."

I nodded, and a long silence followed. Matthew blew out a sigh of deliverance. "Man, I am really glad you saw the SOS. I didn't know what else to do." He smiled and regarded me sheepishly. "It's all rather embarrassing."

"Not to worry. As far as embarrassing goes, I'm the guy who decided to walk into your house, at night, in the dark, uninvited. If I had been wrong about the SOS, that would have made front page news in a lot of ugly ways."

Matthew stood casually with his hands in his trouser pockets. "Well, thank heavens you saw it. I had left my cell phone downstairs. The distress signal was the only thing I could think of."

"So, I'm guessing you were in Boy Scouts?"

At first, he hesitated, not understanding my question. "Oh, actually no. I was in the Navy for several years."

This was a revelation. Matthew hadn't struck me as ex-military. But in reflection, I recalled that at the church, despite his cautious nature, he did carry himself with a kind of understated reserve. Nevertheless, the initial surprise on my face had been too obvious. Matthew's eyes tightened, and I could detect an almost amused grin forming at the corners of his mouth; a response that struck me as odd. Perhaps because of his modest size and bookish manner, he was accustomed to a certain level of disbelief about his military service. I felt awkward at being read so easily and feared that my stunned reaction was likely viewed as a kind of slight. I changed the subject.

"What do you think happened with the lock?"

"Absolutely no idea. The doors and lights of this house seem to have a mind of their own. How did you get in, anyway?"

"The front door was unlocked."

Matthew stared at me, composed but mildly bewildered. "Well, I thought it was locked. But I guess I'm fortunate that it wasn't."

"I noticed the lights are working now. I couldn't get them to come on."

"The breaker box is in the utility room off the kitchen." Matthew paused and glanced at the floor before continuing. His response was hesitant as if he felt the need to choose his words carefully. "I checked it before coming back up. Half the breakers were tripped off." There was something elusive in his manner. My curiosity stirred.

"Looks like that flashlight of yours came in handy." It was a baiting question. I said this noting that he had not returned with it.

Again, Matthew looked away before responding. "Yes. The lights have gone off before, so I usually keep one up here. Earlier I had put the children to bed and needed to get online for a few minutes. I don't even remember shutting the office door. But when I was through with the computer and tried to leave, the door was locked."

He folded his arms and exhaled, visibly perplexed. "Who knows...I seem to be in a fog these days. Perhaps I absent mindedly shut the door."

"But it was locked. Doesn't that require a key?"

He lifted his shoulders in resignation, signaling his mutual understanding of the unresolved details. "Yes. The lock is not spring loaded; it's geared. You must have a key to engage it, just like you did."

"And I take it you don't have a key?"

"No, I don't. There's never been a key in the lock like the other doors. So, I've never really thought about needing one."

My eyes tightened. I spoke slowly. "So, there's no key but the door locked anyway?"

"Apparently."

I stared at him deadpan, wordless. An involuntary tingling bristled down my neck. I wanted to hold tight to the rational high ground. But for this night, it looked like creepy was determined to have the upper hand. "Nice," I mumbled in resignation. "And just like that, we go from curiously odd to mildly terrifying."

Matthew scratched his head and smiled. "I hear you." He shrugged. "But then again, I was told that this place is full of, you know…."

"Ghosts?" I blurted abruptly. The events of the evening had tidily disrupted my previous definitions of reality and left me with half-humored gregariousness. "I mean, hey…why not just say it? Ghosts, right?"

The question hung between us, and I waited for a response that at first, did not come. Matthew's only acknowledgment was an affirming nod and a wary grin. The paranormal was a topic that he seemed to embrace passively. "So, I take it you don't give the supernatural much quarter?"

I grinned and scratched my head. "I've always tended to reject anything ghostly as improbable, lest everyone think I was delusional and regard me with a wink and a nod. Although admittedly, several of my Watervalley experiences during the past eighteen months have somewhat altered that hardened viewpoint. But after the locking doors, the tripping breakers, and the personal performance I received earlier from the Poltergeist Glee Club, I'm considering making a full conversion."

"Poltergeist Glee Club?"

"Yeah, in the front yard right after I arrived. For several seconds there, I could have sworn I heard a whirlwind of singing voices circling me. Needless to say, it wigged me out a little."

"Huh, interesting. The children have spoken of the same thing. I've yet to hear it."

"Does it frighten them?"

"No, actually they describe it as rather warming and pleasant."

"Well, I must have heard the unplugged version. Because it scared the crap out of me."

Matthew had no response but just stared at me woodenly. I exhaled and spoke again. "Anyway, you might think I'm nuts, but I think this place has some non-paying guests."

He grinned, seemingly amused. "You mean, like spirits."

"Ghosts, spirits, whatever. Is there a difference?"

"Ghosts are more shifty-eyed."

I stared at him blankly, not understanding.

"Sorry. That was a joke," he said sheepishly and looked away. Under his breath, he added, "and obviously not a very good one."

"You seem a little more at ease with this subject than I am."

Matthew spoke with bemused resignation. "Well, I guess since you've seen me at my worst, I might as well fill you in." He nodded toward the door. "Come on; we'll talk on the way down." I followed him into the hallway.

"I'll admit," he said, "things go bump in the night here, but they don't have an ominous feel to them."

"Well, that's reassuring, sorta." I wasn't certain what to make of his assertion. "I mean, how do you know. Do they sign a lease agreement with rules attached?"

Matthew smiled as he continued down the steps. "My initiation began in Charleston. A year and a half ago we moved into a huge old house south of Broad Street that had been in my wife Emily's family for generations. Her grandmother had passed and left it to her. Emily was the only surviving heir."

"Hmm, her grandmother you say?"

"Yes. Emily was an only child, and her parents had passed away before we met; boating accident the year she graduated from high school. She lived with her grandmother during the summers of her college years and grew to love the old Charleston place. We had a house north of town. But when Emily inherited the family estate, she insisted we move there. So, we did."

"Okay. And?"

"We heard voices and noises all the time. Every Tuesday after midnight there was a Ladies Bridge Club that met downstairs in the parlor."

By now we had made our way to the second floor. I stopped and turned to him. "You're serious?"

His response was spontaneous and unmistakably matter-of-fact. "Oh yeah. Quite a cutthroat old bunch, too. We'd hear them in the night, chatting it up, snapping at each other, and taking direct hits off a bottle of bourbon. There was a two second grace period to play your card before getting yelled at. I'm pretty sure punching was allowed."

I grinned but still regarded him skeptically. We proceeded down the loops of the grand stairway, and undoubtedly, I was slightly dumbfounded at his casual regard of the subject. Yet, he didn't seem to be joking. I was about to inquire further, but by this time we had arrived at the large room where I had previously bumped around in the dark.

Instantly, the conversation took a dramatic turn.

Chapter 10

SECRETS

The room was spectacular, almost magical, and I stood there gawking in amazement. The grand hall was alight with a magnificent Christmas tree and incredible furnishings. Thick Persian rugs defined the tightly ordered sitting areas gilded with vintage antique furniture. The soaring wood-paneled walls were covered with original artworks of both oil and watercolor. Tall, stately glass-front hutches contained lighted displays of Waterford crystal and bone china. There was a permeating, almost intimidating feeling of old wealth far beyond anything I had known in Watervalley. Oddly, the large chamber had the well-appointed and lush feel of a grand and luxurious hotel lobby, similar to one I had visited in Chicago in years past.

Perhaps the most amazing thing about the room was the balance and symmetry of the space to its belongings as if the furniture had been meticulously selected and placed rather than randomly relocated from Matthew's house in Charleston. I stood for a moment, absorbing everything. Collectively, it was singularly extraordinary.

"Matthew, I've got to hand it to you. For a classics professor, you've got a rather sharp eye for decking a place out."

By now Matthew had regained the reserved and polite demeanor of our earlier encounter at the church. He grinned dismissively. "Yeah, well...I had some help with that."

"Really? Someone locally?" Oddly, my curiosity had caught him off guard. He hesitated.

"I um, I had a service out of Nashville come set everything up." By small degrees, he seemed uncomfortable discussing the room's furnishings. He turned his attention toward the Christmas tree, seemingly to redirect the conversation. "In fact, another Nashville service did the tree, lights, and everything. No way I could have gotten that monster in here by myself."

I smiled and nodded. This explained the series of trucks and workmen who had been seen in the previous weeks. Yet, all the while I was weighing my thoughts about Matthew. I had mistakenly equated reserve with timidity. Now I realized that his restrained manner was more likely a derivative of his military service. Aside from his somewhat disheveled dress code, there was about him a casual urbanity. This was a man who was quite comfortable amid expensive things. All this pointed to a confirmation of Mayor Hickman's assertion. Matthew was wealthy and, given the salary of a college professor, I suspected he had married into it.

I stood with my hands in my pockets, slowly circling to admire the grandeur of the enormous room. Matthew waited politely, granting me this brief indulgence. That was until I became fixated on the painting above the mantle.

The oil canvas was of a young and elegant woman in a sundress, standing in the brilliant light and lavish pastel flowers of a brick courtyard, quite clearly a Charleston setting. She was breathtaking.

In her early thirties, the woman was tall and slender, well made with fine blue eyes and splendid blonde hair that was stylishly swept away from her face. Although polished and reserved in presentation, she was fresh and beautiful with delicate, perfectly balanced features. Her posture and bearing had a flowing, almost regal quality, full of the artful lure and glamour that normally adorned the cover of *Town and Country*. And yet, there was something in her smile that conveyed a feeling of warmth and humor, an approachable, almost girlish nature that was vulnerable, sensitive, whole-souled, engaging. I was immediately and completely enchanted.

At first, neither of us spoke, and we were both conscious of the avoidance. Perhaps I should have turned away, moved along as it were. But the woman in the painting was so striking, so radiant, that she seemed to absorb all the light in the room. I found it impossible not to stare.

In time, Matthew straightened his back, and his appearance projected a varnish of fortification. He exercised great economy in his words. "Yes. That was Emily."

"She was quite beautiful. I can see where the children get their handsome looks."

He spoke modestly. "I would agree. It certainly didn't come from their father."

I smiled and turned to him. "Well, that's not exactly what I meant."

Matthew grinned. But I could tell that his attempt at humor was to mask the deeper emotions of his heart. He stared at the portrait with a mind that was elsewhere, fathoms deep in an ocean of loss. I couldn't help but wonder if he was reflecting upon Christmas Eve's that should be but never would. One thing about Matthew was certain. His grief defined him. Perhaps all else could be understood from there.

He gazed solemnly at the painting for a long moment before finally speaking. "She could occupy a lot of space in a man's head."

Instinctively I stepped toward the portrait to view it more closely. But upon approaching the fireplace, I noticed an array of framed black and white pictures on the mantle. One of the prints was sepia-toned and caught my attention. Carefully, I picked it up. The photograph appeared to be of Society Hill Manor from an earlier time, freshly built with no landscaping. Standing on the front steps was a man in a suit. He was tall and lean with thick dark hair.

"Is this the mansion?"

At first, Matthew seemed reluctant to speak. His gaze tightened, and I sensed that he was talking himself through some inner argument. Then he pursed his lips and smiled warmly. "Yes. It is. It was taken in 1925."

"Well, that is incredible. Did you find it on the Internet somewhere?"

Matthew pondered his answer. "No. Actually, we found it in the attic of Emily's grandmothers' house in Charleston."

I was dumbfounded. "Are you serious? How did it get there?"

Just as before, Matthew was contemplative, slow to respond. But in time, he spoke with a soft, accommodating smile. "The answer is quite simple. The fellow in the photograph is Hiram Hatcher, the man who built Society Hill. He was Emily's great-grandfather."

"Oh," I said lightly, straining not to reveal the full jolt of his statement. For some reason, I wanted to appear indifferent…to act as though I was above all the gossip and curiosity as to why Matthew had come to Watervalley. I returned the photograph and folded my arms, doing my best to seem detached. Still, it was difficult not to speak to the obvious.

"Well, I guess that explains your interest in the old place." But in truth, this information did the exact opposite. His disclosure generated a lengthy list of questions. I was hoping he would volunteer more. He didn't.

A long silence ensued, during which I felt oddly conspicuous. We exchanged an affirming nod, a mutual understanding that the time had come for me to go. As we walked to the entry hall, we traded telephone numbers; a wise precaution.

Once again, he shook my hand in gratitude. "Luke, I can't thank you enough."

"Sure. No problem." I wanted to make light of the whole affair. "I still feel a little funny about coming in unannounced. Good thing you're not the gun-toting-shoot-first kind of guy."

An amused, faintly cunning smile emerged. Matthew spoke impassively. "Well, actually I have a fairly extensive gun collection. Perhaps I can show it to you some time."

I hid my surprise. Matthew was mild-mannered and taught classical languages. So, I had pictured him as more of the stamp collecting type or the kind of person who was the first to finish his science project in elementary school, not a gun enthusiast.

"Sure, sounds good. Although I must admit, having worked at Vanderbilt's ER, I'm more familiar with gunshot wounds than I am with guns themselves."

Matthew smiled. "Yeah, I saw more than a few of those in the Navy. Not a pretty sight." Then, he pursed his lips and spoke guardedly. "Luke, listen. I know this kind of thing makes for a good story in a small town, but if you don't mind…"

I stopped him in mid-sentence. "Matthew, it's not a problem. I have no need to tell anyone… except perhaps, for my fiancé, Christine. She's expecting me, and I'll need to provide an explanation. We don't keep too many secrets." I paused for a moment, wincing at my half-truth. "Anyway, she's discreet. So, no worries."

"Thanks. I um…I appreciate that." He cast his gaze downward, deliberating. "Luke, I have another favor to ask."

I shrugged. "Okay."

"My reasons for buying the bed and breakfast are many-sided. They involve a mix of issues with my wife's final wishes. I'd rather not have it under public scrutiny." Having said this, he paused, gathering himself. Then oddly, he looked to the side and gushed a muted laugh. "Truth is, I wasn't planning on visitors and hadn't expected anyone to see that photo. I probably shouldn't have it sitting out. But, it meant a lot to Emily." For a second, he drifted; drawn to some distant moment.

"So, I guess what I'm asking is that you keep that knowledge under wraps, at least for now. I've got some things I'm trying to work through. I certainly understand confiding in your fiancée. But beyond that, I'd appreciate it if you didn't mention it to anyone."

His request fostered a dozen more questions. What were Emily's final wishes? What things was he trying to work through? Naturally, I wanted to know more. But standing before me was a man with a tremendous loss and a simple request. My curiosity would have to wait.

"Sure. Not a problem."

"Thanks. And thanks for coming to my rescue."

The humility and sincerity in his voice were so unmistakably genuine that candidly, I felt slightly embarrassed. "Oh, hey, no big deal. Besides," I said jokingly. "You never know. Maybe next time it'll be you coming to my rescue."

He casually slipped his hands in his trousers and smiled. "I doubt that. But I'll be on the lookout just the same."

"Well, you've got my number. Call anytime."

"Thanks, we're fine. We'll be right here."

I tightened my coat collar around my neck and turned to leave. But while closing the door behind me, Matthew whispered under his breath, "in omnia paratus."

After starting the engine, I eased back through town and guided the car into the immense and lonely countryside. The road before me was deserted and black, absorbing the beams of the headlights. I rode along in silence, accompanied only by the drone of the engine and the faint wash of the dashboard lights.

The high clouds had cleared, but the unfinished moon was shy and distant; casting only a dimly luminous pale across the darkened landscape. As the slumbering farmhouses and frozen fields vanished in a blur to either side of me, I pondered; wondering what Matthew had meant by quoting the Latin phrase, "ready for anything." Nothing came to mind. It was yet another twist in the tangle of words and events from the past hour. For now, there were no answers.

Grasping the steering wheel tighter, I sighed deeply and pressed onward into the swallowing darkness. Matthew's friendliness was unquestioned. But I was troubled. His casual regard of the spectral world was unsettling enough. But all too often there had been a reluctance, an evasiveness in his words; something that went beyond shyness or a desire for privacy. And strangest of all was his desire to keep his wife's relation to Hiram Hatcher secret.

It made little sense. The people of Watervalley held their family and ancestors in reverence. A bloodline connection would make his interest in the bed and breakfast easily understood and accepted; something that would go far to dispel the rumors that had been created to fill the void. But Matthew didn't seem to care. Nor, by all appearances, did he seem interested in opening the B&B for business any time soon. Yet, one thing remained certain. As much as I wanted my first impression of Matthew to be correct, a crippling doubt had taken residence in my head. Suspicion now clouded the lens through which I had previously viewed him.

Chapter 11

THE CHAMBERS WOMEN

At long last, the distant lights of Christine's farmhouse came into view. Warmed by the knowledge of seeing her, I put my concerns behind me. Inside, only a small lamp in the living room stood sentry. Christine was asleep, snugly coiled on the couch. I sat on the edge, brushing lightly against her, waking her without words. Her eyes opened slowly; quietly absorbing my presence before softening into an affectionate gaze, made perfect by a tender, sleepy smile. She placed a warm hand against my face and whispered in a voice that was sweet, heartfelt, relieved.

"Good. You're finally here."

Drowsy, she closed her eyes again and instinctively nestled closer to me, seemingly content in the knowledge of my safe arrival. I had been irresponsibly late and out of touch, fully expecting to apologize and pay penance for my delay. And yet Christine required none of this, patiently tolerating my absence. I ran my fingers through her hair and knew that I was most fortunate. Soon she was to be a doctor's wife, a role that included some unfair downsides. Knowing this was one thing. Accepting it was another. Christine had already done both.

In time, she sat up and gazed at me through nodding eyes. "Bradford, I'm going up to bed." She rose and walked toward the stairs in a kind of groggy stagger. I turned off the lamp and half-leaned, half-collapsed against the shoulder of the couch. A couple of hours later, I awoke and stumbled to the guest bedroom. We would talk in the morning.

Breakfast was a late and lazy affair consisting of robes, house shoes, and coffee in the kitchen. I leaned against the counter as Christine and her mother, Madeline leisurely went about the business of frying eggs and country ham, occasionally imploring my help with a minor task or two.

In truth, despite my grousing to Christine the previous evening, I adored Madeline Chambers. A banker's daughter, she was a petite and handsome woman with a pleasing, graceful manner. Christine's father, a prosperous farmer, had passed away a decade ago in a tragic farming accident. But there remained between mother and daughter a deep intimacy; a delightful, tender relationship of two who had grown to be best friends.

Our breakfast conversation was light and lively, full of easy laughter. At some point, Madeline made a polite inquiry regarding my late arrival. I casually dismissed it as a house call. An errant glance to Christine conveyed that more was suspected. But Madeline left it at that.

I knew that the two of them telepathically communicated on some mysterious X-chromosome-only frequency. I readily assumed that Madeline was aware of a rift in my response. But, she had far too much tact and courtesy to query further.

After breakfast, we opened gifts and delighted in the small joys and affections of exchanging presents. We were a modest threesome. But even months before the taking of official vows, we were family. In her own way, Madeline was the flawless matriarch, full of warmth and humor and a slow, discerning gentleness. She was engaging and easy company. But this wasn't true for all the Chambers women.

Near noon Madeline left to pick up Christine's paternal grandmother, Mattie Chambers, at the airport in Nashville. This was not good news. I had met Mattie the previous Christmas and somehow had never quite won her over with the Bradford charm. Unfortunately, Christine adored her. Me, not so much. She was a blunt, opinionated, and proud Southern farm woman who generally regarded me as if I were a direct descendant of William T. Sherman. She lived in Florida but always came back to the farm every year during the holidays for an extended visit; similar, as I viewed it, to the off-season equivalent of locusts. I could scarcely wait.

That afternoon, Christine and I decided to take a hike up to Bracken's Knoll, a large, bald hill on the back of the farm that, as a child, had been her favorite place to spend her carefree hours. We set out under a grey, overcast sky that felt close and moist. But our spirits were high, breathing in deeply of the brisk, clean air of late December. The open countryside was a dormant world of neat fencerows, fallow fields, loamy earth, and broad pastures of hibernating, untamed grass. In the distance, the far, shouldering hills were covered in the delicate mist of winter.

Yet, Christine was energized by all of it. She drew from the land a secret strength; a provincial hardiness rooted from many years among constant hills and familiar skies. Even though the farm was in the slumber of winter, the whole of it felt like a sleeping giant, immense, raw, powerful; filled with a living presence and a romantic abundance.

Along the way, we talked. Christine listened as I related the events of the previous evening, responding with the same fascination and curiosity that I had felt regarding the various twists of the story; especially Matthew's desire to keep his wife's ancestry secret. I chose not to mention the paranormal part of the evening, especially the chanting voices. As impacting and real as they were, I lacked the words to describe the situation properly and, in the light of day, felt rather silly trying to do so. When I finished, Christine readily agreed to Matthew's request for discretion.

In time, we arrived at the pinnacle of Bracken's Knoll. Awash in an enchanted smile, Christine stopped, closed her eyes, and breathed in a deep draft of the fresh, cold air. As she slowly exhaled, her face seemed transformed. There welled from within her a contentment found only in the thousand-fold memories of this remote hill. In all directions, the rolling plain of the valley floor extended for miles. Christine held out her arms in a euphoric long stretch, seemingly embracing the whole of Watervalley. Beyond any doubt, her mind and soul were intimately woven to this small place on earth.

After finishing the story about Matthew, I had planned on telling her about the letter containing the research offer from Vanderbilt. I didn't. After seeing her so incandescently happy, my heart couldn't bring me to it.

At the time, I had no idea that events were already in motion that would make this a profoundly foolish decision.

Chapter 12

THE TALK

I returned home that evening to an empty house, an empty bed, and a napkin on the kitchen table with the word "Sorry," written on it. John wasn't a man for elaborate apologies. I worried about him. He had picked an odd time to break a dry spell.

Christmas had been on Sunday, and I had told Christine that I would be scarce on Monday to avail her the opportunity to spend some quality time with her grandmother. She, of course, saw right through this ploy, knowing that I would rather kiss a goat…twice, than spend five minutes with Mattie Chambers. Sooner or later I'd have to be around the old bat. I chose later.

Late Monday morning, I went next door and collected my two golden retrievers, Rhett and Casper, from my kind and accommodating neighbors. Based on the amount of drool, it appeared the boys were quite happy to see me.

Bowl games were on. So, armed with a load of munchies and the TV remote, I settled into the deep cushions of the couch. Soon afterward, I heard a car pull in to my driveway, and in short order, there was a knock at the door. It was Connie.

"Good morning, sunshine. I didn't expect to see you today."

She was carrying a full grocery bag and offered only a puckered frown at my teasing. She headed straight for the kitchen and set the bag on the table. "I brought you some leftovers," she said dryly.

"Ohhhh, that's right. Big Christmas dinner at your place. How'd that go?"

"It was fine. All my children made it except for Rayford. He's working as a commodities trader in Chicago now. He wants me to come and visit sometime."

"You should go."

Connie removed her coat and began putting the leftovers into the fridge. "I will at some point. Maybe when it's not so cold," she said vacantly, leaving the subject at that. "We had two whole pies left over, so I brought you one."

"Is it chess? Please tell me it's chess."

"Yes, Little Jack Horner, it's chess."

I closed my eyes in satisfaction. "Ahhh. And on the eighth day, God created chess pie, and He saw it was good."

She was unamused. "Be careful how you use the Lord's name, doctor. You don't want to appear as a man of low spiritual fiber."

"I'll eat more bran."

"I also brought you all the leftover ham and turkey. I'm thinking about becoming a vegetarian for my New Year's resolution."

"Should I put the houseplants on notice?"

Connie regarded me with tired disdain. "Should I grab those wooden spoons over there and play a little tune on your foolish noggin?"

I held up a hand in surrender. "Fine. Suit yourself. Drink green stuff and jog. But the way I see it, the species fought long and hard to get to the top of the food chain. I'm not forfeiting the benefits so readily."

Connie ignored me and casually changed the subject. "So, how's your day been?"

"Rough. Just before you got here, I broke off a chip in the dip. So, I sent in a recon chip, and that broke too."

She ignored this as well. "By the way, I want to thank you for your Christmas gifts. You shouldn't have gotten me anything, you know."

"So, I'm guessing you found them along with my note to open them." I had put Connie's gifts in her car during the Christmas Eve party. With all the frenzy of the evening, it was the simplest way to be sure she got them.

"I did, but I have to ask, what is the Fruit and Nut of the Month Club?"

"They send you a basket each month. It's supposed to be super, high-quality stuff."

"So, it's for real?"

"Sure. Why wouldn't it be?"

Connie shook her head and laughed, clearly amused. "Luke, dear, I don't want to hurt your feelings, but the combination of fruity and nutty along with your endless capacity for childishness made me think you were up to something."

"Oh, I see. Well, I guess that does sound like me. But, no. It's the real deal."

Connie smiled. "It sounds lovely. Thank you. And thank you for the other gift as well."

"Ouch. That last part sounded a little too diplomatic."

"No, it's fine. I'm just not sure what the point of it is."

"It's an ancestry DNA kit. You put some saliva in the tube and send it off. Or, if you prefer…in your case, venom works just as well."

Connie returned to her task. "Umm hmm," she hummed dispassionately. "And what will that tell me?"

"It will give you a pie chart of what countries your bloodlines are from, you know, like Kenya, Turkey, Sweden...Krypton."

Connie put away the last of the food and shrugged. "I guess it's worth a go."

"Well, try to curb your enthusiasm there, bubbles. All the cool kids are doing it. I thought you'd find it interesting."

"Oh, I'm sure I will," she said absently. The napkin on the table caught her attention.

"That looks like John's handwriting. I'd heard a rumor that he had spent the night here Christmas Eve."

"Yeah, well bad news always seems to have a longer stride than the other kind."

"Hmm, hmm, hmm," Connie muttered. "John will be getting his second liver transplant before he admits to his alcohol problem."

"I know. He didn't seem himself. Except for you and me, I don't think he talked to a soul the other night."

Connie shook her head. "John's not one to make friends with humans. I figured out a long time ago that for him, there are two categories of people in Watervalley."

"Oh, really? What are they?"

"Doesn't matter. He doesn't like either kind."

"Well, Ann will be back in a couple of days. Maybe that will boost his spirits."

"You think they're getting serious?" Connie inquired.

"Hard to say. I think she's been good for him. But here lately, I don't know. I hope he's not falling back into a reclusive funk."

Connie shrugged and rubbed her chin thoughtfully. "I doubt it. Ann's smart and John's not a bad catch. He's a clean, one-owner model with relatively low mileage. I wouldn't be surprised if they were married by summer."

"You think so?"

"Maybe," she said lightly. Then, after a moment's reflection, she looked at me and spoke sternly. "But don't tell anybody I said so. If it doesn't happen, I wouldn't want to lose any street cred."

She paused and looked around the kitchen which, undeniably was in slight disarray from my chosen holiday laziness. "So, you have big plans for the day?"

"I was thinking about inviting some of the regulars from down at the Alibi Road House to come over. You know, slumber party, drinkey, drinkey, limbo contest…just the normal stuff."

Connie spoke dryly. "Umm-hmm. Fascinating. Well, while you're planning your little shindig, you might want to think about taking tidiness for a test drive."

I stiffened, both surprised and amused at her allegation. "Something on your mind, Constance Grace?"

"Yeah. I'm thinking right now might be a good time for the talk."

I shrugged. "Works for me."

Connie nodded. She instinctively pulled out one of the chairs away from the kitchen table and sat down. I followed suit. Her voice was kind but direct.

97

"Luke, dear. You realize that after you get married, I'll no longer be coming around to help with the housework. This will be Christine's house, and she doesn't need me in the way."

"Okay, fair enough."

"The wedding will be a blur, and I'm sure the honeymoon will be glorious. And for the first few weeks after you get back, everything will still be fresh and new and exciting. Both of you will be bending over backward to be considerate and affectionate to each other. It will be like living a dream."

I nodded attentively, wondering where this was going. Connie continued.

"But then one day you'll both wake up and realize that the lawn needs mowing, the bathroom needs cleaning, and the garbage needs to be taken out. And that's where I'm a little concerned. It's about your domestic skills."

"What about them?"

"I think they peaked in middle school."

"I'm not sure what you're saying?"

"I'm saying your housekeeping habits are a train wreck, and pretty soon this is no longer going to be my station."

I fell back in my chair, somewhat stunned. "Well, thanks for the subtlety."

"Now don't be getting all riled up. You're a handsome man, Luke. You're tall and good looking. You've got an easy smile and can be quite charming when you choose. So, along with being the town physician, people naturally want to do for you."

"Gee," I responded skeptically. "I'm not so sure about all that."

"Well, I am sure. So, listen. You know I care deeply for you. But you need to hear me out. You're a doctor, Luke. And not just a good one but a brilliant one. God gave you this…not that you've figured that out and shown Him any gratitude… but anyway, you've lived on your own for quite some time. For most folks, and especially men, when they live alone like that, they get the sincere notion that they're quite easy to live with. And in your case, not only have you lived alone, you've lived a lot of years without a woman's touch in the home."

"Meaning?"

"Meaning your domestic practices have suffered. Sometimes I'm amazed you know how to walk upright. And living with two dogs hasn't pulled up your average either. Not that I'm judging, mind you."

"You sure? Because whole sections of that sounded like judgment to me."

"All I'm saying is that before you bring a woman into this house, I think you need to contact Mission Control because you are nowhere near ready for lift off."

Admittedly, I was mildly indignant at Connie's assertion. "Give me one example."

"Just last week I noticed you were wearing what you found in the dirty clothes hamper that morning. What were you thinking?"

"I was thinking I was going to get away with it and not have to explain it to anyone," I said defensively.

"And you need to learn how to pick up after yourself. The ability to create clutter may just be your superpower."

"I never have trouble finding what I'm looking for. Besides, I do my own laundry from time to time."

"I've noticed. The other day there was enough fluff in the lent trap to make a cushion."

"I cook, too, I'll have you know."

"Umm-hmm. And according to the neighbors, you must be using the smoke alarm as a kitchen timer."

"I get a lot of interruptions."

Connie was unamused and fastened upon me a sharp, penetrating stare whose clear intent was to decompose me. I held up my hands in a gesture of capitulation. "Okay, fine. Out with it. Let's hear this roster of villainy."

By now she was in high gear, her voice both animated and matter-of-fact. It became readily apparent that this was a conversation she had begun long before she arrived this morning.

"For starters, apparently you expect the laundry fairy to pick your pants up off the floor. And your shower. I've never seen anything so filthy. I'd rather take a sponge bath on a garbage barge. There are bacteria in there big enough to be domesticated as household pets."

"Not everybody sees dirt on the sub-atomic level that you do, Connie."

"Are you kidding me, Luke Bradford. You don't notice an accumulation of dirt until it's large enough to pot a plant in it. And your bedroom. Did someone set a bomb off in there? With some photos and the completion of a few online forms, you could qualify for federal disaster relief."

"A little disorder breeds character."

Humph," Connie retorted. "I may have to spray the whole upstairs with disinfectant because of all the character that's breeding up there."

I stared at her blankly, speechless. I couldn't believe what I was hearing. Admittedly, my standard of cleanliness wasn't that of a surgical field. But neither was it the floor of a fraternity house bathroom. I folded my arms, mildly peeved. "How does this happen? One minute I'm a happy guy with bowl games and Cheetos and the next instant I'm assaulted by the Germ Gestapo."

Connie regarded me with a puckered and reproving face. Her voice was both authoritative and instructive. "Luke, this could be one of those times when keeping your mouth shut might be your greatest accomplishment."

I ignored her. "Hey, all I'm saying is that I think I'm a reasonably clean and tidy guy. I'm busy. I'm a doctor for heaven's sake. It demands a lot of my time. So, on balance, I need to be appreciated and understood."

"Could have fooled me," Connie breezed to the general air. "The way you're acting I was thinking you needed to be swaddled and burped."

I wanted to come back with a clever retort, but nothing came to mind. "So, what's your point?"

"The point, Luke, is that since both of you have full-time jobs, you need to rethink the distribution of labor. Keeping up a house involves a lot of repetitive, unglamorous tasks. But you can punch above your weight if you work together."

"Such as?"

The words began in a high-pitched voice and nearly exploded from her. "Such as? How about this! Learn how to fold laundry, lower the toilet seat once in a while, and for heaven's sake figure out why God invented coasters. Be thoughtful and pick up around the house from time to time. Help with the dishes. Change out the bag in the vacuum."

I sharpened my gaze. "What bag?"

Closing her eyes, Connie slowly shook her head from side to side. An agonizing silence ensued. I impatiently drum rolled my fingers on the kitchen table. There was an element in the mix of this entire conversation that didn't fit. Finally, a simple reality washed over me. I leaned toward her.

"Connie, is there something else bugging you here?"

"You mean other than your occasional holiday from hygiene?"

"This is about you and me, isn't it? It's about us no longer seeing each other on a regular basis."

Connie stiffened. "Of course not. You're just trying to change the subject to save your own skin."

"Why shouldn't I. I'm very attached to it."

"That's not the point."

"Look, Connie. I'm sure there is some truth in all the things you're telling me. But Christine and I are both adults. We'll figure things out. Meanwhile, you need to realize something. I know you'll no longer be the housekeeper. That will be a change. But one thing will never change, and I want you to hear what I'm saying... plain and simple. You will always be Connie Thompson, my surrogate mom. That's not going to change."

Connie pressed her lips hard together and nodded lightly. Then suddenly, her face began to crumble. It would seem that I had hit the mark. She exhaled a deep sigh, and a large tear emerged in the corner of her eye. I was quite moved, especially since, as much as I adored her, I didn't think she had a drop of water in her. She wiped it away and stiffened her back in a gesture of determination. "It's just that I want you and Christine to be happy. I want this marriage to be beautiful for the both of you."

"Look, Connie. Obviously, marriage is going to be a brave new world for both Christine and me. But we love each other deeply. We'll be fine."

She paused for a moment and focused her gaze out the windows toward the backyard. "Marriage isn't just about love, Luke."

I stared at her curiously. "You're kidding, right?"

She looked down for a moment, reflecting. "I wish I were." Then she took my hand. "Listen, Luke. For centuries people married for economic and political reasons. It wasn't romantic, but it was a union that both parties understood. Now people marry solely on the impulse of love because they want to make a nice feeling permanent. Now I'm not saying that love is a bad thing because Lord knows it's not. But it's an emotion, a feeling. And a marriage based on feelings has largely been spared the need to justify itself."

"Meaning?"

"Meaning, two young folks say they love each other and think marriage will be a breeze. It isn't. All that love does is give marriage a chance. Beyond that, it's nothing but an optimistic, big-hearted roll of the dice."

"So, what makes marriages last?"

"Compatibility. That's what makes a marriage endure. Love is the fuel that makes two people look for ways to stay together. Compatibility is the achievement of love. It's not a prerequisite of it."

Connie patted my hand. "I love you, Luke. You and Christine are well matched. I know you two will be happy. But as your surrogate Mama, I can't help but want to give you some advice along the way to make sure it's perfect."

I looked down and smiled, somewhat embarrassed by Connie's unfiltered forthrightness. "Well, by all means, Constance Grace. Feel free to toss out any words of wisdom."

She nodded her understanding. "Just tell her every day that you love her, thank her every day for the things she does, and never go to bed angry."

"But what if what I do to make her angry happens after we get in bed?"

Connie's tender countenance de-glossed. "Luke Bradford, you are such an adolescent. I'm fixing to put you in the freezer and make a big kidsickle out of you."

She shook her head and quickly regained her tone of lecture. "Meanwhile, I'll be anxiously awaiting the dawn of a new era in the tidiness department. From now on we're going to do a weekly clean-up-after-yourself report card and put it under the little pineapple magnet on the fridge."

The problem with what Connie said was that I knew she wasn't kidding. I appreciated the marital advice, but this seemed to be taking things a little far. Nevertheless, I held my angst in check and spoke with effusive diplomacy. "What would I do without you?"

Connie rose from her chair and whispered under her breath. "It doesn't bear thinking about." An amused silence fell between us, and my thoughts drifted to a different matter.

"Connie, tell me what you know about Hiram Hatcher."

Chapter 13

HIRAM HATCHER

Connie's eyes tightened. She scrutinized me for a moment, no doubt, curious. "Well, he was long before my time, mind you, but I do know a little bit about the man. He came to town in the early twenties when the phosphate boom happened. I think his family had been in the mining business in Maine; granite if I'm not mistaken. So, he knew a lot about excavating and quarrying and made a fortune, although, I think he showed up with quite a bit of money."

"Why is that?"

"A year before his phosphate business was up and running, he was highly involved in real estate development. From what I understand, he came to Watervalley in a pretty big way. He bought a vacant block of downtown and built the Hatcher Building on half of it. As you know, sister Estelle's bakery is in one of the shops of that original building. The other half was a warehouse, but it was torn down in the fifties. He even built his own railroad line up to Nashville to ship the phosphate. They took the old track up years ago. It's now Leipers Creek Road."

"Wow. He built a railroad?"

"Phosphate was big money. It was during that time that a lot of folks like Hiram Hatcher moved in and built those huge homes up on Society Hill, although it wasn't called Society Hill back then.

"What was it called?"

"Bootlegger Hill. Some of the old folks around town still call it that. Society Hill levels out on top to a pretty broad area. But the backside beyond that leads into a mixture of deep hollows and sharp ravines with lots of caves in them. For decades, all of it was thickly wooded, and it was common knowledge that several stills were tucked away back there. The hollows made it easy for bootleggers to hide their operations and, if need be, escape by the old logging roads. When the phosphate boom came, folks cleared out the level woods on the front side and built houses; the Hatcher estate being the grandest of them by far. I've been told that the original estate had hundreds of acres. I think it's only a fraction of that now. But even after all these years, the ravines and hollows behind it have remained untouched, and the woods have retaken everything. There are no roads, and no one lives back there. I think some out of state trust owns it."

"When did the name change from Bootlegger Hill?"

Connie paused, entertained by some private amusement. "Not sure exactly when, but I do know why. It seems that several of the local blue bloods wanted to build new houses up there as well, especially after the Hatcher estate was built. Needless to say, the name 'Bootlegger Hill' was a problem for the culture crowd."

"So, what happened?"

"During the twenties, some of the ladies of the town formed a book club that met every month in the huge parlor at the Hatcher estate. I think Lida used that room for the lobby and dining hall, but the book club still met there every Tuesday afternoon even when she had it." Having been in the magnificent room the previous day, I knew exactly what Connie was describing. But I made no acknowledgment of this to her.

"I'm guessing Hiram's wife was part of the group?"

"No chance of that. To my knowledge, Hiram Hatcher wasn't married when he lived here. I think he was just very involved with the community and had offered his home as a meeting place to get in good with the locals. Since the ladies met in that grand mansion, their husbands started to teasingly call them the High Society Book Club. The name stuck, and the area became known as High Society Hill. Over time the 'High' was dropped."

"If he wasn't married, why did he build such a big house?"

"Who knows. Hiram liked to live large. The story goes that he always had a ton of out of town guests and threw big parties all the time."

"So, what became of Hiram Hatcher?"

"Don't really know. For some reason, he left town rather suddenly sometime in 1927 or 28. There's always been a rumor that he murdered a woman up in the old mansion one night in a drunken fit."

"Really? Who was the woman?"

"No details on that either, but it couldn't have been anybody local since no one turned up missing. Some say a girlfriend out of Nashville or someplace farther who had come to visit him for a few days. The rumor goes that he buried her in the backyard or under the floor in the basement. Then again, there's no reason to believe that anyone was ever murdered there in the first place."

"Well, still. That's genuinely creepy."

"Sure is. Anyway, he sold the phosphate company to some of his competitors. Several weeks after he left, big trucks showed up and moved everything out of the house. To my knowledge, Hiram never came back to Watervalley again. Several months later the place sold to a banker in Nashville but then the depression hit. The house was boarded up and sat empty for years. Over the decades, it changed hands several times, but nobody's ever restored it to its former glory. Lida converted it into the Bed and Breakfast fifteen or so years ago and had done what she could to bring it to at least a shadow of its original state."

I nodded, assimilating everything Connie had said with what I had learned. I was puzzled. "And no one knows why he left?"

"Hard to say. Hiram was a pretty smart entrepreneur, and it seems that everything he touched turned to gold. Maybe he read the tea leaves about phosphate and got out. The boom ended a few years later."

I stared at her curiously. "So, how do you know all this about him?"

She shrugged. "Most of this is common knowledge. I remember my grandfather, Rayford Coleman, talked about him when I was a child. Evidently, Grandpappa knew him."

"Interesting. Did he do business with Hiram?"

"No. Grandpappa Rayford was an A.M.E minister. When he and Grandmamma moved here, he was fresh out of seminary. He said that Hiram was a generous soul and had quietly given a lot of money to help construct his church building; a pretty big gesture for a white man to do at the time."

"Sounds like Hiram had a little saint in him."

Connie mildly winced. "I'm not sure I'd go that far. Hiram was a businessman and knew how to spread money around to bring folks into camp. I'd always heard that he had a lot of influence with the local politicians as well as with law enforcement."

"Why would he need that?"

"No idea. Apparently, he was a man with big ideas and that was how he got things done."

Having said this, she lowered her chin, regarded me sternly, and spoke with the unqualified authority that's usually the preserve of KGB interrogators.

"Now, Dr. Bradford. I have a question for you. I got a text from Christine after the Christmas Eve party wanting to know if I knew where you were. You want to explain yourself on that one?"

Christine hadn't mentioned this. Apparently, during my lengthy absence that night, she had innocently touched base with Connie. This was a conversation that was best avoided.

"Not really."

Connie was undaunted. "Also, a little bird with a deputy's badge told me your car was seen rolling through downtown after midnight. That's the opposite direction from Christine's place. Seems to me there's a story here."

I had forgotten about the traffic cams downtown. My solitary car rolling through at that hour had probably piqued the interest of whoever was staffing the night desk at the sheriff's office. I sighed. "Yes, Mrs. Thompson. There is a story here."

Perhaps I simply needed to unburden my curiosity. Perhaps there was something larger about Matthew that I wanted to understand and could not do on my own. Or, maybe I knew that Connie was discreet and would eventually leverage the truth out of me anyway. I folded. For the next several minutes, I gave her a full accounting of the events of Christmas Eve, save for the peculiar incident on the lawn and

Emily House's relationship to Hiram Hatcher. Connie listened silently, contemplating all that I said. When I finished, she asked a rather odd question.

"So, you say that Matthew went downstairs to check on his children and left you alone in the third-floor library?"

"Yeah, that's right."

"Was there anything there that you didn't expect to find?"

"You mean besides me?"

Connie responded with a slow drop of her chin, unamused. I thought for another moment. "No. Nothing unusual. Why?"

Instinctively, she leaned in as a precursor of confidentiality. "Lida has always said that people heard voices coming out of that room at night."

"What kind of voices?"

"It was always female. Some kind of singing."

The back of my neck prickled as if something invisible had just breathed upon it. My reaction had not escaped Connie's notice. She regarded me curiously. "What?"

I gushed a weak chuckle in an expression of resignation. "Okay, don't laugh. While I was outside of Matthew's house, I got a little serenade from the spook sextet." I went on the explain as best I could the odd vocalizing I had heard; about how it sounded like several melodies being played on top of each other.

I was half-expecting Connie to admonish me for giving credence to anything in the spectral realm. Her reply, however, was quite the opposite.

"Did you recognize any of the tunes?"

I was slightly taken aback. "Well, no. Not really." But after further thought, I added. "They sounded old, like something...I don't know, maybe from the Twenties."

"From the Twenties?" Connie countered skeptically.

"Gee, I don't know. Maybe. At the time, I seem to recall being more focused on getting my heart restarted. Besides, I guess I'm surprised. I didn't realize you were open to the possibility of a little higher cosmic vibration."

Connie leaned back in her chair. "Well, I have a confession to make. I've been in the Hatcher House only once in my entire life. I was about nine years old at the time. Daddy was a painter, and I tagged along with him when he went there to give an estimate on some work. Daddy told me to stay close. But I wandered upstairs to the third floor to have a look around. Well, I ended up in that old study...all googly-eyed at how beautiful the place was. Then suddenly, I heard those voices just like you did. It scared me to death. I ran so fast I almost time traveled. I thought demons were trying to get me because I had disobeyed Daddy. I felt so guilty, I went home and punished myself by reading the entire book of Deuteronomy, twice. After that, I swore I'd never set foot in that house again."

"You think it was the ghost of the murdered woman?"

"I don't know, and I don't care. For the next ten minutes, after it happened, I was probably as white as a daisy." Having said this, Connie bellowed out a deep throated laugh. "Lord have mercy," she continued, "It still gives me the jitters. I've never been so scared in my entire life."

She shook her head and continued to snicker. But in time she folded her arms and pondered for a moment. "I think it's time I put that

112

silliness behind me. I need to pay our newcomer and his family a visit. Looks like I'll have to overcome the heebie-jeebies and make that happen." Connie tilted her head back and stared at the ceiling, preoccupied. "It's still a curiosity why he came here. It's too dramatic a change. He's either running to or running from something."

I was tempted to reveal Emily's relationship to Hiram Hatcher. But I didn't. As agreed upon, I had told Christine. Connie was another matter.

"Well, by all means, do what you think you should. Matthew is reserved, but certainly a likable fellow." Despite my newly acquired skepticism about him, I felt compelled to describe him in a positive light. Connie noticed my brooding and stared at me with anticipation, expecting more. I changed directions.

"By the way, Matthew mentioned that he was in the Navy. I found that, well, odd. He didn't strike me as ex-military."

Connie shrugged. "Did he say what he did? Was he an officer?"

"No. No details. Although, I guess he saw some level of combat because he mentioned seeing wounded men."

"Do you think he meant the Marines? You don't normally think of someone on a ship being shot."

"I'm sure he would have made the distinction if he were a Marine."

She nodded in agreement. "Well, in any case, I'm glad you've struck up a friendship. I've always heard that knowing people is better than knowing about them." Having said this, she paused and reflected for a moment. Then she said the most curious thing. "If you want to know the skinny on Hiram Hatcher, you should talk to John Harris, although, it may be a touchy subject."

"Oh, really? Why is that?"

"John's maternal grandmother was Hiram's personal secretary. There's an old rumor that the two of them had a fling."

"So? What's the big deal about that."

"She was married to John's grandfather at the time."

"Ohhhh," I muttered in a long, low voice of revelation. "Yeah, that would make for an awkward line of questioning."

"To make it worse, John's mother was born several months after Hiram left town so suddenly. And you know Watervalley, sweetie. The school for scandal is always in session."

"Well," I said thoughtfully. "Thanks for the heads up. I'll tread lightly."

I walked her to her car and on my way back, stopped by my mailbox to check the mail, a duty I had neglected to perform for several days. There was a healthy stack of letters, mostly Christmas cards and junk mail. I vacantly flipped through the pile on the way to the front porch. But one envelope brought my progress to a halt.

It was from the law offices of Levine and Schweitzer, the firm in Atlanta that handled my Aunt's estate. Between my deceased parents and my Aunt Grace, I had been left a considerable inheritance. It would not come into play for several years. That made the letter quite odd and candidly, somewhat troubling. The envelope was legal size and clearly not a Christmas Card.

I returned to the kitchen and opened this peculiar correspondence. What it said changed everything.

Chapter 14

STUNNED

The letter from Levine and Schweitzer read as follows:

Dr. Luke Bradford
205 Fleming Street
Watervalley, TN 38489

Dear Dr. Bradford,

I hope this correspondence finds you well.

As executor and trustee of your Aunt Grace's estate (Lillian Grace Bradford), I am charged with specific ongoing responsibilities regarding the administration of said trust.

Notwithstanding, within the scope of her instructions are allowances for the disbursement of dividends, earnings, and other sourced monies attained beyond the original principal of the trust, provided certain conditions are satisfied. All monies, including the principal, will be made available upon your thirty-fifth birthday which is still several years hence.

As you are aware, your Aunt Grace had a prescribed interest for you to follow in your father's career as a rural physician. However, specific within her instructions was the option to avail funds as identified above, after you completed two years of service in a doctor deficient community. While the language defining the use of these funds is intended toward your "health, education, and welfare," they will nevertheless be disbursed directly to you to be used at your discretion.

Per my understanding, July of the coming year will mark the completion of two years of service in the community of Watervalley, Tennessee, where you remain the sole physician. Thus, the intent of this letter is to inform you that at that time, you will receive a disbursement of approximately $75,000 from your aunt's trust fund.

Please contact my office at your convenience so that arrangements can be made to facilitate a wire transfer of the funds when the appropriate time arrives.

Sincerely,

Jacob Levine, Esquire

I read the letter three times, returned it to the envelope, and then retrieved it and read it twice more. The clause regarding the availability of interest and dividend money after two years was a vague memory that I had discounted because much of my aunt's trust was in low interest-bearing bonds and savings accounts. As well, the phrase "other sourced monies" made no sense but I readily disregarded it as "lawyerese."

I have no idea how long I sat there, vacantly staring at the objects in the kitchen. Suddenly, my life had something it had not possessed: choice. Come next July, seventy-five thousand dollars would pay off the balance of my college loans with a few thousand to spare, effectively releasing me from my third-year obligation to the town of Watervalley. As well, the research position I had been offered at Vanderbilt did not start until July when the Federal Grant money would become available. After being married in early June, I would go on my honeymoon and could then pay off my college loans, move to Nashville and step right into a position at one of the country's leading research hospitals. It was an adrenaline rush, a dream come true. With the opening of a single letter, all the cosmic tumblers had magically fallen into place.

I spontaneously extended my arms and fist in the air. "Yes!" I shouted aloud. My exhilaration was beyond words. The thought of being back in academia, steeped in the world of cutting-edge research and discovery, absolutely thrilled me. It lifted my soul. I was ecstatic, consumed with the realization that a bold new adventure lay before me. Still holding the letter, I began pacing back and forth in the kitchen, thinking of the possibilities and energized beyond belief. In my mindless excitement, my steps carried me down the hall and into the living room.

Then, reality set in.

Before me was the Christmas tree with all its stacks of gifts, canned goods, baked bread, and small crafts; modest offerings of thanks from the plain and ordinary people of Watervalley. I would be leaving them.

I collapsed into one of the living room chairs, dismayed. What had I been thinking? Had I been asked thirty minutes prior, I would have said that my life in Watervalley was practically perfect. I was deeply in love with a beautiful woman, enjoyed many endearing friendships, and was adored and appreciated for doing a job from which I took great satisfaction. I was fortunate, and I knew it.

And yet, my sold-out elation at the prospect of this new opportunity told a powerful story. I had come to define my world with Watervalley being my only horizon. But the dream of doing research had been more deeply embedded than I realized. Now awakened by hope, the thought absorbed me, devouring all else. The letter had become a magic door through which I could pass to a life I had only imagined. I now realized that unknowingly, I had longed to dream great dreams again.

But there were other possibilities to consider. The money could be used to buy the Moon Lake property, an extraordinary and enchanting twelve-acre tract of land a few miles out from town. Christine and I had gone there on our first date, a picnic. A month ago, I had attained a one-year option to purchase the property, allowing me sufficient time to scrape together a down payment and secure the land. My thinking was that on some distant day, we would build a house there. It was my way of assuring Christine that Watervalley would always be part of our future. But the estate money could turn that distant dream into today's reality. Watervalley would pay off my school debt, and we could pursue building a house and starting a family. I knew in my bones that this news would make Christine euphorically happy.

All I had to do was stay.

The hours passed slowly. I methodically opened and sorted all the small gifts under the tree, moving the baked and canned goods to the kitchen and found small places to display the various crafted pieces that had been so proudly given. As a matter of course, I also sent an e-mail to Dr. Bray, my Vanderbilt professor who had offered me the research position, to inquire as to whether the job was still available. In our initial exchanges, he had told me to mull it over for a couple of months and that we would talk after the first of the year. That left me somewhat confident that the job was still mine should I want it. While online, I did a few searches for housing near the university; a likely meaningless exercise but one that my muted excitement couldn't resist.

The balance of my day was spent in much this way, vicariously living between the two dissimilar worlds, the two radically different lives that lay before me. Despite the fretting preoccupation with this dilemma, I was in high spirits. I found it impossible not to be elated at the prospects of such a huge windfall. As well, perhaps I innately knew that there was time. An inevitable decision would have to be made, but it wouldn't have to be made today. For the moment, I could delightfully dwell in the possibilities.

By late afternoon, I grew restless. I loaded up the dogs and drove out Gallivants Crossing to the Moon Lake property. The two-acre lake was on a high bald hill with views that were near celestial, making it the perfect place to build a home in the country. Originally, my thought was to buy the Moon Lake land for Christine. But there was a large part of me that equally loved it.

On the drive out, the boys couldn't be still; frantically climbing over each other between the front passenger side and small rear bench seat of the Austin Healey. They were on full dog adventure alert, excitedly looking from side to side and saturating the small enclosure with steamy dog breath. They constantly fidgeted, explosively looking out one window and then the next. It seemed that they instinctively knew we were going to Moon Lake. They loved the freedom of the open countryside, making the thought of confinement in a Nashville apartment a sour contrast. It was yet one more thing to consider.

In time, we arrived at the locked gate. I opened it with the key that Luther had graciously provided me, and pulled the car into the thick, matted-down winter grass beside the lake. The December sun was still whole in the western sky, but only just so. I gave the boys a stern lecture about not running and jumping into the water. Disappointed, they looked at each other and seemingly nodded their agreement. As soon as I let them out, they strolled leisurely up to the lake's edge and proceeded to walk directly into it, not run and jump. It was a legitimate technicality.

I leaned against the side of the car and took in the splendor of the moment. The air was cool and crisp, suspended under a late afternoon sky of clear, delicate blue. The broad world before me was soundless, satisfied, eternal. There rose within me a contentment that transcended words. I could see myself here, breathing in this same air, staring at this same sunset, living out my life in an unbroken cascade of endless seasons.

Suddenly, I missed Christine deeply and longed for her to be with me. I had grown to realize that part of the joy of Moon Lake was the unspoken delight that filled her when she was here. She had such a rich passion for life, and I wanted to be part of it, to live selfishly in the light of her boundless happiness. Both of our childhoods had known love, but hers had known roots and stability; something that mine had not availed. Her love of the rolling fields and high meadows of

Watervalley centered her, gave her strength. It seemed that she and the incredible beauty of the valley were natural companions. I feared what taking her away from this would do. Perhaps I was a little too full of my own journey.

In time, the distant western hills turned red with ancient light. The day slid into oblivion, leaving behind a vast and brooding darkness. Soon, an endless array of proud and tender stars, the warming particles of night, dotted the unbroken canopy of the heavens. For the longest time, I sat there; pondering, speculating, searching.

Rhett and Casper had spent the last hour energetically roaming the lake and nearby fields, exhausting themselves. With nightfall, they came galloping back and sat at my feet, awaiting some sign of departure. But I was beyond the horizon, unavailable. They eventually collapsed into the tall grass beside me, their heavy panting forming small, steamy wisps that vanished into the dew of the night. A feeling of loneliness permeated the listless evening breeze.

Try as I might, I could find no clear answer, no logical resolve. Even so, the spare, soft light of the partial moon gave the night an immortal stillness, washing away the harsh confusions of the past hours. Either future had the potential for both joy and disappointment. Ultimately, it seemed that everything yielded to a question of the greater good that I might accomplish with my life.

I suppose few would doubt the benefit of my service to the people of Watervalley. They had struggled and been without a town doctor for three years before my taking the position. I feared that my departure would leave them in the same predicament for some time. Still, the research grant at Vanderbilt was to test the efficacy of an experimental fertility drug; one that, if successful, could benefit thousands and thousands of women and couples worldwide. Given that Christine had been diagnosed with premature ovarian failure, a condition that could potentially leave her barren, the research opportunity had tremendous personal significance.

I also knew that I was not irreplaceable. Watervalley would survive, and as well, the research project would be completed without my involvement. Nevertheless, time and circumstance had decided otherwise. Both worlds wanted my participation, and at some juncture, I would have to choose one and forget the other. Each choice had consequences.

Soon, I would need to talk to Christine; to tell her everything. It was a matter that we both should decide. But I needed to know my own heart first, and at that moment, it was clearly divided. I didn't like holding my silence but felt it was the right choice. For the time being, truth and secrecy would have to lie down together.

Chapter 15

PATIENTS

Christine and I talked briefly on the phone that night. Her day with her grandmother had been wonderful, she said. They had talked non-stop and apparently Mattie had recounted a liturgy of hilarious stories from the past, especially her college days.

"Did they have colleges when your grandmother was young?"

"Stop. I'll have you know she graduated with honors from Agnes Scott. Her degree was in the Performing Arts."

"Hmm, interesting. I guess somebody had to play Cruella De Vil."

"You need to spend more time with her. She's a clever duck."

I had a different creature in mind, the kind that shed their skin. How was it that Christine and I saw this woman so differently?

She suggested that maybe the three of us could get lunch the next day. The very thought of being around her grandmother made waterboarding seem like a day at Disney World. My answer was as vague as possible.

I mentioned to her that I had taken the dogs out to Moon Lake but said nothing about the attorney's letter. That conversation was not for the phone, and besides, I had much to think about before bringing her into the equation. I went to bed early, hoping that the morning light would bring clarity.

Instead it brought work.

The Watervalley Clinic had historically observed a practice of closing for the week between Christmas and New Year. This, however, was my second Christmas in Watervalley and I had learned a valuable lesson from the first one. When it came to closing the clinic, everybody but the sick people got the memo.

Thus, I had told the staff that during Christmas week this year, we were going to open the clinic for some limited hours...an idea that didn't exactly receive wild, sustained applause. Nevertheless, Tuesday morning I rolled out of bed and made my way over to Church Street and the old antebellum mansion that housed Watervalley's Medical HQ. I slipped in from the back door and was excitedly greeted by the office manager, Nancy Orman, who zipped by me at her usual administrative Mach-7 speed. Despite her rather short and rotund shape, Nancy was a virtual cyclone of organizational energy. Nuclear power plants were run with less regimen.

The balance of the small staff greeted me with notably less enthusiasm and began the day echoing a low mutter of sullen protest. But their snarls soon thawed into some good-natured teasing. Even though they didn't want to be here, they understood that this was the nature of the profession. We did what we had to do.

And, when we had to, we did without. Ann Patterson, the clinic nurse, and John's love interest, was still out of town. Fortunately, there were only a few people in the waiting room.

The first two cases were common colds brought on by the December weather. But my third patient that morning was somewhat unexpected. It was Hoot Wilson.

Large and loud, Hoot was a third-generation dairy farmer and the single parent of a darling fourteen-year-old daughter. I liked him, a lot. He was a huge man of three hundred pounds with an expansive, mischievous humor, and an ever-present perpetual smile.

I entered the exam room to find Hoot in his standard overalls but wearing a flowery Hawaiian Christmas shirt and a face of tacit worry. The shirt concerned me more. Generally, dairy farmers from rural, bush-hog intensive regions like Watervalley didn't have Hawaiian attire in their style file.

"Wow, Hoot. And here I thought your New Year's resolution would be to wear more camo. Think you could turn down the volume on that shirt?"

He spoke sheepishly. "It was a Christmas gift from my cousin, Paula Jo. We always try to get each other something thoughtful."

"That's nice. What did you give her?"

"A tee-shirt that said, 'Drink till you want me.'"

"Okay, good. Interesting stuff." Despite the peculiar wardrobe modification, Hoot still had the unmistakable ambience of the dairy parlor. It was an odor strong enough to disrupt cell tower signals. He was noticeably unaffected and probably thought of it as "the scent of a real man."

As much as I liked Hoot, I was anxious to move on with the day and attend to the remaining patients before lunch. "Hoot, what seems to be the problem? Do you have a cold? Are you feeling sick?"

"No, I feel fine, doc."

I folded my arms and regarded him with a curious frown. "Hoot, I don't think I understand."

He shrugged. "I feel good, doc. I really do."

I was vacillating between perplexed and perturbed. "Well, Hoot. I guess at the risk of asking the obvious, why are you here?"

He looked from side to side and spoke in a hushed voice. "Doc, can I tell you a secret?"

I stared at him vacantly, not sure where this conversation was going. "I wouldn't recommend it, no."

He ignored this. "I kind of got something I really need to get off my chest."

"Is it your shirt? Please say it's not your shirt."

Once more he looked from side to side. "Me and the doc have kind of hit a bump in the road. I could use a little advice."

Hoot had been dating Karen Davidson, a Veterinarian who had moved to town over the summer. Petite and amiably attractive, she was ex-military, plain-spoken, and had the unembellished manner of a tomboy. For months, she and Hoot had cultivated a close, companionable relationship, much to the surprise of many, including me. I spoke cautiously.

"Okay, Hoot. What's on your mind?"

"Normally, doc, I have a lot of confidence, except around women. Typically, when I walk in a room, they scatter like deer. Those that don't run off regard me as a friend, and I have a hard time shifting that perception. But Karen has been different. She seems to really like me, a lot. And lord knows I've been pretty crazy about her."

"So, what's the problem?"

"She's been a little miffed the last couple of days."

I thought for a moment. "You guys seemed fine at the Christmas Eve Party a couple of nights ago. Come to think of it, I've never seen a woman eat so many ribs, except maybe in a caveman drawing."

"I'm thinking I might have messed up with her Christmas gift."

I sighed. This was my punishment from the universe. It was no small irony that I would be called upon for relationship advice. "Okay. So, what did you get her?"

Hoot dejectedly looked at the floor. "I'm a little embarrassed to admit to it."

I wanted to say, "Okay. Sorry, can't help you. Bye." But I didn't. I took a deep breath and spoke patiently. "Well, can you give me a hint."

He shrugged. "It starts with a b."

"Okay. Bubble bath? Bikini? Brassiere?"

His face squeezed to a tight grimace. "More like bait."

I was dumbstruck. "You mean, bait? As in, you know…fishing bait."

The notable disbelief in my response served to deepen Hoot's embarrassment. His voice was choked with contrition. "Yup. Nightcrawlers. You think that was a bad idea?"

"Hoot, what were you thinking? Good grief, fellow. Do you have a history of mental illness in your family?"

Hoot thought for a moment. "I have an uncle who does yoga."

I chose to disregard this. "Seriously, Hoot. Nightcrawlers. Really?"

"Gee, doc. What was I supposed to do? The woman really likes to fish. I got her a new Zebco rod and reel, too."

This was an improvement. My initial shock ebbed. "Well, okay, good. There's that, I guess." I was caught between stunned and amused. "Why didn't you just get her a frog gig to complete the set?"

"She already has one."

Decidedly, "stunned" had won out. Again, I stared at him blankly. "Hoot, I may be a little out of my wheelhouse with this situation."

He adjusted his John Deere cap and spoke reflectively. "Yeah. I understand, Doc. I guess hindsight is twenty-twenty."

I scratched my head, still anxious to attend to the remaining patients. "I don't know, Hoot. Seems to me that regular sight should have seen this one coming. What did she get you?"

"Not anything. We had agreed not to exchange gifts."

There it was; the "aha" moment. "Well, maybe that's the problem. Maybe when you said, 'Let's not exchange gifts,' she took that to mean 'Let's not exchange gifts.'"

Hoot rubbed his chin. A cunning regard tightened over him. "Hadn't thought of that."

"Look, Hoot. Why don't you just talk to her? Apologize. Offer to give her a foot rub. Grovel a little. Women seem to like that kind of thing. Seems like the easiest solution."

He winced with uncertainty. "I don't know, doc. Sounds too simple."

I was exasperated. "Well, you two could always go at it bare-knuckled. See who's really in charge."

"You serious, Doc? I don't know about that. Karen's pretty scrappy. I'm guessing she could arm wrestle any of the guys down at the Co-op and maintain a winning percentage."

"Hoot, I was kidding. Look, just talk to her. Tell her how you feel."

"I tell her how I feel all the time."

"Really?"

"Yeah. You know…like, I feel tired or I feel hungry."

I pursed my lips tightly. "We're not connecting here. Maybe you should get one of those relationship books, like the men from Mars and women from Venus one."

"Actually, doc, I've got that book."

"And you've read it from cover to cover?"

"No, I mostly just read the cover. Astronomy's not my long suit, doc. I couldn't really get into it."

I stared at him in quiet disbelief, speechless. Hoot sensed my frustration and began to inch off the exam table, a gesture of departure. "Well, doc, thanks for your time. I guess this sort of thing ain't exactly in the medical books. Maybe I'll drop by the Alibi later tonight and throw back a couple with the boys to see what they think."

I was fairly certain that a randomly selected panel of lowlifes down at the Alibi Bar were probably not the best life coaches for Hoot's dilemma. I held up my hand and motioned him to stay.

"Hoot, what's the real problem here?"

"What do you mean, doc?"

"I haven't told you anything you don't already know. So, what's really bugging you?"

Once again, he gazed toward the floor. "Things are just different now than when I was younger. It used to be that if a fella was prosperous and owned his own doublewide, he had it made with the ladies. But Karen's been all over the world. She's seen lots of things, and all those experiences are part of who she is. Me, I'm just a dairy farmer from Watervalley. I barely make it to the Livestock Show at the State Fair in Nashville every year. We're just not the same."

"So, you're telling me that there's a whole side to her that you can't relate to; that try as you might, there's a large part of her life you'll never be able to understand fully."

"Yeah, that's right."

"And here you are with a fourteen-year-old daughter and a tether to the milk barn that prevents you from experiencing some of the things Karen talks about, to share that part of her life."

He exhaled a long sigh. "Yeah."

"Hoot, have you asked the woman if she cares? As I recall, she came to Watervalley to be a part of a community, to belong somewhere, to leave that other life behind her. Maybe a dairy farmer with deep roots is exactly what she wants."

Hoot took off his hat and absently ran his fingers through his hair. Despite his massive size, he wore the anxious face of a little boy. He was searching. I knew that he had been crushed when his wife had walked out on him while Wendy was still an infant. Hoot was no different from anyone else. The loss, the confusion, the abandonment, and the pain had left scars on his heart that served as an unseen reminder of the devastating memories. Instinctively, Hoot had quietly programmed himself to never be vulnerable in that way again.

In time, he nodded with a face of quiet resolve and extended his massive hand toward me. "Thanks, doc. I knew you were the right fellow to talk to. I'll sit down with Karen, and we'll get it all sorted out."

I shook his hand and nodded. "Anytime, Hoot. Let me know how it goes. And, just as a reminder...I really was kidding about the whole fistfight thing."

The next two patients were a couple of well-baby check-ups and immunizations which went quickly and smoothly. That left only one remaining chart hanging outside of Exam Room Two. I grabbed it for a quick review before entering. But upon reading the name, I exhaled a long, deflating sigh. It was Polly Shropshire.

This was nothing new. Polly was a frequent flyer at the clinic. With her petulant, hangdog face and haughty voice, she would come by every few weeks with a protracted litany of non-specific ailments which she would summarily attribute to "upset nerves." Usually, the list was long, and their description was longer. And invariably, Polly would randomly slide into a social commentary about the lesser tribes of men and women of Watervalley.

For some reason, with each visit, she seemed compelled to connect with me on a confidential level. She would assume a whispered, sacrosanct tone to signal the imminent disclosure of some scandalous intelligence. Typically, her facts were laced with a fair amount of fiction. But that did little to dissuade her certainty regarding the pontifical weight of her opinions. When this occurred...and it always did, I would tactfully redirect the conversation.

As I entered the exam room, Polly's face looked thin and sour, as if she had swallowed poison. An enveloping weariness rested upon her like an old perfume. Historically, she would greet me with an effusive cordiality and would detail her complaints with a slow and ponderous enunciation of each word. But today she projected a pricklier nature.

"Good morning, doctor. Thank you for seeing me. I'm not well."

I nodded thoughtfully. "Okay, Polly. What seems to be the problem?"

"I can't sleep," she remarked tersely. Usually, Polly would volunteer a lengthy description of her infirmities. I waited, but nothing was forthcoming. So, I asked the obvious.

"What do you think is the cause?"

"My nerves. I've been very distressed lately."

"I see. And when did all this start?"

"Well," she said stiffly. "It began on Christmas Eve when that maid of yours treated me so rudely in front of Dr. House. It was so unkind and upsetting. I haven't been able to sleep."

And there it was. Polly had cleverly guided the conversation into a discussion of social score keeping. Her complaint clearly called for me to agree with the injustice she felt she had been served. Nor was it lost on me that Polly had referred to Connie as my "maid," denoting a certain lesser standing. Having set the trap, she locked her gaze in sharp scrutiny, awaiting my response. On previous visits, I would do my best to listen patiently to Polly, occasionally nodding my head and frowning with concern. Not this one.

"I see," I said politely. Without emotion, I reached into my pocket, retrieved my prescription pad, and proceeded to write in silence. With each passing second, her stern scowl de-glossed into a face of childlike confusion. "Polly, I am writing you a prescription for some sleeping pills." I ripped the paper from the pad and handed it to her. My tone was reserved and academic. "Hopefully, that will take care of the problem."

Somewhat stunned, she hesitantly lifted her hand and took the prescription. But from her speechless, searching expression, I could tell that she considered the conversation far from finished. Soon enough, her momentary confusion calcified into a lofty, offended inquest.

"Did you not see the way she treated me, pulling me away like that?"

This was a direct question, an awkward and thorny moment calling for both tact and honesty. I did what any highly-educated mature adult would do. I responded with neither.

"I didn't notice."

This did little to satisfy her. Both her resolve and her lips stiffened, and she gave the matter a final salvo. "I would think you would treat this situation with more concern, Dr. Bradford."

Polly was seeking affirmation, wanting me to take sides. I was Polly's doctor, and to that end, I felt called to treat her medical complaint. I was not, however, called to explain to her that she was an insufferable snob and that, in fact, she was the one being rude on Christmas Eve.

I spoke with detached diplomacy. "Polly, if you have an issue with Connie Thompson, I suggest you pick up the phone and give her a call. I'm sure she'll be glad to talk with you."

My response yielded only a stern, unappeased stare that eventually withered into a look of hurt and betrayal. Polly assumed an air of resolve, gathered her purse and stood.

"Thank you for the prescription, Dr. Bradford. Good day."

I went to my office, sat in my desk chair, and gazed out the large window at the grounds of the church next door…wondering how I might have handled the conversation differently. I didn't have long to ponder the matter. Moments later, there was a heavy rap on my office door.

Chapter 16

AN OMINOUS CONVERSATION

John Harris entered the room wearing an aloof air of casual authority. He moved fluidly, swinging the door shut behind him before plopping down in one of the armchairs across from my desk. Unintentionally, it seemed that everything about the man had an intimidating element. His presence was like that of a mountain, reducing you to size. Despite his fifty plus years and his affinity for scotch, he was still lean and athletic, solidly made. I rested back in my chair and knitted my hands behind my head, observing him with a wry grin. John's eyes tightened as he took note of my chosen reticence. A shrewd smile began to form at the corners of his mouth.

Without a doubt, my smirk was nuanced with superior righteousness regarding his Christmas Eve impersonation of Goldilocks. John easily read this. By small degrees, an expression of amused contempt began to emerge. He looked away for a second, gushing a short laugh.

"Forget it, sport. I didn't come here looking for amnesty."

I held my hands above me in a long stretch. "I see. So, you're not here because your conscience told you to make nice. Shocker."

"Didn't you get my note?" He said defiantly.

"The napkin? Yes. I'm having it framed."

"That's right, smartass. Have your fun. Get it out of your system."

"Oh, not the case at all," I said innocently. "I just didn't realize that Christmas Eve was also when you celebrated the repeal of Prohibition."

135

"Clever. Anything else?"

"Hmm, I think that's it for now."

"I saw Polly Shropshire leaving as I came in. She didn't look so happy."

"Does she ever?"

John rubbed his chin. "Yeah, good point, I guess. Polly's not all bad, though. Back in the day, she did a lot for the community. She was almost normal about five cats ago."

"I'll take your word for it. Anyway, what can I do for you, professor?"

"I came by to see how the conversation about the Vanderbilt letter went with Christine."

I shrugged. "It didn't."

"What do you mean it didn't?"

"She seems completely unaware of it. I've thought about bringing it up on a couple of different occasions. But both times, it wasn't the right moment. It hasn't happened."

"But you are going to tell her, aren't you?"

John's question was the Genie in the bottle. A large part of me wanted to talk about the attorney's letter as well, to confide everything to him about the incredible choice before me. But at that moment, I realized that this decision affected him also. John was my best friend. Despite our mutual inability to communicate any sentiment of friendship toward each other, it would be a great loss for both of us if I were to leave. I held my thoughts in check.

"Yeah. I'm sure the conversation needs to happen at some point. I imagine it will soon enough."

"I wouldn't hold my cards for long, sport. Probably best to get that business behind you. Otherwise, it will be the tar baby that fouls everything."

"So noted." I smiled and said nothing more. I appreciated John's advice but wanted no further discussion on the matter. John read this. He changed the subject.

"By the way, has Walt Hickman said anything to you about being on a Community Development Panel?"

"Yeah, he mentioned something to that effect at the party the other night. I think he's looking for ways to attract more business and manufacturing to the valley. Sounds like the kind of thing a mayor should be doing. He hit you up as well?"

"Of course. He wants to know if I have any thoughts about how the old DuPont plant can be retooled."

"Doesn't seem like a bad idea."

John was more skeptical. "Maybe. Maybe not. I like Walt, I really do. As far as local politicians go, he's about as good as we've had. But he also knows how to change his politics based on the prevailing winds. Over the years his opinions have taken more positions than a Sports Illustrated model."

"Sounds to me like he's just trying to build some momentum and consensus."

"Eh, you're probably right. I guess change is inevitable." After saying this, he fell silent.

"John, I need to ask you about something."

"Knock yourself out."

"What can you tell me about Hiram Hatcher?"

His gaze tightened, and I could practically feel the heat of emotion rising within him. "What would you like to know, other than that he's my grandfather?"

"Is that true?"

"Hell no, it's not true. Who told you this?"

"Nobody did. I was asking Connie about Hiram Hatcher, and she mentioned I should talk to you, that you would know more about him."

The fact that Connie had been my source seemed to have a calming effect. He settled in his chair and spoke impassively. "My maternal grandmother, Jessica Ravenel was Hiram's personal secretary. And in her day, she was one damn good-looking woman, the kind that made men ogle and women envious. She married my grandfather, Trenton Ravenel, in 1925. He was no slouch, either. He was over six feet tall, had broad shoulders and a lot of dash about him. He was a manager for the railroad, the L&N, not the one Hiram owned. She went to work for Hiram in 1926, and the three of them became good friends, they were close."

"And you know all this because…"

"Because they told me. They used to laugh at the rumor about Hiram and my grandmother. Said it was all bunk."

"So, what was the rumor all about?"

"As I mentioned, she was his secretary and personal assistant. Well, in early December of 1927, she went on a five-day train trip with him to Chicago to handle some critical business matter. Normally, Hiram always went alone, but there was something very important that he needed her help on. That's when all the talk started."

"But it was all bunk?"

"Yeah, it was all bunk. Because here's the part that most people don't know. Hiram begged my grandfather to come along, pleaded with him to do so. But he couldn't get away and was perfectly fine with my grandmother going. My grandfather told me this to my face, and it was pretty convincing. Look, Hiram Hatcher was a big deal in this town, and my grandparents were the quintessential insiders. A lot of the locals were jealous of that. My mother was born in late August of the next year, close enough to the timing that people were inclined to speculate.

"What was the business trip all about anyway?"

"They were always tight-lipped on that subject. Only that Hiram was going through a pretty tough personal time and needed their help."

"Hmm. But I guess it's easy to see how that kind of thing could be used to stoke the rumor mill, especially from jealous detractors."

John leaned back in his chair, and a broad grin returned to his face. "Well, I guess that's one of the things I loved about my Ravenel grandparents. They didn't give a rat's ass what other people thought."

"Interesting. Apparently, social indifference is hereditary."

John grunted. "Could be. But probably the real reason sport is that they weren't local. They were from Baltimore. My grandfather was transferred here with the railroad just after they married. They were well educated, stylish, and financially successful. My mother was their only child. You know, my dad was a postman. He made a solid living and was well respected. But any wealth that's been passed along came from my mother's side. A lot of the antiques and old books up at the house come from them."

Having said this, John fell silent. He seemed haunted by some deep preoccupation.

"Something else on your mind, John?"

"Hmm, oh…nothing. I was just thinking about my people not being from here."

"And?"

He sharpened his focus at me, and then, oddly, assumed an expression of strained uncertainty.

"Do you ever wish for more than this life has given you?"

Although my blank expression hid it well, dumbfounded would best define my reaction. John was not one for reflective inquiry. But perhaps, more than the question itself, was the intensity and earnestness, the complete vulnerability in which John had said the words. My response was hesitant, stammered. "Well, sure. I guess we all do at some point."

He nodded quietly. I leaned forward in my chair, resting my folded arms on the desk. "What brought that question on?"

With his legs out-stretched, he stared ponderously at the ceiling before speaking with dry precision. "Non sum qualis eram."

Even at this moment where he was compelled to unburden the weight of his troubles, he cloaked his sentiments in Latin. He had said, "I am not the person I once was."

"In what way?"

Again, he looked to the side before speaking, as if he was uncertain about revealing his thoughts. Exhaling, he turned to me. "It was always Molly's idea to move back here."

"Yeah, you've um...you've mentioned that before."

"After she died, with everything we had done to clear the land, to build the house, to establish the orchard and all the landscaping...I couldn't just walk away from it. I couldn't just sell it off to some stranger. It had been her dream." He paused for a moment, deliberating his next words. "But I have to admit. I don't know that it was ever my dream."

I nodded. "So, what are you thinking?"

To my surprise, John shook his head and released a kind of exasperated laugh. "That's the problem, sport. I don't know what I think. Part of me wants to travel, live other places. I feel the need to push back my horizons."

"I didn't realize they were standing so close."

The faint suggestion of a smile hovered around his mouth. "You know what I mean, smartass."

I said nothing. But in truth, I did know. I knew that far-off look, that hunger for journeys, that was written all over him. "Where are you thinking about going?"

John held up his hand, a gesture of indecision. "Not sure. New Zealand, Spain, Patagonia, Big Sky Country...places I've always wondered about and wanted to see."

"Doesn't sound that complicated to me, John. Pick out a place and go there for a few weeks. Try it on for size." I paused, realizing one small complication. "So, where does Ann fit in all of this?"

John crossed his arms and hesitated for a moment. "Yeah. Well, that's the problem. I don't think she does."

His assertion came as a sharp surprise. "Oh! Okay. I guess I didn't see that one coming. I assumed you two had become pretty tight."

"We have. I love the woman and have told her as much. She's told me the same."

"And yet you're thinking about leaving her behind."

John scratched his head. "Yeah, yeah I am. It's just this desire inside of me, this need for adventure. Who knows; wanderlust, middle age crisis... I don't even know what to call it."

"Here's a thought, why don't you call it, 'how to make a really dumb decision.'"

"Not helping, sport."

"Okay, fine. We'll workshop the title a little. But the point remains. Why would you leave and not take her with you? I mean, is this about Molly? Because, let's face it John...not that you care what anybody thinks, but it's been almost three years. I think moving on is an acceptable option at this juncture."

John seemed unaffected, dispirited. He rubbed his chin in a small act of resolve. "No, it's not about Molly. It's about me."

"I don't understand."

"Ann and I are adults, and what transpires between us around here is our business. So, you can laugh if you want, but I'm a little old fashioned. To ask her to go gallivanting around the world with me as my girlfriend, well...that's just not my style."

"Okay. Good to know that chivalry's not dead. But if that's an issue, and you love her, why not just ask her to marry you? Admittedly, I realize that's a daunting thought for any woman."

"I'm not ready for that."

"So, you would just go without her?"

"Maybe. And here's the thing. If I'm going to break it off, I need to do it sooner rather than later. No sense in delaying the inevitable. Besides, she can't just leave for three weeks and expect to have a job to come back to."

I slumped back in my chair, perplexed by all that he was telling me. It made no sense, and candidly, part of me was annoyed at my good friend's foolishness.

"Okay, let me try to summarize all this. Hmmm...you're bailing out on a meaningful relationship with a lovely woman that you adore without even talking to her first. Gee John that doesn't sound like you." Then I slid into a tone of full sarcasm. "No, hold it. That sounds *exactly* like you."

He was unaffected. "I don't think I'm picking up a sympathetic vibe here."

"John, everything you're saying is nuts. This entire conversation should serve as a reminder of the importance of taking your prescription medication."

"I'm not on any prescription medication."

"Then it's a reminder you should be. I can recommend some anti-psychotics. In fact, I'll even make them generic. Just because you're delusional doesn't mean you should overpay."

He grinned. "I know you're trying to humor me, sport. But I'm not getting any younger. I've got some tough decisions to make."

"John, look. You're killing me here. I know in this world that not everyone can be a star, but you don't have to be a cloud either.

He offered nothing in return.

"John, buddy...you need to think this through. Psychology is not my long suit, but maybe you're simply coming to terms with the loss of Molly. Or maybe it's chemical, some kind of serotonin issue. I honestly think this may be a non-situational depression. It's got you in a temporary funk...emphasis on temporary."

He pondered this for a moment. "Hmm, depression, you say?"

"Let's face it. You've been pretty down lately. If you sink any deeper, I might as well shovel dirt on top of you."

"I guess you may be right. I haven't noticed anything different. But apparently, you have."

"John, I've been around diseased and dying people for the past ten years, and the way you've been acting lately is starting to make that look like good times."

He leaned forward in his chair. "Well, thanks for listening, Luke. I care a lot for Ann. I'm not sure what's the right choice. I know you two work pretty closely. I'll let you know before I make any big decisions."

I nodded. "I appreciate that. But let me offer a little unsolicited advice. Forget about talking to me. Talk to Ann before making any big decisions. See how she feels. Not that I want to lose a great nurse, but she may be just fine hopping a plane and traveling with you. And one other thing, John. For better or worse, Watervalley is home to you. It always will be. Maybe there's a life for you and Ann in both worlds."

John said nothing. He pressed his lips together and stood silently, weighing my words.

After a time, he smiled and extended his hand. "Again, thanks for listening."

"Sure thing." I walked with him to my office door. "And not to get all mushy or anything…just know that I'm with you either way, whether you make the right decision or the really stupid one."

"Comforting. Thanks."

"Oh, and regarding payment, if you would, on your way out you could throw a dollar in the slushie fund."

John looked at me, confused. "You mean the slush fund?"

"No, the slushie fund. We actually buy slushies with the money. My favorite is strawberry."

"How did you ever make it through med school?"

"Mostly on my looks."

"Apparently."

"Well, big fellow," I said pointedly. "If you thought it was that easy, why didn't you go to med school?"

"I considered being a doctor, but I didn't like the idea of being nice to stupid people."

"And he's back, folks. For a minute, we thought we'd lost you."

John ignored this. "Hey, you hungry? Why don't you let me buy you lunch?"

"Thanks for the offer. But I'm heading over to the Depot Diner to meet Christine and her Grandmother."

"Mattie Chambers?"

"The one and only."

John smirked. "Lucky you."

"Right, thanks. I'll probably order the hamburger special. I think I'll need a lot of grease and ketchup to medicate my misery."

We shook hands and John departed. I shut the door behind him and returned to my chair, sinking into it, slightly dazed. Even in her death, Molly had remained the center of John's life. It hadn't occurred to me that the grand house in the hills that he and Molly had built together had become a shrine to her memory; a symbol of his everlasting love for her and how their life was supposed to have been. It had defined him. Now, he likely saw his love for Ann as a betrayal. His head and his heart could not reconcile the maze of conflicting emotions, causing him to do the one thing he knew was safe; isolate himself...leave and search elsewhere for the elusive happiness that he believed was missing from his story.

The duplicitous hypocrisy of the morning was not lost on me. First, I'm giving Hoot Wilson relationship advice that open communication was the best remedy for the lovelorn and now, of all people, here I was encouraging John to do the same, as well as to stay in Watervalley. Nevertheless, their situations were clear cut with simple solutions. Mine was a morass of complexities.

But more than I wanted to admit, John's news shook me. It seemed that much of my world was in disarray. My best friend was deeply troubled and in the throes of a heart-wrenching decision. As well, I would have to live with the daily dread that Ann Patterson, my adorable and dear coworker, was in love with a time bomb. I cared for them both, but it seemed I was helpless to do anything for either`.

Churning beneath this was my own anxious predicament. Along with the unsettling encounter with Polly Shropshire from earlier that morning, my day was totally awash with apprehension, angst, and doubt.

On the upside, however, at least I was about to have lunch with Mattie Chambers.

Chapter 17

MATTIE

Noon arrived and the clinic closed for the day, much to the glee of my coworkers who jokingly called me Dr. Scrooge the entire morning. Outside, the day was sky blue and brisk with the cold, fragrant smoke of winter in the air. I was in no hurry and decided to walk the few short blocks to the diner. Along the way, it occurred to me that Watervalley was one of the seven remaining towns in America that still didn't have a fast food restaurant. The Sweet Life Bakery and the Depot Diner were the only eating establishments available... provided you disqualified the concession stand at the ballpark during the summer.

Despite the natural lethargy of the holidays, the diner was packed with the usual assortment of red-faced farmers and local merchants. Upon entering, I was met with a palpable wave of clamorous conversations, clanking dishes, and robust laughter. I found Christine and her grandmother in one of the booths against the back wall. They were engaged in a lively conversation that suspiciously collapsed upon my arrival. Mattie's animated smile promptly soured to a baleful glare. I endeavored to strike a congenial chord, but the task was requiring every bit of my "A" game.

"Hello, Mrs. Chambers. Wonderful to see you again." I extended my hand to her. Reluctantly she took it, giving it a lifeless, clammy squeeze. The experience was akin to holding a recently departed catfish.

I'm not sure why Mattie Chambers intimidated me so much.

She was a small woman, no more than five-feet-two inches and probably weighed less than a hundred and twenty-five pounds, including her brass knuckles. But something in her personality had a magnificent power of torturing amplification. Past conversations with Mattie convinced me that she suffered from a mild form of dementia, an idea that Christine completely dismissed. I released her hand and slid in next to Christine, who greeted me with an unabashed kiss and mirthful smile.

"We were just talking about you," Christine said, giving her grandmother a secretive glance.

"Let me guess. You were talking about how I carry myself with a breezy sophistication and impeccable style." I was hoping that my stab at humor would lighten Mattie up a little. It didn't. She smiled thinly, leering at me like a benevolent vulture.

Rolling her eyes, Christine bumped my shoulder with hers. "No, we were wondering who your groomsmen were going to be. I don't think we've talked about that."

My response was aloof. "That's because talking about it requires that I actually think about it first."

Christine was unamused. "Seriously? That's your answer?"

The noted change in her tone set off some alarm bells. The last thing I needed was to have her upset with me in front of her grandmother, whose happiness seemed to feed upon my disapproval. I regrouped.

"Well, what I meant was…isn't there a kind of parity thing to all that? It sort of depends on how many bridesmaids you're having, doesn't it?"

Christine relaxed. "True. That's a fair point." My response had done the trick, diffusing the momentary angst in Christine's voice. Her grandmother, however, was unimpressed, regarding me like something that scurried under the refrigerator when the lights went on in the kitchen.

"So, how many bridesmaids are you thinking?"

"Seven, at least. Maybe eight."

"Wow. Really?"

"Is that a problem?"

"No. I don't guess. I mean, I may need to have Rhett and Casper fitted for a tux to come up with that many guys."

With this, Mattie Chambers entered the conversation with her blunt, foghorn voice. "Are you not in the habit of making friends with humans?"

I glanced at Christine and endeavored to find a diplomatic response to Mattie's strident inquiry. "I um, I've always been something of a loner."

Her gaze bent upon me with piercing intensity. Ignoring my presence, she turned to Christine and spoke in a voice loud enough for dogs in Nebraska to hear. "Are you sure about this one?"

Under the table, Christine grabbed my hand before smiling warmly at her grandmother. "It's fine, Grandmamma. We'll get it worked out."

Mattie's jaded regard of me continued. Nursing her contempt, she took a sip of tea and spoke to the general air, her voice serving as its own public-address system. "Well, I don't know. He seems dumber than Howdy Doody to me." Exasperated, she shook her head and began to slide sideways out of the booth seat. "I gotta go pee. Order me the vegetable plate." Before departing she gave me a final sneer. The only thing missing was a show of teeth and an accentuated bark.

As she ambled away, I leaned back against the bench, lifted my chin, and gave Christine a stiff sideways glance. She read my thoughts in one swift glimpse and spoke in an accommodating if not apologetic voice.

"Grandmamma can be a little direct."

"I hadn't noticed," I said, nonchalantly browsing the menu.

She melted into a mischievous smile, looking down at her menu as well.

In time Mattie returned, and we managed to pass the next half hour exchanging a few pleasantries that almost bordered on normal conversation. Mattie did manage to further endear herself by noting that when I ate, I sounded like a mule enjoying an order of oats.

We finished, and I asked for the check. My deliverance from family purgatory was finally in sight when, unfortunately, Christine asked to be let out. She needed to be excused to the restroom. I almost said no. Her departure meant I would be left alone with the septuagenarian from hell. After letting Christine out, I sat back down, painfully aware of Mattie's disapproving scowl. She scrutinized me like something from a petri dish and wasted no time in finding a voice for her disdain.

"So, you're marrying my granddaughter, huh. Are you sleeping with her?"

There was an intended shock factor to her inquiry. But after being battered for so long by her unfiltered bluntness, I decided to respond in similar form. Leaning in, I spoke with cool defiance. "Can't say I am. But I sure would like to be." I continued my radar-lock stare and casually took a bite of a French fry. "Think you can help me out with that?"

At first, her neck stiffened, clearly at a loss for words. But then, curiously, her eyes narrowed to a clever softness, and there appeared the faint suggestion of a smile. It was slight, little more than a muscular tremor, but there was something telling in it. She rallied quickly.

"Humph. Fat chance, Dr. Gigolo." She took a healthy sip of iced tea, an obvious stall tactic while she recovered her caustic persona. "By the way, nice save with the whole groomsmen thing. I haven't seen that kind of fancy footwork since Riverdance."

I had had enough. "You know, Mattie, since we're going to be family, I don't feel like we're building team skills here."

Once again, the edges of a crafty smile began to surface. "You're pretty sure of yourself, aren't you?"

My response was notably indignant. "Seems like I'd have to be to win Christine's affection, wouldn't you think?"

Oddly, her face blossomed into a stunned delight that I had never seen before. Her response was animated, almost gleeful. "Oh, I love the way you bring the noise."

"Mattie, I love your granddaughter, and we are going to be married despite the fact that you come with the package. All I ask is that you don't bring your flying monkeys to the wedding."

She was about to respond when Christine appeared at my side. "Well, I see you two are getting along famously."

Instead of standing I moved over so that she could slide in beside me. "Yes, famously," I said glibly. Mattie sat smugly and said nothing, observing me with a guileful smile. I couldn't quite figure out the old goat. Soon afterward I paid the bill, and we parted company.

As I walked back to the clinic, I breathed a sigh of relief. I had survived another encounter with Mattie. But something about this episode was different, as if I had gotten a brief view into the second side of her, one that told of a hidden cleverness. It was yet another odd twist to what had been a mostly out-of-sorts day. Nevertheless, I didn't dwell on her for very long. As quickly as possible I wanted to wash her out of my thoughts. And then, for good measure, rinse and repeat.

Chapter 18

LAYERS OF THE ONION

When I returned home later that afternoon, there was a large and unfamiliar SUV sitting in front of my house. I pulled into my driveway and cut the engine, all the while regarding the vehicle curiously. Seconds later, the driver emerged. It was Matthew. He walked toward me and waved somewhat sheepishly. From under the sleeve of his coat, I noticed that his left hand was wrapped in white gauze.

"Luke. Hi. Wonder if I might trouble you for a minute. I've had a small mishap." Matthew was apologetic but in no apparent distress. "Sorry to catch you off guard like this. I went by the clinic, and it was closed. So, I thought I'd try to find you here."

We shook hands. "Hey, no problem. What happened there?"

Matthew held up his bandaged left hand, observing it casually. "Small grease burn. Pretty clumsy of me. I was wondering if you might write me a prescription for Silver sulfadiazine? That is, assuming you don't carry Exsalt at the clinic?" His request somewhat surprised me; not in its bluntness, but in its accuracy. Silver sulfadiazine or Silvadene was commonly known as an excellent antibacterial ointment for a severe burn. But Exsalt dressings were specialized products used mostly at professional burn clinics.

"Exsalt, huh? That's some pretty savvy medical knowledge for a Classics Professor."

Matthew grinned dismissively. "Well, marry a doctor, and the dinner table talk can be quite educational. So, think I can get that prescription?"

I wanted to be accommodating, but I wasn't used to patients coming to me with a predetermined diagnosis and remedy. Matthew awaited my response. I stalled.

"Um, sure. But let's go inside and take a quick look at it. No sense standing out here in the cold." My response was slightly disjointed, as were my thoughts.

Matthew pressed his lips together, a subtle sign of impatience. "It's just the epidermis. Not a full thickness burn."

His comment readily indicated that he thought my examination unnecessary. And admittedly, he seemed well proficient in the jargon of skin burns.

I grimaced, turning my head to the side in an expression of reluctance. After a brief deliberation, he acquiesced and offered an accommodating smile. "Certainly." He proceeded to open the door of the SUV so that Andrew and Adelyn could climb out. Just as before, they were dressed warmly but in a somewhat ragamuffin style.

"Come along, guys."

I asked the three of them to wait on the front porch while I put the dogs out in the fenced backyard to do their business and to avoid the inevitable licking and love attack for the children's attention. I returned and let them in, taking their coats and asking the children if they wanted something to drink. They politely refused.

"Your house smells like the woods," said Andrew curiously.

"Well, thank you," I replied, unsure if his assessment was a good or bad one. "Must be all the pine from the tree and the wreaths."

"No," said Adelyn in the characteristically unfiltered bluntness of a child. "I think it smells more like a dog in the woods. A stinky dog."

I couldn't help but smile. "I'm sure you're right. My two Golden Retrievers have been skipping bath time. I'll have to speak to them about that."

Matthew calmly took control. "Children, I want you to wait in the living room for a few minutes while Dr. Bradford looks at my hand. Can you do that for me?"

They nodded obediently and sat side by side on the couch, absorbing everything in the room with silent, inquisitive eyes. Matthew and I went to the kitchen where I found a pack of sterile gloves and proceeded to unwrap his bandaged hand.

"This cottage has a lot of charm," said Matthew, endeavoring to make polite conversation.

I almost laughed outright and offered a good-natured response. "That's pretty high praise coming from the owner of Society Hill, the Lord of the Manor as it were."

A knowing, wry grin spread across his face. "Well, Luke." He said slowly. "I guess that proves we have one thing in common."

I continued to unwrap the bandage and glanced up at him. "And what would that be?"

"Neither of us is impressed by money."

There was a telling penetration to his statement. He was right, I suppose. He had quickly distilled that my unrestrained badgering about

156

him owning the old mansion meant that I owed him no reverence just because he had a larger stack of chips than most. Despite my present circumstances, I had come from money. I knew its pluses, but I also knew its limits as a substitute for contentment. I continued to unwind the gauze.

"So, I take it your people have done well?"

For some reason, the question amused Matthew. He smiled, and there was a pleasant warmth in his response. "Yes, I would say they have done well. But not in the sense you're implying. My parents are lifelong missionaries. For the past five years, they've been in Kenya. I suspect they believe they live richly. But their creature comforts are modest at best."

I stopped and stared at him. "That's fascinating. Then, I'm guessing you grew up all over the world?"

"Pretty much. Charleston was home base. But a fair amount of my childhood was spent in Europe and Africa."

"Well," I said inquisitively. "That's quite interesting." He nodded, and I resumed the unweaving of his bandage. My curiosity loomed. I spoke cautiously.

"Looks like you were on somebody's 'A' list. I take it from what you said about Emily's grandmother the other night that you married into Charleston Society." It was a probing question, one that I probably had no right to ask. But Matthew's relaxed and sensitive face seemed at ease, open, receptive. He spoke with a warm smile.

"I don't think I was on anybody's 'A' list or 'B' list or even their waiting list. I just got lucky."

"So how did you two meet?"

"We met ten years ago at the Spoleto Gala, a high society affair before the festival begins."

His response was curious and unexpected, triggering a kind of spontaneous amusement. "Alright, big guy. This has the makings of a good story. You need to fill in a few blanks here. Next, you're going to tell me you were working as a valet and parked her car and it ended up being some kind of reverse Cinderella story."

"No, it was a slightly less dramatic than that. I was there in uniform. I was a Naval officer stationed in Charleston. As a kind gesture toward the military, the organizing committee always extended a dozen or so invitations to the base. My name got pulled out of a hat, and I went."

"Ahh, and you two met, and you swept her off her feet."

"No, actually someone bumped into me, and I accidentally spilled wine on her shoes. I apologized, and we struck up a conversation. Emily was gorgeous, but I didn't really care for her at first. I just figured she was another ditzy socialite with one of those thick southern drawls. I certainly got that one wrong."

"In what way?"

"For starters, she had just finished med school; not exactly ditz status. She was very genuine, very real, but she had a kind of graceful ease about her. She fit in everywhere. She was one of those people who have a kind of energy and joy in them; something that they communicate with everything they touch." As he spoke about his departed wife, Matthew's face seemed to glow, losing its usual sad and thoughtful framing. Words were crowding his brain, seeking utterance.

I finished taking off his bandages. The burn site was on the top of his hand and bordered on being Level Two in severity. Fortunately, it was only about the size of a silver dollar.

"Ouch. That looks pretty nasty." I examined the injury for a moment, and as I did, a curious thing struck me. At the clinic, I saw minor burn injuries all the time, and this one didn't present as anything unusual. But what was different was the bandaging.

Matthew, no doubt, had done the dressing himself and had used Kerlix wrap and Xeroform gauze...items typically found in a hospital ER, not on the pharmacy aisle at the grocery. Then again, his wife had been a doctor, and he would previously have had access to these sorts of items. The dressings had been applied immaculately, and I now understood why Matthew hadn't wanted them removed. His original assessment had been entirely accurate. All the injury needed was Silvadene.

Carefully, I began to reapply the dressings. "Matthew, I haven't helped you here at all. You were right about it from the beginning. There's no Exsalt at the clinic, but I know we've got some Silvadene. If you want, you can follow me over there, and I can fix you right up?"

"Thanks, but a prescription is fine."

"You sure? This is going to need some regular dressing changes. I can get you what you need, or you could just come by every few days."

He gave me an accommodating smile. "Thanks, again. But not necessary. All I need is the Silvadene." I wanted to ask more but didn't. An awkward silence ensued.

Matthew sensed this and endeavored to fill in the gap. "Besides, it's not that bad. I've had verbal insults that have probably taken longer to heal."

I smiled, nodded, and wrote out the prescription. We walked to the living room where his children had been as quiet as mice. Andrew was silently gazing out the front window, but Adelyn was standing in front of a small chest crowded with old family photos. She was studying them with sharp intensity.

"Are you the little boy in this picture?" She asked inquisitively.

"I sure am. That's my Dad and my Mom and my Aunt Grace. We were on vacation at a place called High Hampton. It's in North Carolina."

She nodded and for a moment, returned her gaze to the photo. "They're not here anymore, are they?"

I hesitated. It took me a second to process the question. "No. No, they're not. They passed away some years ago."

She turned and looked up at me with her penetrating, radiant eyes and spoke with all the diplomatic innocence and sincerity of a child. "I'm sorry."

The depth and purity of her delivery were both heartwarming and adorable. "Well, you are very kind to say so. Thank you."

By now Andrew had joined us. He said nothing but simply endorsed his sister's comment with a strong, affirming nod. I looked over at Matthew. He smiled and calmly said, "familia supra omnia."

I helped get the children into their coats and walked with them to the SUV. Matthew once again expressed his appreciation. I held up my hand as they drove away.

Family above everything. My Latin was thin, but I was quite sure that this was what Matthew had said. His children were incredible; practically cherubs and clearly a great source of joy for him. But there was no escaping the impression that Matthew was haunted by a sense of irreparable loss. His love for his absent wife had much hunger in it.

Yet, a large portion of him remained a mystery and secretive, and I began to suspect that he had a powerful talent for concealment. More than ever, I was convinced that he was hiding something that went beyond a desire for mourning and privacy. I liked him and, in some ways, even admired him, especially in his relationship with his children. But my trust in him lagged far behind.

I went to the back door to let in the boys. In their frustration at being excluded from making new friends, they had overturned the trash can and were having a private dinner party. Quickly, however, my initial aggravation soon gave way to a light-hearted thought. Of all the entangling messes in my day, at least this was one that I knew how to clean up.

Though inwardly amused, I put on my stiffest game face and regarded them tersely; lecturing Rhett and threatening Casper with military school.

It would be my last light-hearted moment of the day.

Chapter 19

MAYLEN COOK

I was haunted that night. Darkness came early as it always did in December, leaving me to negotiate a quiet house of lamplight and shadows with hours to pass before sleep would come. I built a fire in the fireplace to occupy the time and perhaps bring some small measure of coziness to the slow hours. Warmed by the embers, the dogs stretched out on their sides and collapsed in a listless slumber on the living room rug.

But I was on edge.

In time I gathered my coat and mindlessly made my way to the backyard, hoping the cold might help me find clarity to the muted confusions of the day. It was not to happen. The dim night sky, fretted with stars, seemed to close; crowding my head and pressing the weight of my muddled thoughts heavier upon me. I returned inside and went to bed. But the ghosts of indecision continued to whisper, to confound and torment me. Sleep that night was both uneasy and broken.

Despite the toss and turn of the small hours, I awoke to a brilliant morning of golden light that fell slantwise, clean, and cold across the hushed, frost-laden yard. The chaotic voices of the night seemed washed away. The day had an air of expectancy, a fresh, brisk vitality. I took care of the dogs, ate a light breakfast, and went for a morning run. Often, I would take the boys with me. But this morning, I chose not to, wanting the freedom to clear my head. Afterward, I showered and in the fog of the bathroom mirror decided that, along with the dogs, I had become quite shaggy. It was time for a haircut.

If gossip was Watervalley's largest industry, then Maylen's Barbershop was the home office. Located downtown just off the square, it was a simple one-room structure made of concrete blocks smothered in fresh white paint. Inside was old and rustic but spotlessly clean with a lone barber chair in the center on an ancient wood floor. An odd assortment of benches and seats lined the four walls. Except for the updated Farmer's Co-op calendar, the room probably looked just the same as it did when Maylen first opened over thirty years ago.

I liked Maylen Cook. He was of modest height, loosely jointed, and slim; belonging to that odd fraternity of Southern men who simply had no backside. A well-worn belt kept his pants clinging desperately to his bony hips. Despite his lanky, lean build, Maylen had uncharacteristic heavy jowls.

Adorned in a short-sleeved barber's shirt with a banded collar, he had droopy eyes and a stoic countenance that gave the impression he was thoroughly bored with life. But nothing could be farther from the truth. He was gifted at listening, had an insightfully clever mind, and a quick-witted sense of humor. And while it was never my habit to hang out at his shop, there was always a sense of anticipation and amusement whenever I went. My day was off to a good start.

I collected my things and headed out the front door both light-hearted and energized, unaware that the untroubled clarity of this early hour would soon be shadowed.

I drove downtown and parked nearby. Upon entering I was greeted with a heavy chorus of "Hey, Doc" from the nearly full room. The air was permeated with the smell of Pinaud's Aftershave and the thick earthy smell of the farmyard. Most of the men wore overalls and flannel shirts accessorized with camo in the form of a hat or a coat or both.

An unwitting patron would walk into this packed house and abruptly leave, thinking his turn would be hours away. But I had long since learned that Maylen's shop was an unofficial men's club; a sanctuary from wives and a hub for news. The only open seat was the barber chair itself, a good sign. After pausing and casting an obligatory searching glance around the room, I was met with a spontaneous response of pointing fingers and kindly voices saying, "you're up doc." As I settled in, Maylen gave his barber sheet a ceremonial unfurling pop and proceeded to drape it around me.

There was an unexplainable ease of mind that always prevailed upon me at Maylen's shop. The room was filled with a comfortable camaraderie that was relaxed, good-natured, oftentimes salty, and invariably bathed with the plain and honest bluntness of the rural mindset. There was a mix of age, but most of these fellows were old farmers who had reached a hearing-impaired mass, leaving many of the conversations to sound like amiable shouting contests. They were a jovial bunch; telling stories, stomping their feet, and laughing themselves into various levels of coronary failure.

And perhaps the best part of it all was that, contrary to urban stereotyping of small towns, on occasion, the local mechanic, Chick McKissick and other men of color hung out at Maylen's just to enjoy the banter and robust companionship. Chick's brother had a barbershop over on South Street, so everyone knew he was not there for a trim. And rather than casting a cloud of hushed silence over the room,

Chick's random appearance would create a cacophonous explosion of warmth and humor.

Someone from beyond the valley would be aghast at the uninhibited exchanges that followed. Hilarious and rhapsodic conversations ensued that openly teased about ethnic differences in food, and music, and language; topics that would have been considered offensive in the city and its façade of cultural homogeneity. But here I had learned that for the most part, there was a deep, abiding bond among the people of Watervalley, irrespective of color. The challenges of weather and crops and the inherent sparsity of rural existence had forced both a familiarity and a dependency. These men served together as volunteer firemen, watched their children play ball together, shared their gardens, served their country, and in many cases, worshiped together. They had their differences, but it seemed that most had gladly moved beyond the harsh vestiges of past decades. Because of the long years of genuine friendship and respect that existed between them, they would laugh and needle each other on a level that few outsiders could understand.

Ironically, the one person whose presence invoked a mild censuring of the conversation was me. The rural culture seemed to automatically pay an unspoken homage to my profession. Despite knowing practically all these men on a first name basis, they seemed to be on their better behavior when I was around...at least, for the most part.

As Maylen began to clip away, the first hot topic of conversation had to do with Lester McFall's plans to paint his tobacco barn green. The majority seemed quite certain that it was God's will that a tobacco barn should be painted red, provided God had had the benefit of tobacco farmer decorator training. This was a serious matter to the group and from the intensity of the conversation the continuation of democracy as we knew it depended on the outcome. Apparently, the fashion sensibilities of the average Watervalley farmer were surprisingly high.

As soon as the barn discussion ended, Abner Dooley held up a wobbly finger and said, "Hey, hey. I've got a story to tell about an old barn." A collective moan reverberated around the room. Abner was a rickety little octogenarian who had random teeth and a tendency to spit when he talked. He was likeable enough, but his anecdotes tended to lose track and take forever to finish. His tale began about a barn but ended up being about catching a catfish the size of a small submarine. Somehow, along the way, an alien sighting got involved. The story had a plot that even Tolkien couldn't follow.

Meanwhile, I had fallen under the trance of the steady clip-clip of Maylen's scissors. My eyes had closed, and I was drifting. Then through the fog, I heard someone mention the name, Matthew House.

My head popped up so quickly that Maylen almost skewered one of my ears. He took quiet notice, but let it go at that. Apparently, during my momentary snooze, someone had walked in with a hot off the press copy of the *Village Voice*, the Watervalley newspaper. On the front page was Matthew House, giving a $3,000 check to Mayor Hickman to help underwrite the Annual Run with Scissors 5K planned for the following Saturday; an event that raised money for the elementary school. The story was read aloud and met by an affirming crowd of raised eyebrows and nodding heads. This was followed by a healthy round of accolades and admiring praise for the new innkeeper. It seemed that between his humble appearance on Christmas Eve and this grand act of generosity, Matthew had transformed his status from one of suspicion to celebrity.

Inwardly, I was stunned. This was completely counter to the secretive and secluded Matthew that I had come to know. He hadn't mentioned anything about so openly engaging with the community. I guess I should have felt happy that he was being seen in such a high regard. But I wasn't. In truth, I was dumbfounded and now more skeptical than ever. Matthew's actions struck me as both astute and calculated. By his own admission, he had no intentions of opening the inn anytime soon, so his immersion into the public goodwill at this point was fiercely suspect.

Then again, in a week his children would be attending the local elementary school, and perhaps this was his way of responsibly enlisting himself into the process. Through it all, I remained silent. I was confused more than ever about Matthew, yet convinced of one thing. He was shrewd. He may not have been impressed by money, but he certainly understood its uses.

In time, the talk of Matthew diminished, and the group turned their focus in a new direction; me. Even though months away, my upcoming nuptials were fair game for taunting. The usual one-liners emerged quickly; about how a bachelor never makes the same mistake but once and, that instead of getting married, I should just find a woman I hate and buy her a house. But the discussion took a definitive downward spiral when Vernon Boshers entered the conversation.

Vernon was a squat, chunky little man who owned the coin-laundry adjacent to the barbershop. With his round face and perpetual clownish grin, he was a loud, ill-mannered, lout whose vacant intellect had remained undaunted despite years of Maylen's quick-tongued censure.

In his typically blunt and bloated fashion, Vernon began to boast about the number of times he and his wife found connubial bliss on their wedding night some decades ago. Then he proceeded to prod the other rustics into his game of braggadocio, and quickly the topic evolved into numerous claims that were beyond the realm of absurd. Having effectively stirred the pot, Vernon stared in my direction with his half-idiot grin, clearly wanting me to weigh into the conversation. But Vernon held no spell over me, and I remained coolly silent.

All the while, Maylen clipped away with a hangdog face of bored disdain. Having no luck with me, Vernon turned his verbal assault on him; badgering Maylen to quote some statistic regarding his wedding night activities. For the longest time, Maylen ignored him. His face remained expressionless, save for the eventual pursing of his lips, the closing of his eyes, and the slow, tired shaking of his head. But Vernon was relentless and continued to press him.

Eventually, the entire barbershop was held in attention awaiting Maylen's response. Finally, he paused his cutting, exhaled a long sigh, and turned to Vernon, speaking in a weary monotone that suggested he was talking to a mentally challenged goat.

"We only did it once, Vernon. My wife wasn't so used to it."

Amidst the roar that followed, Maylen turned back to me, politely used his thumb to reposition my chin, and then continued with the methodic clip-clip of his scissors, his tired expression never changing. Soon after, I paid and left.

Maylen was the highlight of my day.

During the brief hour, while having my hair cut, a cold front had moved in, leaving the sky grey and overcast. Even though the clinic was closed, I spent the balance of the morning and afternoon in my office, going through old files, reading a few articles, and generally squandering away the day. It seemed that spare time and I had become strangers and, having suddenly been afforded so much of it, I was at a loss with what to do with myself. Instinctively I defaulted to the rituals of my daily life, using work and the opiate of responsibility to fill the empty hours.

A large part of me wanted to call Matthew or just randomly stop by his house under the guise of checking on his burn. But in truth, my real curiosity was about the $3,000 and his sudden audacious entrance into the public eye. I chose to do neither.

Later, Christine and I talked briefly on the phone. After that, I gathered the dogs and threw the ball in the backyard until the last light of evening faded. Just as the night before, I was burdened with my thoughts and sleep was elusive.

During the week of the holidays, I seemed to have lost the faculty of estimating time. Unconsciously, the days passed and slipped into January. My movements were driven more by habit and custom rather than purpose. And yet, during every moment of the day, part of my mind was held captive, constantly and silently preoccupied with the horrendous decision before me. But despite this constant torment, I held my silence, attempting to pour myself into the oblivion of work in hopes that somehow, the events of my ordinary life would provide certainty as to which future to choose.

During this time, the decay had begun. With each passing day, by modest degrees, I was confronted more and more by the smallness of my life. From this grew a slow resentment that was blind and instinctive; secretly nurturing a sticking bitterness that tainted everything. I was less patient, less caring, quicker to anger. Sometimes my private irritation seeped to the surface, blooming darkly on my face. Friends and loved ones took notice, occasionally making pensive and concerned inquiries. But my answers were dismissive and evasive, and I would quickly assume a more light-hearted demeanor.

In this fashion, I muddled through the cold, cloudy days that followed the new year, holding on to the reckless notion that once I had passed the tombs of winter, all would be clear. I saw little of John and even less of Matthew. Connie and I would talk on occasion, but I was detached. I knew she was troubled about me, yet she never pressed the matter. It was around Christine that I presented the greatest counterfeit of my true thoughts. I was determined not to upset her until I was sure of my own head and heart.

In hindsight, holding everything in…keeping secrets from everyone, proved to be remarkably stupid. Unwittingly, whole parts of my world were quietly careening off course. Then, late one afternoon at the end of January, I received a most peculiar phone call.

Chapter 20

PHOTOGRAPHS

"Why, thank you, Polly. As a doctor who is hundreds of thousands of dollars in debt and who has focused his entire life on knowledgeably caring for the sick, mending wounds, and listening to the concerns of his patients, I welcome insulting remarks about my shirt."

Polly had been primly sitting on the exam room table and talking non-stop while she surveyed the room with a detached and ponderous air. But after absorbing my comment, her neck stiffened. The sarcasm in my words had bled through a little too thickly. Her bristled response was both haughty and wounded.

"Well, I didn't realize that I was rubbing an open nerve. I was simply observing that your tie didn't seem to match. My dear Clayton, the late Mr. Shropshire, always wanted me to pick out his ties. He thought I had an impeccable eye for fashion."

I ignored her. After retrieving my pen, I scribbled out an anti-anxiety prescription to accommodate this week's edition of Polly's endless ailments. Perhaps it had been the doldrums of winter or the dreary continuum of work separated by nights of insufficient sleep, but I had grown weary of the likes of Polly and numerous other patients whose problems were largely between their ears.

In the Watervalley school for scandal, Polly was the headmistress. Her visit was just another episode of rant and gossip mixed in with some fabricated malady. It seemed the discontent of others was her greatest amusement. When that was not accommodated, she held no qualms at manufacturing misery for whoever crossed her path. Apparently, this morning had been my turn.

I handed her the prescription and, after grunting a salutation, I exited to my office and dropped into my chair, exasperated. Altogether it hadn't been a bad day, and I was determined not to let Polly's visit put me in an ill humor. I swiveled around to face the large windows behind me. Outside the world was already on the cusp of darkness and I blew out a long sigh. Another gloomy winter evening had arrived. Nancy Orman timidly took a half step through the door to tell me she was shutting everything down. I told her that I would soon follow. I stood, gathered my papers, and retrieved my cell phone from my overcoat pocket. I was about to call Christine when I noticed that a voicemail had been left. It was from Matthew House.

Curious, I returned to my chair. Matthew had left a message asking that I give him a call, or better yet, drop by when I had a chance. There were some things he wanted me to see. He further explained that the matter was nothing urgent. I was about to dial his number but then, thought better of it. For some reason, I wanted to mull it over. I gathered my things and locked up. On the way home, I called Christine.

Despite the magic of being engaged and in love, our lives still included the mundane. Work, feeding dogs, shopping for groceries, and paying bills were still part of the daily and weekly regimen. Still, we managed to see each other on most school nights to grab some food, catch up, and of course, talk about the wedding, which now seemed to be costing about the same as an aircraft carrier. I was delighted to hear her voice, but it soon became apparent that seeing her that evening was unlikely. She had a huge stack of papers to grade, another task of the daily grind.

I sat in my driveway, and we talked for a full fifteen minutes. I didn't want to let her go. But in time we said our goodbyes, and I walked to the front door, and the familiar sight of two wet noses pressed to the living room window. The boys always lifted my spirits.

The two of them would come skidding into the front hallway in DEFCON Five, full-alert mode. After an obligatory head rubbing there would be a slippery gallop to the kitchen where both would sit in frozen obedience and stare at the back door in rapt attention. Once I had opened it a minimum of six inches, there followed an explosive muscling dash outside that held all the reckless abandon of a prison break.

While they darted around the backyard with random stops to take care of their business, I would fill their dinner bowls and place them on the porch. Ninety seconds later the bowls would be empty, and a less intensive reconnaissance of the rear domain would resume. After a lengthy playtime, I would call them back in. Rhett would quickly oblige. Casper, however, would ignore my calls and continue scampering around the backyard, tenaciously following some unidentified scent. Lecturing Rhett about how "He's your son. You need to fix this," did little to improve the matter. Inevitably I would have to venture into the cold and be Casper's personal guide to the back door.

Meanwhile, Rhett provided an altogether different problem. Recently he had developed a troubling habit of lying at my feet and emitting certain odors. I had come to realize that the dog contained more natural gas than a Canadian province. So, after showering and scratching together some dinner, I settled into an evening of random TV, light reading, and a pet whose GI tract could be used as a weapon of mass destruction. Yet all the while, in the back of my head was a nagging wonder about Matthew's call.

Around half past seven, my curiosity got the best of me. I considered calling him, but oddly, the idea of paying a visit had a stronger appeal. After all, I reasoned, the intent of his call was for me come by his house. I grabbed my coat and headed out the door. Just as I had done a month before, I started the engine and began the long, curving assent up to the heights of Society Hill.

As soon as I pulled through the iron gates of the old estate, a haunting memory of my previous visit swept over me. I had the peculiar sensation of an unexplainable presence; as if an apparition had casually joined me in the passenger seat to serve as my escort up the long driveway. I gushed a short laugh; an expression of dismissal of this absurd, ominous feeling. But I also took a quick slanting glance at the seat beside me, just for good measure.

With headlights on high-beam, I pulled up to the dark front entry and cut the engine. After getting out, I put a little extra juice behind closing the car door so that it would loudly slam shut. For some reason, I wanted to be obvious, to make my presence known. As I made my way through the shadows and climbed the front steps, I began to whistle, something I hadn't done since grade school. The outside door and entry hall lights were off, but lamplight glowed from the large room beyond. I rapped several times and continued whistling, only to abruptly stop when I realized I was inadvertently tooting the tune to "The Adams Family." Soon the front porch lights lit up, and Matthew appeared in the entrance hall.

I was about to diplomatically explain my presence when he took a step back and opened the door invitingly wide. "Luke! Glad you dropped by. Come in, come in." Even though his actions were modulated with his normal reserve, he was clearly in a buoyant mood.

We shook hands as I stepped past him. "I got your voice message. Hope I'm not showing up at a bad time."

"Not at all, not at all. I just got the children off to bed and, as I remember it, I asked you to come by whenever you could."

Even though we had scarcely seen each other in the past weeks, there was a spontaneous energy between us, an instant comradery. The drudgery of the everyday had made Matthew and my previous suspicions about him a largely forgotten topic.

"Can I get you something to drink? Beer or wine perhaps?"

"Beer sounds good."

He departed to the kitchen, leaving me to wait in the magnificently appointed great room. The splendor of the huge chamber served as an easy distraction for it seemed that instantly, Matthew reappeared. He smiled warmly as he handed me the beer and gestured for me to have a seat on a nearby sofa. He settled into an opposing chair and lazily rested his crossed feet atop the antique coffee table that sat between us.

"So, how's the doctor business?"

We talked casually for several minutes, during which time I noticed that Matthew's comments tended to center around his children and a collective relief that school and their transition to the world of Watervalley were going well. I quietly concluded that this was confirmation of his reasons for making such a sizeable donation to the charity run a month earlier. I also noticed something else.

Matthew had changed. He was more smartly turned out, more relaxed, and spoke with a confident, amiable reserve. His clothes were crisp and well-tailored, and he carried himself with a more definitive social assurance. The haunting cloud that previously shadowed him had largely faded, leaving in its place a strangely sensitive face that seemed full of understanding and patience.

His only note of annoyance regarded the High Society Book Club, who had made several requests about resuming the use of his home for their meetings.

"What is with that bunch?" He inquired, his face framed in an amused incredulity. "I politely told them that I would have to think about it. Apparently, that created some hard feelings."

"Don't let it bother you. For the most part, the people here rarely pretend to be what they are not. The majority are decent, unprepossessing souls. But Watervalley is no different from any other Southern town. There's a hierarchical social system in which those on the upper rungs practice a graciousness to all, but they also staunchly cling to some unspoken lines of inclusion."

"But this is a private residence. Don't they get that?"

"You've robbed the High Society Book Club of their identity. My guess is that the 'Public Library Conference Room Book Club,' doesn't quite attain the same lionized distinction."

"I suppose not," he said, smiling reflectively. An odd lull in the conversation followed. I was likely doing a poor job of concealing the strain of curiosity that, with each passing minute, was churning larger and larger beneath the surface. Matthew had contacted me for a reason, and we both knew that at some point, the conversation would turn in that direction. I decided to press the issue.

"So, is that why you called? Do you need someone to help slay those Philistine blue-bloods?"

Matthew grinned, his head appraisingly cocked a little to one side, and he nodded mirthfully; a non-verbal confirmation that he knew the time had come to discuss what was on his mind. He removed his legs from the coffee table and leaned forward, gently resting his arms on his knees.

"Luke, I need a confidant."

I shrugged impassively. "Sure."

"Allow me to start with a little background. The last time you were here I believe I mentioned to you that about a year before Emily passed away, we had moved into her grandmother's house on King Street in Charleston."

"Yes, I remember."

"When Hiram Hatcher left here in early 1928, he bounced around a few places, but he ended up in Charleston. Later that year he met Sofia Moncrief, a Charleston debutante who was ten years his junior. Hiram and Sophia married in June of 1929. Ten months later, in April of 1930, Hiram bought the house on King Street. He and Sophia had only one child, Eloise Hatcher, who was born in 1931. Eloise was Emily's grandmother."

"In 1953, Eloise married and had only one child, a daughter who, of course, was Emily's mother. She, in turn, married and had Emily who was also an only child. You with me so far?"

"Sure, I think so," I said mechanically.

"Hiram and Sophia Hatcher both passed away in 1961 and ownership of the King Street house passed to their daughter, Eloise. Upon her death, the house would have gone to Emily's parents. However, they died in a boating accident when Emily was eighteen. Thus, upon Eloise Hatcher Duchamp's death a few years ago, she left the house to my wife, the only heir."

I nodded my understanding. "Okay. That all sounds pretty straightforward."

"True. But there is one oddity. I had a title search done when we were bequeathed the property. Originally the old mansion on King Street was owned by the Moncriefs, the parents of Hiram's wife, Sophia. It turns out that Hiram bought the estate from her parents in April of 1930 at a rather exorbitant price for the times."

"Seems odd. Everything I've heard about Hiram Hatcher points to him being a rather shrewd businessman. The house purchase would have been on the heels of the market crash in 1929. Doesn't seem like a time when real estate would be at a premium."

"It wasn't. I did a little further digging and discovered that Sofia's father had been a prominent Charleston banker. As you might guess, he lost his shirt in the crash."

Matthew paused to allow me time to process what he was saying. I began to nod slowly. "So, it would seem that Hiram bailed the in-laws out of debt, allowing them to save face."

"Exactly. And not only that, but I also found in the Charleston real estate archives that around this same time, Hiram bought a very nice house only a few blocks away. That's where the Moncrief's lived until both of them passed away in the late forties. Soon after, the house sold. But it had always remained in Hiram's name."

"Sounds like Hiram was a pretty generous guy."

"He was. I found his obituary in the newspaper archives. It covered half a page."

"Really?"

"Yes. The man was practically a saint. He ran a very successful shipping business, was an elder in the Presbyterian Church, and at one time, or another was the head of every charity in the county. He could surf the waves of Charleston Society as well as anyone."

"Well, okay. Pretty interesting stuff. But, I'm not sure I follow your point with all this."

Matthew calmly scratched one of his elbows and nodded his understanding. He spoke in a kind and engaging manner. "You're a good fellow, Luke. I imagine you're as curious as anyone as to why I moved my family here. But you've been polite enough to not just bluntly inquire. I wanted to reveal all of this about Emily's family because I need your help. There was something that has always bugged me about Hiram's story."

"And that would be....?"

"Where did he get all of his money? I mean...even when the stock market and all the banks failed, apparently, he was still sitting on a mountain of cash."

"Yeah, seems that way. So, what's the answer?"

Right after we moved into the house on King Street, we had some repairs done to the tile roof on one of the attic dormers. The wood underneath the tile was rotten, so the roofer had to replace it. That's

179

when we noticed that the area underneath the dormer in the attic had been walled in, boarded up if you will. It wasn't something you would usually notice. When we tore the boards away, we found an old wooden steamer trunk in there. It was modest in size but quite elaborate. On the outside, there was a brass plate with the initials ELH. It took some doing, but I finally busted the lock with a crowbar. What we found inside was, well, pretty incredible."

By now I was unwittingly sitting on the edge of the couch, absently drawing closer to Matthew to make sure I didn't miss a single word. But without uttering another sound, he stood, walked to a nearby wooden secretary, and retrieved a manila folder from the top drawer. Upon returning to his chair, he extracted an old black and white photograph from the file and placed it on the coffee table between us. "Among other things in the trunk, we found this."

I took the photo from him. The ancient and faded sepia picture was of two men in suits, standing side-by-side and arm-in-arm in an elaborate bar. They were holding up their beer mugs and smiling for the camera in what was clearly a moment of celebration. I studied it for a few seconds before speaking cautiously. "Based on the other picture of him, it seems pretty certain that the fellow of the left is Hiram Hatcher." I turned over the photo and looked at the back where a penciled inscription read, "Gabe and me, January 1927." I flipped it back and examined the two men a moment longer. "But who's the guy on the right? For some reason, he looks incredibly familiar."

Matthew spoke with a kind of odd, amused reserve. "Apparently, Gabe was something of a nickname. He looks familiar because his full name was Alphonse Gabriel Capone."

Chapter 21

PROMISES TO KEEP

"Are you serious?" I gaped at Matthew like a wide-eyed, open-mouthed child. Further words hung in my throat. Matthew patiently nodded his confirmation. I looked at the picture again and deliberated.

"So, you're saying Hiram Hatcher was a bootlegger?"

"Not sure. He might have been…in part, at least. He had some legitimate businesses. It's well proven that he was in the phosphate business here in Watervalley. Prohibition ended in 1933. But by that time, he had migrated into the shipping business."

"Then what was his connection with Capone?"

Matthew reclined in his chair and relaxed his hands on the back of his head, pondering. "I'm not completely certain. But it does look like they were friends and probably had business dealings of some kind."

"How do you know?"

"There was a ledger in the trunk, one that had dates and shipping details."

"What kind of shipping details?"

"It's a little cryptic. First, there is a transaction number. Then there's a to and from entry, like WV to Mobile or WV to Chicago. I assume the WV is Watervalley. Then there is a units entry."

"Units of what?"

"Doesn't say. Also, there are no dollar figures associated with any of the transactions. My guess is that there was a separate money ledger that listed financial details against the transaction numbers. Keeping two separate ledgers was likely a security measure. It would be difficult to build an incriminating case if you didn't have both of them. That is if, in fact, he was doing something illegal."

"So, no second ledger in the trunk?"

"No."

"Well, what else was in there?"

"Several photos of the house, including the one you saw on the mantle. Many were of the inside. It turns out, much of the furniture from the King Street house came from here. I used the photos to return each piece to its original spot."

I lifted my head in a gesture of understanding. That explained the room's incredible glamour and symmetry with its furnishings.

Matthew continued. "There was some clothing in the trunk also. An old tuxedo which I assume was Hiram's and something rather odd; a dress."

"A dress?"

"Yes, a sleeveless number covered in black sequins with matching elbow length gloves. Fairly typical of a flapper dress of the times, I guess. Quite elegant looking, though. According to the label, it was custom made by a Chicago tailor."

"I have to ask this question. Did the dress, by chance, have any blood stains on it?"

He responded with an entertained smile. "Yes, I've heard the rumors that Hiram had murdered a woman here in the mansion. But no. The dress was spotless."

I thought for a moment. "So, any other papers? Anything else significant?"

Mostly travel receipts…mainly from Chicago. Apparently, Hiram went there quite often. There were invoices from both the Drake and the Palmer House Hotels in Chicago along with nightclub and entertainment bulletins. No idea why those would be important. Besides the ledger, the only other curious thing was a Bible."

"A Bible? Really?"

"Yes. It does seem a little out of place. Maybe I'm being unfair but having a Bible somehow doesn't exactly fit the general persona of Hiram Hatcher from that time period. At a minimum, I think it is safe to say he led quite a flamboyant lifestyle. He traveled extensively, entertained lavishly, and always had a house full of out of town guests. I suppose that's why he built such a grand place."

"Makes sense."

"Anyway, there are two curiosities about the Bible. There is an inscription on the inside cover that reads, 'Always know that you have done the right thing.' There was no signature, and the handwriting was a flowing cursive. In all the documents I've seen, Hiram always wrote in a blocked print. So, someone besides Hiram wrote it. No idea who. But then right below the inscription, in what is clearly Hiram's handwriting, he wrote, 'Forgive me. Everything is in the camera. I could not throw it away.'"

"What does that mean?"

Matthew smiled and shook his head. "Again, no idea. I presume there were some old photographs tucked away somewhere at the Charleston house or maybe even an old camera with some kind of note or clue inside of it...but there was nothing."

"So that's a dead end."

"Pretty much."

"Well, the other thing is this. Who was he asking forgiveness from?"

"Again, no idea."

We both fell silent, perhaps hoping that added time would somehow add illumination. "You mentioned that there was a second curious thing about the Bible."

"Yes, the other matter was a hand-written notation in the book of Ecclesiastes."

"Hiram's handwriting?"

"Definitely. He had underlined the second verse from the third chapter, the one about a time to be born and a time to die. Evidently, somewhere along the way, Hiram learned a little Latin. In the top margin of that page, he penned, 'Praeteritis obsignatus est in via,' and then added a second inscription at the bottom, 'Non sum qualis eram.'"

I tightened my gaze at Matthew, a gesture that he ably noticed. He spoke cautiously.

"Did I miss something?"

I was deliberating, trying to recall when and where I had recently heard the latter quote when John Harris's name emerged from the depths of memory. He had quoted the same Latin phrase during his last visit to my office; an odd coincidence. Matthew's imploring silence refocused me.

"No, nothing," I said abruptly. "Just a random thought. I'm somewhat familiar with the second phrase. But just for clarification, what is the translation of both?"

"Well, the top inscription states, 'It is sealed in the past,' and the bottom one reads, 'I am not the kind of person I once was."

"Any idea why he wrote that?"

"None at all," Matthew replied. "All I can gather is that in the waning months of 1927, something big must have happened in Hiram's life. Whatever plans he had for living here all changed."

I recalled John's story about the scandal around his grandmother and Hiram taking the trip to Chicago in December of that year. I was endeavoring to assimilate this with all that Matthew had said when a final oddity occurred to me. "You mentioned that the initials on the trunk were ELH. How does that match up with the name 'Hiram?'"

"Good question. It doesn't. Apparently, 'Hiram' was a nickname. The name on the deed of the King's Street house was Emanuel Lorenzo Hatcher."

"Sounds like a mix of Italian and English. It certainly accounts for Hiram's dark hair and the tan complexion."

"That would be my guess as well. I did quite a bit of digging on Hiram in the months before I came here. He grew up near Penobscot Bay in Maine."

"I've heard it said that he was from Maine."

"He was raised by an Aunt and Uncle in Penobscot. But he was born in Brooklyn and lived there through the sixth grade. No idea what happened to his parents or how he ended up in Maine. His uncle was in the mining and shipping business. Hiram went on to attain a degree from Dartmouth with a major in business and a minor in classical studies."

"Isn't Brooklyn where Capone grew up?"

"Exactly."

"Perhaps the two of them could be childhood friends."

Matthew nodded in affirmation. "My thinking as well."

"So, here you have a guy who knows a lot about shipping and distribution connected with a guy in bootlegging."

"Seems to fit together, doesn't it?"

"Yeah, but why Watervalley? Why make this a distribution point? And how does mining phosphate play into any of this?

"Well, it's all conjecture mind you. Hiram already knew a lot about the mining business, and phosphate was a legitimate boom at the time. But the area was also known for the making of spirits. Let's face it, even in modern day, the Jack Daniels and the George Dickel distilleries are only a county away from Watervalley. For better or worse, this part of Tennessee has a long history of whiskey production."

I leaned back and folded my arms, staring at Matthew inquisitively. "You know, it's my understanding that Hiram built a railroad spur that goes from Watervalley up to Nashville. Along with phosphate, it does seem like a clever way to transport large quantities of whiskey on a regular basis without drawing a lot of attention."

"And a small, remote little town as a distribution center was likely to be under the Feds radar...not in the way a Chicago, a Kansas City, or an Atlanta would be."

186

I gathered my thoughts. "This is all quite incredible."

"So, I guess you can understand why I have been rather discreet about disclosing why I came here. Being the descendent of a likely criminal and possible mobster is not exactly the kind of reputation you want your children to be known for by their schoolmates."

"Well, I certainly understand that. But honestly, Matthew. Why come here at all? I realize that the loss of your wife was tragic and that everywhere you turned in Charleston probably held some memory of her. But I can only assume that you enjoyed your professorship, you had ample friends, a grand house, everything was familiar to the children...why leave all that? Why come to this backward little boondock if you didn't have to?"

With my blunt posturing of this question, Matthew's demeanor eased to that of stoic resignation. He spoke with quiet conviction. "Because it was Emily's dying request that I do so."

I had no response for this. Just as before I simply stared at him, somewhat stunned. Moments passed before I could find words. "But...but why?"

Matthew gazed down at the floor as if he were deliberating his response. "Emily died of synovial cancer. It is rare, and we foolishly didn't catch the warning signs. As cancers go, it took her down pretty fast. She died in a matter of months. But in truth, it didn't feel very fast. I spent hours and hours at her bedside, watching her waste away. She slept often. And in that sleep, she dreamed. In her final days, she kept having the same dream over and over again. She dreamed she was talking with Hiram, her great-grandfather. He appeared to her as a young man. He kept pleading with her to come here, to…to come to Watervalley, to somehow help him heal some great tragedy that happened years ago."

Matthew paused and looked up at me as if he were trying to read my acceptance of his words. He gushed a short laugh. "I know it all sounds rather far-fetched, Luke. But you have to understand, we had this conversation numerous times, and I'm convinced she was completely lucid."

I shrugged and nodded compliantly. "No, um…absolutely."

My tone more than my words seemed to mollify him. He rubbed his chin and spoke with further resolve. "You see, there's something else as well. I wasn't joking when I told you that sometimes, the children could see angels. I think somehow in the crazy scheme of things, they really can. I used to not pay much attention to it all until we were coming home from church one Sunday about three weeks after Emily died. Out of the blue, Adelyn said, 'Mommy wants to know when we're going to move to Watervalley?'"

My eyes tightened. "No way."

Matthew drew in a deep breath and nodded. "I swear to you they knew nothing about Emily and my conversations. Adelyn said her mother had appeared to them during the service and asked the question."

Just like with previous visits to this drafty old mansion, a hardened shiver bristled down my neck and, without passing go, went straight to my toes. The problem with what Matthew was saying was that I believed every word of it. Something about the atmosphere of this place seemed to lend plausibility to virtually anything in the spiritual realm. I did my best to appear unruffled.

"So, what is it that you're supposed to find?"

"Well, there's the rub. I honestly don't know. All I know to do is to keep digging into Hiram's background. And that, Luke, is why I asked you here."

Admittedly, by now I was a little spooked and somewhat reluctant. "Well, okay. Tell me what you had in mind?"

"As I mentioned earlier, I have done some research at the Watervalley library in their microfiche files, trying to look at old newspaper articles. But at least a dozen people came and struck up conversations. Half of them outright asked me what I was looking for and the rest did their best to try and look over my shoulder."

I had to laugh. "That sounds about right."

"Well, I need to go to the courthouse, to the Assessor of Property's office and look at any records I can find out about this place and see if there are any old documents regarding Hiram's phosphate business. My presence raises too many questions. So, I was wondering if I might trouble you to do this if you can find the time."

Inwardly, I breathed a sigh of relief. This I could do.

"Sure. Yeah, that'd be no problem."

Matthew's shoulders relaxed as if he had been wound tight. "Splendid. Thank you."

He said this and nothing more. Perhaps it was due to his military background, but now that Matthew had attained his objective, it seemed that he saw no further need for conversation. I sensed this and stood, a motion toward departure.

But curiously, Matthew politely held up his hand in an act of inquiry. "Luke, I wonder if I might ask a probing question?"

Instinctively, I returned to the couch, somewhat guarded.

"Go ahead."

"I picked up on something earlier that struck me as…well, odd. You referred to Watervalley as a backward boondock. I guess I have been under the impression that you grandly loved it here. But I detected a certain…I don't know, toxicity. Did I get that wrong?"

Matthew's insight had been both astute and accurate. I tightened my gaze, contemplating his question. Then it occurred to me that he was the perfect soul in which to unpack my burden of confession. Matthew had no real ties to Watervalley and was a well contained and cool head. He was the perfect sounding board.

"Well, here's the deal." I spent the next hour unloading the weight of my conflict, rambling a little bit, but giving full testimony to the benefits and disadvantages of both staying and leaving. It seemed that I talked nonstop and yet all the while, Matthew listened patiently and attentively. At long last, when my words were exhausted, he responded quietly.

"Luke, it appears that you have a great love for both your fiancée and the people of this community. It also sounds like Christine is made of pretty strong stuff and she'll go along with you to Nashville… if that is what you want. But as far as the people here go, I get the sense that it's not so much that you fear disappointing them, you just don't want to leave them high and dry…without medical coverage as it were."

"Yeah. I'd say you just summed up in eighteen seconds what I've been trying to say for the last hour."

Matthew pressed his lips together, acknowledging his understanding. "It's a tough one, alright. I wish I had an easy answer."

"Didn't expect you to. I appreciate you letting me bend your ear for a while. I'll figure out a solution. I need to find a way to put all the pieces together. The trouble is, I only have a few weeks left before a decision has to be made."

"Well, like I said. I wish I had an answer."

I stood and extended my hand to him. "Hey, no worries. Thanks for the beer. I'll get down by the courthouse early next week and let you know what I find."

"I appreciate it. I wish I could give you a better clue as to what you're looking for."

"Eh, you've got me curious now. Maybe something will turn up."

We walked to the entrance. But as I turned to shake his hand again before departing, a loud metallic crash echoed from the depths of the basement.

Chapter 22

BUMP IN THE NIGHT

"**D**id you hear that?"

"Yeah," I whispered. "What was it?"

"No idea," he said intently. His light manner hardened into a sharp, focused stare. Quietly, his thoughts were submerging; brooding upon some unspoken apprehension.

I spoke haltingly. "You want to go check it out?"

He was preoccupied, clearly searching for some easy explanation. He nodded. "Do you mind coming with me?"

I shrugged. "Sure." But after a moments silence, I spoke in a confidential, hushed tone, almost not believing the words I was saying. "You think it might be a...you know...ghost?"

Matthew shook his head decidedly. "No, that was no ghost. Not the right vibe. That was more of an in your face kind of noise."

His blunt certainty caught me off guard. Matthew seemed to be itching for a fight... a condition that was decidedly not contagious. The only thing I was catching was a bad case of the sissies. "Matthew, look. Don't get me wrong. I like your confidence, especially coupled with the old-school smack talk. But what makes you so sure? Is there a 'Ghosts for Dummies' that I should thumb through?"

He grimaced, his thoughts still consumed. "It's uh, it's hard to explain. With ghosts, you feel them before you hear or see them." He shook his head again, clearly irked. "No, something or someone is down there. Come on."

We hurried through the living room and down a short hall to an elaborate kitchen that was large enough for a small staff. "Wait here," Matthew said with quiet authority. A moment later he returned with two long flashlights and a pistol.

"Whoa," I exclaimed, poorly masking my alarm. "This looks serious."

Matthew had also brought a box of bullets and set them on the counter. Methodically, he popped out the clip of the pistol and began to load it. "Just a precaution," he said calmly.

"A precaution for what?" I spoke in disbelief.

He glanced at me and continued filling the clip. But he was elsewhere, looking more through me than at me, as if he were rehearsing the steps of some well-practiced drill. He spoke crisply.

"Look, per Lida, the basement is extensive. Down the steps is a sizeable main room but there are several hallways leading off it. There are doors all along those hallways that go to several storage rooms."

"Rooms for storing what?"

"Don't know. Lida said they were part of the original design when the house was built in the twenties. She told me that the lights don't work and that except for the main room she hardly ever went down there. Early on she tried to explore all of them, but according to her, most of the heavy wooden doors were wedged shut from the house settling over the years."

"So, have you been down there and checked it all out?"

"Not really. I've only been down to the main room. It's pretty cluttered. Since there are no working lights, that area of the house is toward the bottom of the 'to do' list."

Admittedly, I was a little rattled by this sudden change of events. In fact, downright scared would likely be a better summation. "Okay, let's break this down. You're saying the lights don't work down there. So, that means it's dark, right?"

"Yeah, completely black. Why?"

"Well, I don't know. It's just that when I was a kid, I was always taught that the dark was a place that nice people didn't go."

"Are you saying you're afraid of the dark?"

"No, I'm saying I'm afraid of what's in the dark?"

"You don't have to come."

"No. I'll come. I was thinking that maybe we should wait and get an electrician to come with us. Preferably one with a concealed weapon permit."

It might have been the complete lack of testosterone in my voice, but Matthew now realized the full weight of my trepidation. His demeanor changed, and he offered me a somewhat forced but accommodating smile.

"I think it'll be fine."

"Yeah, I'm sure you're right. I just have a thing about basements."

"What do you mean?"

"Well, about a month after I moved into the house on Fleming Street I was going to bed one night when I heard a noise in the basement, just like we just did. It's an old root cellar with a dirt floor. Other than opening the door and taking a quick glance, I'd never taken a step down there. So, I tried the stairwell lights and nothing.

Completely dark, just like you're describing. So, I'm thinking, 'no problem.' I get a flashlight and start inching my way down."

"Okay, so. Did something happen?"

I shrugged, wanting to treat the matter coolly. "Well, I...you know. I saw something."

"You saw something?"

"Yeah."

"Okay. You mean something like a ghoul or some creepy apparition?"

I looked down and breathed a short laugh. "You wouldn't believe me if I told you."

"Try me."

I spoke sheepishly. "Well, it was an um...it was a spider."

"A what?"

"A spider. A big hairy spider."

"That's it? I mean...all of this because of a little spider?"

"Alright, alright, I'll admit it. I'm the arachnophobia poster child. But I'm telling you, this spider wasn't just big; it was an evil mutant spider."

"Tell me your kidding."

"Hey, trust me. That thing was scary. I think it was wearing a coat made of chipmunk hides. All it needed was a tiny fedora to look like an eight-legged pimp."

Matthew smiled and returned his focus to loading bullets. "Okay, okay. I get it. But seriously, why not just hit it with a shot of Raid?"

"Because I'm telling you, this guy was huge. Raid would have just pissed him off. If I hit him with a spray of Raid, next thing I know he's locking the door to the basement and chuckling softly."

"Well, why not blind it with the flashlight and just step on it?"

"First of all, I was barefoot. All I had on was boxers. Secondly, I didn't see him. I felt him. He was sitting on my shoulder."

"Yeah, I guess that would freak anybody out. What did you do?"

"I did what any real man protecting his house would do. I screamed like a little girl, brushed wildly at myself, and dashed frantically back up the stairs."

Matthew forced a smile, but it was clear that he was absorbed with what waited beneath. He spoke dryly. "Come on. The basement is this way."

We walked down a short passageway to a large door with a deadbolt. Matthew paused and tucked his flashlight under his arm. Then, once again, he popped the magazine cartridge out of the handle. After a swift examination, he crisply reinserted it and pulled back the slide, loading a round into the firing chamber. The entire process took only a few seconds, conveying that he had done this a million times. It was both impressive and curiously odd.

"You think you might need that?"

"Like I said. Just a precaution." He spoke dismissively, but his entire demeanor said otherwise. I swallowed hard and followed him, plagued with the fleeting notion that I was about to descend into the cellar of Satan. Admittedly though, I had to admire Matthew's boldness. For a modest-sized fellow, his intensity made him seem ten feet tall.

We moved cautiously down the steps. The damp, musty air welling up from the dark vat before us was decidedly cooler, thick with the muddy held breath of decades. It gave me an abrupt shuddering chill. To our left was a stone wall but the right of the wide steps was open to the room. After descending far enough to avail an angled view of the cavernous space below, Matthew stopped. We both crouched and shined our lights into the far corners.

I'd love to say my courage had risen to the moment. But in truth, I was scared senseless. My movements were feverish and abrupt, zooming my light around the large chamber with chaotic uncertainty. Conversely, Matthew was controlled and methodic, systematically scanning from left to right. He adeptly held the pistol in his right hand and the flashlight in his left, crossing his arms at the wrist to move the two in close unison. He was cool and measured. Spiders and creepy basements had my number. Nothing had his.

The chamber below was cluttered with the remains of the mansions previous lives, the heaped and forgotten refuse of many years. The walls and floor were crowded with paint cans and boxes, rusted garden tools, broken furniture, antiquated folding chairs, and lawn game equipment. There was both order and disarray; the surviving remnants of long ago inspiration and subsequent neglect.

Even still, with its stone walls, brick floor, and massive timbers, the wide room held a certain grandness. Beneath the elements of time and desertion, I got the sense that the derelict muddle below was a false veneer, a temporary film on the surface of what was a massive and enduring structure. Despite the eeriness of the moment, it was difficult not to be impressed.

Our lights had penetrated every corner, revealing nothing. There was neither sound nor movement. I was anxious to call it quits, to get this episode over. But Matthew had other ideas. He knelt patiently, and we waited. Finally, he switched off his light and turned to me, speaking in a half whisper. "Turn yours off too."

"What? Are you nuts?"

"It's okay. Just do it."

Reluctantly, I complied. We strained against the darkness, listening. Matthew's tactic worked. Distantly, there came another sound as if something metallic had been pushed across the brick floor.

"Come on. It's coming from one of the far hallways." He switched his light on and stepped quickly. I followed, but with decidedly less enthusiasm.

We navigated our way through the haphazard piles in the central room to a large open door on the far end. Beyond was a broad hallway that extended in both directions. Alternately, Matthew shined his light toward either end, deliberating.

"I'm not sure which direction the sound came from. You go down that one, and I'll go down this one. Shout if you see anything." He headed off.

"Whoa, whoa, whoa!" I called out in an urgent whisper.

He stopped and turned back toward me. "What's wrong?"

"What's wrong? Really? What's wrong is that I have this huge line down the middle of my back and it's painted bright yellow. It practically glows in the dark."

"Are you suggesting you're afraid?"

"No. I'm not suggesting anything. I'm outright telling you I'm afraid. Look, Matthew, you're the one with the gun. That makes you the lead guy in this deal. And in the movies, this is usually the scene where the trusty sidekick without the gun gets bumped off."

"Okay, okay. I get it. We'll stay together. Come on."

He pushed ahead, and I trailed tightly behind. But it was awkward. That was because I was walking backward, shining my light to the rear. I had watched enough thrillers to know how the "getting picked off at the end of the line" thing worked.

The first door we came to was of thick, heavy oak with large iron hinges. Matthew turned the handle and heaved against it with his shoulder. It didn't budge. The same was true of the next door. After that, the hallway turned to the right and narrowed into a swallowing darkness. To my thinking, we had given it the good old college try. It was time to turn back.

"Don't think the noise came from this far off, do you?" I was trying to be as persuasive and analytical as possible under the circumstances. But Matthew was undaunted. We continued deeper. After several steps down this second hallway we came upon a door to our left. Unlike the others, it was ajar, availing an opening of about six inches. Matthew looked back at me and nodded. My heart pounded.

He positioned his flashlight and pistol tightly together and shoved the door with his foot. It swung open sluggishly with a sharp, wincing screech of the hinges. A split second later, we were both inside. What we found was completely unexpected.

The wide room held three long rows of floor to ceiling wine racks, skillfully crafted of wood and still firm and solid. Our search was momentarily suspended as both of us stopped to admire the craftsmanship of the extensive and airy structures. Now empty, they had a capacity of thousands of bottles. It was yet another odd detail about the life of the elusive Hiram Hatcher.

We were about to leave when my light caught a flicker of movement along the back wall at the distant end of the room. "Did you see that?" I blurted out.

"No. What?"

"Down that way. Something moved."

"Something or someone?"

"Definitely not a someone."

Immediately, Matthew walked in that direction with flashlight and pistol in fixed attack mode. I, on the other hand, was open to a little further contemplation on the matter before proceeding. At first, I held tight, content to let Matthew sort out the details. But as he moved farther away, I made an abrupt policy change; one that included staying close to the guy with the gun. I caught up quickly.

At the end of the wine racks was an open space of about eight feet which was empty save for one of the corners where an accumulated clutter of rusted metal bands covered some timeworn apparatus. Closer inspection revealed it to be a vintage metal dolly whose rubber wheels had long since deteriorated into crumbled flakes. Oddly, however, although it had a base on one end and handles on the other, it also had wheels on each end and was slightly bowed across the back. Beside this was a stack of a dozen or so five-gallon cans. Four of them were strewn on the floor, randomly lying on their sides. I picked one up by the metal handle welded to its center. Using my flashlight, I could barely make out the faded label on the side which read, "Frontenac Maple Syrup Company. Product of Canada." These had likely been the source of the noise we had heard. Something had knocked them over.

Hastily, we probed our lights into the corners and then down the length of the wooden rows. But our search revealed nothing. And yet, I felt an odd presence. That's when it occurred to me to focus my light up high to the top of the nearest wine rack. Two eyes reflected back at me. We had found our culprit.

I handed my light to Matthew and then stepped on the bottom rack to reach and retrieve the big fellow.

"So, that's our spook," declared Matthew.

My voice was drenched in relief. "Yup. It's Lida's Siamese cat. His name is Chairman Meow."

"Really? It looks like a female."

I shrugged. "You may be right. But the only way to tell the difference involves some rather impolite snooping."

Matthew grinned. "Doesn't matter. Anyway, he seems to know you. I assume you two have met?"

"We're acquaintances. He usually hangs out down at the Diner with Lida. I guess he decided to visit his old stomping ground."

"I wonder how he got in?"

"No clue. If you speak Mandarin, we can ask him."

Matthew shook his head. "Well, okay then. I guess that's that."

"Yeah. I'll drop him off at Lida's house on the way home. She lives a few streets over from me."

Matthew nodded and handed me the flashlight. I cradled Chairman Meow under my arm and exhaled a huge sigh as well, glad that this basement experience was finally over. But as we began to depart, I couldn't help but notice something odd.

"Matthew, is it just me, or does it seem strange to you that this back wall is brick? All the others are of stone."

Chapter 23

CONSPIRATORS

Matthew stared with strained curiosity. "Luke, I think you're right."

"What do you make of it?"

"Not sure. It doesn't appear to be part of the original structure."

As we stepped closer, our lights gravitated to the same spot, a six-inch opening in the top right corner above the five-gallon cans. The wall rose to ten feet, making the gap far too high for either of us to peer through.

"That must be where Chairman Meow got in," I said probingly.

"And the noise we heard was him knocking some of the cans over."

"So, I wonder what's on the other side?"

Matthew shook his head. "No idea."

I spoke guardedly. "You think it might be...you know, the bones of a woman who once wore a flapper dress with black sequins on it?"

Matthew grinned and grunted a low noise of acknowledgment. "Well, let's hope not."

I focused my light on the pile of metal bands. "I have an idea."

We propped the antiquated dolly up against the wall and used the rungs connecting the handles as a ladder. Matthew held it in place while I inched my way up and positioned my light through the hole.

"What do you see?" He inquired.

"Not much, really. The breach is too small. But there's definitely an open space on the other side."

"Can you get your arm through it?"

I glanced down, regarding him stiffly. "Well, I'm sure I can. But I'm a little concerned that something on the other side might want it for a keepsake."

"What I mean is, how thick is the wall?"

"Looks to be about a six-inch framed wall behind this course of brick."

"Alright, good. Come on back down."

I descended and dusted myself off. "So, what's your plan?"

"In the morning, I'll buy a concrete saw from the hardware store and cut a hole in the wall. Somebody had a reason for wanting to close it off. I want to know why."

Still curious, we silently moved our lights back and forth across this mysterious partition. But there seemed nothing more to be gained. I gathered Chairman Meow. Matthew offered a confirming nod, and I followed as he led the way back toward the stairs. Just as a precaution, I occasionally focused my flashlight on the path behind. Our unnerving quest into the bowels of the old mansion was over. My case of the sissies wasn't.

I had to laugh at myself. Things that brought a paralyzing panic to others, like a mangled and bleeding arm or a flat-lined heart rhythm, did little to faze me. I understood those matters. But the spectral world had no rules, no guidebook. I wanted to dismiss all of it. Yet something primal within my DNA simply wouldn't allow it.

My education had taught me to apply a sobering dose of scientific rationale to all situations, enabling me to find order in the empirical world. Nevertheless, even from the lofty high ground of intellectual indifference, there was always a small, uncertain voice somewhere deep within whispering, "but what if?" Conversely, Matthew seemed unaffected by such notions.

As we emerged from the musty air of below, I was baffled by his easy confidence. "Matthew, you okay going back down there by yourself tomorrow?"

"Sure, why wouldn't I be?"

"Just make sure your work belt has a holster for your six-shooter."

He grinned. "There won't be a need for that. Whatever's on the other side of that wall might be gruesome, but I doubt it's alive."

Matthew shut the door to the basement and locked it.

Still, my curiosity drove me. "So, humor me. The gun. If there's no concern, why did we need it for this little adventure?"

He pursed his lips for a moment, weighing my question before speaking in a voice of calm resignation. "In Emily's dream, she said that Hiram had told her that he had left something in Watervalley. She was never clear on that part. She said it was some 'f' word like fortune, or future, or family."

"Or felony?"

"Well, possibly that too, I guess."

"Yeah, but none of those make sense. From what you said, he clearly had his fortune when he arrived in Charleston. If it was his future, then why did he leave? And it seems pretty common knowledge that he had no family here."

"Welcome to my dilemma."

"So again, why the gun?"

"I think it's safe to say that my arrival has stirred up a lot of interest among the locals. The children are asked questions all the time at school. One of the old rumors is that there is some kind of treasure hidden away here, like a valuable painting or an original Stradivarius violin. I'm certain it's all bunk."

"It's a big place. What makes you so sure?"

"In her grandmother's files, Emily had found a list of Hiram's furniture and artwork. I guess he wanted everything cataloged for insurance purposes before the move to Charleston."

"Sounds reasonable."

"Except for an odd silver spoon or two, whatever has any value has been accounted for. Nevertheless, Lida told me that the stories crop up every time there is a new owner. So, here's the deal. We heard a noise. I've lost my wife. I'll take no chances with anything happening to my children just because the wrong kind of person got curious."

His solemn response made perfect sense. I nodded and, cradling Lida's cat under one arm, we made our way to the front door. Before leaving, I turned to him.

"Look, Matthew. For a couple of guys who tend to be loners, it seems that suddenly we both have a lot of skinny on each other. Do we need to spit in our hands and shake or anything?"

He grinned. "You're contemplating leaving town, and my wife's ancestors were likely mobsters and murderers. I think we're good."

"Right. Nice summary. Well, since we're an item now, let me know what's behind that wall. I'll call you after I go by the Property Assessors office."

"Thanks for coming up."

As we shook hands an unspoken confidence passed between us. Despite its unnerving aspects, the evening had been extraordinary.

Outside the winter air had a biting edge, leaving Chairman Meow blissfully content to be snuggled under my coated arm. I walked briskly to my car, awash in a beguiling mix of weariness and exhilaration. But before opening the car door, I hesitated, captivated by the frozen night and its attendant silence.

High above was an infinite black canopy, an immense and lonely sky illuminated only by the reluctant light of a shy moon. The great house towered before me, seemingly watching me, taking measure, weighing me in the scales. Slowly, once again I begin to feel the haunting presence of invisible things, as if something deep and ancient within the brooding stones were trying to whisper to me, imploring me to listen. I waited. But there was nothing.

I began to open the car door when the corner of my vision caught a flicker of light. It was the lamp in the window of Matthew's office in the high tower. It flashed two dashes and three dots...the ending of an SOS signal. Then, it went dark.

Suddenly, Chairman Meow stiffened, straining against me as if something had alarmed him. I stroked his head and continued to stare at the distant window, dumbfounded. Fleeting seconds had elapsed since Matthew had closed the front door, making it impossible for him to have crossed the grand room and scale the two flights of steps to the high tower, even at an all-out sprint. This wasn't Matthew. This was something else altogether.

My pulse accelerated. A dozen thoughts consumed me. The worst scenario was that of an intruder. Then again, no intruder would be flashing an SOS signal. I dismissed the possibility. After a long minute of nothing but shadowy silence, the cold began to penetrate, dissolving my momentary alarm into a numbing lethargy. I began to doubt that I had seen anything at all. Deciding that no further heroics were needed, I slid into the car seat and headed back out the cobbled drive.

After dropping Chairman Meow off in Lida's front yard, I made my way home, took a quick shower, and fell into bed. Despite the incredible revelations of the past few hours, I soon submerged into a deep and consuming sleep. Buried within the larger events of the evening had been the opportunity to tell a sympathetic listener the depths of my quandary.

There was an abiding solace in that act that I was yet to understand fully.

Chapter 24

ANTIQUES

The clinic was unusually busy the next day, especially for a Friday. My plan of slipping away at lunch to the Property Assessors Office never materialized. Nancy Orman went by the bakery and bought me a sandwich which I swallowed whole between examinations. After finishing my last patient around four-thirty, I retreated to my office, hoping to make a quick dash to the courthouse before it closed at five. But as I gathered my things, the office door swung open and a lovely, familiar voice inquired, "is the doctor in?"

It was Christine.

She stood in the open doorway with her hand outstretched against the frame. Though unintended, her raised arm allowed her overcoat to drape wide and loose, revealing the alluring flow of the contours beneath it. Basic instincts alone immediately had me under her spell. But the effect was doubled by her adoring gaze which seemed to mask something rich and secretive; a musing expression of irrepressible affection. I was lost to her. The Property Assessors office was all but forgotten.

Putting my things aside, I stepped toward her. "Hello, gorgeous. How goes the razor's edge life of elementary school?" She closed the door behind her and offered only a daunting grin. By instinctive habit, we embraced in a long, delightful kiss.

Afterward, she did something quite unusual. She walked behind my desk, removed her coat, and sat...rather authoritatively, in my chair. There was a mischievous grin on her face and a light of higher purpose flickering in her eyes. "So, how was work?" She inquired casually.

Following her lead, I plopped into one of the leather armchairs across from my desk. "Oh, you know. Just the routine hypochondriacs complaining about weird twitches, skin rashes, unusual body sounds, and the occasional speech impediment."

"Glad to know you had a good day."

"How was school?"

"It was good. I love my class. They're a great bunch."

I nodded. "As it should be. Anyway, this is a nice surprise. I'm guessing something's on your mind."

"I've got a great idea about a little side trip I want us to take tomorrow."

"Be still my beating heart."

She dropped her chin in reproach. "Careful, Bradford. Don't make me put you in time out."

"Is this where I make some nuanced remark about being spanked?"

"No. This is where you choose your words carefully, or you may have to spend some time in the principal's office. I've got a small adventure I want us to go on tomorrow. It's going to be a lot of fun."

"You mean fun as in more fun than talk like a pirate day?"

"Wow, Bradford. Epic failure on the whole 'choose your words carefully' thing."

"Alright, pretty girl. I'm all ears."

"In the morning, let's drive down to Lawrenceburg and go antiquing."

"I'm quite sure my expressionless face did not render the desired response. Try as I might, my answer was forced. "Okay. Sure. Anything, in particular, we're looking for?"

"No."

I nodded thoughtfully, doing my best to mask my disinterest. But Christine knew me too well.

"Oh, come on, Luke, you'll love it." Her voice was annoyingly confident and instructional, a telling sign about how she saw this conversation ending.

"Love the idea of being with you. Not so sure about the whole antiquing thing." I hesitated and made a quick glance to the side. "I mean, is antiquing even a real verb?"

Ever so slightly, Christine narrowed her eyes. "It is for this conversation. Do I need to explain to you what antiquing looks like?"

"No, no. I think I've got it. It's where you go to some huge, drafty building and look at old black and white pictures of other people's grandparents."

Christine aloofly folded her arms. "Okay, no problem. I'll just go by myself."

My gushed response was automatic. "Oh, now don't be like that."

"Like what?" She replied innocently.

She had me off balance. "Like, you know...dismissive because I'm not all giggles about looking at what is usually a lot of junk." My comment brought no response. "Look, I have a better idea. Why don't we hop in the car and drive to Atlanta tomorrow? All of my parents' and my Aunt Grace's furniture are in two huge storage units there. Many of the items are vintage antiques. We'll make a day of it. You can look through it all and pick out anything you want."

Christine's face softened into an amused smile. Then oddly, she stood, circled the desk, and knelt beside me, resting her elbows on the soft arm of the chair.

"Luke, I'm sure your parents' things in Atlanta are nothing short of incredible. I do not doubt that I will fall in love with all of it. But you and I are the same. We're both only children. So, all the generations of furniture and oriental rugs and silver at the farmhouse will one day be mine as well. I doubt we'll ever have a house big enough for all of it. But the reason I want to go antiquing tomorrow is so that at least one thing in our house will be our own, not from my family or from your family, but ours."

She was entirely correct, and I was hard-pressed not to appear as stupid as I felt. The moment called for nothing less than absolute contrition, for me to do nothing short of telling her that she was completely right and that I was a moron. So, I did the only thing a real guy could do. I said nothing and sat silently, hoping that the feeling of complete shame would be replaced by a more palatable emotion…perhaps something more on the order of reserved acceptance.

Ultimately, I smiled and spoke penitently. "Well, gee. I guess since you put it like that, now I feel like it's a moral imperative that we do a little antiquing tomorrow."

Christine's gaze tightened into a guileful, knowing smile. She had me. She knew that my atoning response along with its spontaneous but failed humor meant that I knew I was wrong. She also knew that I would likely not openly admit it. But that didn't seem to bother her. She leaned seductively close and kissed my forehead, never losing her artful smile.

But she wasn't quite through with me. She looked down and spoke provisionally. "We don't have to go. It's only if you want to."

I responded with a wary grin. I didn't mind that she so overpowered me; that her intuitive cleverness, her unselfish tenderness, and mesmerizing effect of her sensuous lure always held sway over me. But I did mind that she pretended not to know it. My amused glare spoke volumes.

"What?" She finally countered, her tone replete with innocence.

"I'm just a big gullible puppy dog to you, aren't I?"

"That's not true," she said aloofly.

"Au contraire, brown eyes. I think you know better."

By subtle degrees, her manner became more relaxed and sportive. Wearing a mirthful smile, she leaned in. "I have no idea what you're talking about."

"Humph," I lightly retorted. "It's pathetic. I bet if you scratched my tummy I'd automatically start shaking my leg."

"You want me to give it a try?"

"Best not. It would only serve as confirmation."

Christine laughed yet all the while she gazed at me with an absorbed affection. "Oh, Luke Bradford. I do love you so. You crack me up."

"Said the woman with her hand on the short leash."

"I think a little road trip will be a great opportunity for us to talk." Her eyes were cast downward as she spoke as if there were something leading about her comment.

I shrugged. "Okay, sure. Talk about what?"

She seemed preoccupied and began to draw small loops in the hair above my ear. At first, she said nothing, content to let her gaze follow the slow circles she was making as if she were secretly dialing the combination to unlock what was inside. There was something evasive in her response. "Oh, about the wedding, the honeymoon, and then…you know, what will happen after that."

"Well, I've thought a lot about the first two but haven't really gotten to the 'after that' part." Even under the most liberal use of rationalization, this was a naked lie. But somehow, I justified my response by viewing my "stay or leave" decision as a colossal fork in the road. I was stuck there. And honestly, I hadn't thought in detail about the next steps of either option. Fortunately, Christine's focus was on the middle topic.

"Oh, so you've been doing your honeymoon homework? Now would be a good time for the big reveal."

"Nice try, brown eyes. I've told you I'm keeping it a secret."

"Oh, come on. Not even a hint?"

"Nope."

"Don't I have even a little say in this?"

"I'm certainly open to suggestions."

"How about Paris?"

"As in Paris, Tennessee?"

Christine offered a calculated grin. "No, it's a lovely town, but I think I had a different Paris in mind."

"Never saw that coming."

She lifted her chin and fell silent, coolly assessing me.

"You know, Dr. Bradford. I get the feeling you like keeping secrets from me."

"And what makes you think that Miss Chambers?"

She looked down, seemingly consumed in an impish and artful humor. She seemed in terrible want of telling me something. Instead, she simply made a quiet nod of resolve. As she spoke, just as she had done with my hair, she took her finger and began to draw small, slow circles over my heart.

"What makes me think that, Dr. Bradford, is that I believe you are entirely and eternally in love with me. I think you would do whatever you could to make me happy."

"True. But the going antiquing thing may have raised the bar."

"Oh, admit it. I know you think it's a fun idea."

"Well, not so sure about the whole 'fun' component. But, being with you has its upsides."

"Such as?"

"Not sure if I've mentioned this, Chambers. But you're pretty easy on the eyes. And rumor has it that you might even be a fair kisser."

"Well," she said, looking down shyly. "Maybe if you weren't talking so much, you could find out."

I got the message.

The next morning, we set out on the road to Lawrenceburg,

Tennessee. The February sun, normally timid, emerged brilliantly above the frosted hills to the East, casting long, clean shafts of light across the frozen fields. Even though the vast and silent countryside was still in the slumber of winter, the crisp, vaporous air had a muted excitement, an unexplainable, elated feeling of discovery. The morning was fresh, and bright, and perfect as if it were the first day of the world.

Save for the occasional ambling tractor, the idle two-lane roads stretched for miles before us, availing a measure of stress-free solitude to our journey. We talked nonstop and the hour plus drive seemed like an opportune time to reveal everything to Christine about the research offer and the incredible letter regarding the payout from my Aunt's estate. But I seemed powerless to reveal my thoughts and feelings on the matter because, in truth, I was still unsure of what they were. And for much of the way, Christine did not stare out at the road or passing woods but instead was turned toward me, enraptured, as if I glowed. She had this powerful, sensuous way of expressing her affection even with the language of her body. It made me all the more fearful of doing anything that would plunder her happiness. I kept my silence.

Along the way, we stopped by several small and isolated shops that were little more than converted sheds. Their exteriors were cluttered with odd pieces of wrought iron, old wooden windows, and disorderly stacks of abandoned items that didn't warrant shelter. Inside was equally brimmed. While there were a few articles of worth, most of the congested shelves were filled with memorabilia that had only nostalgic value and could only be treasured by those whose meager funds prohibited them from collecting anything else. Christine and I would casually edge our way to the rear before looping back, all the while wearing faces of polite interest. With a silent nod of confirmation, we would thank the proprietor and make a methodic exit.

After returning to the car from a third fruitless foray into the world of hoarding turned enterprise, I started the car and spoke dryly. "Well, that was certainly fun."

Christine was undaunted. "It's not just the destination, Bradford. The journey counts too."

"Although I will admit, I was tempted to buy the old Smother's Brothers and Herb Albert albums. My parents had those when I was a kid."

"Yeah, I noticed you looking at the girl on the "Whipped Cream," album like she was an old friend."

"Actually, I was thinking about what you would look like under similar circumstances."

Christine shook her head dismissively and turned her gaze to the farm fields rolling past us. "Eyes on the road, Bradford. Eyes on the road."

On the outskirts of Lawrenceburg, we came across an old Victorian home with a large "Antiques" sign at the road. Our approach down the long gravel drive revealed that the house's paint-flaking and sagging exterior had long been left unattended. But the classic lines of its central turret, asymmetrical shape, and generous porches spoke of former glory. The place itself was an antique, worthy of renewal.

Once inside we were met by a rather rotund but perky woman in her sixties who welcomed us with an amiable warmth and told us to look anywhere we pleased. We thanked her and began ambling from room to room. The place smelled of the past. The sharp, pungent, yet musty fragrance of wood, smoke, and time had fermented together over many decades, saturating the air. It gave the packed but orderly rooms a feeling of mellow abundance. Unlike the bric-a-brac of the earlier stops, the old house was filled with marvelous furniture. Christine was in her element.

It was all grand until a fellow appeared behind us and began to talk as if we had been familiar friends for years. Being short and equally plump, he was, no doubt, the husband of the woman we had met upon entering. He was thick-jowled and heavy with a flabby roll of flesh under his chin. He walked with the waddling gait of a man who had overeaten his lunch. But despite his friendliness, there was a certain stiff-backed and banty nature to his demeanor. After the initial exchange of pleasantries, he seemed perfectly content to stand and monitor us, injecting himself uninvited into our conversation and observations.

Christine didn't let it bother her, but I found him downright annoying. She was intensely focused on an old oak washstand with her lips pressed together, completely absorbed. I took this as an opportunity to excuse myself, telling her that I was going to check out the upstairs. I departed, and fortunately, the nosy little proprietor elected not to follow.

The upper floor rooms had less furniture and more clutter. Nevertheless, I strolled through them until I came upon the small, square turret room. Upon entering, I practically laughed out loud. The walls were covered with old black and white photographs. Additional piles of framed photos were stacked on the floor around the perimeter of the room. Before me were unnamed faces of the past; images captured for some obscure occasion whose meaning had long been forgotten. Admittedly, I folded my arms and scoffed at it all. "Who would collect such a thing?" I thought to myself. "And furthermore, what kind of idiot would buy them?"

I shook my head and turned to exit. But after one stride into the hall I stopped abruptly and hastily back stepped into the room. A framed picture hanging by the door had caught my passing notice. I drew closer. The sepia-toned photograph was of a cluster of workers on a crowded and busy railroad loading dock. The great doors of the freight cars stood wide open, their insides stacked high with five-gallon cans. All of the men in the picture were slightly blurred, evidence that they were going about their work, seemingly oblivious of the photographer. All of them, save one.

A man was standing in the foreground staring squarely at the camera. He was wearing a sharply tailored suit and a jubilant face. Beside him was a small wooden crate whose lid had been removed and left askew on the platform. In much the same way that someone boastfully presents a newborn baby, he was proudly holding a beautifully crafted Victrola Phonograph. Unmistakably, the man was Hiram Hatcher.

Chapter 25

SCANDAL

I impulsively lifted the picture from the wall and walked to the window for better light. My mind was swimming. I wanted to immediately memorize every detail, to absorb every particular; the writing on the crates, the lettering on the box cars, the make and model of the truck being loaded. When was the picture taken? What year? What month? And most importantly, why the phonograph? Hiram was a wealthy man with many fine things. And yet for some reason, he clearly had a captivated attachment to this one item…so much so that he wanted to archive its arrival.

For several minutes, I poured over the photograph looking for significance, for some story. But nothing was forthcoming. I did, however, notice one small detail. Tucked under one of Hiram's arms was a package. It was slim, like a large envelope, and yet not the right size. The item was square and wrapped in plain paper, likely brown. I wanted to take the photo out of the frame to see if there was any notation on the back of it. But that seemed inappropriate for the moment. The small, orange price sticker had a hand-written amount of two dollars. Purchasing the picture was a foregone conclusion. But before departing, I quickly scanned the prints on the wall to see if by chance there were any other pictures of Hiram. There was nothing. Satisfied, I returned downstairs.

Christine was in a friendly haggle with the portly proprietor over the price of the oak washstand. I slipped by to the front entry to find the shop owner and make my purchase. She was absently working a crossword puzzle but came to life upon my entrance.

"Found something you liked?" She cheerily inquired.

"Oh, just an old photo." I handed it to her along with a few dollars, hoping to facilitate a quick transaction. But instead, she took the picture and studied it.

"Is there a relative of yours in this?"

Something in my private nature always disliked this kind of invasive question even though it was just a courtesy.

"No. I um, I like trains."

My clipped reply wasn't lost on her, and she responded with an accommodating smile and a low noise of acknowledgment. As she slipped the picture into a paper bag and handed me the change, I heard Christine call out to me.

"Luke, come look at this washstand. I like it a lot. It could be a versatile piece for us."

In truth, she could have taken a picture with her phone and sent it to me. If she was happy with the item, then I was ecstatic. But I dutifully followed her and did my best to appear discerning and contemplative about how this small piece of furniture would play various roles in the evolving stages of our lives. The nosy little husband of the shop owner seemed quite content to stand and eavesdrop on this private conversation, much to my irritation and Christine's unconcern. After several minutes, it seemed to me that a proper vetting had been accomplished.

"Well, by all means, why don't we buy it?"

"Are you sure?"

I was sorely tempted to reveal my indifference. But Christine's voice was full on gentle yearning, a telling sign that this decision carried much weight with her.

"Absolutely. By the way, how much wampum are we talking about?"

She nodded toward our plump and prying companion. "We've already agreed on a price including delivery to your house."

"Oh. Well, okay. Sounds good."

Christine gazed at our new purchase with total adoration; as if a long dreamed of and cherished event had finally arrived. She seemed enraptured, fully absorbing the bliss of the moment. I astutely followed her lead and warmly admired the piece in silent reverence, all the while contemplating lofty thoughts such as, how heavy that sucker was and if I would be able to lift it by myself.

Nevertheless, I was amused by her unexpected elation. "You're just floating in the clouds, aren't you?"

Remaining focused on the washstand, she breathed a slow, satisfied, "Yes."

But a second later she turned to me and spoke flatly. "Okay. We're good. Go ahead and pay the man. I'm going to look around a little more." Before I could utter a response, she was gone. I stared in the direction of her departure and muttered under my breath.

"Good to know you've landed safely."

When I turned around the little rooster with suspenders was regarding me with a rather disdainful and puckered scrutiny.

"That check local?"

As we walked back to the car, Christine inquired about my purchase. I took it out and handed it to her. "I bought it for Matthew House. I'm pretty sure the man with the phonograph is Hiram Hatcher."

"Really? I've never seen a picture of him."

I started the car, and we headed for home. "He's the spitting image of the fellow in the photograph at Matthew's house." I had to catch myself, remembering that Christine knew about the picture of Hiram standing in front of his home but not the one in the bar with Capone. "If you don't mind, take it out of the frame and tell me if anything is written on the back."

"There's a handwritten date. June 19, 1927. Are you sure it's him?"

"Best I can tell."

"It's funny, isn't it? Hiram Hatcher's name is all over Watervalley, the Hatcher Building downtown, the library is named after him, and people still refer to Society Hill as the old Hatcher Mansion. Until now, I don't ever recall seeing a picture of him."

"From what little I've learned, there are plenty of unknowns about Hiram, even though he clearly immersed himself into the life of the town."

"How so?"

"Well, he created a lot of jobs, he developed real estate, he built a railroad, and as you mentioned, he gave money to build the library. He was quite generous to a number of local charities and churches. The list seems to go on and on."

"But then he suddenly left town and was scarcely ever heard of again."

"True. And that's where the unknowns come in to play."

"Does Matthew have any ideas about why Hiram Hatcher left so suddenly?"

I paused, wanting to choose my words carefully. "I get the impression it's a mystery to him as well."

"And he still doesn't want anyone to know his deceased wife was related to Hiram?"

"Apparently not. We haven't talked about it recently. But I guess that's still the case."

Christine's questions were all understandable. But I feared she was probing too close, even though part of me wanted to tell her everything about Matthew; about the bootlegging, about the picture of Al Capone, and about things that went bump in the night. But it seemed best to steer the conversation elsewhere.

"Are you aware of the old rumor about Hiram and your uncle John's grandmother?"

"Well, of course. Now it's ancient history, but evidently, it was quite the scandal at the time."

"I talked to John about it a while back, and he said it was all garbage, that people were just looking for an explanation for Hiram's mysterious departure."

Christine gazed out the window and spoke vacantly. "Well, I'm sure Uncle John would like to think that."

"Oh? You believe there's something to the story?"

She followed the passing countryside for a moment longer. Then she shifted and turned toward me. Now, it seemed, her words were the ones being carefully chosen.

"Look. As you know, Uncle John is related by marriage. I've only seen pictures of his grandmother, Jessica Ravenel. But believe you me, in her day, she was lethally gorgeous."

"So, I've heard. Doesn't exactly make her an adulteress."

"No, it doesn't."

"So, why the doubt about Jessica Ravenel and Hiram Hatcher?"

Christine paused before answering. "It's because of things my mother has said."

"Your mother, really? I'd think she would be the last person to prattle on about some old scandal."

"And you would be correct. Mom is uncommonly discreet. But she once told me an interesting story about my grandfather and Hiram Hatcher."

"Really? And...what is this story?"

"Soon after Aunt Molly and John became engaged the rumor about John's mother being illegitimate surfaced again."

"Why?"

"Small town stuff. It was started by several of the society mothers who wanted Aunt Molly to marry one of their sons rather than the son of a postman."

"So, evidentially your Aunt Molly was quite the catch, as was certainly your mother."

"I'm sure that's true in their own right. But you also have to remember that they were the daughters of Sam Cavanaugh, the owner, and president of the local bank. My mother and my aunt came from money."

I shrugged. "Fair enough. No doubt, an added plus."

"I think I've mentioned before that my grandfather Cavanaugh married late in life. He was quite a bit older than my grandmother. He was born in 1900 and personally knew Hiram Hatcher and the Ravenels. Everything I've ever heard about my grandfather Cavanaugh was that he was a quiet, well-respected leader in the community and an exceptionally gracious and humble man. But, as a father of the bride to be, he was not about to let a bunch of gossips slander his daughter's new family. So, he stepped out of his normal reserve to let a few of the community leaders know that their wives needed to put a lid on it or there would be consequences."

"And did it work?"

"At an epic level from what I understand. What's so funny about that story is that it is completely out of character for my grandfather."

"Hmm, interesting. But I'm missing something here. I gathered from your earlier comment that you think there's still an air suspicion around Jessica Ravenel?"

"Because a couple of years later, in private, my grandfather told my mother that there was a lot more to the Hiram Hatcher story and Jessica Ravenel than people knew, and that it would be best if it never came out."

"Did he tell her what?"

"No. Never a word more. But whatever it was, he thought it was important enough to wield some heavy influence to keep it secret."

"So, you think he was trying to protect John's mother?"

"It would seem so. And yet, that doesn't make sense. Because if he considered the adultery story to be true, then he would not have staked his reputation on squelching it. My mother doesn't believe he would have done all that to cover a lie."

"I don't know," I said pensively. "Sounds like he was protecting somebody or something."

"Yes. And that's why I've always had a lingering doubt about the Jessica Ravenel and Hiram Hatcher affair."

I mulled over her words, wondering. "You know, I've heard another old rumor about a murdered woman whose body is buried up at the old mansion. Do you think he was referring to that?" Stirring in the back of my head was the discovery of the trunk and the elegant flapper dress and what may lie behind the masonry wall in the basement.

"I've heard that too. I asked Mom about it once. She said my grandfather just laughed about that story, saying that it was the farthest thing from the truth."

"Oh, really? I guess Matthew will be glad to hear that." Privately, so was I. The thought of there being a skeleton behind the wall in the basement was a gruesome prospect.

"Why? Does Matthew know anything? Has he talked about it?"

"I don't think he knows more than anyone else. But he's heard the rumors."

A reflective silence followed. Christine looked at the photograph one last time before returning it to its paper bag and placing it on the rear seat. It seemed odd that almost ninety years later this brief, captured moment was a small window into the curious life of a flamboyant yet enigmatic man; that with all the worlds he seemed to be conquering, the arrival of a phonograph appeared to be at the pinnacle of his expectations. Bathed in the glorious light of that day, Hiram was blissfully unaware of what lay ahead, of tangled events, of something ruined and irretrievable, of something yet undiscovered that would compel him to leave forever his life in Watervalley. The fence posts lining the vast and untamed fields began to fly by. I drove on, lost in thought.

The touch of Christine's hand upon my knee stirred me from my mindless daze. I turned, and she was smiling adoringly.

"What are you thinking about, Bradford?"

"Oh, I don't know. Everything. Nothing."

She looked away and laughed. "Oh, Bradford. You're just like my Grandfather Cavanaugh and Hiram Hatcher, aren't you?"

"That's pretty interesting company. Not sure I understand."

"Just like them, you have your little secrets, don't you Luke Bradford?"

"You're talking about that macramé class I took once, aren't you? I should have known word would get out. It had to do with a girl."

"And there's my guy, always ready to use humor as a deflection."

"Humph," I grunted. She watched me silently, waiting for my response. There was a baited cunningness in her smile; a clever, alluring feint of expectation.

"Secrets, huh?" I said sportively. "How about this? Come closer, brown eyes, and I'll tell you a little secret."

This conjured the lowering of a skeptical chin. "Hmm, so said the spider to the fly."

"Oh," I said, gushing a laugh. "You're good."

Christine inched closer to me, speaking in a near whisper. "Good? Whatever do you mean?"

I glanced at her slyly. "Spider and fly, huh? I've been caught in your little web since the first time I saw you, Christine Chambers. Not that you haven't noticed." Having said this, I continued my focus on the road ahead.

She leaned in ever closer. Her voice was low and soft. "So, what's this little secret you want to tell me, Bradford?"

"I, Miss Chambers, am ridiculously, foolishly, and pathetically in love with you."

Her face warmed to a tender regard. But there remained an element of curiosity, a searching thoughtfulness in the hemmed movement of her eyes. In time, she leaned in and kissed my cheek, breathing her words. "I know you are, Luke Bradford."

We traveled home in a silence that was warm, content, and happy; a mutual feeling of accomplishment with the simple act of buying a piece of furniture...*our* piece of furniture. But all the while, with all the talk of secrets, a distant and haunting voice from deep within me whispered the words, "Oh the tangled web we weave..."

Chapter 26

TREASURE MAPS

I dropped Christine off at her place with plans to come out later for dinner. I excused myself for the afternoon, noting that I would probably drop off the picture at Matthew's house. This was true, but I also had larger plans.

It was rare that I took privileges in my role as the town doctor, wielding influence or requesting special accommodations. But I needed access to the Courthouse where the county archives, deeds, tax maps, and plats were kept. All the government offices were closed on Saturday, which struck me as actually being ideal.

On the way back to my house, I called Walt Hickman, the mayor. I explained that I needed a favor and that, among other things, I needed to do a little research on the Moon Lake property. It was a pliable truth, but accurate enough. I further explained that with the demands of the clinic, it had been impossible to do this during normal office hours. That said, I inquired if I might borrow the keys. Walt was more than happy to oblige, so much so, that he met me at my house with them.

Ever the politician, he took the opportunity to once again enlist my engagement in his newly formed Economic Development Council, the idea he had pitched at the Christmas Eve party. Just as before, I consented to participate but had to endure another ten minutes of Walt's ramblings before he departed. As he drove away, I looked at the keys and smiled, having skillfully accomplished the first step of my plan. Despite the subtle shades of deception, there was a rather consuming and delicious thrill in being clandestine. I shook my head at this reality. My life definitely needed expansion.

I drove downtown and parked inconspicuously a block away from the Court House. Merchants were open, and a few shoppers were milling about the streets, but the afternoon was generally cast with a drowsy lethargy. On the back of the Court House was an outside concrete stairwell that dropped below the level of the ground to a door accessing the basement. I used this for my entry. The Register of Deeds office and the Property Assessors office were both on this level. After several tries from the ring Walt gave me, I found the key to each, only to realize that once inside, there was an unlocked door in the wall between them. Not wanting to draw attention, I switched on only a couple of desk lamps.

Fortunately, one of the public computers and the microfiche machine had been left on, and as well, there were laminated instruction sheets in large lettering everywhere regarding how to access records. These had undoubtedly been provided by the clerks in this office who had long ago grown weary of repeating the same instructions to the daily public. With all this at my fingertips, I went to work.

Sadly, most of what I found over the next two hours was largely routine. Deeds and records showing the transfer of property bought and sold by Hiram Hatcher generally fell in line with what was already known. I had hoped that by some stroke of luck I might find an old set of blueprints to Society Hill. But even in the modern day, Watervalley didn't have a building and codes department. So, there would have been no requirement to file a copy of the blueprints with the county. However, after quite a bit of digging, I managed to find the cardboard tube that housed a copy of the original plat for the development of Bootlegger Hill which later became Society Hill. By happenchance, a sitemap labeled, "Hatcher Property," showing the footprint of the house and the location of the utilities was rolled in with it. I carefully spread the document out on a nearby desk.

The property was a deep rectangle of fifty acres with almost eight hundred feet of road frontage extending away from the street for almost half a mile. The house was located in the front third, after which there began a significant drop in elevation toward the rear. Although it was an interesting find, there was little about it that was remarkable. But one detail did catch my attention. Toward the back of the property was the outline of a small building. The notation beside it read, "Spring house and holding tank. To be added later." The curious part about this was that the sitemap already noted the location of two existing wells on the property. And the odd thing about the location of the holding tank is that based on the topographical markings, it would be at least a hundred feet below the level of the house, requiring that water be pumped to yet another holding tank nearer to the level of the residence. It didn't make a lot of sense, but then again, for my purposes, it didn't seem to matter.

I was about to roll the document up when I noticed one other odd detail. Although the adjacent tracts were not shown in their entirety, the owners of the bordering properties were listed in small print just beyond the boundary lines of the sitemap. In small but clear print, the notation on the property behind Hiram's fifty acres read, "928 Acres, Frontenac Corp."

For a long moment, I stood there dumbfounded, desperately trying to remember where I had before seen the word Frontenac. I suddenly remembered that it was the name on the five-gallon metal cans we found in Matthew's basement, The Frontenac Syrup Company. I wasn't yet sure what to make of this, but it was clearly more than a coincidence.

I sat down at the computer and pulled up the Tennessee Property Map program to gather the details on the Frontenac tract to see who now owned it. To my astonishment, it was still held by the same company, The Frontenac Corporation. It had been purchased in April of 1925 and was still an intact 928 acres, having never been subdivided. I switched my view to the topological map which revealed the property to be a tangle of steep ravines and hollows shouldered by ridges that rose sharply. The rings reflecting the ten-foot elevation drops were almost on top of each other. A review of the satellite map revealed much the same. The property was a morass of high unruly hogbacks adjacent to plunging washouts. The steep terrain had no potential for development, leaving it worthless with the possible exception of logging value.

I clicked on the tax information. There were no names associated with the Frontenac Corporation, only an address. It was a Post Office box in…of all places, Charleston, South Carolina.

I had been hovering tightly over the keyboard but now collapsed to the back of the chair and stared at the screen in front of me. It wasn't much, but it was something; a fascinating, intriguing something. Someone in South Carolina knew about the Frontenac Corporation. Someone had been paying the $1,728 levy of property tax every year. Someone was sending a check. I gathered that Sue Dell Calloway, the County Treasurer, would probably know. But I decided to let Matthew pursue this in whatever manner best suited him. It seemed that for the moment, I had discovered all that I could. Committing a small act of larceny, I took the sitemap and locked up. No doubt, Matthew would want to see it.

Shortly after four in the afternoon, I arrived at the mansion. Matthew met me at the door holding something rather unusual, a toilet plunger.

"Now that's an odd weapon of choice for a guy who supposedly owns a lot of guns."

He offered a tempered smile. "Come in. I'm doing a little plumbing work. One of the toilets. It's not clogged at the moment, but it keeps acting up."

"You're fixing the toilet yourself? That can't be good. Isn't that outside the natural order of things, like a rift in the time/space continuum?" I followed him back to the bedroom wing of the downstairs.

"So," he responded dryly. "I take it you've never worked on a toilet? Sooner or later, all guys have to work on the toilets. Being a guy means fixing things. When I fix something, I feel one with the cosmos."

"Unfortunately, I happen to know plenty about toilets. Although I'll admit, my original goal in life was to be loosely familiar with the use of the handle. But yeah, I've worked on plenty of toilets. Not successfully, mind you. I finally gave up once and called a plumber. He fixed the problem in about fifteen minutes in exchange for the title to my car."

We walked to a brilliantly tiled downstairs bathroom with vintage fixtures. Matthew set to work. I was fully content to lean against the door frame and observe. He scratched the side of his head and deliberated on his plan of attack, all the while speaking casually. "You have to remember, Luke, I was a missionary kid. Poverty made me a plumber, a mechanic, a carpenter, and probably a few other things that I'm not very good at."

"Well, I can't exactly go toe to toe with you there. For some reason, my prep school in Atlanta didn't have a shop class."

"No shame in that. But bouncing around Africa as a kid developed a kind of do-it-yourself, pioneer mentality."

"Point taken. I guess Daniel Boone never called a plumber."

Matthew grinned passively. "Yeah, something like that."

"Well, you're in the company of a man who has made peace with his ineptitude."

Armed with a small crescent wrench, Matthew began to contort himself to reach the rear of the toilet. But before doing so, he made a gesture with his head towards the items I was carrying. "What you got there?"

I explained to Matthew what I had found at the property assessor's office and the discovery of the site plan. After a quick adjustment to the valve, he elbowed his way clear and stood. I handed him the drawing and, after examining the details, his eyes tightened. "A couple of weeks ago I hiked to the back of the property. It's all wooded, thick with privet and undergrowth. But I came across the spring house noted here. I didn't see a holding tank."

"Really? So, the spring house was actually built?"

"Yeah, it's nearly swallowed in the woods down at the bottom of a ravine. I saw it below me as I climbed down the steep slope of the hill. Other than a small gouge in the metal roof, it looks to be a pretty stout structure."

"Did you go into it?"

"No. I really didn't even get close. From a distance I could see that the door was padlocked and there were no windows, so I didn't pursue it."

"Was there a road leading up to it?"

"Not that I could tell. There probably was at one time, but it's long been overgrown." He returned his focus to the document. "It does seem incredibly odd, doesn't it? And you're saying that all this property behind is owned by the Frontenac Company?"

"Yes."

"Hmm," Matthew murmured reflectively. "Hic autem dracones."

"What did you say?"

"Oh, sorry. It means 'here lie dragons.' Mapmakers used to put them on areas that were unexplored."

"It does seem odd that it is the same name on the five-gallon cans in the basement. By the way, did you get the masonry saw and cut into the wall."

Matthew's face softened into a look of amused resignation. "I did. I did indeed. And after several hours of blood, sweat, and lungs full of masonry dust, I discovered a whole lot of nothing."

"Seriously? Nothing?"

"Well, there is a room on the other side. It's about ten by ten with concrete walls and a concrete ceiling. It's below a storage room that's on the back side of the house that I think was used for keeping coal. That upper storage room has only an outside entrance to it. Anyway, in the basement room, there's a small offset, I'd say about a couple of feet square that was partially boarded up. I removed the planks, and it looked to be some sort of chute leading to the coal storage room above. The rusted remains of a miniature elevator were in there, like an industrial grade dumbwaiter. I'm guessing it was used to move coal down for the basement furnace. I suspect that's how the cat managed to get in."

"So, did you find anything else?"

"Mostly dirt and time. There was an old fuse box and some heavy wiring on one wall. It looked to be original with the house but apparently had been disconnected long ago. Oh, and there were two other rather curious things."

"Which were?"

"There was a long coil of metal cable. Pretty rusted and on an old spool. Probably several hundred feet of it."

"Interesting. And what was the other thing?"

"A good-sized drain pipe coming out of the far wall. Probably about eighteen inches. I pointed a light down it, but it was caved in after about twenty feet.

"What was it for?"

"No idea. I guess it may have been a drain for any water that may have flooded the basement." He paused. "Come to think of it; it leads in the general direction of that spring house at the back of the property. But that's a fifth of a mile away. I can't see where that would serve any purpose."

A silence fell between us as we both tried to fill in the gaps of what we now knew.

"Matthew, I'm no engineer, but none of this makes sense. Why would coal be brought down so far away from the furnace and through a room with all the wine racks? And why would a drain pipe be in the room where there was no plumbing?"

"Beats me. Maybe there was a design change, and the wine racks were built after the fact. Who knows?"

"So, I guess we're no closer to unraveling any big secrets about Hiram Hatcher then we already were."

"Looks that way. Although I would like to know more about this Frontenac Company."

"You want me to follow up on that?" I asked.

"Thanks, but no need. I'll make some inquiries. Maybe when the weather gets a little warmer the two of us can hike back down to the spring house and take a closer look."

"Do you think there's something creepy about it?"

"Not so much creepy, just puzzling. Might be good to have a second set of eyes."

"Fair enough."

He cocked his head slightly to the side and looked at the large envelope under my arm. "Did you find something else?"

I removed the photo. "Yes, but not at the property office. Christine and I were antique shopping earlier today, and I came across this. You recognize the guy?"

At first, Matthew held the print casually. Then he instinctively drew closer, completely absorbed, as if the man in the picture was whispering to him. "Sure do. Where did you find this?"

I explained the details as he quickly flipped it over and back, scrutinizing every particular.

"Didn't you mention once that Hiram had made an inventory of everything for the move to Charleston? Was the phonograph on it?"

He gazed up from the photo, but he appeared to be looking through rather than at me; his thoughts in a distant place. Slowly, hesitantly, he shook his head. "No. No, it wasn't. I don't ever recall seeing a vintage phonograph at Emily's grandmother's house either."

I shrugged and rubbed my chin. "Well, chalk up another chapter in the Hiram Hatcher mystery story. It seems that anything new learned about him only raises more questions."

Matthew offered a nod of concession. "Yeah. I'm beginning to think there's nothing there to find. I may never know why Hiram left town so suddenly or why Emily dreamed about him."

"Sounds like you've had a change of heart."

Matthew grinned and held out his arms in a gesture resignation. "I don't know. Over the last week, the oddest thing has happened. I feel like I'm slowly waking up from a deep sleep."

Chapter 27

LOST DREAMS

I followed Matthew to the kitchen. As he washed his hands in the large sink, he gazed out the window, speaking reflectively. "Ever since we talked the other evening, I have to admit, I've felt a little bad about asking you to be all cloak and dagger about gathering information at the property office."

"Why is that?"

"It's starting to all seem silly now, all the secrecy."

I pressed my lips together, contemplating the question stirring in my head. "So, if that's the case...are you saying it's no longer important to keep Emily's relationship to Hiram private?"

He dried his hands with a towel and turned to me. "Perhaps. Other than the picture I have of Hiram and Capone, nothing is linking him to any kind of bootlegging or anything illegal."

"True. I've not heard any mention in that regard."

"There's some speculation about his swift departure, but he clearly did a lot of good for the town. And even if all of this bootlegging business did come out, I don't think it would matter either way. The truth is, the children completely love living here. School has been wonderful for them. They've made oodles of friends, and I'm beginning to think that the people of Watervalley aren't that swayed by what happened nearly a hundred years ago. They might find it interesting and want to chat about it, but they seem a lot more interested in the here and now."

"No argument. And if people knew about Emily's relationship to Hiram, I think it would go far to help them understand why you came. You have to realize, this is still the South, and ancestor worship is a valid form of religion. In a sense, this is your family's ancestral home. That's reason enough. Emily's dreams never need to be known beyond this room."

Matthew leaned against the kitchen counter, absorbing all that I had said. "I don't know, Luke. Perhaps I'm just looking for a quick resolution. I'm still haunted, still curious about what she meant. Maybe I'm just looking around at the positives and trying to make those fit into the answer box."

I nodded my understanding but had no words of comfort in response. Matthew lived with a perpetual ache; an imbedded sense of loss that time would slowly dull. But without some measure of closure, it would become part of his character, leaving all of his days tinged with a faint sourness. I opted for a change of subject.

"By the way. The children. Are they here?"

"No. Birthday party for a classmate. It's amazing really. For such a little town, they have a constant social life."

"Well, maybe you should start thinking about having one as well."

Matthew offered a tenuous smile. "I don't think so. The garbage goes out more than I do."

"Matthew, look...I know you've been a widower less than a year. But that doesn't mean anything to the single women of this town." I gushed a short laugh. "Or the married ones for that matter. The married ones believe it's their mission in life to find a mate for a single guy like you, irrespective of your thoughts on the subject."

This topic must have struck a chord. His mood lightened, and he spoke with great animation. "Oh, I've already learned that in spades."

"How so?"

"A few weeks back I showed up to a PTA meeting and practically got mobbed. They were like seagulls going after a piece of bread. The kids have had a few classmates over to play in the afternoon. There are some single moms in the mix, and you wouldn't believe the way they dress just to drop their kids off. One of them was wearing clothes small enough to be an outfit for one of Adelyn's dolls. I don't want to be rude, but I'm just not interested. I mean, how do you make them stop?"

"Talk with a Yankee accent."

"Very funny. I'm not kidding, though. It's an awkward business. Some of these single moms can be embarrassingly forward. One of them asked me to go see a movie with her."

"What's wrong with that?"

"From what I could gather, it was playing on the big screen in her bedroom."

I responded with a stifled laugh, not wanting to divulge my amusement fully. Matthew continued.

"How can such a little town have so many single moms? Burning the cornbread must be grounds for divorce."

"I think it has more do with their available options. You're probably in a vast group of one."

"Humph," he replied. "The other day I'm in the grocery store and this girl...young woman, I guess...passes by me. She was very attractive but couldn't have been a day over twenty. Anyway, as our buggies pass, she winks and says 'hi.'"

"And what did you do?"

"I lost the power of speech. I was a complete idiot. I grunted something and practically ran to the checkout line."

"Face it, Matthew. I know you miss Emily and rightfully so. But you're not dead."

"Listen, Luke. I'm thirty-eight with twin six-year-olds. At my age when I'm at the grocery, and a young, attractive woman smiles at me, the first thing I think is, 'I wonder if she babysits?'"

"Well, you can't blame them for trying to get your attention. They know you're in mourning. But they're hoping to be the reason you come out of it."

"It's just not that simple. I'm not looking for another wife."

"That's not going to keep them from auditioning for the part."

Matthew folded his arms and spoke in a mix of dismay and amusement. "Perhaps you're right."

I shook my head. "Well, I'm glad to hear you're getting to know some of the locals. And listen, if sometime you ever do need a babysitter, Christine and I would be happy to accommodate."

"Thanks. It's not a big deal, really. As I said, I'm not looking for companionship. It's just that sometimes, it might be nice to go sit somewhere and drink a beer and remember what a crowd feels like. Anyplace like that around here?"

"There's a roadhouse called the Alibi. It's a good place to see the local lowlifes in their natural habitat. You're not going to find many look-a-likes. The highest skill set most of them have is how to put backspin on a cue ball."

"Rough bunch?"

"They cheer by firing their guns in the air. I think some of them were born with tattoos."

"Seriously?"

"I'm probably not being very fair. The majority are pretty good fellows. And when it comes to farming and mechanical things, they're unbelievable. Half of them probably know how to hotwire a stealth bomber."

"You seem to have connected well with them."

"They're different. But I do like them. Even the rough ones. They are as good and genuine a people as you'll ever know. Granted, there are a few that make me want to put a high voltage fence around my house. But all in all, they've been kind and accepting of me...even though admittedly, I've always practiced a certain self-imposed exile."

"That, my friend, is a little hard to believe. Even from the few conversations I've had, you've practically been canonized by the locals."

"Nice to hear. But it doesn't exactly help my larger dilemma. Besides, if they discovered I was leaving, my status would quickly drop to that of a Nazi war criminal."

"I understand. I've actually thought a lot about your situation. It was good medicine to hear you talk the other night. Lately, I've spent a lot of my time in self-pity. You helped me remember that everyone has struggles."

"I'm a little embarrassed about it now. I generally like to find the answers to my own problems without having to divulge my soul's squalor to anyone else."

"Have you decided what you're going to do?"

"Not really. I still love the idea of doing research, but I can't see my way clear to leave the people here. Looks like my dreams of fame may never occur. Like innocence and hope for mankind, I now number it among the lost things."

"Do you think you would be good at medical research?"

"Truthfully, I think I would be very good at it."

"Then you should pursue it."

"It's just that this town, these people; their need is real. It's here and now and I've grown to accept that, to own it. It's part of who I am. Research is only a hypothetical good. So, every time I do the mental gymnastics on the two choices, I find myself leaning toward the known good."

"Everyone wants to lead an extraordinary life, Luke. The trick is to figure out what extraordinary looks like."

I smiled and nodded. "Fair enough. It's just that the stars seem to be lighting a one-way road that ends in Watervalley, Tennessee."

Matthew smiled and offered a subtle nod of understanding. "Astra inclinant, sed non obligant."

"Meaning?"

"The stars incline us; they do not bind us."

"I wish I shared your confidence."

He again pursed his lips thoughtfully, driven by some private entertainment. "I wish I could do more to help." He paused and gazed around the kitchen. "Truth be known, I do well to take care of the twins. A lot of the time the house looks freshly bombed. I've come to realize that my cooking is only slightly preferable to hunger. I need a housekeeper. Do you know of anyone?"

Chapter 28

HOUSE CALLS

March disappeared into vapor.

Somewhere about mid-month, the first scattered days of spring began to advertise themselves. As warmer, southerly winds passed across the wide plain of the valley floor, the fallow earth with all its abundance, began to stir and swell. Soft breezes pulled at the heads of the emerging buttercups, their brilliant yellows coloring the woods and fields. The normal silence of my morning runs in the countryside became progressively invaded by the distant groans of tractors. The lilting fragrance of fresh grass and clover began to permeate the air. In both mind and marrow, I felt the promise of warmer days.

Caught up in all the anticipation of bridal showers and wedding plans, Christine was in an endless blissful state. I dutifully went along to all the meetings with the event planner, the minister, the florist, the photographer, the baker and all the other players required to be officially betrothed. But candidly, I found it all unbelievable. D-Day had been launched with less preparation. Invariably I hovered on the periphery of all the conversations and decisions, content to be the poor cousin in the mix and finding great satisfaction in watching Christine's excitement with the selection of every detail.

During the month it seemed that Connie and I only saw each other in passing. I had mentioned to her that Matthew might be looking for a housekeeper, but the prospect received only a lukewarm response. Something in Connie had changed. She seemed distant, preoccupied.

Perhaps she was following in form with my own reticence of the past couple of months. But there seemed to be something more to it; a secretive and worried state that offered nothing to the few nuanced inquiries that I made to her.

As the days passed, I fully expected to find Ann Patterson, my incredible nurse, in a puddle of tears...knowing that John would likely follow through on his previous assertion to break things off with her. What played out was quite the opposite. More than ever, John made almost daily appearances; taking her to lunch, showing up at day's end, or arriving with flowers for a minute's visit. He and I would exchange a few words of sly comradery and move on, never having so much as a conversation that included an entire paragraph.

Curiously, the one person who was omnipresent in my world was Matthew. Not with me personally, but in the general life of Watervalley. It seemed that more and more I would see him at the Depot Diner, the grocery store, or the Farmers Co-op. For some reason I expected him to stand in the corner like the shyest boy at the dance. But instead, he would call people by name, and they would respond in turn. He carried himself with a certain confidence, a kind of understated friendliness. Smartly turned out, perfectly tempered, his capacity for blending in was slowly emerging.

As well, the realization that his departed wife was the ancestor of Hiram Hatcher had quietly become common knowledge. Whether by accident or by design, it had been his children who had disclosed the information to some friends at school. Since this truth came from out of the mouth of babes, it was met by the larger adult world of Watervalley as a wholesome and proper thing, the rightful return of the family of a prominent citizen from a more glorious time.

It was seen as a good sign, and no one was trying to read the prosperity tea leaves more than the Mayor, Walt Thurman. He had finally assembled what was, in his words, "an All-Star, Cream of the Crop, Top Drawer, Nobel Prize-winning, Blue Ribbon Panel." I did not doubt that after many long and intense hours of meetings Walt would be able to issue a lengthy and comatose report on the problem. Our initial gathering was set for the first week of April. I could hardly wait.

During the second week of March, I called Dr. Bray at Vanderbilt with the simple intention of telling him that I was likely turning down the research position. I had expected a five-minute conversation, at best. But after an hour of patiently listening to all of my reasons, my wise old med school professor told me that he still thought I was the best man for the job and that he was in no hurry. I suspect he read the uncertainty buried within my words. He asked me to call him mid-April. We would talk then. There was something cathartic about weighing out this tremendous decision with a trusted colleague. As I hung up the phone, I saw little that might happen over the next month that would change my mind. For better or worse, I was staying in Watervalley.

Despite the consolation that came with having the decision made, I found myself haunted by the finality of it. Lying in my bed at night, when there were no longer any patients, or decisions, or noise to occupy my thoughts, I would listen to the great moaning of the wind outside my darkened cottage and wonder if my disillusionment were inevitable. That even with the many fulfillments of my life in

Watervalley, I would look back ten years from now and think of these days as my lost chance. I had thought that the disenchantment with the daily routine that had begun months earlier would be dispelled once I had made my choice. But it seemed that in those lonely hours during the watches of the night, a kind of subtle despair occupied my soul. Despite my resolve to be grateful for the wonderful life before me, I could not seem to shake this thin veil of despondency. As I had done before, I chose to pour myself into the oblivion of work and the rituals of daily life.

Oddly, for the entire month of March, the clinic was only mildly busy. The days seemed to pass slowly, accentuated by the monotony of everlasting repetition. And for some reason, loneliness appeared to top the list of my patients' ailments, especially for the elderly. Many of them spoke of symptoms that were non-descript and soon enough it would become imminently clear that they just wanted someone to talk to, to assure them. I had long accepted this as part of the job, and most of the time I would simply sit back and listen, occasionally nodding my head and frowning with concern. But about mid-morning on Thursday in the last week of March, I reached my saturation point.

Cletus McFarland, who was a kindly little septuagenarian had come to the clinic to get an annual check-up. His last annual check-up had been two weeks prior which had followed another yearly check-up two weeks before that. Nancy Orman did her best to gently remind him that two weeks and not a year had passed. But after a moment of, what I suspect, was a bit of feigned confusion, Cletus shrugged and said, "Well, I'm already here. I guess I might as well go ahead and see him."

Admittedly, I was slightly exasperated with Cletus before ever entering the exam room, and not just because he tended to spit when he talked. He would always begin the conversation by detailing some recent but no longer present pain in one of his appendages. I would examine the offending ankle or elbow, looking for wounds and checking flexibility, while Cletus would launch into some interminable drawn-out tale. He would get confused along the way, and there would be long pauses. Magellan had circumnavigated the globe in less time.

My typical response to Cletus's manufactured ailments was to throw out a few Latin names for possible diseases he might have and rub my chin thoughtfully. But something in my slightly frustrated state induced me to take a different tact. I interrupted him in mid-sentence and spoke gravely. "Cletus, according to my notes, this is the third time in the past year you've come in about pains in your left ankle. I'm glad it's feeling okay now. But frankly, if you have to come back again because of aching in either your arms or your legs, I'm afraid we'll have to amputate."

Instantly Cletus's back went ramrod straight. His wide-eyed face lost all its color, and he uttered a single choked word. "Amputate?"

"I'm afraid so, Cletus. Just cut that sucker right off. Next time you come, bring one of those big pickle jars. Whatever we have to cut off, we'll just put it in formaldehyde, and you can take it home with you."

His previous slouching lethargy promptly changed, and he was now exhibiting movements as perky as a squirrel. I barely had the opportunity to shake his hand before he was out the door. Gathering my things, I followed him into the central hallway, but he had already exited to the parking lot. The only thing missing was a roadrunner dust trail.

Nancy Orman had emerged from behind the receptionist desk and was now staring in the direction of Cletus's departure. Clearly mystified, she looked back at me.

"What on earth happened to Cletus?"

"Beats me," I responded innocently.

She was unconvinced and regarded me with a raised eyebrow. Not wanting to endure further scrutiny, I quickly retreated to my office. The waiting room was empty and the day outside was warm and splendid. Perhaps I was feeling a tinge of remorse for my handling of Cletus because I chose to do something that for some reason I had been avoiding; house calls.

From early on when I first began my practice in Watervalley, I kept a list of patients who were shut-in or lived alone as well as some who had chronic conditions and tended to be non-compliant with their treatment. Every month, as time availed, I would drive out to the country and make rounds on them. Invariably, the visit would mostly be a pep talk, encouraging them to be diligent in their care. Despite the trepidation that accompanied these un-announced visits, their completion commonly brought about a great sense of satisfaction, something my day desperately needed.

I retrieved the list from my desk drawer and studied it for a moment. I felt a reluctance. But getting out of the clinic and connecting with a few of my more marginal patients might very well be good medicine for the doctor himself. I told Nancy what I was doing and asked her to call me should any emergencies arise. Then, on the way out the back door, I reminded her that it was Thursday, and that no emergencies were allowed to happen on Thursdays.

I drove out the north road and decided to make my first stop at the farm of Charlie Peach. A small-time pig farmer, Charlie was a likable but independent little fellow with a weathered face, lively eyes, and a constant cigarette. He was in his early fifties and lived alone except for an Ark full of dogs who lived in the house with him. He always greeted me with an amiable warmth, and while it was good to see him, he tended to be on a perpetual holiday from hygiene. I suspected that he likely had to stand upwind of himself just to get through his day.

Like many of the bachelor farmers in Watervalley, Charlie had a rather independent spirit and perhaps a bit of a wily side to him. He worked hard. But on the weekends, he tended to fall under the influence of Bacchus and likely had a regular barstool at the Alibi Roadhouse. He had been a smoker for thirty years and acquired lung cancer for his trouble. I had diagnosed him six months prior and luckily, caught the disease early. He had made a full recovery but not before offering up part of his right lung to the god of bad habits. Charlie wasn't particularly reliable about keeping to his follow-up appointments, so I had made a habit of going to see him.

Having heard my approaching car, he emerged from his barn in a slow and cautious manner. But after recognizing me, he pulled off his work gloves and greeted me with great enthusiasm. He immediately began a lengthy declaration, stating that he hadn't touched a cigarette since the operation, that he had been getting regular exercise, and that the pain hadn't been too severe. Charlie looked well, and it was all good to hear. But the readiness of his confession along with his congenial but crafty temperament made his declaration suspect. It wouldn't have surprised me to know that he was treating any pain by smoking a homegrown medicinal; the kind of substance that also helped him take an intense four to five-hour interest in individual blades of grass.

As I drove away, I had to smile. I liked Charlie and, in many ways, even admired him. He and his like cut no figure on the small stage of Watervalley. And yet, despite the obvious petty frustrations of his daily routine, Charlie had a certain contentment with his life. I envied him.

My next stop was to see my favorite octogenarian in all of Watervalley, Lilly Dell Logan.

Lilly Dell was a small, diminutive farm woman who had a lively spirit and a sharp intellect despite her years of deteriorating health. She had a generous warmth about her and a clever wit which led her to be boyishly direct whenever she spoke. She lived in a large, white clapboard farmhouse that formerly reigned over a large farm. Her husband had passed ten years prior, and every few years Lilly Dell would sell off a small parcel to keep some cash in the till. However, I was never under the impression she lacked money.

Nor was she lacking house guests. It seemed that the grand farmhouse with its high-pitched roof and generous porches served as temporary quarters for one wayward grandchild or another from time to time. Lilly Dell had had six children of her own and they in turn had been equally prolific…all except for her youngest son known as Mutt who was well into his late forties and still lived with her. But Lilly Dell handled in stride the matriarchal responsibilities of such a large clan.

When I pulled up to the house, I noticed Mutt in the side yard near the barn. He was bent under the hood of one of a half-dozen vehicles randomly parked there. He surfaced for a moment and offered a voiceless wave before returning to his half-submerged position. Lilly Dell greeted me at the door with a grand smile and immediately offered coffee and cake as if she had been expecting me.

We settled at the kitchen table and I inquired about her health. She brushed the question off with the wave of her hand. "The last thing I want to do these days, Doctor Bradford, is prattle on about the pathetic state of my wellbeing. Besides, you should have come yesterday. It was my birthday. I had seventeen grandkids and five great-grandkids here."

"So, didn't any of your own children come?"

"Yeah, but they don't count."

"I saw Mutt outside. Quite a few cars out there."

"Yes, yes. Two of the grandchildren are here for a little bit. Sally, my oldest daughter Edna's youngest, is taking a semester off from college. She wants to get into country music and be a singer, so she asked if she could stay here and work on her songs. She's up there with her guitar right now."

I paused and listened, catching the faint lilt of a rather twangy but soulful female voice. "Sounds like she sings from the heart."

Lilly Dell looked at me dryly. "I've heard howler monkeys with better voices." She took a sip of her coffee and continued. "I love the child, but I'm afraid she has misplaced visions of grandeur. The only thing that sparkles about her is a pair of small diamond earrings she bought herself. I'm sure she showers with them. Anyway, she's just going through the stages."

"The stages?"

"Oh, you know. Youthful idealism, inevitable disillusion, eventual reconciliation."

I smiled and nodded.

"I could go ahead and explain to her that life is just a series of stubbed toes. But I think it best she figures it out for herself."

"So, you said that two of the grandchildren were staying here?"

"Bill Junior's boy Ernie has been here since Christmas. He's going through a bit of a rough phase. He's twenty-seven and just got out of rehab for the second time. He says he's trying to find himself. Meanwhile, he says he's found Jesus. I'd be happy if he just found a comb."

"Is he going to church somewhere?"

She nodded. "Some little independent congregation in the south part of the county. They meet in a barn." She snickered lightly. "I think you have to have dual membership in AA to join."

"Sounds like it might be a good thing."

Lilly Dell regarded me with a seasoned scrutiny. "I'm not so sure. I think it's a rough church, with bouncers and a smoking section."

She followed this with a wink and an entertained laugh. "Apparently finding yourself requires a lot of time doing nothing. I think his superpower is sitting on the front porch watching the traffic go by."

I stifled a laugh. "Well, Lilly Dell, I hope they're not driving you crazy."

"No, Dr. Bradford," she grinned cleverly. "Trust me. They're not driving me crazy. I'm close enough to walk."

As we continued to talk, I pressed her again about some of her health issues to which she was mostly dismissive. I was always amazed at her humor, her quiet dignity, and at the way, her eyes were so patient and understanding. Her home and her heart were a refuge for her larger family, and despite the demands it placed upon her, she found both purpose and solace in that role. As I left it occurred to me that perhaps Lilly Dell's greatest fear was that of an empty house. She insisted that I come back again, and soon. I nodded and waved goodbye. Admittedly, there was a part of me that wondered if that might never happen.

I made several stops over the next two hours and was delighted to find those I visited in generally good condition. It had been a successful afternoon, one that had reminded me of the significance I could and should play in the lives of those in this small community. I felt a sense of satisfaction, an uplifting of spirit. And perhaps that's what compelled me to make one last stop before returning to the clinic. As I made my return into town from the far end of Walnut Street, I pulled down the drive of a large yellow Victorian house that brightly dominated everything around it. This was the home of Polly Shropshire.

Chapter 29

POLLY

I rang the bell and waited. In time, Polly opened the front door, awash in a mix of alarm and taut courtesy. She was immaculately dressed but stiffer than an iron post.

"Dr. Bradford?" She anxiously inquired.

"Hi, Polly. I was just out doing rounds this afternoon and thought I would stop by to check on you." Having said this, I smiled broadly. But inwardly I was kicking myself. The wave of euphoria that had washed me to her doorstep had evaporated, and I again remembered how unpleasant her company could be. She stared at me blankly. Painful seconds passed. She seemed to be gathering herself from the shock of my presence. But quickly enough she assumed a gracious but rigid cordiality. As was her norm, she operated behind a wall of impenetrable politeness.

"That's very kind of you. Please, do come in."

I passed through a central hallway and entered an oak-paneled parlor with heavy drapes and stiff Victorian furniture. To no surprise, the room was spotlessly clean. Some original artwork covered the walls, and every level surface was filled with framed photographs of Polly and her late husband, Clayton. The marriage had produced no children, so invariably all the images were just the two of them.

As I settled into a large chair, Polly asked if I would like coffee. Normally I would have declined, but I accepted the offer if for no other reason than to avail a moment to regroup my thoughts. She disappeared to the kitchen, and I continued to study the myriad of framed photos that blanketed the room. Apparently, they had been great travelers for many of the pictures were of exotic places ranging from Polynesia to Africa to Egypt. In all the captured images, I would be hard pressed to say that there was anything glamorous or handsome about either of them, even in the younger snapshots. Yet, I couldn't help but notice that in every photo the two of them seemed idyllically happy.

Minutes later Polly returned bringing coffee with a silver tray and pot. She had regained her equilibrium because she now spoke in her usual patently aristocratic voice, invoking a ponderous pronunciation of each word. "I hope you don't mind me being formal. I don't often have company anymore, and sometimes it's nice to get the silver out of retirement."

I sipped my coffee and made a few of the standard inquiries to Polly about her health. In return, she offered polite but somewhat clipped responses, and the conversation progressed awkwardly, lacking rhythm and flow. To her credit, Polly moved the discussion to a more effortless plain.

"How are your wedding plans coming along?"

I breathed an easy smile. "Wonderfully, I assume. I do my best to keep to the periphery of things. It's all pretty overwhelming, though. I think the first moon landing was launched with less preparation."

Curiously, Polly's eyes softened to a warm regard. "Oh, let the girl have her fun, Dr. Bradford. You're quite the lucky fellow, you know. Christine Chambers is splendidly beautiful and a darling young woman. There's not a soul could speak ill of her. You've made the catch of a lifetime."

"Well, I certainly won't argue that," I said clumsily, slightly surprised by Polly's charmed affirmation of my bride to be. I usually recoiled at Polly's assertive pontifications. But it seemed that an endearing sentence or two about my sweetheart was all it took to win my kinder regard. She wasn't finished.

"Nor should you. She's full of life, that one. She'll always have you guessing, but you'll love every minute of it. There are elements in each of your personalities that make you a perfect fit. I hope you have many wonderful years together."

"Thank you. That's very kind of you to say so." I was doing my best to demonstrate a kind of casual urbanity but no doubt I was blushing, thrown by Polly's unexpected kindness and candor. Clever old bird that she was, she sensed my uneasiness and spoke in a diffusing manner.

"Oh, don't mind me, Dr. Bradford. When you get old, you become philosophic and direct about things. You spend a lifetime honing what you know, and you want to save others the trouble, whether they want it or not."

I endeavored to make some conciliatory or accommodating remark, but the words seemed stuck in my throat. An uncomfortable silence fell between us, and Polly's gaze drifted toward the floor. I spoke hesitantly.

"It, umm. It looks like you and Clayton had quite a few adventures together."

Polly was about to speak, but it seemed that a weighty pause attended the mention of his name. She gazed out the window for a moment, passing into a deeper contemplation.

"Clayton was blessed with the ability of enjoying to the utmost, the most ordinary thing." A smile had re-entered her voice. "He amazed me. He lived with the conviction that attitude was destiny. He was pragmatic, mind you. But he had this remarkable ability to smile at whatever came his way. He saw life as an adventure." She paused, turned her eyes toward me, and spoke in a voice of warm gratitude. "And for all those years I was lucky enough to tag along."

I nodded and smiled, my thoughts still off balance. "So, since we were just talking about weddings, I'm guessing that you and Clayton had a grand one?"

Polly's eyes drifted tenderly toward the floor. "Oh, yes. There were so many parties. We met at Vanderbilt and became engaged right after we graduated. I grew up in Belle Meade, and Clayton's family had been here forever. We always laughed because it seemed our parents were in competition as to who could throw the largest and most elaborate bashes. Mind you, this was when the world was quite a bit younger. But they were a lot of fun; highball evenings, big earrings, Chinese lanterns flickering on neatly cropped lawns, and loads of laughter and champagne. It was quite wonderful really. Clayton and I were so amused by it all. You see, Dr. Bradford, we both had come from money, but we knew who we were. We weren't a glitzy couple. We were rather plain, actually, compared to the opulent crowd we ran with. But we had each other. We were in our early twenties and thought we could simply dream our future."

I nodded politely, letting my silence encourage her to continue.

"But then, shortly after we moved here Daddy's business fell apart. Bankruptcy. They had to sell everything. What was left was all

261

family name and no fine china. After that, all of our friendships in Nashville seemed to evaporate. I was devastated, but Clayton never thought twice about it. I think he spent the rest of his life trying to make it up to me like it was his fault. Absurd, I know. But he loved me like that. We had one incredible adventure after another."

I smiled warmly. "Well, it sounds like the two of you had an interesting life together." Even as the words left my mouth, I realized how patronizing they must have sounded. It was little more than superfluous commentary and not reflective of the deeper empathy that I felt for Polly's story.

But the damage was done.

Polly again looked toward the floor, seemingly self-conscious, if not a little embarrassed at having spoken so openly about her past. I searched for something else to say, but it seemed a barrier had come between us. She exhaled a small gesture of fortification and stood. "Would you like more coffee?"

Spontaneously, I stood as well. "No, thank you. I probably should be going. But let me help you get everything back to the kitchen." I set my cup on the silver tray and proceeded to pick it up.

Polly spoke with kind resignation. "Dr. Bradford, there's really no need."

I responded briskly, trying to proffer a kindness with my actions that I was unable to do with my words. "No, I insist. Please, let me help."

At first Polly resisted, but ultimately, she shrugged. "Very well."

I followed her to the kitchen and set the tray on the counter near the sink. She thanked me, and I made a movement toward departing when a question came to mind. "Polly, how are you with your medications?"

At first, she seemed at a loss. "What medications, Dr. Bradford?"

For a moment, her uncertainty was contagious. I stared at her blankly. "Polly, I'm pretty sure I've written you a prescription for anxiety and one to help you sleep."

Her eyes were searching. Her air of confusion persisted. "Do you mind waiting a moment? I'll be right back."

"Certainly." She exited down a hallway. While waiting, I folded my arms and leaned against a small built-in desk, casually glancing at the stacks of bills and magazines. That's when I noticed something interesting. There was a letter size calendar on Polly's desk that oddly, was open to June. There were two handwritten notes. In the small box of June first was written, "The day I married Clayton. The best day of my life." Three days later, in the small box of June fourth was written, "The day Clayton died. The worst day of my life."

I looked up as Polly re-entered the room. She was oblivious to my nosy curiosity. "Here they are Dr. Bradford. They were in my medicine cabinet. I guess I had completely forgotten about them."

The two prescription bottles were full. "It's fine," I replied. There's no call to take one unless you need it."

Polly shook her head, still in a kind of frustrated disbelief. "I guess being forgetful is just a part of age."

I stared at her for a moment, weighing out what she said. Polly was more than a little distraught with this realization about her medications. There seemed to be something larger troubling her.

"Polly, we all forget things. Is there something else bothering you?"

At first, she didn't respond, still wanting resolution for the doubt that clutched her. But as she returned to the present, she schooled herself to a more ordered manner. "No, I'm fine," she said, doing her best to appear recovered and at ease. I pressed my lips together and nodded. She followed me to the front door. As I said goodbye I couldn't help but notice that Polly had a veil of weariness upon her, something she wore like a vague perfume. More than I had ever noticed before, it seemed to define her. She thanked me again for stopping by, and I walked to the car.

By now the sun had set. I drove home, fed the dogs, and ate a bite of dinner. Afterward, I walked out into the backyard to see the stars. The night was dark as velvet; silently intense, and gorgeous. I had seen a different side of Polly Shropshire, one that I was uncertain as to how to categorize. In her own home, surrounded by the strength of her things, she had been courteous and vulnerable. And our conversation weighed upon me because I had handled it so poorly. Previously I had only known her as a haughty woman who seemed to keep a list of every social injustice served upon her. No doubt, the list was long and its keeper sour. Yet now I understood how her husband had been the center of her heart and life. His death had dismantled the order of her world, and without him, she felt incomplete. And perhaps I was a little haunted by her words about Christine and me. It seemed they rang a bit too true. Christine was the one with the strength, with a zest for life, and a seemingly unassailable optimism. It was impossible not to make comparisons. This left me as the uncertain one who could easily turn bitter when life failed to unfold as I planned. The thought struck a little too close for comfort.

I stretched my arms high above me and gazed into the vast ocean of stars, exhaling a deep and glorious yawn. As I turned to make my way to the back porch, I thought of Polly's words. "We thought we could simply dream our future," she had said. Perhaps this one statement impacted me so powerfully because my conversation with her had somehow availed an encapsulated understanding of their life together; of its joys and its richness.

And in that moment, I realized my grand failure, the grand fallacy of my previous logic. *I* had been dreaming our future, not *we*. It was time to tell Christine everything; about the offer, about the money, and about my resolve to stay in Watervalley. It also occurred to me that revealing such a long-held secret might appropriately invoke some hurt feelings, doubts, and mistrust. The matter needed to be handled with some careful forethought. Then, an idea struck me about "how," and most importantly, "where" to do it. "When," would take a little planning.

Chapter 30

PLANS

Christine sat studiously in the leather chair across from my desk. She was leaning forward with her elbow firmly planted on the top of her crossed legs, her chin in her palm, and her lips together in a small pout of concentration. Spread out in front of her were five different examples of wedding invitations displaying various fonts and wording. She was scrutinizing them with the kind of intensity normally attributed to Russian chess players. I was seated in the chair beside her doing my best to exhibit great facial interest. But in truth, I was studying her more than the invitations, and my thoughts had delightfully drifted to a much more primitive realm. Soon enough, this side trip of my wanton imagination was detected. Christine glanced at me reproachfully.

"Bradford, you need to be focused."

"Oh, I'm very focused." I countered innocently.

She responded with a sly, admonishing smile and returned her gaze to the invitations. "Luke, dear. It's the first week of April. The wedding is June tenth. We have to get things decided. I don't think you're taking this seriously enough."

"Sure I am. Wedding invitations are fun."

"Humph," she gushed under her breath. "Said no man ever."

"No, really. This is…you know, great."

"Shouldn't your pants be on fire right now?"

I needed to redirect this inquisition. "Which one do you like best?"

"You go first."

"Okay." I thoroughly reviewed the five options for a full and exhausting two seconds. "I like that one."

Christine's face knotted into a twist of disapproval. "No, that one's a little too pretentious. I like this one better."

"Gee didn't see that coming."

"You don't like it?"

"No, no. It's perfect. I mean, look at it. All the letters are swirly, and there're no misspelled words. What's not to love?"

Christine leisurely collapsed to the back of her chair, a telling sign of uncharmed resignation. "Bradford, sometimes I think you're just a toddler on growth serum."

I thought for a moment. Then, I partially stood and shifted my chair so that it faced her. I leaned back, extended my legs, and laced my fingers behind my head. "Christine, the only thing that is important to me about this wedding is that in ten weeks I hear the words, 'I do.' Every one of these invitations tells who, what, where, and when. The fact that everybody in Watervalley and most of their pets already know these details makes it even less critical. So, whichever one makes you happy is grand with me."

She smiled artfully and tucked a lock of hair behind her ear. "Well, okay." She said reluctantly. "I guess you've redeemed yourself. But only a little."

"I'll take what I can get."

She returned to business quickly. "So, here's the next question. Mom and I have been putting together a list of names, and it comes to over two hundred. It could easily jump to three hundred."

"Three hundred? Are you inviting people from an alternate universe?"

She ignored me. "The problem is your side of the equation. Everybody in town knows you. You're their doctor. For many of them, they   think   of   you   as   family."

"Which means they will be hurt if I don't invite them."

"Correct. It seems to be an everyone or no one proposition."

I nodded thoughtfully. "I guess you're right. I hadn't thought about it."

"So, how many people are we talking about here?"

"As far as how many would show I'm thinking maybe two to three hundred."

"The sanctuary at First Pres will hold seven hundred. That shouldn't be a problem. The problem is the invitations. Do we send one to every patient or do some blanket invite."

"I don't know," I said, slightly bewildered. "We would be talking about almost four hundred families along with your three hundred invitations.

"Taking out the likely overlap we're looking at five hundred plus invitations. And all of them have to be individually addressed by hand."

"By hand? Seriously?"

"Yes, Luke. By hand."

"We have everybody's address on the computer. We could just run labels."

For a long moment, she stared at me with a face that I could only describe as a mix of affection and disbelief. "Luke," she said patiently. "This is a wedding invitation, not a notice to get your flu shot. They have to be hand addressed."

"I guess an e-vite is completely out of the question?"

Christine crossed her arms, offering only an indignant drop of her chin.

"Okay. Hand-addressed it is. And, contrary to my profession, I actually have excellent handwriting. I can help."

"Good. That settles that," she said. Once again, she seemed energized with a sense of progress. But then, reality sunk in. "Luke, how long do you think it will take to do that many?"

"Well, let's think about it for a minute. Provided we don't take any breaks, I'd say probably until the end of time."

She said nothing, and I couldn't quite tell if she wanted to laugh or hit me. But eventually she shook her head and proceeded to gather the five invitations. "Look, we've decided which invitation. So, we've made a little headway. Let's table the 'how many' question and let me talk to the wedding planner. Maybe she can think of a creative way to invite your patients."

"Perfect. What's the next order of business?"

"I'd like your opinion on something."

"Sure."

"Well, as you know, the reception afterward is going to be outside on the lawn at the farm. The photographer has quoted an option to have a drone make aerial photos and videos which sounds like such a great idea. What do you think?

I shrugged. "Sure. I guess. How much is he talking about?"

Christine retrieved a paper from her folder and handed it to me. I blew out a short whistle and handed it back. "Wouldn't it be cheaper to just re-task a satellite."

"It is quite a bit. But grandmother Chambers loves the idea and has offered to pay for it."

"Fine by me. If she's buying, I'm flying." I paused, shaking my head lightly. "You know, by my calculations, this wedding is costing about the same as the Hoover Dam."

Christine raised an acknowledging eyebrow. "Don't remind me. I mean, I have thought about it, about doing something small and simple. But then, so many people that I care about and who care about me would be left out. I don't think there's an alternative."

I leisurely scratched the back of my head. "Hey, a girl only gets married once."

A soft smile eased upon her. She leaned toward me. Her voice was warm and yielding. "That's certainly my plan, Dr. Bradford."

To admit that I was charmed would be an understatement. I could do little more than plunge delightfully into the deep well of her brown eyes. But a moment later, she put her hands together and spoke with great animation.

"Oh, by the way. Mr. Clancy has offered to drive us away from the reception in his horse-drawn carriage. It's white with an open top like the ones used for tours in Charleston."

"Are you talking about Lester Clancy, the little fellow out on Williamsport Pike?"

"Yes. You know him?"

"I know him and his horse. They rode with Roosevelt over San Juan Hill. I mean, don't get me wrong. The whole carriage thing sounds nice, but have you seen Mr. Clancy's horse? He voted in the last three elections. I'm not sure he'd win out against a strong headwind. And Lester is no spring chicken either. His eyesight is terrible. It'll be like being chauffeured by Mr. Magoo."

Her response was affectionate but noticeably instructional. "I think that he could take us from the reception down the driveway to the front entrance. It's only a few hundred yards. From there we could hop in your car and make our getaway." I could tell by both look and tone that this was an idea in which the decision had already been made.

"Come to think of it, I've always wanted to ride away in a white carriage."

Christine responded with contented diplomacy. "Good answer, Bradford. I thought that's how you felt. Now, a couple of other things. I've got three bridal showers coming up in the next few weeks, and Uncle John and some of Mom's friends want to throw a big party for us."

The mention of John's name made me curious. "Have you talked to your uncle recently?"

"Not really. Why? I thought the two of you were big chums."

"Well, I'd say we are. But lately, he seems to be spending most of his spare time with Ann. Not that that's a bad thing."

"I do remember that mom said he's not drinking as much as he was."

"That may not be saying much. To drink any more he'd have to be doing it in his sleep."

Christine nodded and spoke wistfully. "I know. Uncle John. I love him dearly. But his drinking worries me." After a moments reflection, she added. "But you say he and Ann are a steady item?"

"Yes. It's amazing, actually. Ann is as smart as they come, and you'd think the key to loving a man like John is to have a poor short-term memory. But lately, they've been inseparable."

Christine seemed pleased with this news. Then as she gathered everything back into her folder, she spoke with fresh exuberance.

"So, how are plans for the bachelor party coming along?"

"Not sure on that one. John hasn't really mentioned anything."

"Well, surely he'll come up with something. Have you said anything to him?"

"Only that I wanted it to include a bouncy house."

"Very funny, Bradford. And have you decided who the groomsmen are going to be?

"Yes. I've chosen the groomsmen very carefully, based on their ability to answer yes to a critically important question."

"Which is?"

"Do you want to pay for your own tux and be in my wedding?"

Christine gushed an exasperated sigh and for a long moment, stared blankly into the room. She spoke to the general air in a searching, reflective voice. "How did I ever fall in love with you? There is not an adult bone in your body."

She uttered an exasperated "ugggh," and playfully shoved my shoulder. Yet all the while she was doing her best to stifle an irrepressible laugh.

Before I could respond there was a simultaneous knock and opening of my office door. Nancy Orman leaned in. "We're getting ready to close up Dr. Bradford. Do you need anything?"

Christine and I were bubbling in smothered laughter. "Yes," I said buoyantly. This woman just assaulted me. What do you think should be done about that?"

Nancy paused, pondering the question before speaking dryly. "Do you think the rest of us could line up and take a shot?" Christine placed her hand over her mouth, shuddering with delight.

"Love you, too, Nancy. Go home and come back tomorrow as a nicer person."

She smiled and winked at Christine, before closing the door.

"You know I haven't thought to ask you," said Christine. "How was your day today?"

I tucked my hands under my arms and thought for a moment. "Well, let me think. I saw a few cases of the sniffles. I did exams on a pilonidal cyst, two hemorrhoids, and three cases of bunions. It's just been a buffet of healing."

Oddly, for the longest time, Christine said nothing. When she did speak, her voice carried a deeper tone of concern. "Doesn't sound like you enjoyed it very much."

I played this off. "It is what it is."

She nodded her understanding. But buried within her expression was a deeper contemplation, something she seemed in want of saying. I changed the subject.

"What's going on this weekend?"

"I have a shower Saturday afternoon. But it will be over by four."

"Good. I have an idea. The weather is supposed to be sunny and warm. What say we go out to Moon Lake Saturday afternoon, build a fire, and, I don't know, maybe talk about the future."

"The future?"

"Yeah. Sure. The future."

Oddly, a long silence fell between us, during which, Christine studied my face probingly. In time an affectionate smile emerged. "Sure. I'd like that."

Chapter 31

THE MEETING

On Friday the clinic was modestly busy with a few of Watervalley's more colorful personalities in the mix. Having made the decision to stay, I rediscovered a mild contentment with the daily rattle and hum of patients. Although far from inspiring, the day was routine and for the most part, enjoyable. Admittedly, the highlight was the lunch meeting of the newly formed Community Development Council; a reality that hit me as I started my car for the drive downtown. My threshold of thrill had sunk to an all-time low.

I arrived late for the meeting at the Courthouse only to find an empty conference room. After checking my cell phone calendar, I realized that the meeting was at noon and not eleven thirty. Weighing my options in the balance, I decided to simply take a seat and wait. This proved to be a fortunate choice because a minute later, John Harris walked through the door. Instantly, there was a spontaneous humor between us.

"Hello, professor. I'm glad you're here. We need to have a little chat....you know, just between us girls."

"What's on your mind, doctor?"

"As I recall from our last episode, you were expressing some heavy concerns about leaving Watervalley behind and discovering new worlds. 'Finding yourself,' I think you called it. But the only place you've been finding yourself is down at the clinic hovering around Ann. Am I missing something here?"

John offered nothing more than a derisive grin. He took off his coat and drug one of the heavy wooden chairs away from the conference table, turning it askew. It was neither against the wall nor square to the table, but rather sitting in space, as if John were instinctively asserting that this was now the center of the room. In similar fashion he casually seated himself, exhibiting a composure secured by the chemistry of wealth and intellect. But there was something different about him, a kind of submerged ease that supplanted his normal brooding air.

I was prepared for a healthy round of his clever-tongued invective. Instead, he held his hands up in a gesture of concession. "Doc, I don't know what to say. These past few weeks have been, well…incredible. My face hurts from smiling so much. She's funny, she's beautiful, she loves me just the way I am. Hell, even I don't like me the way I am. And lately I've been experiencing this really weird feeling."

"John, let the doctor explain. That feeling your talking about, it's called happiness."

He shook his head, amused. "I just find myself thinking about her all the time."

"It's simple. You're in love, big guy."

His gaze sharpened. I leaned forward in my chair. "Look, John. I realize that our normal topics of conversation are limited to news, weather, and sports. But being in love is considered normal for most humans. It's one of the six basic emotions."

"Oh, really? What are the other five?"

"Gee. I don't know. Greed, lust, envy, fear of used car salesmen, getting the munchies…what does it matter?"

"You left one out."

"Which is?"

"Anger. And you know what's a primary cause of anger?"

"Enlighten me."

"Marriage."

"So is driving in Atlanta. What's your point?"

"The point is, sport…" John's voice seemed to stick in his throat. His expression withered. "Hell, I'm not sure what the point is. I just know I don't want to screw things up."

As I was about to respond, Connie Thompson entered the far end of the conference room. "My, my. Looky here. Watervalley's brain trust is already on the job. The town is saved."

John turned to her, his words thick with salt and humor. "Connie, I'm surprised you're here. Isn't this about the time of year you normally shed your skin."

She came and seated herself in the chair next to him, unfazed.

"Keep it up, John and your organ donor card may come into play a lot sooner than you think."

"Oh, come on, Constance, play nice. Besides, you know I'm just wanting your attention. I've always had a big crush on you."

"Hmm. Why do I have my doubts?"

"Have I ever lied to you?"

"All the time."

"Then you should be more used to it."

John glanced at me, winked, then fluidly changed his tone to one of genuine concern. He reached over and lightly placed his hand on top of Connie's. "Hey, before I forget. How's Rayford doing?"

"Oh, he's fine. He's going back to work Monday. I need to go pay him a visit."

I stared at Connie, confused. Rayford was her oldest son who lived in Chicago. "What happened to Rayford?"

"Acute appendicitis. Last Sunday. He was on his way home from the hospital on Monday before I even got a call. I was ready to drop everything and catch a plane, but he insisted that I stay home. Said he wanted me to come when he was well and not when he was recovering from surgery."

Admittedly, I was a little stunned. Not just with the news but with the fact that I knew nothing of it. "Well, I'm glad he's doing alright." My response seemed forced and diplomatic, but I gave it the full measure of facial concern, attempting to make up in dramatic delivery for what the words lacked in novelty. Oddly, Connie only nodded and lapsed into a distracted silence.

Soon afterwards other committee members began to arrive, and the conversation migrated to the typical salutations of acquaintances. There were about nine altogether including some merchants, a bank officer, and a couple of prominent farmers. Watervalley was still largely an agricultural community and the mayor knew where his bread was buttered. Insightfully, Walt was seeking input from a variety of viewpoints before launching any campaign to attract new industry. If Walt was anything, he was a politician.

He was the last to make an appearance, scuttling in as if he were late and anxious with a kind of prancing nervousness. He greeted everyone effusively and offered at least two rounds of thanks to all the participants. After detailing the need to cultivate some moderate growth in the local economy, he began the discussion by tossing out several "brainstorming" ideas he had in hopes of getting the conversation started.

His first recommendation regarded promoting tourism and hovered around Henrietta, the dancing chicken.

Apparently, some decades ago, a local chicken farmer named Butterbean Taylor made a home video of one of his chickens he claimed could dance. Butterbean thought it would be a good marketing ploy. His pitch was, "The Taylor Egg Company, Home of Henrietta, The Dancing Chicken." He scrounged up enough money to buy come commercial air time on a Nashville TV station and Henrietta became an overnight sensation. For a time, people flocked to Watervalley to see Henrietta in action.

"I'm thinking," said Walt enthusiastically, "that we could build on that by having a "Dancing Chicken Festival." The Fall Festival is our biggest tourism money maker. So, I thought we could do this in the spring. Have a fried chicken competition, a Funky Chicken Dance off, maybe even a dancing chicken contest with real chickens."

Having made his spiel, Walt surveyed the room. "Well, what does everybody think?" His inquiry was met with deafening silence and most of the committee members cast their eyes downward like truants in the principal's office. Finally, John replied, doing his best to be diplomatic and kind. "Walt, I'm not sure that being the birthplace of

279

Henrietta the Dancing Chicken should be claimed as our proudest moment. I realize that we're not trying to qualify as a World Heritage Site, but I think we might want to put our efforts toward something more sustainable than a one weekend festival."

Walt responded in stride. "Good point, John. Which brings me to the next idea. I think we should try to capitalize on the valley's natural recreational value. There's a five-acre tract of land available at the north end of Akin Ridge. What if we were to get one of those paragliding outfits to come in here and set up. It could bring in several jobs and a steady flow of tourists."

This scheme prompted a few approving nods and a more open-minded reception. That was, until once again, John spoke in a polite yet informative voice.

"Paragliding from Akins Ridge isn't going to be particularly popular with anyone who is familiar with gravity. You need a place to land as well. Given that the only safe landing zone is Lester McFall's pig farm, the whole experience would probably be considered something less than cosmic. And convincing Lester to sell would probably require a Papal Decree."

Walt nodded his understanding, his enthusiasm clearly waning. For a moment, the conversation stalled. The mayor's intentions were good but figuring out an approach to the task seemed beyond his depth. Fortuitously, Connie, who had a certain knack for seeing the dominant color in any situation, entered the discussion.

"Walt, it seems to me that we need a plan on multiple fronts. For starters, we need to see how we might open greater markets for the agriculture we're already producing. The cabinet factory is here because the surrounding hills have thousands upon thousands of acres of inexpensive hardwoods. Maybe we should look at recruiting some furniture manufacturing here as well. There's plenty of timber to go around. As far as industry goes, our best shot is to find someone to retool the old DuPont plant. We still have a working railroad track coming through the valley and that will prove beneficial to any new industry. New retail is fine, but we need to find ways to bring new dollars into the community, not redistribute what we have. We find new dollars, retail will follow. We all know these things and talk about these things, but we need to devote some focused attention to them. I say we make some sub-committee assignments to look into each area and meet back to discuss the possibilities."

Seamlessly, Walt followed in step and began to assign chairs from the various group members. Appropriately, John was asked to look into the plant revitalization since in years past he had been the manager. The farmers agreed to meet with the Co-op and look into expanding the agricultural markets. Walt and the bank officer would reach out to possible furniture manufacturers. Luckily, given my busy schedule and upcoming wedding, Walt didn't assign anything to me. Connie wasn't so considerate.

"Luke, you're friends with Matthew House. Why don't you ask him when he thinks he might reopen the bed and breakfast? If we're going to attract new business, people will need a place to stay when they visit."

Suddenly, all eyes turned to me. My voice stuck in my throat. Apparently, Matthew had remained tight lipped about his intentions. I had assumed that his desire to keep Society Hill as a private residence was general knowledge. I now realized it wasn't. I stammered out a response. "Um, well, sure. I'll make a point of asking him."

Soon after, the meeting adjourned, and Connie quickly exited before I had any chance to speak with her. The room emptied leaving only John and me.

"Wow, Connie more or less parted the waters for everyone in that discussion."

John's eyes tightened. A shrewd grin foretold that he knew something more.

"What?" I inquired.

"Sport, do you think she and I walk into these things blind? For years the two of us have sat in meetings like this until we were about to die from fanny-fatigue. These days we're a little more intentional. Everything you heard was well discussed several days ago. My job was to defuse any bozo ideas Walt came up with and Connie's job was to bring some structure to the gathering."

"You're not making this up, are you?"

"Of course not. Look, I like Walt. You like Walt. Everybody and their dog likes Walt. But other than having a knack for bringing the right people together, he has the IQ of a croissant."

John's summary of Walt was no surprise. But his comments answered a larger question. "I guess that's how you knew about Rayford?"

"Yeah, she mentioned it when we talked earlier this week. I take it you didn't know?"

"No, I didn't. I haven't seen Connie this week."

"You know," John said reflectively. "I kind of picked up an odd vibe from her about that. It seemed to be about some discussion the two of you needed to have but one that she was wishing to avoid for the time being."

"That's odd. She mention anything specific?"

"Not really. It just struck me as peculiar that a woman who has avenging angels with fiery swords on speed-dial would be hesitant to have a discussion with a welterweight like you." John laughed, clearly amused with himself. "Come on sport. I'll walk you out."

As I drove back to the clinic, my mind raced. Connie and I had already had the "Talk." Perhaps she thought I needed a refresher course. But I was at a loss as to why she would have any reticence in approaching me on the matter.

I debated the question around for several minutes with no resolve. Soon enough, my focused changed. Tomorrow was Saturday and I was taking Christine out to Moon Lake. I had my own "talk" for which I desperately needed to prepare.

Chapter 32

CONFESSION

I wanted everything to be perfect.

The accumulated weight of my guilty conscience had burdened me with the need to impress, to be romantic, to vividly assure Christine of the depth of my affection. The fact that I had been deceitful about a galactically important matter for the past half year was just a trivial detail in a larger story. It simply needed some perspective. My original intentions had been honorable, mostly. And my sins were ones of omission; misdemeanor sins as it were. At least, that's what I kept telling myself. Saturday morning, I anxiously put my plan into action.

I borrowed Hoot Wilson's pickup truck to take my push mower out to Moon Lake. Along the way I stopped at the hardware store and bought some tiki lamps, a couple of canvas chairs and a small wrought iron table. I drove to the property and locked the gate behind me, not wanting any unwelcome intruders. Certain aspects of my scheme took hokeyness to an Olympic level, and I was profoundly self-conscious that no one but Christine knew of it.

The rains and warmer days of April had already produced a thick carpet of orchard grass. Using the push mower, I neatly clipped a small level area beside the lake in the silhouette of a heart. Admittedly, even while I was shaping it, the idea struck me as embarrassingly corny. I knew that if I was ever questioned about it, I would have to do what any normal guy driven by ardent love would do: lie with impunity.

But Moon Lake was my private world and I felt emboldened. I was so proud of my landscaping prowess that I decided to engage a second grand idea. I moved to the opposite side of the lake where the bank sloped more sharply. Using the push mower, I carefully sculpted stick figures of a man and a woman followed by progressively smaller children and two dogs; a figurative depiction of our future. I returned to the near side and smugly admired my handiwork. Despite my sense of satisfaction, the moment was mixed.

I was torn between pride of cleverness and a sickening vulnerability for this open display of sappy melodrama. I considered going back and mowing over the whole business. Then again, Luther, whom I was buying the property from, never came out here. I was the only other person with a key. And besides, my confession needed all the style points it could get. Christine was far from gullible, but there was no harm in doing everything I could to set the stage for a charmed evening. Nevertheless, for a guy who typically hid his feelings, I felt practically naked.

In the early afternoon I made a second trip out to the lake, this time bringing a white table cloth and two dozen freshly cut roses from the flower shop. I positioned the chairs, spread the covering over the table, and centered the roses in a large glass vase. Before leaving, I paused to take in everything. The intoxicating smell of clover and warm grass poured over me. The world seemed to be holding its breath in anticipation. Satisfied, I ambled back to my car, all the while rehearsing the words I would say. The stage was set.

Unfortunately, I had an hour to kill before picking Christine up at four and the idle minutes permitted me to slip into a pool of my most woeful feelings. I was filled with a nagging uncertainty. It's not that I feared losing Christine but rather, I feared losing her esteem. As well, in my heart of hearts I knew that my choice to stay in Watervalley was far from unassailable. By degrees I had simply talked myself into it. Yet I felt that I must steel myself to reveal nothing of those doubts; to demonstrate a complete resolve to stay, lest my indecision cast an even darker cloud over Christine's trust. Perhaps my real trepidation came from the knowledge that I hadn't stopped dreaming, I had simply gotten better at hiding it.

I arrived at her farmhouse at the stroke of four. The day had been gloriously warm, and I drove with the top down on the Austin Healey. After parking the car, I began to make my way to the front door. When I reached the second step, Christine emerged onto the porch. She was wearing a sundress that was neatly molded to her warm and fluid curves. I stopped and gawked. She looked incredible.

The moment held me still. Her fresh and eager face and the sensuous flow of her every move was full of seductive grace. As I stood gaping, she dipped her chin, regarding me with luminous eyes and a smile touched with both tenderness and humor. In that moment, all my forebodings melted away. There was nothing but her, whole-hearted and beautiful. Christine brought clarity to all things. Suddenly, my world, my thoughts, my decisions seemed all black and white, not a jumble of finer shades. There fell between us a natural and casual intimacy.

"Wow, I'm stunned. You look like...I don't know...like, dessert."

She stepped toward me and took my arm, all the while wearing the mirthful smile of one who knew many secrets. "Come along, Bradford. We have to eat our vegetables first."

We drove through an April-drowsy countryside of clear streams and rolling fields. The breeze of the open convertible playfully teased Christine's long black hair away from her face. Consumed in a blissful air, she melted back against the headrest. With her slightly lifted chin, her dark sunglasses, and her seductive red lips, she seemed the very picture of grace and glamour.

She spoke with a flirtatious and entertained tartness. "Gee, this is big. We're going to Moon Lake and you're not taking the dogs along. What about you, Luke Bradford? Aren't you the romantic devil?" Despite her teasing I could sense the affection in her voice.

"They weren't too happy about not making the invite list. Besides, I haven't talked about it, but lately Rhett's been having a bit of a flatulence problem. I need to talk to the vet about his diet."

"Thanks for the share," Christine responded. "Did I just use your name and the word 'romantic' in the same sentence?"

"Scoff if you must. I'm only thinking of you."

"You might need to explain that one."

"Well, in case you've forgotten, brown eyes, in a couple of months, you'll be the new roommate. A dog whose GI tract is akin to that of a neutron bomb might not compliment the nesting instincts."

Christine laughed and spoke with genuine empathy. "Poor Rhett. Maybe Karen can figure something out."

"By the way, have you talked to our friendly veterinarian lately?"

"Not really, why?"

"Just wondering how she and Hoot are getting along."

"Don't know. I like them together, though. They seem like a good match."

"I think they're more than just a good match."

"In what way?"

"Are you kidding? Karen can field dress a deer, bait her own hook, and back a boat down a ramp. For Hoot, she's practically the perfect woman."

"I can do those things."

"Should I let Hoot know?"

"Maybe. But I feel kind of bad about it. I mean, you did ask first."

"Hey, I don't want there to be any second guessing here. I couldn't bear the thought of you seeing Hoot out on his tractor some day and thinking, 'what if?'"

She smiled dismissively. "Not to worry, Bradford."

By now we had reached Gallivants Crossing, the road to Moon Lake. I eased the car into a lower gear and turned down the tree-lined lane. In my head I was practicing the things I needed to say.

"You've turned awfully quiet. What are you thinking about?"

I evaded. "Oh, you know. Just wondering if everything was in order for the wedding."

She lowered her chin. "Nice avoidance you big liar. But, yes, all the wedding plans are on track. Mom and I went to Nashville this morning to do the final fitting on the wedding dress."

"And, how did that go?"

"Oh, it was wonderful, of course. How could it not be? I love the dress. It has a long train, almost eight feet."

"With a caboose and everything?"

"Not funny, Bradford."

"Well, I don't know," I said jokingly. "This wedding is starting to feel more like a coronation. Maybe you should wear a crown?"

"An actual crown?"

"Sure, like a princess."

"I think not," she said with dismissive politeness. And yet, there was a noted hesitation.

"Huh, your words say no but your eyes say yes. And why not? You're kind of Watervalley royalty."

She spoke instructionally. "Every girl wants to be a princess on her wedding day, Bradford. But Watervalley would see it as pretentious and so would I. Of course, that doesn't apply to you."

"Meaning?"

"Meaning, to you, I am a princess with a crown. So, whenever you look at me, just pretend I'm wearing one." Quite pleased with herself, she did her best to suppress a gleeful smile. Her gaze rolled to the passing countryside and an amused silence followed.

We sped along under the spell of the warm day and the mesmerizing drone of the engine. The sunlight dappling through the trees flickered across Christine's face, illuminating her silhouette in a soft, almost ethereal radiance, like the kaleidoscopic frames of an old film. The effect was surreal, magical. In that very moment, I was once again reminded that she was the most beautiful woman I had ever known. I suspect every man felt that way about the woman he loved. But I feared my well-rehearsed lines were becoming a blur.

We reached the entrance to the property. I unlocked the gate, pulled through, and then locked it behind us. We rolled through the tall grass to the side of the lake. The warm breath of spring floated in the air and a golden light bathed the entire area, offering a hazy luster that shimmered across the water. We were in the deep green heart of April and the afternoon brooded with a lazy, drowsy enchantment, like a day from an unfallen world.

I came to a stop alongside the table and flowers. Christine immediately gushed into a gape mouthed astonishment and with both hands she pulled herself above the windshield to attain a better view. "Look at this! Luke, this is so wonderful!" She absorbed everything for a few seconds before collapsing back into her seat. Wrapped in a pleasant euphoria, she looked at me and seemed to pass into a deeper reverie. "Wow, now I really do feel like royalty."

"Well…there's wine and roses in it for you but no tiara I'm afraid."

She turned and hit me on my shoulder, an act of delighted admonishment. "I love it. What's gotten into you?" She was radiant and looked at me with willing lips and adoring eyes as if I were the answer to every prayer she had ever offered. The moment was powerful and delightful, and I couldn't help but linger in it, letting the earth rotate just a little bit farther.

"Come on, gorgeous. Let's go smell the roses."

We settled into the chairs and talked casually for a time. But all the while, I began to feel a baffling torture of doubt. A strained unease crept over me. Despite the churning in my stomach, my heart was packed with its burden for confession. For a long moment, I vacantly stared out over the lake and into the middle distance.

"Christine, there are some things I need to tell you, things that I've kept to myself for, well…for a variety of reasons."

Her lively expression tempered. With strained uncertainty she made a low noise of acknowledgement. Yet even then she looked at me with eyes that were patient and undemanding.

I need to clear the air about something." She nodded softly, saying nothing. A wispy breeze carried the faint scent of early honeysuckle. I took a deep breath and began.

I told her everything…about receiving the research offer, about my anguish during that time regarding her medical condition, and about how my decision to keep the matter quiet was driven by my desire to protect her. Then I told her about the letter from the estate attorney and how the money could be used to pay off my debt to the town, allowing me to pursue the research opportunity. I told her that I had thought about it, seriously. But I finally decided that what I wanted more than anything was for us to be happy, for us to live in Watervalley. I would use the money to buy the Moon Lake property and we would use it for building a house.

During the entire time I was speaking, Christine sat silently. She simply listened, heard, breathed. I finished by saying, "I'm sorry. I should have told you all of this sooner. I just wanted to be certain of my own mind first."

I awaited her response and a knotty silence ensued. When she finally did speak, her words were soft, almost fragile.

"Luke, I have something that I need to confess to you."

I stared at her blankly. This was not the reply I was expecting. My mind churned, and it occurred to me that the only logical confession regarded some previous boyfriend or tryst that she wanted to reveal. My words grew quick with expectation.

"Look, Christine. It's okay. If there's something about a previous boyfriend, don't worry about it. We all misplace our hearts a few times before we find the right place to put it."

"No. No, Luke. It's nothing like that." There was a naked pleading in her eyes.

I was dumbfounded. "It's not?"

"No."

"So, no skeletons in the closet, no mad moment of weakness at a fraternity party, no 'Girls Gone Wild,' video appearances?"

"No, no, and no." My failed assumption had eased her trepidation. Her gaze grew tender and the light of higher purpose seemed to flicker in her eyes.

"Then…what? What could you possibly need to confess?"

"It's about everything you just told me, about the research letter and the money."

"What about it?"

"I already knew."

Chapter 33

SPLENDOR IN THE GRASS

"I don't understand? What do you mean you already knew?"

"Don't be upset with me, Luke. Please." She said the last word as if it was a sentence unto itself.

I starred at her, searching, dumbfounded. "Well, no, I'm not upset. A little baffled, maybe. I mean, how could you have possibly known? John knew about the research offer. But I've told no one about the attorney letter."

Before speaking she reached over to hold my hand, a gesture of needed assurance. "Do you remember last November, after the Veteran's Day ceremony, when we drove to the concert in Nashville?"

"Sure."

"Well, for several days following that, I couldn't find my sunglasses. So, after school I stopped by the clinic to look for them in your car. I didn't see them, but I thought maybe you had put them in the glove box. And that's when I found the letter from Vanderbilt. I know I shouldn't have read it, but I did."

Her words brought back the events of that day. Before leaving town, I had checked my mailbox on the way to the car. After reading the letter I had wadded it up to throw away. But after a moment, I thought better of that idea and tucked it in the glove compartment. That's where it had remained, even to this moment. Christine continued.

"I guess I thought you would eventually say something about it. But when you never did, I wondered why...why you wouldn't pursue your dream. That's when I realized it was because of me. Because you thought I would be unhappy to leave Watervalley."

I nodded solemnly. "That would be correct."

"I guess at the time your assumption was true. But as the weeks passed I began to grasp what you were giving up and I came to realize how much you truly loved me. My roots are in Watervalley, Luke, and I draw a lot of strength from being here. But you've changed that. You had your dream job within reach and you never said a word. You put your love for me before everything else. I'm amazed at it, really, and I'm not sure I deserve it. But being with you is where my world is now. I had always assumed that being loved would bring me happiness. But I never realized how much courage it would also give me. I love Watervalley, Luke. But it's just a place. My home is with you, wherever that may be. That's why we came up with the plan about the money."

"We? What we?"

"My grandmother Chambers is a wealthy woman and quite a while back she set up a trust fund of $100,000 to be given to me the day after my wedding. She's old fashioned and I guess it's kind of a dowry thing. Or, I don't know, maybe she thought I was going to be an old maid and was using it as a bribe. In any case, mom and grandmother and I came up with the idea of contacting your attorney and offering $75,000 so you could pay off your debts and take the research offer. It seemed like such a simple plan. I never dreamed you would think of using the money to buy the Moon Lake property."

"So, you're saying that the $75,000 is your grandmother's?"

"Yes."

"And she agreed to this?"

"Yes."

"How did you even know how to contact my attorney?"

"It was during the Christmas Eve party, when mom and I were upstairs in your room. She stood guard while I went through your filing cabinet. That's how we got the name and address. On her way back home to Florida after Christmas, Grandmother Chambers stopped in Atlanta to see the estate attorney. She can be very persuasive."

"This we know."

"That's why the letter said the money would be distributed in July. Grandmother wanted to hedge her bets a little just in case the wedding didn't happen. Her idea, not mine...just so you know."

"I'm shocked she consented to any of this. Look, Christine. I know you love your grandmother. But every time I've been around her, she acted like she wanted to debone me. I've never thought she liked me. And listen...I'm just going to say it. I think she's mental. I don't believe she limits her madness to March."

Christine laughed, placing her hand over her mouth. "Oh, dear Luke! I haven't been very fair to you. Grandmother Chambers adores you. She truly does. But she's a prankster and was a drama major in college. Around you she's acted out this tough farmwoman persona, but she's really not like that. I shouldn't have let her little ruse go on this long, but you see her so rarely."

"You mean it's all been a game with her?"

"Mostly. I'll agree, she's a bit eccentric. But she really does have a heart of gold."

I stiffened my neck, unconvinced. "I'll take your word for it."

The conversation came to a lull. It seemed that we had allowed the discussion to follow tangents and had avoided the larger subject. I was searching, still trying to grasp everything Christine had told me. I stared at her curiously.

"So, question? Why all the charade? Why not just tell me about the money?"

"And would you have felt good about saying 'Oh, by the way. I've gotten this research offer so let's use the money to leave Watervalley?'"

"Probably not. I would have felt guilty for not having already told you about the job."

"And besides, I've already said it was wrong for me to read the letter. I felt guilty, but I couldn't change what I knew. Now it sounds like a whole lot of silliness. I wanted you to be free to choose. I never expected this." Christine made a glancing gesture toward the lake. "I never expected you to use the money to buy the property and stay here."

"I want you to be happy."

"And I want you to be happy."

"So, what does that look like?"

"I think you know what that looks like, Luke. It looks like a research position at Vanderbilt. It looks like living in an overpriced apartment in the West End, me teaching at a private school, and us loving every minute of it."

A grand, deeply born euphoria began to well within me. "You think so, really?"

"Yes, I do," Christine said emphatically. She fell silent and dropped her gaze, pondering. Ever so carefully, she placed both her hands on top of mine. Her voice was low, deliberate, penetrating. "And I'll tell you what else it looks like. It looks like you going to work each day and doing fertility research and then coming home each night and us spending some delightful hours putting those theories into practice."

There was no missing her intent and her modest but resolute message sent my primal instincts soaring. After a time, she looked up at me with a soft and inquisitive regard. "Everything okay?"

"Oh, couldn't be better." I gushed a short laugh and looked across the lake. "Sorry. For a moment there I lost the power of speech."

Christine smiled wistfully, no doubt aware of the incredible gravity she held over me. "Luke, listen. Yes, one day I would love to come back to Watervalley. And part of me would like to think that you feel the same way. But this research opportunity is the future you want."

"But it will take months for Watervalley to find a new doctor. I would be leaving them in the lurch. After everything this town has done for me, it doesn't seem very fair."

"All of that can be worked out. You know it can. Watervalley went without a local doctor for years. Arrangements can be made to cover a few months until another physician can be settled."

I searched her face. "You're willing to do this?"

"Absolutely."

"Are you sure? I thought this was the only place on earth you could be happy?"

Christine looked away for a moment. "Luke, to climb the same hills, to walk the same meadows, to breath the same air my parents and grandparents did for almost a century before me is unaccountably rich in satisfaction. It's a gift, a strength, a sense of belonging that I carry with me. It's hard to explain. I can't show it to anyone and they can't see it. My roots here define me, and I like who that person is. But they don't bind me. They don't limit my happiness to this one place on earth."

I collapsed back into my chair and once again stared at the lake, speechless. My thoughts and emotions were muddled. Exhilaration, apprehension, and guilt all converged upon me. It was an incredible business. I had not allowed myself to entertain the possibility of taking the research position. But Christine's assured endorsement swept all doubts away. The elation I had felt months ago when I first opened the attorney letter and dreamed the possibility of taking the Vanderbilt job now returned. It seemed I had been sleepwalking the last half year, living under a veil of a self-induced melancholy. Christine's voice broke through my temporary muddle.

"Well?"

"Well what?"

"Have you decided, or do you want a few moments to overthink it?"

"Well, yes. I want to take the position." I heard myself say the words and yet, my own senses held them in disbelief. Christine said nothing, but her eyes softened.

I looked at her wide-eyed and began to shake my head, repeating the words. "Yes. Yes. I want to take the research position."

For long after that, it seemed that all both of us could do was laugh spontaneously. We teased and chided each other for our secretiveness, our scheming, and our collective foolishness. It was as though a magic door had opened to a splendid, more abundant world and we both were intoxicated with the freshness, the sense of adventure of our life to be. Christine spread the blanket over the grass and we stretched out, our eyes transfixed across the water. The sun shimmering upon the surface mesmerized us, enveloped us in a transcendent feeling and we lazed in the glory of Camelot. After a time, while perched on her elbows, Christine placed a hand over her eyes and focused on the distant shore.

"Did you do something to the grass over there?"

I spoke sheepishly. "Yeah, I mowed some images on to the bank. Can you make them out?

"Not really." She sat up, continuing to shield her eyes with her hand.

"Oh, I see it now. That's us with three kids, right?

"That would be correct."

Christine collapsed onto one elbow and turned to me, her face framed with a charmed and melted adoration. Then without uttering a word, she rolled toward me and pushed my shoulders to the ground, pressing herself upon me for a long, delightful kiss. In time, she folded her arms across my chest and spoke with whispered affection. "You can be such a sweetheart." Once again, she turned her head and focused back across the lake.

"What are those other two things?" She asked. "Are those cows? Are you wanting to raise cows?"

"No. They're dogs. That's Rhett and Casper."

She sat up and studied the far bank. "Kind of big for dogs."

"A push mower is not exactly a precision instrument."

She laughed and once again playfully grabbed my shoulders and pushed me to the ground, delightfully yielding the full measure of herself against me. She was smiling irrepressibly and probing deep into my eyes. "You make me very happy, Luke Bradford."

After kissing me on the forehead, she continued to search my face. "Do I make you happy?"

At first, all I could offer was a gushing smirk. "Miss Chambers, I am in love with you, and I find that everything about you brings me tremendous happiness. But in the spirit of full disclosure, the fact that there are only a few pieces of cloth between me and your delightfully perfect body invokes larger emotions that make happiness a poor cousin. I won't apologize for it. I am a man in love with a beautiful woman, and I cannot wait to consume every inch of you."

Christine lowered her gaze and spoke thoughtfully. "I know. I think about it a lot, too." She shrugged lightly.

I simply nodded, there being little more to say on the matter.

She fell silent as well. A soundless, balmy breeze floated over us. Despite our longings, we had made promises to each other. Promises not born out of some rule book or some hope for heavenly upgrades for good behavior. But rather, promises of what we wanted our life together to be despite the norms and opinions of the larger world. It was who we were. And yet, that didn't mean it was easy.

Often, the incredible weight of our emotions begged us to think differently.

After a time, Christine's reflective manner began to melt away. In a gesture of fortification, she nestled close and looked at me with undaunted resolve. "Luke, listen. All the teasing you did earlier about me being a princess and wearing a crown...I know that, well, that there may be a grain of truth to it. I know that the wedding is all about me and I admit it's a little selfish on my part. I also know that you've been patient. You've done everything to make my wedding day all the things I've ever hoped for, all the things I ever wanted that day to be. But, mind you, Luke Bradford, that's the wedding day."

"Okay." I shrugged.

"So, I can promise you one thing about what our wedding night will be."

"Oh, and what's that?"

With unabashed certainty, Christine leaned in close and whispered a single word in my ear.

"Epic!"

Chapter 34

FINDING CLOSURE

I woke up Sunday morning in an odd mix of apprehension and exhilaration. Before going to bed the previous night, I had sent an e-mail to Dr. Bray at Vanderbilt telling him that I was planning on taking the research position. I wanted the decision behind me. The conflict had clouded me for so long that I willfully chose to cross the Rubicon, knowing that the light of morning might engender second thoughts.

It did.

Sunday mornings in Watervalley owned a certain serenity and stillness. The world turned more leisurely, breathed more gently. By the time I awoke in my sequestered attic bedroom, the morning sun of April was showing its muscle, casting warm, bright squares across the wooden floor. The room was filled with a hazy, ethereal glow, leaving the spellbound air languid and heavy. Moving slowly, I placed my feet on the floor and stretched, twisting my arms high in a contorted yawn, as if I might wring the sleep from my body. Eventually, I headed downstairs, fully enjoying the luxury of an unhurried day.

After taking care of the dogs and making coffee, I decided that I would polish up a little and attend the morning service at the Presbyterian church. Although I would hardly consider myself a devout person, my convictions had been part of me since childhood. The on-call duties of my profession had made my attendance sporadic, and I suspect that a few of the First Pres regulars saw my occasional harkening of the narthex doors as only taking religion for a test drive. I knew better. Besides, although I had decided to leave, I could not deny that part of my heart would remain here in Watervalley. That morning, haunted by an odd sense of loss, I felt a quiet need to sit among the people I had come to know.

The pastor at Watervalley First Presbyterian was Joe Dawson, a young, likeable fellow who had an easy smile and endless energy, which made everyone slightly jealous and wondering if somehow, he was getting better sleep than them. In the last year he had brought some needed change to the worship service of Watervalley's frozen chosen whose previous rule of thumb was not to sing any hymn written after 1800.

I eased in and sat in one of the open pews toward the rear. Yet as I quietly gazed at the modest lives around me I couldn't help but contemplate the explosive news I was harboring and the effect it might have on them. The hushed and reverent setting of the long, lofty sanctuary was sobering and reflective, conjuring up childhood memories of biblical narratives. And try as I might, I was unable to quell the nagging comparison of myself to Judas. To my relief a moment later, Matthew arrived. He and his two children joined me. We exchanged hearty handshakes and smiles but the start of the service prohibited further socializing.

Despite my infrequent attendance and the weight of my news, I found that I always enjoyed the Sunday service. There was something medicinal to the mind and soul about simply pausing for an hour to reflect, to ponder, and to escape the treadmill of a busy life. Christine normally sang in the choir. But on this particular Sunday, she had nursery duty. As the opening hymn began I once again gazed around the room at all the lives, all the stories around me.

I had come to Watervalley foolishly thinking that these were small people; people who had no power to make a new life for themselves and whose greatest impulse was to simply keep in the swim. But I had discovered them to be quite the opposite, fiercely independent and self-determined. And while it was true that they cast a curious eye toward distant horizons, they lived here by choice. Underneath their plainly fashioned exteriors were noble capacities. They were brave, faithful, earnest, and had an unsparing friendliness toward strangers like myself. They tended to stick to their roots, their traditions, and their families because they found strength and security in the familiar.

And yet the larger world from which I had come thought of them as narrow minded and ignorant because they were indignant toward the vast, impersonal forces that intruded upon their daily lives and tried to dictate to them what their values and morals should be; that they should accept and normalize behaviors that they believed were wrong. They were not perfect people, nor were they saints. There was a fair share of them who were ethanol challenged to the point of excess and who fell prey to a little mattress hopping along with the other frailties of the human condition. But their occasional indifference to right and wrong didn't mean they didn't know the difference between right and wrong. They felt no inclination to redefine truth because it was inconvenient. In my way I admired them deeply, and I would miss them. The reality of leaving hung like a troubling veil.

Meanwhile, I noticed that the twins were once again about the business of gazing into the far corners of the sanctuary and pointing and counting before whispering to each other behind a protective hand. As before, Matthew seemed oblivious. I, on the other hand, quietly found it fascinating. If this was a game, it would seem that its' freshness would have expired long ago. Yet, here they were, engaged as ever in the same odd practice. It was baffling.

The service ended and thus began the inevitable slow departure. The post-service period was the supreme opportunity to meet and greet. Many of the regulars felt like they shouldn't leave the church until fifteen minutes after the Holy Spirit did. As well, it seemed that Matthew's and my presence was something of a novelty, and immediately we were both surrounded by a lengthy list of greeters. In time the crowd dissipated, leaving us the opportunity to catch up.

"Well, Dr. House. What's the latest with you and yours?"

A broad grin emerged. "We, my friend, are immersed into the extraordinary world of the Watervalley T-Ball Baseball League."

"That's great. What team does Andrew play for?"

"Mahlon's Barbershop. They're the Barbershop Pirates. Apparently through some distorted Watervalley interpretation of the words, everyone calls them Mahlon's Barbary Pirates."

I nodded my understanding, knowing the propensity of some of the locals to fuse a small fact to a larger fiction. Matthew continued.

"The funny thing is this. As it turns out, all the uniforms are a little big and the 'P' and the 'S' are hidden around the side under each player's armpits. So, it looks like the name of the team is 'irate.'"

"That's hilarious."

305

"You would think. But actually, the name fits pretty well for some of the parents."

I understood his implication. "Pretty intense, huh?"

"Oh, my gosh," Matthew exclaimed. "It's insane. You would think the future of Western Civilization depended on the outcome of each game. Some of the parents act like the Braves or the Cubs have scouts in attendance. Last Saturday, two of the moms almost got into a fist fight."

"Mmm, sounds about right."

Matthew leaned in. "Listen to this. The other night, Andrew got tagged out sliding into home base. So, I tried to be encouraging and shouted, 'Good try, son. Good try.' A second later, this hefty, redneck mom sitting behind me tapped me on the shoulder. I turned around and she rather flatly told me, 'Mister, this ain't no good try league.'"

"Let me know the next time he has a game. I'd love to come watch…both the game and the parents."

Matthew seemed curiously surprised at my offer. "Oh. So, were you a big baseball guy back in the day?"

"Not really. I pretty much sucked at baseball. I was however, exceedingly good at infield chatter."

Matthew nodded, exhaling a short laugh.

"Seriously, though. Give me a call."

"Well that would be great, but I can't imagine there aren't better options to occupy your time."

"No, actually, the ball park is pretty high on the list of entertainment choices for Watervalley."

"Really?" He paused for a reflective moment. "I'm not so sure how I feel about that. What else do people here do for amusement in the evenings?"

"Typically, people just sit on their porch and talk, mostly about other people."

Matthew smiled, letting the subject drop. "So, how are things with you?" He paused, lowering his voice. "Any developments regarding future plans?"

I quietly motioned for us to step outside to ensure that we were out of earshot. Once clear of the church steps, I told him about my conversation with Christine and my plans to leave. Matthew listened patiently.

"So, how do you feel about it?"

"Mixed. I think it's the right decision. But it's not an easy one."

"Understandable. When are you going to go public?"

"I'll need to let the Mayor know immediately. That way he can begin corresponding with the state's med schools for a replacement. But I'll also ask that he be discreet. It will probably be best to hold off on any larger announcements for a few weeks."

"Why is that?"

"I'd hate for all that business to overshadow the wedding, especially for Christine's sake."

"Ahh, I see. By the way, I had a conversation with Mayor Hickman the other day. He's really pressing me to reconsider reopening the house as a bed and breakfast."

"And?"

"Not interested. At least, not at present."

"Do I detect a slight change in the prevailing B&B winds?"

"Not really. I'm just not as dead set against it as I was."

"Fair enough. Any more progress with the house...you know...in terms of finding anything?"

Matthew shook his head, "Nothing. And I guess I have to admit, I've lost some steam on the whole matter. It turns out, the kids are happier here than I ever imagined. Admittedly, I'm doing okay, too. I'm starting to think that maybe that's what Emily meant for us in the first place. Maybe a little small-town happiness was what we were supposed to find." Matthew shrugged. "It doesn't seem like that should be all of it. But, who knows?"

"Could be." I said. "Watervalley grows on you. And I have come to realize that there is something oddly charmed about this place. It has a way of healing wounds. But I understand what you're saying about being unsure, about figuring it out."

"Yeah, I know. I just wish I knew what 'it' was. Meanwhile, I'm just getting on with the business of living and maybe in the fullness of time, whatever it is I'm supposed to find here will become obvious."

I shrugged. "Probably a smart plan. In the interim, I may need a lifeline."

"Why is that?"

If word does get out that I'm leaving, I may need to come and hide at your place."

"Why? Do you think the locals will be storming your house with torches and pitchforks?"

"No, but I don't think they will have a parade and carry me around shoulder high through the streets either."

Matthew grinned. "Another thing, if you get a chance sometime, I was wondering if you'd mind taking a little hike with me."

"Sure. Where?"

"Remember we talked about investigating the old spring house at the back of the property?"

"I do."

"I'm still thinking I want to take another look at it to see if there is something in it that sheds any light. I'd appreciate it if you'd come along."

"Be glad to. Just let me know. By the way, did you ever find out anything about the property behind you, the nine-hundred plus acres?"

Matthew grimaced. "No, that's kind of fallen through the cracks. But it would be good to know more about this Frontenac Company. I'll go by the Trustee's office this week and see what I can find out."

I was a little surprised at Matthew's inattention to this matter but saw it in keeping with his general retreat from trying to find answers to his departed wife's haunting request. Perhaps this change of heart was part of the grieving process, an acceptance of what his life is now and a realization that perchance he had been looking for meaning where there is none. I took the conversation in a different direction.

"So, since it looks like you and the kids are truly settling in, what do you think you're going to do with yourself?"

He slipped his hands in his pants pockets and grinned. "Good question. I'll admit, I've been feeling a little adrift lately. I'm starting to catch up on the projects at the mansion and I'm pretty certain the high school is not looking for a Latin teacher."

"Probably an accurate insight."

"So, I don't know." He paused for a moment, clearly scrutinizing some distant idea. "The whole bed and breakfast thing…the truth is, it's just not my cup of tea. Maybe if someone ran it for me I could possibly get my head around it. The town definitely needs some place for visitors to stay."

"And look at you, the previous recluse is now the concerned citizen. I'm impressed."

"Well, I'm just trying to be practical about it all."

"No, no. Absolutely. I get it. I didn't mean to sound insincere. It's small town fever. It creeps in under the door and just takes up residence. Trust me, I understand. I mean, despite my decision to leave, I hate the fact the town will probably have spotty medical coverage, at best, for several months to come. Perhaps even longer. But I have no answer for that."

Matthew nodded and offered nothing in return. Oddly, his eyes narrowed, and he cocked his head a little to one side, leaving his face framed in a distant pondering. Then again, there was little he could say. The medical coverage dilemma was one of my own creation and not his problem to solve.

Soon afterwards, Christine joined us. She invited Matthew and the children to come for Sunday lunch out at the farmhouse. "Mom generally cooks enough fried chicken to feed the Third Infantry, just in case they're in the neighborhood. So, there will be plenty."

Matthew politely refused. Curiously, he seemed distant, preoccupied, as if something in our conversation continued to privately absorb his thoughts.

We bid our goodbyes and departed.

I spent a leisurely afternoon at Christine's and left around five. I drove to John's house to tell him about my decision. This was a discussion that needed to happen face to face. I knew that he would respond with detachment, as was his way. But part of me dreaded telling him. John was my friend and I would miss him. And perhaps in some odd way, the foreknowledge that he would feign indifference to my news troubled me. But I was saved from the entire episode. He wasn't home.

I drove back to Fleming Street to take care of the dogs and hopefully enact an early bedtime, fearing the week would be a busy one.

At half past eight, I turned out my lamp and endeavored to close my eyes. But sleep was elusive. I was thinking about Matthew and his evolved perspective about his life here. In many ways I was happy for him, maybe even a little envious. He had found a contentment in permanently defining himself as part of Watervalley.

Lying there in the shadowed darkness of my room, I knew that part of me had done the same. Albeit, there was a key difference. He had come here by choice. I had not. Nevertheless, our arrivals shared one common denominator. We both were here because of the wishes of family. The key difference was that he had somehow progressed to a place where he had accepted his life here. And while his curious brooding toward the end of our conversation was still a mystery, it appeared that he was sincerely ready to move on.

Yet the researcher in me was still troubled. There were question marks that remained from what little we knew about the life of Hiram Hatcher. The photograph with the phonograph, the hidden trunk, the dress and the Bible, and more than anything, Hiram's sudden departure were seemingly part of a larger story. But it was a story with whole sections that had been absorbed into the folds of time.

Perhaps there were chapters in everyone's life that were turning points; significant events that forever changed their path. The consequence of those actions rippled across the decades, affecting those who follow. But try as we might, we regretfully discover that those family stories of years ago are closed narratives, leaving scarce enough information for us to fully understand. I suspected that Matthew was coming to terms with this reality. His heart wanted to find peace, to have closure. Perhaps investigating the old spring house was somehow a last tangible act in his quest of understanding the tragic loss of his wife. It wouldn't seem so, but as his friend, I was open to his request.

Sleep finally came. A good thing, especially given that the next morning the news on the front page of the local paper would throw my life in a tailspin. And things would only get worse from there.

Chapter 35

ESTELLE

I decided to forego my morning run the next day. Connie still came on Monday mornings and I felt a desperate need to talk with her about my plans. She wouldn't be happy about it, but just as with John, I wanted to tell her before talking with the mayor. They were my best friends in Watervalley and I owed them as much. As well, she had been reclusive and not herself for several weeks. I wanted to know why.

Usually she was in the kitchen before I came downstairs at seven. But this morning she was late. As I waited, I let the boys have an extended run of the back yard before walking to the front porch to gather the paper. As I picked it up I heard a car approaching from down the street. I stood there, fully expecting it to be Connie. It wasn't. The whole business was strange. "Connie," and "late," were not words normally found in the same sentence. Checking my watch, I noticed it was only ten after. I exhaled an impatient sigh, turned to go inside, and casually unrolled the paper. Normally the headline was something earth shattering like "Man From Connecticut Seen In Farmer's Co-op." The reality was quite different.

The front page was an aerial photo of Moon Lake with a headline that read "Watervalley's Version of Crop Circles."

My shocked response was automatic and audible. "Oh, craaaaaap!"

One of the local amateur pilots had apparently flown over during my absence on Saturday and taken the photo. It vividly showed the images I had mowed into the grass on the far bank as well as the heart shaped area with the table and flowers. I hungrily consumed the typed words, blistering through them in disbelief. The paper read:

It would seem that Watervalley's most adorable and soon to be betrothed couple had romantic plans this weekend. Perhaps a certain physician may soon be exercising his option to buy Moon Lake and get a family started...that is, along with raising a few cows.

I was dumbfounded, embarrassed, and slightly angry. Who could have ever seen this coming? And worst of all, the article closed with a ghastly assertion.

Looks like Dr. Bradford and his bride to be are making plans for a long and happy life in the valley. We wish them both the best!

This was not good on so many levels. Dazed, I staggered back to the kitchen and sat at the table, reading through the entire story at least two more times, trying to find some upside to this. There wasn't one. I stared blankly into the room, trying to think of some narrative, some way to spin this that wouldn't make me look like a total traitor to my neighbors once word of my departure got out. Nothing came to mind. I began to read the article through a third time when the doorbell rang...which was odd, because it was already unlocked, and Connie had a key. When I went to answer it, the person standing before me was totally unexpected.

It was Estelle.

Estelle Pillow was Connie Thompson's flamboyant sister. She was ten years Connie's junior and had recently taken early retirement from teaching chemistry at Vanderbilt to return to Watervalley and open the Sweet Life Bakery. She was a large, loud, hilariously lovely woman and a far cry from her typically stoic older sister.

"Estelle!" Hi. Good morning. Please...come in."

She immediately wrapped me in a consuming bear hug that always seemed to linger a moment longer than it should. "Hi, sweetie! I brought you some rolls from the bakery. You're looking skinny. Is my sister not feeding you well enough?"

She immediately pressed past me, bustling straight for the kitchen with no expectation of an answer. As she disappeared down the hall, I rolled up the newspaper and hid it under some magazines. I wasn't prepared to navigate that discussion. Donning my game face, I quickly followed.

In typical Estelle fashion she was wearing lightweight lavender colored sweats with enough sequins to be seen from space. There was no category of Estelle's life that could be appropriately defined as "understated." Her presence and Connie's absence concerned me more than the headlines. I did my best to be cordial.

"So. Estelle. How are you?"

"Sweetie, I am fine. Just like I look." Having said this, she struck a pose, lifting one hand to her hair, the other to her hip, and pressing her lips together in an impish smile.

"No argument here. Mighty colorful outfit you have there."

"Luke, honey. I decided a long time ago to never let the world dull my sparkle."

"Well, mission accomplished. So, at the risk of asking the obvious. Where's Connie?"

Immediately, Estelle's face lost a degree of illumination. "My sister, has gone to Chicago." Her tone was awash with a distinct aloofness.

"Chicago, really? Did she go to visit Rayford?"

"Beats me," Estelle continued in an overly theatrical air of indifference. "She said she had a list of things she wanted to do."

"So, she didn't tell you why? That's odd."

"Tell me about it," she declared sullenly, flipping her hand for dramatic flair. "Listen, I know my sister can be a starched old fuddy-dud, but lately she's taken that persona to an industrial level. Something about her is just not right."

"You mean like a personality disorder?"

"Oh, heavens no. It's more like a 'I have no personality' disorder."

I let this pass. "So, she didn't share anything with you about her trip?"

Estelle turned to reach some plates from the cabinet. There was a noted resentment in her response. "No. We haven't been in much of a sharing mood lately."

"How so?"

"Humph," she grunted. "Based on how she's been acting recently, let me explain how I feel about sharing with my sister. Let's say I have five cookies and she wants one of them. You know how many cookies that leaves me with? Umm hmm. That's right, five."

Despite her present angst, I knew that Connie and Estelle were extremely close. What I was witnessing was thinly veiled hurt feelings.

Realizing that nothing more would be learned with further questions, I let the matter drop,

"Well, I appreciate you coming over in her stead. I'm sure I would have been fine. Do you need to get back to the bakery?"

Her radiant demeanor promptly returned and once again, she dismissively flipped her hand at me. "Oh sweetie, not at all. The staff has everything covered there. Besides, Connie wanted me to remind you to keep the place tidied up."

Having not yet to come to terms with Connie's assertions about my housekeeping habits, I was somewhat indignant at this last comment. "Oh, and what if I'm not up to par."

"She said I should slap you around like a sock monkey."

"Really?"

"Of course not, sweetie. I just made that up."

I shrugged. "Right. Okay. I guess it just kind of sounded like Connie."

Still giggling, she put the pastries on plates and we sat at the kitchen table. After a long silence, she spoke reflectively. "I don't know what's going on with my sister, Luke. Heaven knows I love her but sometimes she can be a difficult person. That girl can start an argument with an empty room."

I took a bite of pastry. "I don't know either. But, I'm sure she'll come around."

"Well, I'll admit. It has hurt my feelings...her being all secretive and what not. But I've decided that even if she doesn't come out of it, I plan on being my glamorous, happy self. You know what they say, a smile is always in style." She said the last sentence with

317

prophetic flair, as if she were making a speech in the Miss America Pageant.

"Sounds like a good mantra," I responded passively, content to let the subject drop.

Estelle wasn't. She placed her hand on mine and looked at me imploringly, using the solemn voice people have when they are about to tell you that the president has just been shot.

"Luke, I think it's important to always be one's self." Satisfied with this pronouncement, she took her fork and ate another bite of pastry. "Unless, of course, you're a princess. Then you should always be a princess."

As was normal, talking with Estelle was a magic carpet ride in an alternate universe. My angst about the headline article began to re-emerge. But I still thought it best not to broach the subject. I strove for nonchalance.

"So, Estelle. How have you been?"

"Oh, Luke. I have to tell you this story. The other day, the most terrible thing happened."

I did my best to nod thoughtfully, unsure of what was to follow.

"I was in the yard, down on my knees pulling weeds from the roses and a yellow jacket flew up my gym shorts and stung me, right on my booty-bone."

"On your what?"

"On my booty-bone. You know? You want me to show you?"

"No, no. That's fine. Are you okay?"

"I couldn't be better. But I'm telling you right now, after the sucker stung me, I didn't care if I was out in the yard in front of God and all creation, those fluttery gym shorts were coming *off.* I mean *off,* baby."

"You took your shorts off in the front yard?"

"Oh, you know I did," she declared with unabashed detachment. "So what if the rest of the world learns that big girls like to wear leopard panties like the skinny ones do. When you get stung on your booty-bone, vanity has to take a back seat."

I was doing my best to take this trip to Neverland in stride. "Estelle, I just have to ask. You've got a PhD in chemistry. You're a highly educated woman and an accomplished baker. But, seriously...booty-bone? I've heard better English from Tonto. That's the best you've got?"

She paused and looked at me sheepishly. "I guess you have a point." But after pondering the idea for a moment, she crinkled her nose with a girlish grin. "But it does sort of roll off your tongue, doesn't it? Booty-bone, booty-bone, booty-bone."

"I'll think about it."

"Oh, my! Would you look at that?" Estelle's molecular attention span had moved on.

"Look at what?" I said aloofly. I was still trying to process the newspaper article, to think of a narrative to bring it into perspective. I liked Estelle. But she was a drama queen, and I was finding it difficult to pay attention.

"My nails! Goodness, I can't believe what bad shape they're in." She turned her hand for me to see. "My, my. That's just criminal."

"Should I notify the media?"

She cut her eyes in feigned admonishment. "Don't be playing, Luke Bradford. A girl's nails are an important business."

"Good advice. I'll make a note."

By now she had moved on to her toes. "Heavens, would you look at those. If my toenails get any longer I could swoop down and catch dinner from a lake. Mmm, mmm. I've got to get a Mani Pedi today." After a reflective, self-consumed moment, she looked up at me with an animated face, as if she had solved the secret to cold fusion. "You know, Luke, you should get one too. You should call Christine and the two of you go together, like a date."

"Hmm. Not so sure about that one, Estelle."

"Oh, piddle. There's nothing wrong with having attractive hands. Think about it, you could put the man back in manicure."

"Thanks, Estelle. But I think I'd rather put the pro back in procrastinate."

She offered a puckered frown and returned her focus to her hand, speaking wistfully. "You know, when I was younger there was a time when I thought about being a hand model."

"Oh, really?"

"Why yes. People have always told me I had beautiful hands. And listen to this. When I was a lot younger back in Nashville, I once had a painter ask me to pose for him, in the nude."

"Gee," I said, mildly surprised. "Did you do it?"

"No, but I did think about it. He was so dashing and cute."

"Oh yeah?"

"Yeah. And very talented, too. He was painting my kitchen at the time."

I chose to finish my pastry in silence.

Soon after, I thanked Estelle and gathered my things before heading to work. Between making the front page, Connie's peculiar absence, and my imminent conversation with the mayor, my stomach was in knots. And to make matters worse, on the way to the clinic, with my hand on the steering wheel in front of me, I couldn't help but notice that perhaps Estelle was right.

I could use a manicure.

Chapter 36

BREAKING NEWS

There was no shortage of teasing remarks from the staff about the newspaper article. I did my best to be dismissive but the contradiction to my real plans made the matter all the more foreboding. As much as I wanted to talk to Connie and John first, I had a burning need to move forward with the whole business. It was time.

I had a lull in patients around mid-morning and decided to walk over to the mayor's office. Walt Hickman was probably the least intimidating person in Watervalley, but my painful trepidation over breaking the news coupled with the expanding heat of the day made the short journey feel like a death march. By the time I climbed the steps to the courthouse, I was consumed with dread. Fortunately, Walt was in and able to see me immediately.

His assistant amiably invited me to have a seat in his office and said that he would join me shortly. A moment later Walt arrived in a whirlwind of bother and fluster, apologizing for having kept me waiting. Despite oily politician demeanor, it was simply impossible not to like the fellow. He had a chubby, affable appearance that appeared to have never lost the round contours of infancy and a personality that was completely free of guile, rendering his face captive to his immediate thought or mood.

I began with a kind of clumsy gratitude, thanking him for all his assistance over the past two years. It was an awkward and indirect start. Despite having practiced my exact words a dozen times, I was suddenly incapable of speaking directly to the point. I rambled, making conciliatory remarks that by their nature assumed that my departure was already understood. I guess that in some way I had hoped that Walt would grasp my intent by inference and deduction. He didn't.

"Doc, I'm not sure I understand what you're telling me here."

I exhaled a deep, decisive breath. "Walt, I'm leaving."

For a moment, his mouth worked silently at attempted speech. I continued.

"I've been offered a research position at Vanderbilt, and I'm going to take it. This has been an incredibly difficult decision, but I think that for me, it is the correct one."

I went on to explain as diplomatically as possible all the factors that weighed into my choice and to again express my gratitude to him and the town. All the while his mouth formed an "O" of surprise, and I felt quite certain that for the next few minutes the rest of my words fell away. In time he gathered himself enough to offer a few understanding nods but beyond that he was largely silent. It was not the meeting of minds I had hoped for.

I brought the encounter to a close by repeatedly asking him to keep the matter strictly confidential until after my wedding. Thirty days-notice was all that was required, but I told him that I wanted to give him the opportunity to discreetly begin the search for my replacement as soon as possible. He again nodded his understanding and thanked me. But his whole demeanor was one of wide-eyed shell shock. There was nothing more to say. I stood and extended my hand. We exchanged a hearty shake, something Walt knew how to do instinctively. But his clasp lingered, as if he didn't want to let go.

On the court house steps, I stopped to gather my thoughts. It was done. There should have been an accompanying feeling of relief with the moment. But it was scarcely present. I wanted Walt to understand, to see the rationale of my decision, to maybe even be happy for me. But his devastated response was all too clear. It troubled me, and I was still consumed with a brooding uneasiness. I decided to take a circuitous route back to the clinic in hopes that perhaps a stretch of the legs would allow me time to find some balance. For the next half hour, I ambled along the sidewalks of the downtown shops. It seemed that at every step I was met with warm smiles and friendly waves. As always, the grand show of acceptance was gratifying. But I had mentally prepared myself for this. I had come to terms with the realization that I would have to steel my emotions. I cared for the people of Watervalley, but the decision had been made. Unfortunately, Walt's speechless acceptance had left me with an embedded frustration.

I entered through the rear door of the clinic and proceeded to the front to check with Nancy as to which patient was next. But she was nowhere to be found. Conversely, during my absence to meet with the mayor, the waiting room had accumulated a small crowd. I turned down the main hall and noticed that all the exam rooms were empty, which made no sense. Curious, I proceeded to the break room at the very end. The door was shut, and, as I drew close, I could hear the rant of some very animated female voices. I stepped into the room and spoke above the chatter.

"Well darn, ladies. Somebody went and left the front door unlocked again and now we have actual patients in the waiting room."

My teasing remark was met with immediate silence. The four women exchanged dour, petulant glances. None of them looked directly at me. A hard, uncomfortable silence ensued.

"What's going on here?" I queried coolly.

All eyes turned to Nancy. She lifted her chin, made a short swallowing gesture, and spoke in a voice that was both bruised and indignant. "So, Dr. Bradford. When is your last day?" Her chill tone dropped the room's temperature by no small measure.

Blood rushed to my head so quickly that I felt momentarily dazed. Instantly I was gripped with a complete and humiliating embarrassment followed by a sharp, provoked anger. Walt had done this. I had asked for discretion in order to avoid this exact situation. It was now clear that my request had been completely disregarded.

Now, all eyes were upon me. I took a deep breath. Try as I might, my terse words were tainted with acid infuriation. "Ladies, I apologize. Yes, I am leaving, and I'm sorry I wasn't given the opportunity tell you directly. The mayor hired me. So appropriately, it was my responsibility to inform him first. I did this less than thirty minutes ago and specifically asked him to refrain from making it public just yet. But apparently the only sure way to diplomatically inform everyone is to drive around town with a blasted bull horn."

I was seething and needed to check myself, lest I allow my rage to do all the talking. After pausing and pressing my lips tightly together, I spoke firmly. "Again, I apologize. At an appropriate time, we'll all sit down and discuss this. But right now, we have patients. I think it best we take care of them first." I returned to my office and shut the door. Every fiber in me wanted to slam it, hard. But I refrained.

I sat in my chair and simmered. On two different occasions I picked up the phone and began to dial Walt's number. Each time I stopped and hung up. What would be the point?

For the next couple of hours, I worked among a low mutter of sullen protest. To the staff's credit, it seemed that none of the patients were aware of the news. All of the exams went without incident or inquiry. I took a late lunch and sat at the counter of the Depot Diner. For the most part I was politely engaged but I couldn't help but notice that the busy chatter of tables dropped as I went by. On the short hike back to the clinic I passed Hoot Wilson and Karen Davidson, walking hand in hand. As they approached, I fully expected them to stop and talk. They didn't. Instead, I was greeted with an expressionless nod. They never broke stride. It seemed that word was spreading fast.

I returned to the clinic and, after taking care of a few more patients, I retreated to my office, in no mood to meet with the staff. I was still boiling and needed more time to gain a calmer perspective. After only a few minutes, however, there was a sharp rap on the door.

"Come in," I called out in an irritated, surly voice.

It swung open. John Harris's tall, broad shouldered frame filled the opening. He didn't enter but instead stood there, casually assessing me with a laconic, cagey smile.

I said nothing, regarding him deadpan. But slowly a stout, calculating grin began to emerge. Ever so slightly I shook my head from side to side. Then slowly, I spun my chair around to gaze out the windows behind my desk. I held my hand up and motioned with two fingers for him to come in. After that, I heard the door close. No words had been spoken, but we had already exchanged volumes.

I continued my focus out the window at the grounds of the Episcopal Church next door, allowing John time to seat himself in one of the wingbacks across from my desk. After a considerable silence, I spoke unceremoniously.

"So, I guess you've heard?"

"Needless to say, sport, the entire town is in full blown hyper-gossip mode."

I slowly rotated my chair to face him. After doing so, I laced my fingers behind my head and slumped, extending my legs and crossing them at the ankle.

"So, it would seem. Sorry. I wanted to tell you beforehand."

"I see. Hmmm. If only Watervalley had some kind of small, electronic devices where people could talk to each other."

"Hey. I came by your house yesterday. I wanted to talk face to face, not send you a text message. I met with Walt this morning out of courtesy, so he could start looking for my replacement. I asked him to keep the matter quiet. I had no idea he would do this."

John gushed an acerbic chuckle. "Sport, Walt Hickman makes his living by running the town. But he makes his bones by running his mouth. What did you expect? You knew that when you got in that saddle, you had better be ready to ride."

"Great. Thanks for the non-help."

"Ah, don't be so hard on Walt. You already knew he had the spine of a tube worm. There's no way his Coco Puff sized brain could keep a secret about you leaving contained. If he had, the first thing people would ask him was how long he had known. You're leaving,

Luke. He's still got to live here. What kind of choice do you think he believed he had?"

I rubbed my chin. "Yeah, I guess you have a point. Still, I was trying to do the right thing and he just screwed me royally."

"Walt has a way of interpreting things to his own satisfaction. But let's face it, if he wasn't mayor, his only value in life would be that of an organ donor."

I indifferently gazed up at the ceiling and grinned. John was right. I probably hadn't thought through the whole matter regarding Walt.

"Well, I guess what's done is done. The problem is, the staff found out through the grapevine, so now they're hacked. I went to lunch at the Depot and I'm already getting the cold shoulder. The whole business is just a disaster."

John offered an unmoved shrug. "Small town, small minds, big mouths."

"You say that like it's a major philosophical position."

"Look sport, at some point you finally get to an age where you figure out that pleasing everyone is impossible. But pissing everybody off is pretty easy."

"And at what age did you come to this amazing insight?"

"Hmm, I don't know. Somewhere between eight and nine."

Despite my angst, I simply had to laugh. That was John's magic. "Sounds about right. But then again, John, if you knew how many enemies you really had, you'd probably carry a gun."

"Who says I don't?"

"Never mind."

"By the way, at the risk of asking a pretty dumb question, where is my niece on all this?"

I sat up in my chair, leaned in, and placed my elbows on my desk. "My fiancée and your beloved niece, my dear friend, is at the heart of it."

I went on to explain to John about the money, Mattie Chamber's involvement, and Christine's complete endorsement of me taking the research position. John nodded thoughtfully. But I could tell that even he was a little surprised with the whole story. When I finished, he said nothing and simply folded his arms together, his face framed in a pleased contentment. What followed was a long silence in which we both speculated, I suspect, about the changes that would soon be upon us. For most people, John's personality had a certain woven density that made him hard to understand. But he wasn't that way with me. Despite our difference in age, we understood each other, could read each other's insights, and without the benefit of words we had an implicit appreciation and acceptance of each other. In time, he broke the silence.

"By the way, Christine has asked me to give her away. With her father gone, I guess I'm the closest thing to a surrogate dad."

"Makes sense."

"So, along with being your best man, looks like I'll be doing double duty."

"You know, John. You being…well, you, and playing such a major role in the ceremony, it almost gives the whole business an ominous aura."

"I know. Scares me too. But I have to ask a question?"

"Shoot."

"The groomsmen. They're all locals. None of your buddies from med school or your college days. Why is that?"

Once again, I collapsed back in my chair. Despite the diversion of John's company, I was still livid from the events of the day. I plopped my right foot on top of my desk and crossed it with the other one, stewing for a long moment before giving John an answer. He was unaffected and waited silently. I turned my gaze back toward the windows. "I guess I just didn't want to listen to all of it."

"All of what?"

"All the smartass remarks. All the jabs and the digs about how redneck the town is and all the 'Deliverance,' comparisons." I pressed my lips together, brooding over my thoughts. "Maybe I'm not being fair. It's not like all my old friends are jerks. It's just that, if you're only here a day or so, you don't have a chance to understand the people of this little town. You don't get them. And typically, what you don't get, you make fun of."

I turned to face John, rubbing my chin. "So, instead of a bunch of sarcastic frat brothers, I went native with the groomsmen list. Chick McKissick, Toy McAnders, Warren Thurman, Maylen Cook, Hoot Wilson and the others…they don't show up on anybody's social register. But they're all good men; men who would do anything in the world for me. And I have to tell you. The look on their face when I asked them was priceless. Every one of them acted like I had bestowed knighthood on them. They were honored. Truly honored. I'm not sure I can properly explain it, but it was a pretty extraordinary thing."

John responded with a slow, intentional nod. He understood.

"Now, on the other hand…I ask the same thing to my buddies back in Nashville…it would be, 'let me check my schedule and get back with you,' and 'how long of a drive is it to Watervalley.' So, on the groomsmen choice, I have no regrets. Other than the fact that none of them may be willing to do it now that I'm leaving."

John laughed. "I wouldn't sweat it, sport. Those kinds of relationships aren't water thin."

I wanted to change the subject. "And since we're on the topic of relationships. How goes it with Ann?"

At first, John was silent, as if he were contemplating his answer. He leaned back in his chair and inhaled deeply, his eyes probing the far corners of the room. When he spoke, his voice carried an unusual gentleness. "It took me a while to figure it out, Luke. But now I know what's troubled me about Ann."

"I'm all ears."

He looked squarely at me and spoke resolutely. "Ann is perfect. She's pretty, she's smart, she's funny. She's completely at home in her own skin and no doubt about it, I'm in love with her."

I shrugged. "Sooooo, what's the issue?"

"The point is, I finally realized that while I was ready for another love like Molly, I wasn't so sure I was ready for another loss like Molly."

Immediately, I understood. I realized that John had lived the unthinkable. He had lost his life companion far short of a complete lifetime. When I thought of Christine and me, I only thought of the many years ahead of us. My mind simply wouldn't allow me to consider any other reality. I'm sure that John had done the same. But

Molly had died. For the longest time, he had simply been unable to cope. Ann had breathed new life into his world. Yet, he knew that the unthinkable could happen again. Perhaps more than ever before, I saw the emotional depth of my good friend.

"So, where does that leave things?"

John sharpened his gaze at me and his mouth slowly formed an artful grin. "Good question." He offered nothing more.

He stood, signaling his imminent departure.

"Look, sport. Keep your head up. People will need some time to get used to the idea, but they'll come around. It's all like a fog. A wind will come through and blow it all away."

"You think so?"

"Sure. You know, after a decade or so."

"That's what I like about you, John. Ever the optimist."

"Well, all kidding aside, this may sound a little odd coming from me, but by all means, Luke, follow your dreams. Make your plans and don't look back. Just know this. Sometimes, when we plan, God laughs."

I paused and mulled over his words for a long, reflective moment. In time, I exhaled and spoke in a low voice of acknowledgement. "You're right, John. That does sound odd coming from you."

"Thanks, smartass."

"No, really, it's good. A little on the profound side, maybe. Especially for you."

"I can be profound."

"So, it seems. And all this time I thought you were just another pretty face."

He grinned warily. We shook hands and, as I walked him to the door, a thought occurred to me.

"Do me a favor and try to explain things to Ann. Maybe she can soften things up with the rest of the staff."

"Don't sweat it, Luke. If they didn't like you, they wouldn't be so pissed."

"Nicely put. You're a brick as always."

"Hey, I guess I'll see you Friday night at the big party."

"Yeah, that's right. Might want to go easy on the food prep. Attendance may be dropping off sharply."

"I doubt it. Free food and an open bar. They'll show. Meanwhile, you stand your ground."

"Easier said than done but, probably good advice."

We reached my office door. Before opening it, John turned to me. "But just in case, if standing your ground doesn't work, you might want to consider hiding under the porch like a kicked dog."

I shut the door behind him and leaned against it. With the wedding only a few weeks away, I was wondering what the next days would bring. It didn't look promising.

Chapter 37

AN UNEXPECTED VISIT

Christine and I talked on her front porch that evening to well past twilight. The story had roared across the whole of Watervalley. It seemed she was handling the situation far better than I. Over the years she had weathered the storms that erupted when personal choices didn't parse with Watervalley public opinion. In her high school days, she had been an All-State basketball player. She was offered full scholarships to Tennessee and Vanderbilt but instead had chosen Agnes Scott, a small school in Georgia where her mother had gone. Many in town wanted her to play on the big stage for a national championship and acted personally wounded when she decided differently. They didn't suffer in silence.

I was heartened by her resolve that we were making the right choice. But secretly, I had reservations. My situation was different. I was their doctor, not an athlete who had garnered a healthy dose of local pride. My leaving affected them personally. I drove home that night fearful that the journey of the next several weeks before the wedding might be a rather awkward and lonely one.

The next morning, I received a phone call from Luther Whitmore, editor of the local paper, *The Village Voice*. Luther had historically been a rather acerbic character who cared a lot for facts and little for feelings. He printed the truth, period. Those who didn't like it could find a support group, a liquor store, or God. But Luther and I had history. I was more than just his doctor.

Luther was like most human beings in that he had reached adulthood with two hundred and six bones. In his case, two hundred and five of them were snake-biting mean. But in our dealings, I had uncovered his one bone of compassion. Between us was not so much a friendship as it was a bond. The net of our relationship was that I greatly admired Luther, and he regarded me with extended gratitude. So, when I got the phone call from him on Tuesday morning, he likely expressed something to me that he had never said in his entire forty years of editorial life.

"Luke, how do you want me to handle this?"

The front-page article of the Wednesday morning paper cast my departure in as fair a light as possible. Luther did an admirable job of capturing my great reluctance at leaving yet empathetically detailed the importance of the research with which I had been tasked. The story even suggested that my selection should be seen as a point of pride for the community. I had grand hopes that this would quell much of the angst as well as the disappointed smiles I was receiving. The result was mixed.

I had met with the clinic staff on Tuesday afternoon and once again apologized for the manner in which they learned the news. I did my best to explain my decision. They all politely nodded their understanding and offered the appropriate words of congratulations, but it seemed clear that below the surface was a genuine sense of loss. For the balance of the week, the daily routine continued, but there seemed to be fewer smiles, less friendly banter, and a kind of clipped formality to all the exchanges.

A few of my patients were bluntly inquisitive, inquiring in incredulous tones as to why I wanted to leave. Others were quietly courteous. Admittedly, even these were disheartening. Patient relationships that had once been marked by an amused familiarity were now framed with reserve, awkwardness, and arrested gestures. Most said nothing, which, unfortunately, said everything.

In many ways, it seemed as if the clock had been rewound, and I once again felt the exile and loneliness of the first few weeks after my arrival in Watervalley. During the evenings when I wasn't with Christine, I endeavored to busy myself with the final details of the honeymoon trip, the eventual packing and moving of my things, and searching online for a place to live in Nashville. Admittedly, all of these actions seemed surreal, as if in some way part of me thought it would not happen. And more than anything, I desperately wished I could talk to Connie. She was still away in Chicago and, per Estelle, would not return until Friday morning. Life was truly in the doldrums. The looming reality of what the engagement party on Friday night might bring began to absorb me with a smothering trepidation.

But then late Friday afternoon, an odd thing occurred.

Polly came by the clinic. She didn't want an appointment and simply asked Nancy if she could meet with me in my office. I agreed, rose from my chair, and walked to the door. When I opened it, Polly was standing there, preparing to knock. I smiled and invited her into have a seat. She entered, and I closed the door behind her. However, after only two steps she stopped and turned to me. I wasn't prepared for what followed.

Polly had always struck me as haughty, one whose best attempts at friendliness yielded little more than cold cordiality. Her tight urbanity was always attended with an air of social judgment and seasoned indifference. But the woman standing before me was none of those things. Her face was framed in a fragile, transparent, almost affectionate gaze.

"Dr. Bradford, there's really no need for me to sit. I simply wanted to come by to thank you for taking care of me this last year and to wish you the best with your new position."

My stunned reaction was poorly masked. "Um, well, thank you, Polly. That's very kind of you." A difficult silence followed in which her kind gaze only grew warmer, and I stammered like a truant schoolboy. I felt a frantic need to assure her. "Listen, the mayor has already begun a search for my replacement, so hopefully there won't be any significant gaps in ongoing care."

Polly listened attentively but then briefly looked down with an amused smile that was patient, thoughtful, resolved. "I'm not concerned, Dr. Bradford. I'll be fine."

I nodded, searching her face, trying to grasp and understand this baffling change in her demeanor. But she remained silent, regarding me with a soft and undemanding gratefulness. She seemed unassumingly small and frail. "Polly, I've kept good records of your visits, so whoever follows should be able to come up to speed quickly."

She pressed her lips together in a reflective smile, seemingly suppressing some secret amusement. My eyes tightened, searching. She discerned this and after a moment, offered a pursed nod of resignation.

"You have been very kind to me, Dr. Bradford. But I haven't been completely forthright with you."

I slowly folded my arms, a reflexive gesture of attention and concern.

"You see," she continued. "I'm quite certain I'm suffering from dementia. My mother had it, and her mother had it. So, it seems to be an inevitability. At first, I thought it was just age. But then I found myself taking a walk around the neighborhood, and I couldn't remember how to get back home. My friends at Bridge Club began to notice it, and instead of saying anything, they quietly decided to dissolve the group. I guess they thought it was kinder than telling me I was losing my noodle and making the game intolerable for them."

I shrugged. "Surely that's not the case."

"Oh, I'm quite certain it is," she said with amused resignation. "Nobody wants to be around someone whose mind is slipping. Dementia is a natural repellant."

I was at a loss for words. Of all the hours I had spent with Polly, I had not picked up on the signs. I had let my emotions about her prevail, regarding her with short indifference. In that moment, I felt an unbridgeable gap between us. She continued, speaking reflectively.

"You know, there's an old rhyme that goes,

'*Death leaves a heartache no one can heal.*

Love leaves a memory no one can steal.'

The best parts of what I have of my life are my memories of the years with Clayton. So, I guess the old jingle isn't true," she said, gushing a kind of tragic, ironic laugh. "Now, I won't even have those anymore."

"Polly, I'm so sorry. You know there are treatments available; medications, mental exercises, and even some theoretical diets that can help."

"I know Dr. Bradford. And I've read about all of them. But they're just a temporary stall. Eventually, the condition will take over. Look, you've been kind, and I have been unfair. I simply wanted to come by and thank you and wish you the best."

"Well, again. Thank you for that. But I was only doing my job. And now I fear that I wasn't doing it very well. In the time remaining, I wish you would let me try and see what we can figure out to help you."

"It's not necessary," she said shyly, clearly appreciative of the offer. She looked to the side for a moment, obviously contemplating some thought in want of surfacing. "Can I offer you a bit of advice, Dr. Bradford?"

"Certainly."

"I've thought a lot about my life lately, and I've come to realize that when it comes to happiness, for most of us, our minds are not much engaged with the present. We let remembrance and anticipation occupy most of our joyful thoughts. We don't know how to find delight in the moment, and yet we observe the same life at a distance, and our imagination believes it to be desirable. But perhaps worst of all, we all secretly hold the fear that our happiness may never be found but fervently believe that others possess it. For most of my life, I've always thought of myself as being a half-step outside of the circle. And perhaps I was. But now, it all seems so silly."

Having said this, she paused, and I got the sense that she was no longer looking at me, but rather through me and far beyond, her mind cascading over a thousand sounds, a thousand conversations, a thousand sunsets. Her peaceful continence of a minute earlier had dissolved into a face that was distant, confused, lost.

"Polly?"

My voice pulled her back, and for a second, she seemed to be gathering herself, opening her eyes widely as if to rally her thoughts. "Anyway, Dr. Bradford. My point is this, of the opportunities, the blessings life gives you, make a selection and be content. Have no regrets, Dr. Bradford. Because in time, your regrets will consume you."

I nodded my understanding. She continued. "I will miss you, but I admire you for following your passion. We all want to live an extraordinary life. I hope that when you are my age, you will look back and feel that you have done so."

Having said this, she took my hand and clasped it between hers in a brief squeeze of affirmation. I could do nothing more than smile at her with a warm regard. Considering the long parade of disappointed comments and disheartened glances I had endured over the week, it was hard to conceive that the one shining voice of encouragement I would receive would come from Polly Shropshire.

I exhaled deeply, uncertain of the moment. "Polly, are you sure you don't want to sit and talk for a bit. I've got time."

"No," she said with retiring politeness. "You have a big evening ahead of you, and there's no need for me to keep you from it."

"Well, I know for a fact you're on the guest list. So, I hope you can come."

She looked at me with a rather sad-sweet musing. "Perhaps. In either case, give my best to your beautiful fiancée. I'm sure it will be a splendid affair."

"I hope so. But I will confess, I have my concerns. My departure hasn't been universally appreciated."

Polly offered a dismissive shrug. "Oh, piddle, Dr. Bradford. You'll be fine. Calm seas don't make a skilled sailor."

I responded with a wide-eyed nod of acknowledgment. "Good advice, I'm sure."

With this, she stepped toward the door in a signal of departure. I opened it and spoke one last time. "Polly, take care of yourself."

"Don't worry about me, Dr. Bradford. I have my routine and a few memories still. And as well, I have my medications. I've been making plans on what to do. I'll be fine."

Polly stood for a moment, seemingly searching my eyes. She was smiling gently with that musing and tranquil expression touched with sadness that people have when they remember lost faces and long-ago laughter and the pureness of old joy. She turned and departed, and I reluctantly closed the door behind her, listening to it shut with a frail click.

Despite the simple delight of having at least one soul express congratulations regarding my decision, the whole episode with Polly was odd and unsettling. For the longest time, I sat in my chair and stared out the window, doing my best to make sense of it. Eventually, I looked at my watch and realized that I needed to get home to shower and dress for the big gala. I methodically gathered my things and turned out the lights, filled with a cautious excitement about the evening's celebration. But deep, deep within...I was haunted.

Chapter 38

A GRAND AFFAIR

The party was being held at Ravenoak, the home of Franklin and Baby Beth Stilwell. Located on Summerfield Road, Ravenoak was an imposing antebellum mansion that distantly emerged at the end of an arrow-straight driveway lined with ancient oaks. Replete with massive front columns, crowded boxwoods, and a tightly manicured lawn, it had been an equestrian farm of considerable acreage for decades. Some history buffs believe that General Grant slept there. Others claim that he only stopped to ask directions. All agree that it probably wasn't for the way back to Ohio.

Despite her name, Baby Beth Stilwell was in her fifties and well showed it. She was the youngest of five girls, and the childhood name had simply endured the decades. A slim and somewhat weathered blonde, she and her attorney husband Franklin had insisted on hosting the gathering. Baby Beth was a vivacious, outgoing sort who would readily confess that she and Franklin had more money than taste. Noting that her decorating choices had taken shabby-chic to an art form, most tended to agree. Notably, however, she gravitated to the upper crust more so than the crumbs and lived under the mantra that you could never be too thin or have too much silverware. Her audaciousness and approachability had allowed her to float successfully among the Watervalley blue bloods even though she had come from a dirt-poor family in Mississippi, a fact she often alluded to with self-effacing charm.

Known for her rather thick moonlight-on-the-old-plantation drawl, she had just the right balance of panache and plainness to deftly negotiate the broad range of social strata who would be in attendance. Several of Madeline Chambers' longtime friends who were definitive WFF's, Watervalley First Families, had expressed an interest in playing hosts. But Madeline wisely knew that those chosen few would have pushed for more exclusivity on the guests list. The people of the valley were my patients, and my patients were my invitees. I had quietly let it be known that if they weren't included, neither should I be. The Stilwells and their farm made for the perfect solution.

The event was held behind the old mansion where the steps of a wide brick terrace swept down to a broad velvet expanse of lawn. A large, open tent to shelter the food had been assembled on one side of the sprawling rear yard while across the way a wooden stage for the band had been constructed. Dozens upon dozens of tables with neatly aligned chairs sat in orderly rows upon the open span of lawn in the middle. They were covered in white cloth, a vase of beautiful flowers, and a multitude of flickering candles. Around the distant perimeter, an endless array of Chinese lanterns and twinkling lights had been laced among the trees and landscaping. On scale alone, the entire scene was instantly impressive. Yet, something about the incredible panoramic setting lent it an ethereal, almost magical feel. As twilight fell, an indescribable swell of excitement and energy permeated the evening. The world seemed dressed for a grand occasion.

Although the affair was catered with mounding, cluttered food stations, and a sizeable open bar, as they began to arrive, the plain and accommodating people of Watervalley also brought covered dishes with them, a gesture of hospitality that they innocently thought appropriate. Baby Beth quickly and graciously instructed the staff to set up a couple of long folding tables in the food tent. These were promptly covered with white cloths and gatherings of flowers. Thus, along with the elaborate displays of shrimp and cheeses and prosciutto hors de oeuvres, there was also an extensive array of lima beans, pineapple casseroles, Jell-O molds, and congealed salad with tiny marshmallows. As well, several of the rustics made the journey from the parking area in the front field and rounded the back corner of the house toting large coolers of beer. Everyone was proud to be there.

Christine was as gorgeous as ever and floated among the crowd effortlessly, her every movement full of faultless and distinctive grace. She was animated, relaxed, clearly in her element. I did my best to do the same, grandly shaking hands and conversing with people whose names always seemed to escape me in the moment. But it was exhausting. As well, all the congratulations were accompanied by a kind of awkward reserve and small talk seemed to be in short supply. I was leaving, and the knowledge of this was written on the faces of all who spoke to me.

In time I discreetly slipped away and blended into one of the food table lines. But I had chosen poorly. I found myself behind Lester Clancy, the carriage owning octogenarian who was going to drive Christine and me away from the reception. We spoke briefly, but he quickly exhausted my ability to pay attention. Finally, he proceeded forward. But in the process of filling his plate, he moved so slowly I probably could have declared him legally dead. Mountain ranges had been formed in less time. And to top it off, as I waited, I gradually realized that the old fellow was apparently cursed with weapons-grade flatulence, a troubling harbinger regarding the first moments of the honeymoon.

I managed to find a vacant table in one of the darker, distant corners of the yard only to realize that Maggie Chambers, Christine's grandmother was staring at me from a distance. She had me in radar lock and was closing rapidly. Despite her five-foot-four-inch height, she walked with a rather imperial stride. I started to eat faster. Previous encounters with Maggie included flannel shirts and farm boots. But tonight, she was elegantly turned out with a startling tilt toward the edgy; big earrings, layers of pearls, and a black dress with a dangerously plunging neckline that was likely to keep all of the old fellows at the party on their toes. This was a Maggie I had never seen, a blossom that was not yet content to fade. It was our first meeting since learning of her generosity. So, I hastily swallowed a sausage ball and prepared to assume my gratitude game face.

Upon her approach, I stood and smiled as if I hadn't previously noticed her. She was carrying a martini glass and curiously, never broke stride, embracing me in an enthusiastic hug followed by a brisk kiss on the cheek. With Maggie, it was always a game of one-upmanship in which the last person off balance was the loser. Her unabashed show of affection had thrown me, but only momentarily.

"Hi. I'm Luke Bradford. I don't think we've met. But I'm pretty sure I know your evil twin."

Maggie's face creased into a foxy grin. "My, you are witty." There was a flowing and elegant charm to her voice. Maggie was revealing her theatrical side.

"Well, I do appreciate the hug, although I can't help but think it was done for show. Pandering to the crowd, eh, Maggie?"

Her cunning regard continued. She spoke with dry authority. "If I was doing it for show, handsome, I would have grabbed your ass."

Shock factor was one of the prime arrows in Maggie's quiver. I was undaunted.

"I'm sure that's a Kodak moment Christine will want for the wedding album."

She demurred, clearly noting that her shot had missed and took a sip of her martini. "You're not as much fun as when we first met."

"That's because early on I didn't recognize you. I mistook you for an attack dog."

Maggie grinned, pressing her lips together in a moment of deliberation. "Christine said you could be a charmer." She stepped beside me and gazed back across the lawn; body language that suggested a cease-fire. Presently she was silent and followed my example of staring out across the crowd. In the near distance, the band was tuning up, and the loud and lively party goers were beginning to gravitate in that direction. Despite our history of hostile exchange, her simple gesture of rubbing her shoulder against mine made it easy to engage in conversation that was effortless and intimate.

She absently ran her finger around the rim of her glass. "So, why are you out here on the periphery like the ugliest girl at the dance?"

"Given my pending departure, I've taken the notion that the guests would enjoy themselves more freely in my absence."

"I think you're being a little hard on yourself."

For some reason, confession came easy. "The truth is, I've never been much of one for small talk. I mean, I like these people...I really do. I just don't always know what to say to them."

She nodded. "A lot of the people of Watervalley don't have a lot to say. Unfortunately, sometimes you have to listen for a long time before figuring that out."

I looked to the side and raised a curious eyebrow toward her. "Now that's interesting. Do I detect a note of condescension in the wind? I thought these people were your tribe."

"They are my tribe. But you also might notice that I chose to live fifteen hundred miles away."

"I thought that was because the last time I checked, Watervalley doesn't have a beach."

"True. But the main thing I have here are memories. Mind you; memories are a good thing. But I don't want a life where they outnumber the discoveries. And often times I do miss this place. After all, I have a husband and a son buried here. But there is life beyond Watervalley."

"I would certainly agree." I let that small bit of common ground rest in the air for a moment. The revelry in the distance was beginning to escalate, but we seemed a world away from it. I spoke in earnest. "I'll admit, I have grown to envy Christine's sense of roots, the strength and security of knowing there's a place on earth that will always be home. There's something to be said for that."

Still facing the distant crowd, Maggie wrapped her arm around mine, an expression of affirmation and confidence. She spoke in a relaxed, elegant voice, richly enunciating her words.

"The funny part about that is that after we buried her father, we couldn't get Christine to cross the county line for years. She hid in Atlanta and wouldn't even come home for Christmas. It took her mother getting sick to bring her back. Then you showed up and overnight, it was like she came alive. She fell in love with Watervalley again, she fell in love with the people here again, and she definitely fell in love with you. I've never seen that girl so smitten. She was nuts about you from the first minute."

"Hmm," I grunted skeptically. "She must have kept that detail to herself. Granted, the Bradford charm eventually won her over. But as I recall, she did a pretty good job of playing hard to get for quite a while."

Maggie shook her head lightly. "She was just protecting her heart. After the day you disrupted her class, she came home that night and ranted nonstop to her mother about what a jerk you were, how rude you had been, and all the things she wished she would have said in the moment. Madeline texted me later that night and said, 'I think she's met the one.'"

I cut my eyes toward her, confused. "I am definitely not getting the logic here."

"Most men don't," she said with a casual shrug. "Madeline knew because she had never seen Christine so worked up about a guy. And, in all fairness, it was probably a pretty good tell that several times during her tirade, Christine mentioned that you had incredible blue eyes. You must have hit her like a lightning bolt."

I stood for a moment, absorbing everything Maggie was telling me. "Well, I can tell you from my side of the narrative that I had a life-threatening crush on her instantly. Christine Chambers has occupied a part of my brain ever since. And, I must say, while it's delightful to hear all of this now, the version of the story you're telling is a pretty significant re-write from the one I remember."

"Does it matter?"

"Not in the least."

"Good."

Maggie tightened her hold on my arm, clearly content in the moment. But given that reality, a thought occurred to me.

"You know, as I remember it, this whole lightning bolt condition was not contagious with some of the other Chambers women."

She understood my point, smiling modestly. "I love my granddaughter, Luke. I needed to be sure about you."

"And has that box been checked?"

"Oh, I well think so," she said dismissively.

I offered her a pleased smile and gazed at the distant crowd. A long silence ensued.

"You know, Luke. Now would be a good time for you to mention how much you adore me." Having said this, she winked precociously.

For a moment, I looked at her blankly, pondering my answer. Maggie Chambers was certainly unabashed and clearly well-schooled in knowing how to get what she wanted. But I couldn't resist the opportunity. "Well, let's give the storyline some time. I wouldn't want the plot to develop too quickly."

She glanced up at me with a mordant, leering smile. "What I'm asking, doctor smart alec, is, are we good?"

I didn't answer immediately. Perhaps there was still some residual angst that Maggie had so convincingly fooled me for such a long time. But, she was endeavoring to bury the hatchet... this time figuratively and not in me, as was her norm. Still gazing distantly, I reached with my opposing hand and patted her arm. "We're good."

After a short silence, I added. "Besides, Maggie, I have to say. I certainly owe you a debt of gratitude for enabling me to take the research position. It's a very generous offer."

"You're welcome," she said with a pleased diplomacy. "If you felt trapped here Luke, eventually you would be miserable. Christine would feel the burden of that as well. I didn't want that. Not for her, not for either of you."

"Understood. But I have to ask, why all the subterfuge?"

Maggie flipped her hand at me in dismissal. "Oh, allow an old thespian her fun. A little bit of theater just adds some spice to life."

It wasn't a particularly satisfying answer. But it was an answer. I exhaled a long sigh.

"Well, Maggie...fair enough. But I'm just going to say it, you're quite the drama queen."

"Guilty as charged."

"But in the future, is it okay if I don't attend every performance?"

She laughed, spontaneously lifting her hand to her mouth. "I will say this, Luke Bradford, if you're anything, you're clever. If you're half as good at research, I think Christine's dowry will be well expended."

"Thanks. Although I suspect you are only one of six people here this evening that think that."

"That many, huh? Who besides immediate family?"

"My friend, Matthew for starters. Although I think he has mixed feelings. And my old college professor and new boss, Dr. Jackson Bray. He's coming tonight. In fact, I probably need to be getting back to see if he's arrived yet. If word gets out about who he is, there could be a lynch mob."

"Sounds best you should," she said tactfully. Then with some dramatic pluck, she added, "So, come on sailor. Buy me a drink first."

I looked at her artfully. "What's in it for me?"

"About $75,000," she said bluntly.

"Point taken." Arm in arm, we began to walk toward the crowd.

"Oh, and Luke. I have one more favor to ask."

"And what might that be?"

"Promise me a dance later."

"What kind of dance?"

"A slow one, of course. I don't want the paramedics involved in the evening."

"I'll treat it like a summons from the Pope."

"Good." Then, after a few more steps, she added, "Would it be okay if I do grab your ass then?"

I stopped abruptly, clearly dismayed. "Can I just tell you how disturbing that is on so many levels?"

"Oh, chill out, blue eyes. I'm just kidding. But you have to remember. I grew up here. There are still a few old bats from high school that I want to get an eye full of me dancing with the best-looking man at the party."

"Well, if that's the case," I said with detached shrewdness. "Maybe I should grab your ass?" I was about to laugh out loud when Maggie stopped and studied me with an air of contemplation.

"Let me think about it."

Chapter 39

A PECULIAR QUEST

U pon returning to the crowd, I immediately found Dr. Bray talking with Baby Beth. In his mid-fifties, Jackson Bray looked every bit the distinguished doctor. He was tall, immaculately dressed and carried himself with a rather well-washed urbanity. Baby Beth's socialite radar homed in on this unknown newcomer immediately. As I approached, they were in an animated conversation with Baby Beth embracing his arm and disclosing a jovial confidence, melting him with her infectious laughter. Dr. Bray seemed to enjoy the moment.

"Oh, there you are, Luke!" Baby Beth said gushingly. "I was just admonishing this handsome fellow for taking you away from us. But I don't think it's had a bit of effect on him. He's just been bragging about how brilliant you are and what a great job you will do."

Dr. Bray and I shook hands heartily. There passed between us a kind of amused, unspoken understanding. We both knew that the evening would be a potential minefield of anti-departure prods. He seemed quite un-rattled and took Baby Beth's teasing in stride. Fortunately, Baby Beth, who had the attention span of a bumble bee, saw some social prize across the way and waved to him wildly. "You boys excuse me. So nice to meet you, Jackson!"

Dr. Bray responded politely, barely saying the words before Baby Beth had glided away.

We engaged in comfortable small talk for a few minutes, after which, he asked me a rather curious question. "Do you by chance know an Estelle Pillow? I think she's from Watervalley."

"Yes, I know her quite well. You two are acquainted, I presume?"

"Very much so. Dr. Pillow is a little on the flamboyant side, but while she was at Vanderbilt, her research on enantioselective bifunctional catalysis using hydrogen bonding was absolutely groundbreaking."

Instantly, it seemed, a forgotten language returned to me. The vocabulary of academia had been hibernating, replaced by such phrases as "he up and ran off." And yet, I completely understood the processes that Dr. Bray was describing and how they contributed to the studies of disease. It was an absolute moment of clarity regarding the distinction between the two worlds I was straddling.

"Luke?" Dr. Bray's voice woke me from my temporary fog.

"Oh, sorry. I was thinking about Estelle and how her world has changed. It would seem that her groundbreaking discoveries are now with macarons and tarte tropezienne. She owns the local bakery."

"I see." He paused, contemplating this reality for a moment. "Well, I guess people need to follow their passions. For an academic like myself, though, it seems like a waste of a brilliant mind."

I had no answer for him and could only nod reflectively.

"Anyway. Do you think she's here tonight? I'd love to catch up with her."

"If she is," I said wryly. "We'll certainly know it soon enough."

He stared at me blankly, clearly not grasping my assertion.

"Estelle has a talent for making her presence known."

He lifted his head and mouthed a silent "ahh."

As if on que, an audacious shriek exploded from behind us. "Jackson Bray, you big teddy-bear! Come and put some loving on me!"

Spontaneously, we both turned to find Estelle making a beeline toward my reticent and stoic professor, smothering him in an all-embracing hug. The normally reserved dean yielded to her both in body and demeanor; evidence that his regard for her went past academic respect. Candidly, he seemed in awe of Estelle.

But the greatest delight of the moment was in Estelle's wake, her sister, Connie Thompson. She stepped toward me wearing a warm, affectionate smile, a look that immediately conveyed an eager openness. It seemed that the Connie I knew was back. She was singularly focused on me, oblivious to all the animated antics of Estelle's conversation with Dr. Bray. After an instinctive hug, she held my shoulders in a moment of pure adoration. "How are you doing, sweetheart?"

"I'm good, Mama T. Maybe the bigger question is, how are you doing?'

"I'm alright. It's been a troublesome past few weeks, but I'm better now. We'll find a time soon to talk about it."

I immediately took her arm and gently began to lead her away from the crowd, speaking with quiet authority. "I have a better idea. Let's talk about it now. You've had me pretty worried."

Thankfully, Connie readily conceded to my appeal. We found a table in the distant shadows of yard, and I pulled two chairs side-by-side. I was uncertain where to begin and opted for the informal. "So, how was the flight back from Chicago?"

She stared at me blankly, as if the question had caught her off guard. She quickly offered a weary smile. "Terrifying. The flight took so many dips and turns I thought the pilot was skywriting something. And on top of that, the passengers were a rowdy bunch of young hoodlums. Next time I'll be sure to request a non-high-school-senior trip flight."

We laughed lightly. I continued. "And did you have a good visit with Rayford?"

"I did. It's always good to see my boy. But as you might guess, I had some other things to attend to. The real confession is that I wasn't just in Chicago. During the week I flew to Texas and Ohio also. It's been quite an adventure."

"Texas and Ohio? Good grief, Connie. What on earth for?"

"Well, it all started with that DNA test you gave me."

Her words took me a moment to assimilate. "The one I gave you for Christmas? What about it?"

"I had forgotten the silly thing. Then about six weeks ago I came across it in the bureau drawer and decided to send it in."

"And?"

"What it told me made no sense. According to the results, I'm twenty-two percent Portuguese."

"Portuguese? Really?"

I sat back in my chair, dumbfounded. "You're right. That doesn't make any sense. That means that either one of your parents was half or one of your grandparents was practically one-hundred percent Portuguese."

"And none were. All of daddy's people were from right here in Watervalley. Been here for generations. Mama's parents, Grandfather and Grandmother Coleman were from Ohio. Their ancestors had been slaves from Western Africa. No one ever mentioned having an ounce of Portuguese blood in the mix. So, it got me to wondering." She paused, her face framed in apprehension.

"Wondering…what?"

"Maybe I was adopted. I was ten when Estelle was born, so I witnessed first-hand Mama being pregnant with her. But I never recall seeing a picture of Mama when she was pregnant with me."

"I don't know, Connie. That seems to be a bit of a reach. Granted, it was the fifties, but babies just didn't appear overnight without somebody taking notice."

"That's true. But daddy served during the Korean War. He stayed stateside the entire time, stationed in Fort Hood, Texas with the First Cavalry Division. He and Mama had been married three years when he was drafted for a two-year enlistment. After a year, Mama couldn't take being apart anymore, so she moved to Texas and the nearby town of Killeen and worked as a waitress. She was gone for eleven months and I was born during that time. So, no one in Watervalley ever saw her pregnant with me."

"Still doesn't prove anything."

"I know. But that's why I went to Texas. The base hospital where I was born is long gone, replaced in the sixties. There were no

358

documents to be found there. So, I went to Austin to the state archives to find my birth records."

"And?"

"I found a certificate of live birth that shows me as the daughter of Thomas and Maylene Pillow."

"So, that settles it, then. You weren't adopted."

"Correct. But, I'm still twenty-two percent Portuguese. And that leaves one disturbing possibility."

I spoke hesitantly. "That maybe...Thomas Pillow wasn't your real father."

"Umm hmm," Connie confirmed dryly. "It's been a hard prospect for me to swallow, but I guess anything is possible."

"You do know how to figure that one out, don't you?"

"Yes. I explained everything to Estelle, and she sent a DNA sample off earlier this week. If her profile comes back the same, it will mean we both share the same mother and father."

"And if it doesn't, then I guess you'll have your answer."

"Yes. It has had me pretty worried. But, I think I've come to terms with it. That is, should the worst come to be true."

I nodded silently, somewhat at a loss as to how to reassure her. "Connie, look. How you feel about this is your business. But it doesn't change anything about who you are, regardless of the outcome."

"I know you're right, Luke. And candidly, I'm almost a little too old to let it bother me too much. But still, I would be lying if I said I don't think about it."

"Wait for Estelle's results before you travel too far down that path."

She nodded, forcing an accommodating smile. But another question struck me. "So, why did you travel to Ohio?"

"Mama was born in Wilberforce, Ohio. Grandpapa was there in school at Payne Theological Seminary at the time, just before he came here to be an AME Minister. I couldn't find any birth records online, so I went to Columbus to visit the Vital Records office in person. There was no certificate on file, but they advised me to go to the county where she was born. So, I rented a car and drove to Xenia, Ohio. Wilberforce Seminary is in Green County, and Xenia is the county seat. That turned up nothing as well. But the clerk there told me not to be surprised. A child born at home by midwives back in the twenties to a poor seminary couple was likely never recorded. So, that was a dead end. I've been through all of Mama's old papers, but there is nothing in them either, certainly no copy of a birth certificate."

"Well, do you think there is a chance your mother was adopted? Maybe that's where the Portuguese blood comes from."

"The thought has occurred to me. But Mama and Grandmamma Coleman were the spitting image of each other. Granted, Mama's black skin was more porcelain. But they could have been twins. Add that to the fact that she and Grandpappa Coleman were very humble, devout people…I just have to dismiss the idea that any hanky-panky was in the mix of that situation."

Unfortunately, Connie's insights and her dismissive confidence about her grandparents were quite convincing, leaving me to agree with her conclusion that the likely variable had to do with her biological father. Estelle's DNA results would tell the ugly truth. For Connie's sake, I wanted it not to be sor. My mind rambled, grasping at other possibilities. "Did you look for your grandparent's birth certificates in Ohio? Maybe that might tell you something?"

"Like what, perhaps?"

"I don't know. I guess I'm just grabbing at straws here."

"Well, to answer your question, no, I didn't. But I grew up around them. I know neither of them was Portuguese."

"Yeah, good point," I said reflectively. "Connie, I'm sorry. I just thought the DNA test would be a fun gift. I had no idea it would stir up such a can of worms."

She reached over and patted me on the hand. "Don't you worry about that one bit. It has been upsetting, but it's also been a blessing, visiting all the places where my family came from and wondering what their life was like. In a way, it has made me feel closer to them. Besides, I can't imagine them loving me any more than they did."

Having said this, she lifted her chin and regarded me with her familiar stern persona. "So, regarding other business, I hear you are leaving us?"

I spent the next few minutes explaining everything that happened including the offer and the money. "I wanted to talk to you before it got out, but you had already left town. Then Walt betrayed my confidence, the little weasel. Since then he has avoided me like the plague. I'm still pretty miffed at him."

"You need to let that go, honey."

"Oh, I will. In a decade or two. But right now, the only thing I would enjoy more than seeing Walt Hickman gamma ray zapped by a stealth bomber is to see Walt Hickman gamma ray zapped by a stealth bomber in slow motion."

Connie ignored this. "Luke, dear...if this research position is what you want, then that's what you should do. I'll miss you. But I'll still be happy for you."

"Thanks, Connie. You may not find many converts to that way of thinking, though."

"How's John taking it?"

"Fine, I think. But he did say something rather odd."

"Which was?"

"He made a comment about how God has a way of changing your plans. Let's face it; John is not one to bring the almighty into the conversation, at least not in that context."

"True. I think he actually tried to read the Bible once, but when he realized that the books named John weren't about him, he lost interest."

"By the way, have you seen him tonight?"

"Only from a distance. Why?"

"Nothing, really. I always get a little concerned when he has the opportunity to fall under the influence of Bacchus."

"He was with Ann, and, as I recall, he wasn't on all fours."

"Well, that's a good start."

By now the band was in full tilt, and people were beginning to dance, some with rhythm, some with grace, most with neither. The female lead singer, who was actually quite good, turned out to be one of the high school math teachers. She belted out one country song after another, singing from the heart and a little through the nose.

I rose from the table, noting to Connie that I probably needed to find Christine and mingle a little more. She stood as well but grabbed my arm.

"Luke, I need to ask you a question about another matter."

"Sure."

"This new fellow, Matthew House. You've gotten to know him pretty well, haven't you?

"I guess." Having said this, a curiosity came to me. "Connie, have you not met Matthew yet."

She looked away and spoke in a voice of contrition. "No, I'm afraid to say I haven't. I know it's not very neighborly of me. But he almost never comes by the bakery, and I guess I have to admit, Society Hill still gives me the heebie-jeebies. I haven't been able to force myself to go up there."

"So, what do you want to know about him?"

"Do you think he has any real intentions of opening the B&B back up for business?"

"I think I'd be more comfortable if you asked him that question."

"As I recall," Connie said stiffly. "It was your job on the committee to ask him that question."

"Okay, fine. Here's what I know. He didn't come here with the intention of restarting the B&B. But I think the town has grown on him, and now he may be open to the idea. Why do you ask?"

"Let's just say I've learned some things about our little newcomer. He's a man with a few secrets."

The ancestral link to Hiram Hatcher had been common knowledge for some time, so clearly Connie wasn't alluding to that. I couldn't imagine how her trip to Chicago could have yielded information about the Capone connection. But then again, Connie had a way of parsing the truth out of any situation. I feigned ignorance, not wanting to betray anything confidential. "What kind of secrets?"

Connie began to speak, but then seemed to think better of the idea. "I don't want to spread any false information until I'm one hundred percent certain. Best I hold my tongue until I know for sure."

"Well, whatever these secrets are, how do you plan on confirming them?"

Connie exhaled a deep breath, seemingly to collect her resolve. "I'm going to drive up there to that spooky old house and ask him."

Chapter 40

CASTLES IN THE AIR

As I returned to the thick of the crowd, the evening's energy and clamor had spiraled to a full, raucous crescendo, bordering on a kind of blissful pandemonium. I found Christine with drink in hand, amidst a lively gathering of handsome fellows and a few of the bridesmaids. They were tapping their feet to the heavy boom of the band and talking in riotous conversations filled with explosive laughter. Upon seeing me, she promptly abandoned them and wrapped her arms around my neck. She kissed me in an uncharacteristic public show of affection that brought out a few applauding whoops from her friends.

Her adoring smile was crafty and spontaneous. "So, where have you been hiding all evening?"

"You seem to have taken mastery of the middle ground, so I've been working the periphery."

"A lot of folks have been asking about you."

"And I've noticed that more than a few of the young men have been keeping you in steady company," I said teasingly.

"Just a few guys from high school."

"I see. So, have any of the bush hog boys changed your mind about marrying an outsider?"

"So far I haven't seen any reason to trade up. But a girl has to keep her options open, you know."

"Completely understood. Hey, before he gets away, I want to be sure you meet Dr. Bray. He's here. I spoke to him earlier."

"We've met. Estelle introduced us just before you walked up. He seems to have a rather high opinion of your intellect, Bradford. I think I heard the word brilliant bounced around."

I dismissed this, turning my gaze toward the band. "That's only because he got a good look at the woman I'm marrying."

Christine offered a rebuking smile then stepped beside me, wrapping my arm in a yielding embrace. She followed my example of watching the band and the joyous abandonment of those dancing, many of whom were notably rhythm challenged.

Before long a steady stream of well-wishers bided for our time. Invariably they gravitated toward Christine first. Her response to everyone was warm and natural, conducting all conversations with flowing ease and an engaging spontaneity. I was more characterized by a feeling of naked insecurity, repeatedly parroting the same words with as much sincerity as I could manage. Nevertheless, the evening was filled with euphoric magic, overflowing with food, music, and rapturous laughter. Time became blurred, suspended, forgotten. Consumed with a contagious joy, it seemed that everyone found themselves in the moment, reveling in a dizzying and uninhibited celebration.

At some point long past midnight, the crowd, the music, and the laughter had all faded into the mist and dew. Wrapped in the silent, dreamy flicker of Tiki lights and candles, Christine and I offered our final thanks and hugs. Exhausted, we collapsed onto the seats of my car and began the isolated, moonlit drive to her farmhouse. High above the cool air was charged with blue starlight and the great bowl of heaven provided a tender covering for our lonely passage.

Both of us were awash in a kind of warm, sublime lethargy. Christine turned toward me, curled up her legs, and rested her head and left shoulder against the back of the seat. She reached over to hold my hand and breathed a deep and luxurious sigh of contentment. Her hoarse, sleepy voice was husky, delicate, sweet.

"So, did you have fun?"

"Of course, I did. I danced with the prettiest girl at the party."

A contented smile melted across her face. "Well, aside from that, how was your evening?"

"It was interesting. Had a rather fascinating conversation with your grandmother."

"Oh, and what did you learn?"

"I learned that she knows how to wear senility like a costume. I saw a rather different side of her tonight."

Christine exhaled a small, satisfied laugh. "She said she was going to make amends with you this evening."

"She did just that. But I have to admit, it was delightful and terrifying all in the same breath."

"Maggie's a sweetheart. But I guess she can still be a little intimidating."

"She was certainly dressed to the nines tonight, maybe even a tinge on the risqué. She asked me to promise her a slow dance sometime during the evening, but it never happened. All the older fellows kept her dance card pretty full."

"I guess grandmother can be a little spirited. But I think it's all in fun. You know, a wink and a glance and you dream about romance."

I briefly looked at Christine; her guileless, sleepy face illuminated by the dashboard lights. "I wouldn't be so sure, sweetheart. There was quite a bit of gusto between your grandmother and one of the older fellows. I think she had something a little more expedient in mind."

"Oh, like what?"

"Like a drink and a dance and then you take your chance."

She shook her head in a quick note of dismissal. "You need to periscope down on that assumption, Bradford. I don't think she has anything of the sort on her radar."

I cut my eyes sharply. "Okay, fine. We'll go with your theory. But, answer this question for me. Is she staying out at the farmhouse tonight?"

Christine paused for a moment, searching. "Well, actually no. She said she was going to stay over at Betty Hudson's house tonight. Betty is an old friend, and they had some catching up to do." Having said this, she stared impassively into the darkness beyond the headlights, her uncertainty continuing. "What made you ask?"

Late in the evening, I had walked to my car because I had forgotten to grab my hostess gift when I had first arrived. I was on my way back through the dark field when I noticed Maggie Chambers in a rather passionate lip-lock with a tall, older gentleman. I skirted wide and wasn't seen. But in the still air of the night, I heard enough of the exchange to know that plans were being made for a later rendezvous. This foray into a little passion was Maggie's business and not mine to divulge, although I would never let her know it. I was definitely going to keep this knowledge in reserve in case it was needed at a future date.

368

It seemed that the cosmos was finally rewarding me for all I had endured under Maggie's theatrical capers.

I responded innocently.

"Oh, no reason. Just a lucky guess."

Christine's face was still framed in a bemused disbelief. "Her staying with a friend doesn't prove anything. Although…I suppose it is a little suspect."

"Ahhh," I said, brushing off the topic. "You're probably right." It was time for a subject change. "So, how about you? Did you have fun tonight?"

She smiled sublimely. She took my hand and held it to her cheek before softly kissing it. "Yes, Luke Bradford. I had a perfectly splendid time." Dissolving back against her seat, she exhaled a long, enchanted breath.

"Well, you certainly seemed to be in your element."

Her words were slow and affectionate. "That's because I have lived this evening a thousand times."

"I don't think I understand."

She rolled her head toward the side window. The broad, moonlit fields slipped by. Her words were solemn, reflective. "I grew up a little girl on a big farm, Luke. I had a lot of time on my hands; a lot of time to daydream. I took those daydreams and made castles out of them, castles in the air." She looked down for a moment, seemingly embarrassed at her confession, before returning her musing gaze toward the darkness.

"The years come and go. You grow up, and life happens; you go to school, you go to work… loved ones die. You cry, you laugh, you move on. Some days you live, some days you exist, and slowly each day becomes so much like the last that over time they merge into an unchanging pattern and slip away unmarked."

For a moment longer, she focused on the shadowy world stealing by before turning toward me; her face tender, warm, adoring. "Then one day there's a knock on your classroom door. But when you open it, it doesn't lead into the hallway; it leads into an entirely different world; a world you had forgotten, a world you had buried deep in the past, a world with all those castles. And a fellow is standing there with an easy smile and sky-blue eyes, and something about him makes all those memories come flooding back. So, yes. I've lived this evening a thousand times, Luke. But all those times before they were just little girl imaginings, whims, silly fantasies. You changed all that. You made them real. You made them true again." Her voice softened to barely a whisper. "Oh, Luke Bradford. I don't think it's possible for me to be a drop more in love with you."

Just as she had done with mine a few minutes earlier, I took her hand and gently kissed it. The headlights pierced into the darkness and soon I made the turn down the long driveway to the farmhouse. I walked her to the door and held her for the longest while. It was not a time for words.

After that, I made my way home, parked the Austin-Healey, and walked to the backyard to reacquaint myself with the stars. I moved leisurely. Knowing that the evening would be a late one, my next-door neighbors, the Foxes, had suggested they keep the dog-boys. I had gladly accepted the offer.

In reflection, it had been a wonderful, near-perfect evening. To see Christine so blissfully happy filled me with an unspeakable joy. Conversely, Connie's news was troubling, but not consuming. If there was infidelity on her mother's part, it would be a blow for her, but not a knock-out punch. Connie was made of sterner stuff.

Perhaps of all the people I spoke to and saw that night, I was most intrigued by two that I didn't. Neither Matthew House nor Polly Shropshire had come, and their absence bothered me. As to why, soon enough, I would have an answer for one of them.

The other would come later. Wretchedly later.

Chapter 41

INTO THE WOODS

I was awakened Saturday morning by a ding on my cell phone, a text message. I lazily reached for it on the bedside table. The time was half past ten. The text was from Matthew. It read, "Are you up for a hike today?"

After washing my face and ambling downstairs to make some coffee, I texted him back. "Sure, what time?"

"Whenever you get here," was the immediate reply.

"Be there in thirty," I responded. I dressed, ate a quick bowl of cereal, and went next door to retrieve the dogs. My thirteen-year-old neighbor, Will Fox, answered my knock and we talked briefly. Astutely, he took notice of the fact that I was about to leave again and offered for the boys to stay until I returned. Will was a great kid, albeit, a little on the nerdy side. I surmised that his day was probably more fun with them than without them. I easily agreed.

Fifteen minutes later, I was on Matthew's front porch.

He opened the door in full hiking gear and his cell phone pressed to his ear. He motioned for me to come in and I followed him to the kitchen. From the overflow of the conversation, I gathered that his children were at a friend's house and sleeping over that night. After finishing the call, he extended his hand.

"Thanks for coming. The kids are gone for the day, and I thought it might be a good opportunity to go explore the old spring house."

"Sure. Works for me."

"I've rounded up a machete and a pair of bolt cutters. Anything else you think we might need?"

"How about a nine-millimeter?"

In his mild, quiet way, Matthew smiled. "And listen to you talking all sexy."

"Yeah, well...I was also thinking some silver bullets, wooden stake, garlic necklace...the usual stuff."

"Come on, Captain Courageous. The gear is on the patio."

I followed him through the rear service door where a small backpack and the aforementioned tools sat on a small outdoor table. He strapped the bolt cutters to his pack and handed me the machete. "Here. You can carry this if it makes you feel any better."

"I'll channel my inner ninja."

"I was more hoping you would channel your inner weed-eater. The undergrowth is pretty thick down there."

"Either way."

As was often his nature, Matthew seemed preoccupied, contemplative...making him something of a difficult read for me. We stood for a moment as he seemed to be working through some private mental checklist. In time he nodded, made a head gesture toward the rear yard, and set off. I followed.

After a few steps, however, he stopped and turned toward me, his face transformed into a more engaging persona. "Listen. I should have mentioned this sooner. But I apologize for missing the party last night. My sitter bailed on me at the last minute."

"Oh, no worries," I said lightly. "Sorry, you couldn't make it. I think you would have enjoyed yourself. Several women asked about you."

He acknowledged this with a dry nod, notably not interested. We resumed our trek, walking side by side. Matthew returned to his reflective mood, but a few steps later, he spoke without breaking stride. "Well, I guess I'm curious. Any of them particularly eye-catching."

"A few of them had features that merited attention."

"Anybody I know?"

"Not sure. But they all seem to know you."

"Humph," he grunted under his breath. "They just think they know me."

"Meaning?"

He gave me a quick glance as if he hadn't meant for me to hear his last remark. His response was dismissive. "Oh, nothing. It's just that, I've got baggage."

"Well, if you need your luggage sorted, I think there's a waiting list of volunteers."

"Not helping."

"Just saying."

"Anyway, how was the band?"

"Loud."

"You know, did I hear this right? It was Sheriff Thurman's band?"

"Yup. Warren and the Blue Lights. Watervalley's finest."

A slight air of annoyance nested into Matthews's voice. "Yeah, well…Sheriff Thurman is not high on my Christmas list right now."

"Why is that?"

"He gave me a ticket the other day for going twenty-eight in a twenty-five zone."

"Really?"

"Sure did. My kids were in the car. It was a little embarrassing. I mean, Warren's talking to me with that big smile of his, and I'm sitting there thinking the whole thing is a joke. Then he hands me the ticket. Meanwhile, all these teenagers are blowing by in their pickup trucks with expired tags and boom-boom music blasting out the neighborhood. Half of them were probably drinking beer and smoking God knows what. Not that I'm bitter or anything."

"Doesn't sound like it."

"Anyway, I'm not going down without a fight."

"So, what are you going to do?"

"I'm taking it to court."

"You're not going to just pay the ticket?"

"Nope. I'm putting together an intricate legal defense plan."

"Oh, yeah? And what does that look like?"

"The main strategy is called groveling."

I laughed, and we walked on in silence. The day was thick and rich and green, full of warmth and fragrance. The June air brooded with a drowsy lethargy. But with each step, the expanding heat of the day brought the sweltering breath of the Southern wind. We crossed the long field behind the house and saw some thick woods in the near distance. But along the way we passed by an iron gated enclosure that was some twenty by thirty feet in size. It was a small cemetery of about twenty or so small markers.

Instinctively, Matthew volunteered an explanation. "According to Lida, Hiram set aside this small plot as a burial site for the men who helped build the place and continued to work for him. Their families maintain it, so it's fine by me."

I gave the small enclosure a fleeting glance as we passed by but spoke under my breath. "As if this place wasn't already creepy enough."

In time, we arrived at the edge of the woods. Here the terrain began to fall sharply. We found a drainage washout and more or less followed it as we descended cautiously into the deep hollow before us.

The farther we journeyed into the tumbling depths, it seemed that Matthew's mood darkened. He seemed consumed with a strange disquiet; his face a carefully drawn mask that gave nothing away. Unlike myself, he had an accomplished ability to weather silence.

Finally, our efforts brought us to a narrow ravine that flattened to a level plane only forty or so feet wide. We came to a stop to get our bearings. The opposing slope was thick with trees and undergrowth that rose sharply like a nearly impenetrable wall. To our right the ravine continued, gradually winding into the distance and shouldered on both sides by the steep rise of woods. Only by careful observation of the trees could it be discerned that there had once been a road cut through this narrow gulch. But the signs were there. It was while studying the remnants of the lost lane that I noticed something odd.

"Matthew, does it seem strange to you that almost every one of these trees are maples."

He un-shouldered his pack, walked to a nearby branch and pulled off one of the leaves. "I think you're right. This is a sugar maple. In fact, most of these are sugar maples."

"You say that like you're surprised."

"I am a little. Tennessee is the extreme southern edge of where sugar maples grow naturally. Red and silver maples are more the norm." He paused, surveying the surrounding terrain. "I think these were planted intentionally. There should be a broader mix; more oaks, black gum, locust, walnut."

"So, what do you make of it?"

"Not sure."

We stood for a moment, waiting for the other to offer an insight that neither of us had. Finally, Matthew broke the silence. "Come on; the spring house is this way."

We turned to the left and made our way carefully. The remnants of a wet weather creek bed threaded to the side of the ravine. All that remained of it in the June heat was the occasional small muddy bog. The strong, dank smell of stagnant water rose to meet us. About a hundred feet ahead the ravine ended in a u-shaped bowl. Rising rudely from the thick, untamed tangle of trees and undergrowth was a brick structure about twenty by twenty feet square. As Matthew had mentioned from his earlier visit, the metal roof had suffered a long-ago blow from a falling tree, creating a sliver opening from which rain and leaves had likely penetrated the old structure over the years. But the ten-foot-high brick walls showed no such compromise. Covered in an untidy profusion of ivy, they stood solid, timeless. Our progress toward it was painfully slow.

The thick foliage of the trees crowded out all but the occasional slender shaft of sunlight, leaving the air still and the heat thick. The atmosphere was like a bath. We made our way through the briars and tangles, occasionally chopping the thicket with the machete. And for some reason, the closer we came, a strange unease crept over me. Something wrong was pressing in, smothering away the air. The place seemed dark, decayed, unhallowed.

Matthew's temperament had grown ever murkier, his focus intense, his face a twist of impatience. It seemed that now we only spoke in muted undertones. Having finally reached the old building, we instinctively walked around one side and then the other. The back half of the structure was cut into the hillside, covering nearly the first five feet of the rear wall. The large wooden door on the front looked heavy and solid, hanging on three sets of rusted but stout hinges. The vintage padlock was of similar definition.

By elusive measures, it seemed that in the last few minutes, the small tuck of ravine had grown ominously darker. I gazed upward, searching for some fragment of sky amidst the thick cluster of limbs and the high shoulders of the steep ridges above. The previous pale blue had been replaced by a leaden gray. A sudden gust of air stirred, a harbinger of changing weather.

Then distantly, I heard it again. I heard the myriad chanting of voices that had encircled me in the frozen darkness outside Matthew's house back in December.

"Do you hear that?" I said anxiously.

Matthew halted, holding himself silent. "What is it?"

"I hear singing. A woman's voice. Or more likely, several women. They're all singing at once. But not the same tune. Do you not hear it?"

He stared at me blankly, waiting, listening. Long seconds passed. His eyes made a slight twinge of acknowledgment. "Maybe. I'm not sure. Could just be the wind."

I wasn't quite so dismissive. "That's not the wind, Matthew." I paused, slightly irritated, straining to listen. "You do hear it, don't you?"

He pressed his lips together in anticipation. A few seconds later, the voices faded away. He spoke reluctantly. "I might have heard something. But, seems like it's gone now."

"If you know it's gone then you knew it was here."

"Yeah. Okay, fine. I heard it. I heard some voices."

"So? What gives?"

Matthew shrugged. "I don't know. Around here you just hear stuff like that from time to time."

I gawked at him incredulously. "That's it. I mean…the Ghoul Glee Club sings an aria, and we treat it like traffic noise?"

He said nothing. Despite my alarm, the matter seemed to warrant only a passive deliberation on his part. He shook his head indifferently. "I don't know what to tell you." Having said this, he refocused his attention on the padlock.

Just that quickly, it seemed that a door had closed between us. I was startled and dumbfounded, but Matthew was undeterred. A spark of higher purpose seemed to flicker in his eyes.

Conversely, I was anxiously unnerved. The chorus of cryptic voices, the strange and eerie presence of the deserted structure, and the entrapped closeness of this cramped and gloomy basin served to swallow me in an involuntary fear; of what, I could not rightly say. But at that moment, it seemed that I could have poured all of my courage into a thimble. I had nothing to prove here and was content to simply leave. Matthew's hardened face said otherwise.

He dropped his pack and removed the bolt cutters.

"So, what's your plan?" I inquired.

He looked at me, confused. "My plan?"

"Yeah, you know. A plan."

"What did you have in mind?"

"Well, we don't know what we're up against here. So, I thought that after you snap the lock, I'll kick the door open and you could rush in with your 9mm. You know…guns a blazing style."

Matthew responded dryly. "I doubt anything in there is packing heat."

My unease had exasperated me. I promptly held up my hands, placing the fingers of the right into the palm of the left…the clear signal for a timeout.

I spoke bluntly. "Look. You're my friend, Matthew. But, cut me some slack here. I don't deal with whole ethereal world stuff quite so casually. This whole business is creepy. And I mean real darn creepy. Let's face it. You didn't need me to come along. You could have come down here by yourself. But you wanted someone with you, just in case. So, don't tell me that you're not just a little bit rattled by whatever kind of weirdness may be behind that door."

He pursed his lips together and nodded, a gesture of appeasement. He looked down for a moment, endeavoring to find his words. "It's not the creepiness, Luke. It's me. I just want answers. I guess I've been kidding myself, trying to think it didn't matter. But it does. I asked you to come along because you're a smart guy. You don't miss much. And what I'm afraid of more than anything is overlooking something. I thought that between the two of us if there is any clue here that offers any solutions, we'd find it. This is the last place to look, Luke. I just have this feeling that if we don't find anything here, then I'll probably never know…never understand what Emily was trying to tell me."

I tucked my hands under my arms and nodded. I understood. His earlier comment about baggage now struck me with resolute clarity. It wasn't just his wife's request he was trying to understand, it was her absence as well. Despite his assertions to the contrary, Matthew wanted to make sense of a senseless loss. I nodded and exhaled deeply. "Okay, then. Let's do this."

He angled the bolt cutters around the old lock and squeezed hard. It snapped and fell to the ground. After taking one last look at me, Matthew turned the handle and pushed on the door. Surprisingly, it swung open easily, availing a full view of the inside.

Chapter 42

THE SPRINGHOUSE

We were immediately hit with a palpable wave of putrid air. The rank smell of desertion, of years of decay and neglect, had fermented into the walls and floor. The room was a chaos of dirt, rusted metal, rotting leaves, collapsed wooden boxes; a disarray of piled and forgotten junk.

The daylight ebbing through the door and the small crack in the roof offered only modest visibility. Matthew retrieved two flashlights from his backpack, handing one to me. We endeavored to make our way inside, both of us filled with a cautious, curious anticipation.

Despite a thick layer of filth, it was soon apparent that the floor was brick, the same as the walls. We moved to the center of the room and began to take inventory. A disarrayed and rusted collection of five-gallon metal cans littered the wall to our right. They bore the same Frontenac label as those found in the basement. I lifted a few of the intact ones. They were empty.

The remnant of some half-rotted wooden shelves lined part of the left side wall. They were cluttered with tarnished oil lanterns, boxes of antiquated hand tools, grease cans, containers of rusted bolts, nuts, and washers of various sizes, and a myriad of other small items sorted in vintage glass jars with corroded lids. Beside all this was another of the bow-back, four-wheel dollys like the one we had seen in the wine rack room.

Matthew broke the silence. "What do you make of this place?"

"Well, for starters. It's definitely not a springhouse. There's no pump, no pipes, no nothing."

"Yet it's built into the hillside like you would expect a springhouse to be. So, if not that, then why is it even here?"

The question hung in the air between us. I made my way toward the rear wall where a decades-old pot-bellied iron stove sat in the far-left corner. It was blanketed in rust and grime and its flue extended only three feet and left open to the room. But upon further inspection of the rear wall, I noticed a spot about eight feet high where the brick had been filled into a circular pattern. No doubt, at some point, the flue had elbowed and extended through that opening. But for some reason, it had been closed.

Matthew had made his way to the other rear corner where two small and decaying wooden crates sat under a covering of muck and leaves. Dropping to one knee, he brushed off the top one. Then, he took his knife and pried away the lid. Inside were twelve bottles neatly separated by thin pine partitions. They were unlabeled and empty with no metal cap…apparently, undisturbed from their day of manufacture. Matthew retrieved one for closer inspection. It had a narrow three-inch neck that beveled out to a squat, cylindrical body. By all appearances, it was an unused whiskey bottle.

He looked at me curiously. "Is this what I think it is?"

"I think so. Looks to be a booze bottle. Although, I guess you could put maple syrup in it."

Matthew scoffed. "Not likely." He held it out at arm's length. "It looks big."

"It's probably quart size which is thirty-two ounces. Whiskey used to be bottled on the Imperial measurement system. You know, quarts, pints and so forth. These days it's on the Metric system which is 750ml. That works out to about twenty-four ounces."

He nodded his understanding but continued to regard me curiously. "I still don't get it, Luke. None of this fits together. We already knew Hiram was probably into bootlegging. But this building and these few bottles...none of it makes sense."

I heard Matthew's words, but I wasn't completely listening. My attention had been drawn to something odd on the center of the back wall. It looked like a patch had been made in the brick similar to the one where the flue had been. The telltale signs of broken mortar joints revealed a repaired area just above the floor measuring about two feet square. I scrutinized it for a moment. Then, an idea struck me.

I found an old hammer among the box of tools and began to stoutly beat against the area of the patch. Surprisingly, the brick quickly crumbled and broke away easily. After two minutes effort, I had completely removed the last of the patched area. As the dust settled, I bent down and aimed my light beyond the small pile of rubble, revealing the opening of an eighteen-inch pipe.

Matthew knelt beside me. "That looks like the pipe coming out of the wall in the wine rack room. Why would it end up here?"

I stood and scratched my head. Piece by piece I began to link everything together, to figure out just what the wily Hiram Hatcher had been up to when he had built all of this over ninety years ago. Matthew saw the broad smile spread across my face.

"Tell me what you're thinking, Bradford."

I shook my head and laughed. "Okay. Keep in mind that some of this is just spit-balling, but here's what I got."

"I'm all ears."

"I think Hiram Hatcher not only knew how to make money; he liked making money."

"Okay. Not sure I see your point."

"What I'm trying to say is this. I don't think Hiram particularly loved the phosphate business, or the real estate business, or even the bootlegging business. But he liked living large, and he liked doing things that made him money. He's already a wealthy man when he comes to Watervalley. But as he's building his house on Bootlegger Hill, he sees an opportunity. Even in the twenties, whiskey is being illegally made all over this region. Hiram's got his own fleet of trucks and his own railroad line up to Nashville. He's not interested in making whiskey. He's interested in distributing it. So, he networks with his old childhood buddy Capone to cover himself politically and dives in. I'm guessing that he got Canadian whiskey shipped here in the maple syrup cans. As well, he became a collecting point for bootleggers making bourbon and rye in this area. That's why he immersed himself in the local social and political scene. His activities were probably well cloaked, but it's a small town. People would know."

"So how does this place tie in?"

I stepped around the five-gallon cans strewn across the floor and grabbed the old metal dolly. I returned and placed it on the floor and loaded four of the cans on to it. Then, kicking the rubble away, I rolled it into the end of the large pipe where it fit easily with a couple of inches to spare.

"I remember you telling me that the bricked-in room had an old fuse box and wiring and a large spool of cable. I think that at one time, there was an electric motor in that room. That's what the wiring was for. So, here's how it worked. Booze was brought here in the five-gallon cans, probably at night and by a single truck. Or who knows, maybe even during the day. It was probably just a logging road. So, seeing an occasional truck come in and out would have seemed normal.

Anyway, using the pipe, it was smuggled up to the basement room where it was then put into bottles and boxed up. The dumbwaiter you saw was used to lift the boxes to what we thought was the coal room. As I mentioned, Hiram lived large, always throwing one big party after another. So, trucks coming and going making deliveries wouldn't really stir much notice. Besides, even if people did know, they probably didn't care. Hiram was good for the local economy."

"But why not do all the bottling here?"

"My guess is that it would have created too much truck traffic on the old ravine road. And those trucks would have had Hiram's name on the side of them. People would notice. But trucks in town going back and forth to the railroad depot probably wouldn't get anybody's attention. Hiram also needed a secure place to warehouse the bottles. That's what all the wine racks were probably for. Meanwhile, as far as anybody knows, this place is just an old springhouse."

Matthew nodded silently. "Well, I'll admit. Everything you say makes sense." Slowly, he looked around the room, absorbing everything before us and mentally composing the room to its original purpose. Despite the noted gestures of understanding, his face was still framed in a tacit unrest. He exhaled a deep sigh of acknowledgment. "I think you may have figured it out, Luke. I have to say; I'm impressed."

I shrugged, awkward in the face of such a direct compliment. "Sure. I guess that's where the whole 'I want to do research thing,' comes into play."

Once again, Matthew nodded but said nothing more. In the moment, I felt a mild satisfaction, a sense of closure to a few of the unknowns surrounding Hiram and the past. It would be short-lived.

Matthew was moving in a completely opposite direction. His mood had grown dark again. He seemed distant, removed, searching for something far-flung and unreachable. And with that, a simple reality occurred to me. We had found some answers, but not to the questions that troubled him most. A knotty silence fell between us, and it was only then that I wholly understood that for the past months, Matthew had simply been nursing his anger. Months of smoldering frustration now surfaced fully upon him.

He seemed in want of lashing out, of erupting in an explosive tirade, of blasting anything and everything in this world and the next with the full weight of his pain and loss and disillusionment. I understood. It was impossible not to be drawn in by the profound injustice of his vanquished hope. We stared at each other, wordless. A mutual feeling of exasperation hung in the air like a vapor, difficult to name but impossible to ignore. I exhaled a deep sigh of resignation. Not knowing what else to say, I said the obvious.

"It definitely looks like Hiram was in the whiskey distribution business. But there's nothing here that reveals anything more about what happened in Chicago or why he left town or how that relates to what Emily was trying to tell you."

Still holding the bottle in his right hand, Matthew stood silently, clearly discouraged.

"Matthew, man…I'm sorry."

"Yeah, me too." His well-masked desire to find answers had been seething beneath the surface. Now, he saw no further reason to hold them in check. In his frustration, he threw the bottle across the room, shattering it against the bricks. Disgusted, he pressed his back against the wall behind him and slid to the floor. He sat, resting his elbows on his upturned knees, seemingly defeated.

"I don't get it, Luke. I've been over every inch of that house, every room, every closet, every nook and cranny, and attic. There's nothing. No documents, no letters, no buried bones, nothing. It's all just bull. Hiram was a bootlegger, and for some reason, he decided to bail out of it. That's all I get. What that has to do with Emily, I'll never know."

I couldn't help but share his disillusionment. "Matthew, like I said, I'm sorry. I guess I was hoping we'd find something here that told a larger story, that made some kind of connection. But this is just a dead end. The only things Hiram left behind were a few odds and ends and camera photographs in the attic in Charleston."

For the longest time, Matthew stared blankly ahead. Then slowly, his eyes rolled toward me, his expression was hard and penetrating. "What did you just say?"

The sharp edge of his tone had caught me off guard, and for a moment, it seemed that he was ready to stand, clench his fist, and confront me, as if in some way I had offended him. I replayed my words, my tone accommodating but deliberate. "I said that the only clues were in the attic. Hiram left everything there…up in the attic."

"No. You said something else. You said the word camera."

I shrugged. "Okay."

Matthew's stern regard paled to an open-mouthed disbelief; stunned. He let his head collapse back against the wall, staring through the hole in the roof to the distant sky. "I'm an idiot."

"I don't understand."

Slowly, a clever smile emerged. "Do you remember the inscription on the inside cover of the bible I found in the trunk."

"Not word for word. Something about asking forgiveness for not throwing everything away."

"That's right. Because he put everything in the camera."

"Yeah. And…I have to say, that one still has me stumped. So, why are you an idiot?"

"Because Hiram knew Latin."

"Okay, and?"

"Camera is the Latin word for room, and in particular for a high room, like an attic. So what Hiram was saying was that he left everything in the attic."

It took a few seconds to grasp Matthew's meaning. Then, it hit me like a hammer. "Oh! I get it now. But hold on…you said you had been all through the attic of the house."

"I have. But that was all through the attic over the second floor. I've never been in the attic over the third floor where the study is."

"Why not?"

"There's no access. Months ago, I looked at the ceiling in all four rooms on that level and even the closets. There was no way to get up there and candidly, no reason to get up there. So, I wrote it off."

My mind was racing, searching, trying to connect the dots. "Do you remember the Latin inscription Hiram wrote in the Book of Ecclesiastes, the one about the past being sealed forever?"

"Sure."

"Christmas Eve night, when I came to your study and stayed there while you went down to check on the twins, I remember looking at the room and thinking it odd that there were no bookshelves on the right side of the fireplace. That wall comes out flush with the firebox. You think there might be a stairwell behind it?"

Matthew paused for a moment, his thoughts churning. "I don't know. It all appears to be solid paneling."

"But maybe there's a hidden door. Or maybe Hiram simply had it sealed up like the inscription said."

It seemed that within seconds, the pendulum of Matthew's emotions swung hard in the opposing direction. An irrepressible expression of eager discovery welled upon his face. "Hell's bells. You may be right. It's been right there in front of me all this time."

I slid my hands into my pockets and gazed up at the open rift in the roof, feeling the need to temper Matthew's hope. "Well, let's don't jump to conclusions just yet. But it does sound promising." It was then that I realized that my last sentence was said to an empty room. He was already out the door. I mumbled to myself. "Okay. Jump to conclusions it is. Right behind you there, buddy."

Outside, Matthew was already shouldering his backpack, and from all appearances, appeared ready to sprint back up the steep hill. I was contemplating a more controlled ascent. Soon enough, larger forces would motivate both of us to make haste.

I no sooner had pulled the door closed when a deafening explosion rattled the entire gulch. Thunder, so violent it seemed to shake the bones of the earth, stunned both of us; forcing us reflexively to stoop for cover if not outright dive to the ground. Instantly, a cutting gush of wind swept through the ravine, hitting us full force. The ominous and swollen clouds that I had noticed twenty minutes prior had now achieved full strength. The downpour was sudden and brutal. Finer wisdom would seem to dictate that we return to the shelter of the springhouse and let the worst of the storm pass.

But Matthew was undaunted.

With singular focus, he headed down the ravine to find the path we had used for our descent into the gorge. With noticeably less conviction, I followed. We found the washout and headed up. But our climb was viciously challenged. It seemed that we were facing the elements in all their ferocity. The rain came in sheets, and the wind poured against us. Lightning flashed against the black canopy above and was instantly followed by thunder that quaked the entire woods. The washout quickly became a small torrent and had to be abandoned, forcing us to cut our way through brambles and hedges. The steep incline and slippery ground made for unsteady traction. More than once, each of us slipped and fell; sometimes catching ourselves, sometimes not.

We finally surfaced from the woods covered in mud and thoroughly soaked. The course and the footing across the rear field were now more certain, but the wrath of the storm had not diminished. With the rain stinging our faces, we leaned into the wind and slogged our way forward. Long minutes later, we reached the shelter of Matthew's back porch; drowned and battered, but with an irrepressible sense of exhilaration.

Without words, we both instinctively took off our muddy boots and made a dripping path to the kitchen. But before either of us spoke, we both heard a hard, distant rapping. It stopped for a moment and then resumed with seemingly greater force and velocity.

"That sounds like someone's at the front door," Matthew said.

In our pathetic state, we both walked lightly across the broad living room rug to the front entrance hall. I stood back a couple of feet while Matthew swung the door open. Standing there before us with a raincoat, plastic rain bonnet, and umbrella was none other than Connie Thompson.

Upon seeing us, what had started as an engaging salutation quickly soured to an arrested, critical scrutiny. With stoic, unmoved authority, she methodically assessed the two of us, taking ample time to look down at our dirty feet before carefully working her way back up. Peering over the top of her gold inlay glasses, she was noticeably unamused at our soaked and filthy presentation; regarding us like foolish schoolboys who didn't have the sense to come in from the rain.

In her typical deadpan manner, she spoke vacantly. "I catch you kids at a bad time?"

Chapter 43

THE WOMAN IN THE SHADOWS

Before Matthew could respond, I stepped forward, consumed in a sportive grin.

"Matthew, I'd like for you to meet the one and only Connie Thompson. She's my dear friend, housekeeper, and adopted mother."

His initial confusion quickly dissolved to a face of amused and knowing recognition. He smiled at her warmly. "I'm delighted to meet you, Mrs. Thompson. Luke has spoken of you many times."

Connie responded with equal courtesy. "Good to meet you, as well, Dr. House." An awkward silence ensued. Matthew and I suffered a brief moment of social paralysis, but Connie had the grace to carry the conversation. She spoke with tempered politeness.

"I'm sure you gather, Dr. House, that the mother title is figurative." Having said this, she dropped her chin and regarded me sternly. "And impeachable."

I was unfazed. But Matthew, unfamiliar with Connie's sharper edges, went slightly wide-eyed. After a moment of recovery, he spoke cordially. "Umm, won't you come in, Mrs. Thompson?"

Connie pressed her lips together, deliberating. "Well, I did come to pay a long overdue visit. But it seems I've interrupted you boys in the middle of something."

Matthew hesitated. He shot a few probing glances towards me, searching for a workable response. "Well, umm, not completely. We were, umm…"

"Matthew," I said calmly.

He stopped and looked at me blankly. He spoke again, still trying to construct a workable response. "It's nothing terribly important…we were just about to…"

"Matthew," I said, speaking with all the calm in the world.

He hesitated, somewhat confused and sharpened his attention toward me. He spoke in a whispered, unsure voice. "What?"

"We're going to have to tell her everything."

His eyes tightened and his whole manner stiffened. He said nothing but was clearly not in concert with my assertion.

In prelude to my next words, I closed my eyes and shook my head lightly in a gesture of composed certainty. "We're not going to get away with any half-truths here. Trust me, Connie is going to get to the bottom of all we know and probably faster than we do. But you can be sure of one thing. Whatever we figure out, it will go no farther."

Matthew squared his stance and tucked his hands under his arms, pondering my advice. I glanced at Connie who stood there silently, watching the two of us with tight-lipped curiosity. I suspect she wanted to appear detached. But I also knew that in the minutes before I spoke to Matthew, she had already gathered from the general air that something huge was afoot.

Finally, Matthew lifted his chin in an expression of composed resolve. "Okay, then. Looks like we have a co-conspirator."

We both turned to Connie, who was quickly realizing that it was now her turn to enter the conversation.

She did so with unleashed gusto. Her words came hard, fast, and firm.

"Just what kind of foolishness are you two involved in, anyway? And Luke Bradford, where are your manners? Standing there talking about me like I'm off stage in a sound proof booth. Furthermore, whatever it is you two were about to do, you need to change out of those filthy clothes first. Otherwise, you'll be making a mess that somebody will have to clean up. And that somebody will probably be a woman." By the time she had finished, everyone in the room could feel that the power balance had shifted.

I looked at Matthew with a boyish grin. "And there you are."

He smiled in return. "I'll go change and gather some tools. I can grab some towels for you, but I doubt I have any clothes you can borrow that will fit. Meanwhile, you can fill Mrs. Thompson in on all the details."

"No worries. I think I have an old pair of jeans and a tee shirt in the car."

"Good. We'll regroup in the kitchen."

The rain had slackened so I made a quick dash to the car and found the clothes in question tucked in a corner of the trunk. By the time I returned, Matthew had already left some towels with Connie. She handed them to me and turned around, facing the living room.

"You can change right there. I'll keep my back turned. So, Sherlock. Let's hear it."

I took off my wet tee shirt and in an economy of words, did my best to relate everything about Matthew's story; about the connection with Al Capone, about the Charleston trunk and its contents, and about Emily's dying request. I told her about the bricked in room downstairs, the false spring house, and what we had figured out. As I was putting on my jeans, I told her about Matthew's revelation with the camera-attic word play and of our suspicion regarding a boarded-up stairwell.

Connie was fascinated. On two occasions she almost forgot herself and began to turn around in a spontaneous act of confirmation. Having finished, I stepped beside her.

"So, you're telling me that the creepy study upstairs where years ago I heard that scary singing may be connected to some kind of hidden stairwell."

"That's what we're about to find out. Why?"

Connie shook her head warily. "I don't know. Just the thought of going up there makes me a little weak-kneed. Maybe I'll just stay down here, and you can shoot me a few text messages."

I laughed and put my arm around her shoulder. "Come on, Constance Grace. The kitchen is this way."

Moments later, Matthew joined us, arriving from the utility hall with two large crowbars and a couple of hammers. We exchanged nods of affirmation and, with the air of conspirators, we proceeded to make our way up the grand marble stairs to the third floor. Matthew and I were energized with an overwhelming feeling of immediate and impending discovery. But Connie wore a face of strange disquiet, following a few steps behind.

Once we reached the study, Matthew and I immediately began tapping on the wall to the right of the fireplace, seeing if our untrained ears could detect a hollowing difference. In all honesty, we couldn't. There was only a low, thick, thud. We ran our hands over all the raised molding and panels, occasionally pulling at it with our fingers, trying to find some kind of breech or hinge; anything that would reveal an opening. There was none. Having exhausted that option, we stepped back, endeavoring to scrutinize the entire wall on a larger scale.

I lifted my hand in signal of uncertainty. "I don't know, Matthew. I can't say anything obvious is jumping out at me."

He made a swallowed noise of acknowledgement; not so much one of frustration as one of calculation. Connie spoke into the silence. "What was the exact phrase Hiram used about the past?"

Matthew responded. "The Bible we found is on my desk over there. Ecclesiastes, Chapter Three." Connie found it and turned directly to the Ecclesiastes inscription.

Innocently, Matthew continued. "The phrase, 'Praeteritis obsignatus est in via,' Mrs. Thompson, means 'it is sealed in the past.'"

For a brief second, Connie looked at Matthew dryly. She pursed her lips and refocused on the inscription. Politely, she spoke to the general air. "You know, the way this phrasing is structured, this could also be interpreted, 'the way to the past is sealed.'"

Immediately, Matthew turned to me, placing Connie to his back. Dumbfounded, he half whispered. "How does she…"

I made a gesture with my hand and mouthed the words, "just go with it."

Connie continued. "If the way to the past is sealed, I don't think you're going to find a hidden door in that wall. If Hiram Hatcher put something or someone up there, he boarded it up where no one would ever find it. At least, not without taking the wall apart."

After a moment's contemplation, Matthew and I nodded our agreement to Connie's conclusion. We grabbed the crowbars and returned to the wall. Within minutes we had popped off the baseboard, crown molding and side molding, revealing the seams of a two-foot wide board that ran from floor to ceiling. With each of us taking a side, we started at the top and began wedging the board outward, unpinning it from the studs behind until it fell with a large whap on the floor. Behind it was a covering of sack-like brown paper that contained sound proofing insulation; most likely vermiculite which was widely used at the time. I was about to punch my way through this with the crowbar when from behind me, I heard Connie gasp loudly.

"Oh, my!" She bellowed.

I turned to see her with one hand over her heart and holding Hiram's Bible with the other. She was looking at the inscription written inside the front cover.

"I know this handwriting."

Before I could respond, I heard the sound of Matthew ripping the brown paper away from the wall. Using the hooked end of his crowbar, he cleared all of it down in one long sweeping movement.

Before us lay the dusty risers of a narrow stairwell.

Chapter 44

MELODIES

"Connie, are you okay?"

Her face was framed in a demoralizing fear. I moved quickly and helped her ease into Matthew's desk chair. She held up her hand, signaling that she was alright.

"I just had a start, that's all."

"What happened?"

She again waved her hand in a gesture of dismissal. "It's not important right this minute."

Matthew had gathered two flashlights and joined us. "Everything okay here? His concern was genuine, but his eager face was easily read.

"You two go see what's up there," said Connie. "If there are no dead bodies, yell down to me and I'll come up."

"And if there is a dead body?"

"Then yell run."

Matthew and I exchanged wry grins. "You sure you're okay?"

"Go, go, go."

Matthew went first.

There were two dormer windows in the third story attic that partially illuminated the room above us. Using the flashlights, we climbed up the tight stairwell to a floored area about twenty feet square. In the center of it, covered in an undisturbed layer of dust, was a writer's desk with a short wooden filing cabinet. Centered among the things on the top of the desk was a vintage Victrola phonograph.

Matthew and I looked at each other with speechless fascination. Undoubtedly, this was the same phonograph in the picture of Hiram taken that long-ago day at the railroad yard. I probed my light into the far corners of the room to see if anything grisly presented itself. There was only an overturned wooden chair, a small pile of deteriorating newspapers, and the musty air of nearly a century.

I went to the stairwell and called out to Connie.

"It's all clear. Come on up."

"What's up there?" Came the cautious reply.

"Just come on up. You'll see."

I returned to Matthew who was examining an elaborate record case, one of several stacked beside the phonograph. He opened the cover, revealing a felt lined interior. Inside was an odd sized vinyl record. He carefully removed it and examined both sides.

"What do you make of it?"

"Well, at first I thought it was a record. But I think it's something a little more. I think it's an original master. He glanced back at the table. There looks to be about ten or so of them."

"I guess that explains the elaborate packaging. Who recorded it?"

"There's a printed record label. Okeh Records. Never heard of them. There's also some handwriting on it." Matthew wiped it lightly with his finger. "Looks like it says, 'The Man I Love,' April 19, 1927."

"That sound's familiar."

"It's an old Gershwin song. Billie Holiday made it famous in the forties."

Curious, I opened the next record case. The handwriting on it was the song, "It Had To Be You."

"These are some pretty big tunes. Do you see anything that tells who the singer is?"

Matthew shook his head. He placed the record on the table and turned his attention toward the filing cabinet. In the top drawer he found a cardboard shoe box. It was secured with a string which he carefully untied. Inside was a cache of vintage photographs along with an assortment of papers and envelopes. The photo on top was of an exquisitely beautiful young black woman standing on stage and holding a microphone. She was clearly posing for the camera. Matthew held it to light. "Look at this, Luke. You see what I see?"

I took the photo from him and examined it. "That's the dress, isn't it? The one in the trunk."

"I think it is."

"She must be our singer. But I don't recognize her."

From behind me came a low, somber voice. "I do."

I had been so engrossed that I had not heard Connie approach. I handed the picture to her. "So, pray tell. Who is it?"

She looked at it sternly. But soon the hard lines melted into a disbelieving smile. "That's my grandmother, Vera Coleman. Her maiden name was Vera Jamison." Connie took the picture and fanned herself with it, needing a moment to reconcile her thoughts with this revelation. She looked at it again; this time, hesitant and puzzled.

"Connie, are you sure? Because, this doesn't make any sense."

"I'll admit, it's a quantum leap from this to an A.M.E. minister's wife. But that's her."

"Something doesn't add up here. That dress she's wearing was in the attic trunk in Charleston along with the Bible. What would Hiram Hatcher be doing with it?"

Matthew spoke before Connie could answer. "Maybe that's because she had a double." While Connie and I were talking, Matthew had continued to peruse the photographs. He pulled one from the stack and handed it to me. It was of two teenage girls standing in choir robes. Penciled on the back were the names Vera and Violet Jamison, 1923. The photo was small and somewhat faded. But the reality was unmistakably clear. The two girls were biological twins.

"Let me see that," said Connie, practically snatching it from his hand.

"You didn't know your Grandmother was a twin?"

"I never knew she had a sibling at all. Much less a twin sister. There was never a mention of her, ever."

With the face of a lost child, Connie studied the picture. It would seem that for her, the room began to fall into a slow spin. Speechless, she looked at me, then at Matthew, and then back at the photo. I was silent, dumbfounded; but Matthew had the presence of mind to gather the overturned chair and bring it to her. Reflexively, she sat; her mind occupied far away from this small attic room. She was retracing an entire lifetime through a completely different lens. I knelt beside her and held her hand.

"Connie? Talk to me. Tell me what you are thinking."

She looked at me blankly as if she hadn't heard me. Then, she spoke with quiet resolve. "I'm thinking this is not the day I imagined when I first woke up this morning."

402

During this time Matthew had returned to the box and continued his perusing of its contents. "There seem to be quite a few official documents here. Why don't we return to the study to examine them?" We all agreed.

I went first to help Connie negotiate the steep, narrow steps. Matthew followed carrying the box and a few of the record cases. He cleared his desk and set the box on it. But before continuing, he turned to Connie.

"Mrs. Thompson, can I get you anything? A glass of water, some tea?"

She spoke with dry resolve. "Thank you, no. I think I'm about to swallow a heavy dose of reality. That should hold me." Connie's no-nonsense persona was making a quick recovery.

Matthew began to lay all the documents and photographs in neat rows on his desk. Included with the photographs were several playbills from various Chicago night clubs, a birth certificate, a marriage license, numerous letters, and finally, a death certificate. At first, what connected them was unclear. But over the next hour, the three of us uncovered a long-hidden story about Hiram Hatcher and the woman he had fallen in love with.

Connie's Grandmother, Vera Jamison did, in fact, have a twin sister named Violet. The two sisters were from a modestly prosperous family in a small Ohio town. Vera married Rayford Coleman who was several years older, and the two of them moved to Xenia, Ohio where he attended seminary. But her twin sister, Violet chose a very different path.

Violet wanted to be a professional singer and moved to Chicago where she eventually found work performing in night clubs. It was there that she gained the attention of the enterprising Hiram Hatcher. We already knew Hiram was a frequent visitor to Chicago where he conducted his business dealings with the bootleg industry and perhaps Al Capone in particular.

The letters pieced everything together. They were both from Violet to Hiram and, oddly, from Hiram to Violet; the latter being collected and saved by Hiram after her death. Initially, it was quite clear that Hiram saw Violet Jamison as an undiscovered diamond. He more or less became her sponsor; buying her clothes, using his influence to get her night club appearances, and ultimately securing a recording contract for her with Okeh records. A quick internet search revealed that Okeh was actually a subsidiary of Columbia records and modern-day Sony Music. With Hiram's help, Violet Jamison was on the verge of hitting the big time.

Along the way, what had started as a business arrangement apparently grew into an infatuation and ultimately a love affair. In July of 1927, Hiram received a letter from Violet telling him that she was pregnant and that he was the unquestioned father. The baby was due in January. She wanted to know if he intended to marry her. He wrote her back and said no.

Although the exact events in the following months remained unclear, there were several more letters from Violet pleading for Hiram to marry her. There were no responses. Despite this, it seemed evident that Hiram was often in Chicago and that the two of them were still lovers. Given her obvious maternal status, either Hiram or Okeh records decided not to launch Violet's recording career until after the child was born. But that never happened.

Violet went into early labor in December and apparently, from the onset, things did not go well. This was the reason Hiram rushed to Chicago in December 1927; taking Jessica Ravenel, John Harris's grandmother, along with him to help out. The marriage license we found was dated December 12, 1927. The next few documents in Violet's life told a grim story. She gave birth to Maylene Anne Hatcher on December 13, 1927. Four days later, on December 17, Violet died. Cause of death was noted as complications of pregnancy.

There were several letters from Rayford Coleman to Hiram revealing that he and Vera agreed, at Hiram's request, to adopt Maylene. The wording revealed that the relationship between the two men was strained at best. Rayford didn't approve of Hiram. His angst at Hiram for his role in the unfortunate death of his sister-in-law was only thinly veiled. But it appeared that the death of Violet had left Hiram a broken man.

Much of what occurred between Hiram and Rayford is speculative. But the three of us agreed that Rayford and Vera consented to move to Watervalley, likely at Hiram's insistence. Hiram was fundamental in underwriting the building of a modest chapel for launching Rayford's ministry. Whether Hiram saw himself as an unfit father or whether he foresaw the social challenges his mixed-race daughter would face is uncertain. Even with light brown skin, Maylene would be viewed as a black child. In the segregated world of the 1920's, Hiram must have concluded that being raised under the stable love and security of Rayford and Vera was best for her.

Perhaps Hiram's original intent was to continue his life in Watervalley just as before, knowing that his daughter was nearby. But very soon after, it seems, he had a crisis of conscience. He had the basement bootlegging room and the springhouse pipe bricked up. He sold his business and his house, and shortly thereafter moved away. It seemed, Hiram had lost his taste for dealing in illegitimate enterprises.

The last letter from Rayford conveyed a mutual agreement between the two men to dispose of anything associated with Violet's past. To my thinking, this seemed an insensible thing. But the social norms of the 1920's were vastly different. Perhaps the society of that time would have condemned Maylene's birth with much greater shame, placing an unfair stigma on the child. I could only conclude that this was done for her protection.

But somehow, Hiram couldn't completely let go. In the attic trunk in Charleston, he had kept the dress of the woman who had bewitched him and the bible from the man who had helped him, along with an apology for not wanting to totally say goodbye. Perhaps his dreams for Violet had too greatly consumed him and the magic of her voice was something he simply could not destroy.

Hiram never returned to Watervalley and likely never saw his daughter again. He may have tried to correspond with Rayford or even send money, but Rayford Coleman took the answers to those questions to his grave.

It seemed that Matthew, Connie, and I had been talking non-stop for more than an hour; each of us injecting one revelation after another into the story unfolding before us. We had found consensus on the major events and mutually dismissed the smaller turns and motivations that could only be left to conjecture. Having expended our words, a reflective lull suddenly consumed our small threesome. We sat and looked at each other in a mix of wonder and fatigue.

Connie broke the silence. "There's one thing I still don't quite understand."

"Which is?" I responded.

"The twenty-two percent Portuguese thing. Where did that come from?"

"Have you heard back from Estelle's DNA test."

"She got the results this morning. We are a near perfect match."

"Then it must be from Hiram," I concluded.

"But Hatcher isn't an Iberian name."

Matthew responded. "Actually, his real name, as best we know, was Emanuel Lorenzo Hatcher. Hiram was a nickname."

"Good heavens, then!" Exhorted Connie.

"What?"

"Emanuel and Lorenzo are the most common Portuguese names out there. That explains everything."

I looked at her incredulously. "Do you just sit around all day Googling this kind of stuff?"

She ignored me. "The point is, I guess Estelle and I are going to have to get our heads around the fact that the Hiram Hatcher was our biological grandfather."

Matthew's face was consumed in a broad, contented smile "More than that, I'm afraid, Mrs. Thompson, it would seem that you and my children are distant cousins."

After a moment's contemplation, Connie returned the same gladdened smile. "Yes. Yes, it does." She lifted her chin, clearly delighted. "That being the case, I think you should start calling me Connie."

"Matthew," I said soberly. "Maybe this is it. Maybe this is what Emily was referring to…about finding family."

He beamed so grandly I thought he might start levitating. "Yes, Luke. I think you're right."

Wearing irrepressible smiles, we were absorbed in the wonder of this new reality. It seemed that the three of us were consumed in a moment of indescribable satisfaction; an unspoken, gratifying awareness that the fullness of time had provided clarity and understanding where there had been mystery and confusion.

Grandly at ease, I spoke playfully. "I noticed the resemblance between you and the twins months ago."

Chapter 45

REVELATION

Driven by a boiling curiosity, Matthew and I returned to the attic and retrieved the phonograph. After a modest cleaning of the dust, I positioned one of the records on the turntable and rotated the crank. Matthew placed the needle, and to our delight, it worked. What we heard was nothing short of amazing.

The voice of Violet Jamison was deep, rich, and sultry. She was mesmerizing with a near four octave range; easily floating in the stratosphere or flowing effortlessly into a throaty, stylistic contralto. One after another we listened to each recording, absorbed and captivated by her seemingly celestial yet seductive singing. And as I listened, I couldn't help but wonder what fame she might have attained had her life gone differently; about what might have been had time and chance not taken it all away. With what I had heard over the last hour, I could only suspect that she might have been practically immortal.

It was mid-afternoon by the time we finished the last one. Despite the exhilaration of the past hour, the day had other demands. Connie asked Matthew about revealing everything to Estelle. He seemed somewhat surprised at her request.

"Connie, it's your story now, yours and Estelle's. By all means, tell all of it. And tell it to whomever." He seemed sublimely contented. The three of us shared an unspoken awareness that we had witnessed something incredible. Now bonded in mutual wonder, we made our way downstairs.

When we arrived at the entrance hall, Matthew turned to Connie. "I'd like to arrange a time for you to come back. It would seem that we have much to talk about, and I would like for you to meet my children."

She readily agreed. Then, Matthew added. "Perhaps you can bring your sister as well."

Before responding, Connie discerningly looked to the side. "Let's just start with me. We can expand it from there."

Though noticeably puzzled, Matthew conceded with a quick nod. He turned to me and gratefully shook my hand. "Thanks, Luke, for everything." His entire demeanor was one of temperate reflection. While the events of the day had not brought him happiness, they had given him solace. Perhaps his troubled heart could finally begin to mend.

We bid our goodbyes, and I walked Connie to her car under a cloudless blue June sky. The savage storm from earlier had washed the haze from the heavens, illuminating the lush green day in a softer, more brilliant light.

Admittedly, we were both still a little stunned. "Well, Connie. I normally don't like to talk about these things, but now I know where that creepy tornado of songs came from when I was here Christmas Eve. I think your grandmother's spirit has been trying to get somebody's attention for a long time. She sure got mine."

Connie looked down reflectively and gushed a small laugh. "It's funny you would mention Christmas Eve. I knew something wasn't right even then."

"In what way?"

"You remember how I shied away from meeting Matthew that night?"

"Actually, I do. I remember thinking it odd but not worth questioning."

"It was because of the children. I saw them counting angels. They can see them. It's a gift."

My gaze tightened. "Connie, that's almost scary. Matthew has told me the same thing about them. How did you know?"

"Because from time to time in my life, Luke. I've been able to see angels." She held up her hand in a gesture of acknowledgement. "I know, I know. People think you're nuts when you say such things. And I spent a lot of time being confused as a little girl."

"I guess so if no one else saw them. Probably felt like a bit of a curse."

"No. It honestly was a blessing. I'll admit, it took a while to figure out. But think about it, Luke. If you saw angels; if in your heart and mind and soul you truly believed you saw angels, think about how easy it would be to have an unshakeable faith."

I crossed my arms and shrugged. "You make a good point."

"When I saw those children counting angels, it threw me. I'm not sure why, but it stirred up all of that awkwardness from years ago. I knew there was a connection, but it scared me. That's why I've avoided meeting Matthew. Now it all seems kind of silly."

"Connie, Matthew and I have been exploring every basement crack and crevice of this place and I'd be humiliated for you to know what a whiney little chicken I've been. There's no need to explain any trepidation to me."

She leaned in, speaking confidentially. "I have to confess, it took all the courage I could summon just to go back into the upstairs study, much less climb up into that musty old attic. I always knew there was something about this house, some kind of unexplained feeling that all the prayer and positive thinking in the world couldn't shake."

"So, how do you feel about it now?"

Connie paused, taking a moment to look up at the high roof and broad shoulders of the stately old mansion. "It may sound strange, but now I feel kind of connected to it. Like it's home."

"It should. Your grandfather built the place."

Connie looked down with a reflective smile. "Perhaps that's true. But I wouldn't want to change a single minute of my life with my Grandfather Rayford. I recognized his handwriting in that Bible of Hiram's. That's what rattled me."

"Your grandfather sounds like a good man."

"He was both good and wise. And my grandmother will always be a saint to me. Whatever decisions they made about keeping Violet's life a secret, they made them because they loved my mother."

"Well, are you okay with this new revelation about your ancestry? About being part Portuguese?"

Connie smiled sublimely. "In the end we're all part something, Luke."

I nodded in agreement. "Besides, looks like you inherited your grandfather's knack for making money."

Connie raised her chin and spoke with casual detachment. "I was thinking that now I understand where mama got her beautiful skin, which, as you know, she gave to me. Hiram passed that along too."

I could only shake my head and laugh at Connie's rare grab at vanity. "So, what happens now?"

"I think what Matthew said was correct. He and I have a lot to talk about." Having said this, she twisted her mouth into a disenchanted frown. "Then we'll add the sister to the equation and we'll talk about everything again. Only louder."

I laughed, gave Connie a hug, and said goodbye.

After stopping by the house to clean up, I spent the balance of the afternoon and evening at Christine's house. During dinner, I took particular notice that her grandmother, Mattie was unusually quiet, especially when asked about what news her old friend Betty Hudson had to offer. I counted her silence as a blessing and let the matter pass.

Later, as the evening edged toward twilight, Christine and I took an ambling walk down the farm lane through the fields behind the house. I told her everything about Matthew. But this time, I included the details about his wife's dying request, about Hiram's picture with Al Capone, and most importantly about Violet Jamison Hatcher and her connection to Connie.

Christine listened with muted amazement. "So that picture you found down in Lawrenceburg, the one of Hiram Hatcher at the railroad. That old phonograph he was holding was up in this hidden attic?"

"Sure was. Along with all the recordings, letters, and documents."

Christine absorbed everything I had told her for several steps. "Luke, that's a pretty incredible story."

"Isn't it, though," I said in agreement.

"So, based on what you're telling me, Hiram Hatcher certainly never killed a woman up in the old mansion. If anything, I guess you could say he kept her alive all these years."

"In a manner of speaking, that would be correct."

"Then all of this was what my Grandfather Cavanaugh was referring to when he said there was more to the Hiram Hatcher story than people knew."

"Likely so. I'm guessing he may not have known about the secret attic. That seems to be a private matter that Hiram had completed by some trusted workmen. But your grandfather probably knew about Maylene's adoption. To his credit, he saw it as no one's business and never told."

"Mother and my Uncle John are going to want to know all of this. Especially Uncle John, since it clears any doubt about his grandmother."

"I don't think he's losing any sleep on that one."

Christine offered a bemused smile. "Even still."

"And, I guess I need to apologize for not telling you earlier about the Capone picture and Matthew's wife's request. He trusted me to keep that secret."

Christine brushed this off. "I had no need to know and you gave your word. I'm sure there are plenty of interesting details about your patients that would make for noteworthy conversation. You don't tell me those things, and, nor do I care to hear them."

I was again reminded of Christine's depth of character. Despite the vulnerabilities she revealed to me, she was beyond the petty insecurity of needing to know everything, of allowing no room for discernment and discretion between us. At least, on some things.

"On the other hand, Bradford. If, say for example, there's going to be a stripper at your bachelor party, then that's a matter that needs to be thoroughly detailed and vetted."

I laughed out loud. "At this point, I'm not sure there's even going to be a human at my bachelor party. Right now, it's only the dogs and me. The bachelor party is typically organized by the best man, who happens to be your uncle; a man who tries to keep his interaction with humans down to three sentences a week."

"So, Uncle John hasn't mentioned anything?"

"Not a word. Besides, this is John we're talking about. If, in fact, he was to plan a bachelor party, I'd probably have to sacrifice my liver to get through it."

"But what will you do? You have to have a bachelor party."

"Okay, time out. Two minutes ago, you were going all Gestapo about what kind of debauchery my bachelor party might be getting into and now you're concerned that it won't be happening."

"I just want you to enjoy the whole process, that's all."

"Well, let's think about it," I said, rubbing my chin. "I guess as a fallback I could go out to the Alibi Roadhouse and round up some of the bubbas. We could hang out at the bar. Bend our minds a little and our elbows a lot. Then we could swing by the Bingo and Line Dance Club and pick up a few hotties from the denture crowd. After that, maybe we could all go back to my place. You know; drinkey, drinkey, naked dancing."

Without losing stride, Christine teasingly hit my shoulder, all the while looking down and smothering an eager laugh. "Stop it, Bradford."

"Look, if my groomsmen were a bunch of guys from the old days in Nashville, I'm sure they would have something appropriately crude and raunchy all prepared. But as you know, the groomsmen are all friends from here. Most of them are married and probably in bed by eight-thirty. Just going bowling may be a stretch for them."

"Okay. I get it. I just hate it for you, though."

"Well, here's an idea. I could come crash your bachelorette party. What time does the naughty nighty part begin?"

"Not funny."

"And speaking of which…are you guys having a stripper? Because, it looks like I'm going to be available."

"Now, really not funny."

"Sounds like someone's afraid that the bridesmaids might get tired of just looking at Lake Bradford and decide they want to take a dip?"

Christine stopped and put her hand to her mouth, laughing uncontrollably. "Where do you come up with this stuff?"

"Okay, now I'm hurt," I said in mock displeasure. "Careful how you play your cards here, Chambers. Chicks still dig me, you know."

Christine's something short of an eruption. She could barely catch her breath.

"Geez, I didn't think it was that funny."

Having momentarily lost the power of speech, she did, however, detect my slightly wounded tone. Spontaneously, she gathered my face into her hands and kissed me, a gesture that said more than a few conciliatory words.

We both laughed. Albeit, her more than me. "Sweetheart, you're a good looking, very desirable man. Especially for someone your age."

My appeasement was short lived. "You were doing okay until that last sentence. What does that mean…for someone my age? It's not like I wear Old Spice or anything."

"Oh, stop it, Bradford," She smiled at me dismissively and resumed her steps down the grassy farm road. I joined her.

"Good thing the assisted living place has a honeymoon suite." Unknowingly, my attempt at humor prompted Christine on an entirely different matter. "Speaking of honeymoons, Dr. Bradford. You still haven't told me where we are going. I could use some hints about what to pack. You know, like a general theme."

"The word skimpy comes to mind."

"Not helping."

"Let's see. Passport, toothbrush, some jewelry, and a big bottle of unbridled passion."

"Check, check, and check. But you've told me we're going to be gone for two weeks. That list might be a little light."

"Okay, fair enough. So, bathing suit, light jacket, shorts, cocktail dress, and a top or two and you should be fine."

"That's it?"

"If you want, we can go over a detailed list of lingerie."

Christine stopped and placed her hands on her hips. "Luke, I know you want it to be a surprise. So at least tell me when you're going to let me know."

"I'm thinking the carriage ride as we're leaving the reception might be a good time."

"Seriously?"

I spoke softly. "It's okay, dear. It really is. We're not going to another planet. If we need anything, we'll just buy it."

Christine smiled, shook her head, and said nothing more. She took my hand and we resumed our stroll, awash in a grand awareness that we were both foolishly and splendidly happy.

In the far rim of the valley, the western hills glowed with the last vestiges of orange light. Cooler air tumbled in and we made our way back to the farmhouse under a canopy of distant, delicate stars. Soon after, I left for home.

As I made my way down Summerfield Road, I felt a sense of completeness, a kind of mellow awareness that my time in Watervalley was coming to a close. The wedding was only a week away and all the plans were finally set. Matthew's troubling quandary had been resolved, Connie's disconcerting DNA discovery had found a resolution, and the town appeared to be slowly accepting my decision to leave. It seemed that everything was settled and that my path to the future was finally certain.

That was all about to change.

Chapter 46

FAILURE

The next morning, I arrived at First Presbyterian for the eleven o'clock worship service. I was at seven minutes late and slipped in feeling somewhat disheveled and panicked. Fortunately, one of the rear pews was empty. But the creaks and groans of the old floor and bench made for a noisy landing. Heads turned, and I whispered small apologies. Afterwards. I settled in and took a deep breath, finding equilibrium. My clamorous arrival now past, attentions returned to the pulpit. The organ played and the familiar words echoed through the long hall. The hymns washed over me, lulling me into that grand sense of solace that one can only feel in a sanctuary. With each passing minute I was absorbed into the reverence and pace of the service. Time slowed.

As was normal, I grew reflective and observant of those in the room; slowly taking inventory of the stories and the lives that I had come to know. To my mild surprise and delight, I noticed Matthew and his twins were seated several rows ahead on the far side of the sanctuary. Beside the children were Connie and Estelle. I quickly surmised that the powerful realization of a common ancestry had created an irresistible gravity. Instead of leisurely scheduling some future day, it seemed that phone calls, exchanges, and likely visits had occurred within hours.

Perhaps what was more amazing was that from time to time, Connie and Adelyn exchanged small, animated whispers. For a woman who historically thought that there was a special place in hell for anyone brazen enough to talk during a worship service, this was practically a sign of the apocalypse. But collectively, to see them there together was a gratifying and splendid thing.

And yet, something wasn't right.

Despite the captivating satisfaction of the moment, there was within me a nagging sense of something wrong, something missing. Immediately my attention went to the choir. Christine was there; silently, attentively listening to the sermon. Her mother was beside her. I briefly glanced around for John. He wasn't there but this was hardly cause for alarm. Relentlessly, however, the unexplainable feeling of trepidation continued, occupying my thoughts more and more.

I endeavored to dismiss this misplaced sense of dread, for it made no sense. I couldn't think of a time when my life had known such simple harmony or sense of purpose. I closed my eyes, refusing to be bullied by some unnamed anxiety. And in that moment, it seemed that mentally I was slowly surveying the room, that somehow my subconscious was wanting me to see what my eyes could not. That was when I realized what was wrong. It wasn't something that was missing, it was someone. Polly Shropshire.

I opened my eyes instantly, like one who had been roused by an explosion, and quickly scanned the room; practically standing in hopes of catching a glimpse of one of Polly's absurd hats. Nothing. Whatever her personality failings may have been, Polly was a fixture for Sunday worship service. The certainty of her absence now began a cascade of alarming realizations.

Polly had not come to the party Friday night. This was the social event of the season and her affinity for the society limelight made it unthinkable that she would be a no-show unless something was terribly wrong. Unconsciously, my breathing had accelerated. The heat thickened in the corners of the room. Desperately, I began to replay our conversation from the previous Friday. The impact of Polly's words now hit me full force. She had said, "I have my medications. I've been making plans on what to do. I'll be fine." Among other things, I had written Polly a prescription for sleeping pills. The day I stopped by her house she affirmed that she hadn't taken any of them. But on Friday, she had spoken of her medications and her plans in the same breath.

How could I have been so absent minded, so stupid? None of her prescriptions were for dementia. My mind was racing, searching; trying to find some way to defuse the horrific thought that was now consuming me. Then, my subconscious screamed forth a final detail. I recalled the calendar in Polly's kitchen and the notation about Clayton's death; the worst day of Polly's life. The date was June fourth.

That was today.

In a mixture of fury and panic, I leapt from my seat and bolted to the narthex doors, shoving them recklessly open. I was oblivious to the world around me, uttering in an ever-louder voice, "No! No! No!"

Polly's house was seven minutes away. The Austin Healey's engine screamed as I frantically raced to the yellow Victorian home at the far end of Walnut Street. Along the way I had the presence of mind to call the EMT's and told them to meet me there. If I was wrong, if my assumptions were incorrect, then so be it. Watervalley could have one final story to tell about me. But in my bones, I feared that I was not. Moments later, I careened into Polly's driveway.

Her car was there, parked under the portico. I ran to the front door and immediately pounded on it, calling out Polly's name. I waited. There was nothing. I stepped to one of the front windows, cupping my hands around my face. But the curtains were drawn, and the inside was dark. Nothing was discernable. I rapped on the window as well, again calling out for Polly. My summons was met with only an eerie silence.

I returned to the front door to see if it would open. But it was locked and solid. Instinctively, I ran to the rear of the house. The back door off the kitchen had glass panels on the top half. I did my best to peer inside but just like the front, no lights were on. I knocked on the door stoutly and for a final time, yelled Polly's name. There was no answer.

That was it.

I picked up a terra cotta pot from the porch and broke one of the glass panels. Seconds later I was inside. "Polly! Polly! It's Dr. Bradford. Are you here?"

Intuitively, I ran to the bedroom hallway, turning lights on along the way. I was expecting the worst, but all three bedrooms and the bathrooms were empty.

"Polly, are you here? It's Luke Bradford."

I returned to the kitchen and for a flickering moment, thought that perhaps I had been impulsive and foolish. I found the light switch to the short hallway that led to the living room. Once there, I flipped on the overhead light. Polly was on the couch. Upon seeing her, I instantly knew. She was dead.

Her body was contorted and askew to one side; as if she had been sitting and collapsed upon losing consciousness. Her mouth was slightly open, and all the color had drained from her face. A plastic prescription container was on the end table beside her. The top was off, and it was empty. A quick glance confirmed it was the sleeping pills. For nearly fifteen seconds I stood there, frozen, shocked. Then, a hard, angry resolve hit me.

This wasn't over.

I moved to her quickly and felt of her jugular. He skin was cool but not cold. For a half second, I thought I felt a thready pulse. There was nothing more, but it gave me a small grain of hope. I lifted Polly from the couch, hastily laid her on the floor, and began doing chest compressions, hard and fast.

After several cycles of compressions and rescue breaths, I caught the faint wail of the siren in the distance. It felt like an eternity had passed. On the outside I was controlled and methodic, mechanically doing textbook CPR. But inwardly I was frantic, hysterical, losing it. Along the way I began to talk to Polly; at first in my head and then audibly.

"Don't be dead, Polly! Don't be dead!"

I checked her pulse again. Nothing. It seemed useless. I was pounding on the chest of a lifeless body; foolishly cracking the ribs of a woman whose heart was already broken. The howl of the siren grew louder. I kept pushing, harder and harder. I needed to focus, to think medically. Yet all I could do was desperately replay all the words, all the conversations, all the signs, and all of my indifference. Polly had done this. But I had played a role. I had handed her the gun. Rage, shock, panic, fear, desperation...all gripped me simultaneously, wanting to paralyze me. I pushed on, continuing the hammering compressions.

Finding no other outlet, the convulsive storm of emotions within me manifested in tears. They streamed down my face unchecked, falling on my hands. Out of breath and exhausted, I pressed and pressed. Unknowingly, I found myself repeating the words, "I'm sorry. I'm sorry," with each downward push.

Finally, the roar of the ambulance could be heard out front. I left Polly only long enough to unlock the front door. One of the EMT's continued with the compressions while the other gave her oxygen through an ambu bag. Within seconds, I had placed the defibrillator pads. Normally a dose of epinephrine would be given first. But as of yet, we had no IV access. I didn't wait for the defibrillator to analyze her. I programmed it and shocked her. If she was dead, it wouldn't matter.

Polly's body lurched. I was blindly hopeful, searching to see if the heart wave yielded anything. In the intervening seconds, one of the EMT's got an IV started. He was about to administer the first dose of epinephrine when the machine announced, "shock advised."
We all looked at each other, stunned. This meant that Polly had some kind of rhythm. A faulty one, perhaps, but a rhythm that could be shocked into a normal one.

"Clear!" I yelled.

Her body convulsed again. Immediately, the oxygen was restarted. I held up my hand to stop the EMT doing the compressions. Slowly, steadily, the monitor began to beep. It was a sluggish, lazy sinus rhythm. But it was a rhythm, nonetheless. Polly was alive.

We moved quickly. I gave her a dose of atropine to speed up her heart. Within minutes we had her on the stretcher and into the ambulance. But before leaving, I ran back into the house to Polly's bathroom. Fortunately, I found what I was looking for. I had prescribed an anxiety medication for Polly, benzodiazepines. The bottle was full. Had she taken the two together, her death would have been assured. With only the sleeping pills, there was a chance.

On the ride to the regional hospital in the next county, we gave her a large bolus of saline to flood her system and dilute the medication as much as possible. She would need to have a gastric lavage, a stomach pump. But in her unconscious state, this was best done at the hospital, not on a bumpy forty-five-minute ambulance ride. Polly would live. Coma and kidney failure from the overdose were now the next looming concerns.

We arrived at the ER where Polly was quickly evaluated and sent to a procedure room. Their work done, the EMT's asked me if I wanted to ride back with them. I refused. Polly had no one. I could find some means of getting back when the time came.

For the next several hours, I sat in the waiting room mulling over everything that had happened, gathering a composite of all that I knew about Polly. My apathetic regard of her had been triggered by the harder edges of her personality. But I had failed to see the deeper wounds, to look past the pretense.

I came to realize that Polly had lived much of her life as most of us do…in fear of discovery. Fearful that those around us would uncover our secret self, that they would realize that we are not as smart, not as confident, not as good as we projected ourselves to be; that our defenses of authority and self-assurance were often a ploy, that in our heart of hearts we longed for that one voice, that one smile, that one warm expression that tells us that maybe, just maybe, we are wrong... that our presence is valued, our friendship needed, our words important. I had foolishly failed to regard Polly with my most fundamental understanding of the human condition, the need for one. Despite all my rationalizations, I was consumed with shame and guilt. I was leaving Watervalley and running away from the people who needed me most.

By late afternoon, Polly was assigned to a room. She was stable but still unconscious. As well, the blood work results for her kidney function looked promising. I went to her room and sat in the chair beside her bed, determined to keep watch over her. Sometime later however, exhausted from all the physical and emotional drama of the day, I fell asleep. It was the only escape available to my burdened mind.

I was awakened by the soft squeeze of a hand on my shoulder. It was Christine. Connie was standing beside her. I immediately stood, as if embarrassed to have been found dozing.

"Hey," I said reflexively, still endeavoring to wake up.

Christine's gaze was soft and undemanding. "Hey."

She stepped toward me and embraced me in a long hug, an expression that communicated far more than words might have. "So, how is she?"

I relayed all that I knew, noting that now it was a wait and see game as to when she might wake. I shrugged. "Then, we'll have to see about her mental state. That's why she has the restraints. The biggest challenge might still be ahead."

They both nodded their understanding.

"I drove your car here," Christine said. "I'm here to take you home."

I held my hand up. But before I could speak, Connie interceded. "We drove separately. I knew you wouldn't want Polly left alone, so I'm here to stay with her. A couple dozen folks from the church have signed up to take turns watching her. More are on the way. You go on home, Luke. You've done enough."

After a moment's contemplation, I pressed my lips together and nodded reluctantly. We said our goodbyes to Connie and before leaving, I took one last look at Polly. It seemed that hers was a pathetic state. The turns in her world had brought her to this wretched moment. My heart broke for her. No one's story should have such an end.

Christine and I walked to the car in silence. Upon reaching it, she turned to me and spoke crisply. "How about I drive?"

I easily agreed, and we set off into the twilight for the long road back to Watervalley. I could do little more than stare blankly out the side window and into the vast darkness. Christine, in all her grace and wisdom, said nothing, only occasionally reaching over to squeeze my hand. Sometime soon after we crossed the county line, I exhaled deeply and looked at her.

"How would you feel if we didn't leave Watervalley?"

Chapter 47

LAZARUS REVISITED

The next day, the news of Polly's attempted suicide swept through Watervalley like a hurricane. Remarkably, it was met with an outpouring of sympathy and concern. Despite her often-prickly nature, it seemed that over the years, Polly's volunteer and charity work had won her an enduring regard in the fabric of Watervalley life. Notably, her personality was an acquired taste, but she was nevertheless respected and appreciated. Instead of contempt and indifference, her desperate actions invoked a universal sadness and the good people of the town expressed their grief for her in more than just words. Her hospital room overflowed with flower arrangements and dozens of get-well cards. So many volunteers came to hold vigil and watch over her that many had to be turned back.

Ironically, I was given high praise for finding Polly and saving her life. But I didn't see it that way. Candidly, I didn't want to talk about it; a position that was wholly unpopular with the multitude of well-meaning inquiries I received. Only Christine knew my real thoughts. I blamed myself.

As we passed through the darkened landscape on Sunday night, she listened patiently as I poured out the full measure of my anguish and guilt.

I knew.

I knew that I had failed Polly; that my indifference had contributed to her attempt on her life. Perhaps I could have rationalized that this was confirmation that I should leave, that I should not be a small-town doctor. But it had only confirmed the opposite. I knew that despite my attempts at vindication, Watervalley would be left destitute of medical coverage. I could easily change that. I also knew that in part, my desire to do research was to some degree a chase for applause. I was grieved and frustrated but felt that quite possibly I was making the wrong choice.

In her calm and beautiful way, Christine assured me that she would support whatever decision I made. But wisely, she suggested that I give it some time and perhaps talk the matter over with Connie or John or perhaps Dr. Bray. In the moment, I agreed. I would withhold comment to anyone on the idea for a few days. Admittedly, however, I saw little that would change the inevitable choice to stay.

Monday found me in better spirits although I moved through my day with an odd mix of resolve and melancholy. Patients came and went, but I was different. I lingered with them longer, talked with them more, and found a mild sense of contentment in doing so. Late that afternoon I called the hospital to check on Polly. Nothing had changed.

Tuesday passed much the same except that the day was more infused with comments and congratulations about the imminent wedding. Admittedly, the delight of my approaching marriage and honeymoon began to occupy my thoughts. But the simmering uncertainty still remained.

Then, late Tuesday afternoon I received a phone call. It was from the hospital. Polly was awake and asking for me. Within the hour, I was knocking on the door of her room.

Her eyes met mine with a somewhat embarrassed yet desperate, unspoken gratefulness.

I began the conversation the same way I did all awkward discussions, with a stab at humor. "Polly, I am so sorry. I should have had the pharmacy leave instructions that you're only supposed to take one of the sleeping pills at a time."

She smiled at me, and I felt my cheeks warm. Her face melted into a kind and tender gesture. "How did you know to check on me?"

I pulled the chair to the side of her bed, sat down, and held her hand.

"Gee," I shrugged. "I was sitting in church Sunday and couldn't find a fashionable hat anywhere. It set my whole week off on the wrong foot."

She cut her eyes at me dismissively. "You're a good soul, Luke Bradford. Thank you."

I nodded, saying nothing more. A knotty silence fell between us, but Polly seemed unaffected. She released a small, satisfied breath and fixed her gaze out the window. She spoke with a notably new and unveiled bluntness.

"Lately my life has been a gapping sinkhole. But it was one that I dug for myself. Clayton and I had such a wonderful life together. I realize now that I've never gotten over his loss. I thought I had, but in truth I think I've been angry. And I've taken that anger out on everyone around me."

She paused for a moment and again looked reflectively out the window. "After his death, I used to host a lot of dinner parties. I guess in some way I was wanting to bring life and laughter back into the house. But it didn't work. In hindsight I was a terrible hostess; making bitter comments and biting people's heads off. I imagine they all went home, got down on their knees, and prayed to God they would never receive a dinner invitation from me again." She seemed quietly amused, clearly poking fun at herself.

"I thought I had burned every bridge imaginable. And yet, look at this. All the flowers and the cards. I've had a dozen visitors this afternoon, and I understand that while I was asleep, someone was at my side the entire time." She turned to me and smiled warmly. "Including you."

"You're more liked than you know, Polly."

She blew out a short, disbelieving gush of air. "A little patronage is fine, Luke Bradford. But now you're just outright lying."

I grinned and mulled over her words for a moment. "Then let's say it this way. People want to like you, Polly. You're independent, you're colorful, you're intelligent, and over the years you've given of yourself to the community. People revere and value that. They want to be friends with you. But maybe you haven't always made that easy."

She nodded. "Fair enough." Then she smiled, and her demeanor took on a lighter air.

"You know what they say about you when you are teetering on the brink, how your whole life flashes before you?"

"Sure."

"Well, I have to tell you. That happened to me."

"Oh, really? And?"

Polly held up her hands in a grand measure of exasperation. "What a letdown. Huge parts of it were really boring." Having said this, she burst into a high-pitched, wheezy giggle; openly quite entertained with herself.

I laughed along with her and then squeezed her hand. "I think now you've got a chance to change all of that, Polly."

Her face softened. "Yes. Yes, I do. I feel like Lazarus, back from the dead. I've got a second chance at life because of you, Luke."

She paused and looked down, seemingly fortifying herself. "I'm going to have to go through a series of psych evaluations, first though. Seems that when you try to off yourself, there's a lot of concern you may attempt a repeat performance. But, perhaps that's a good thing."

"It has its place."

She nodded with a tight-lipped smile of resignation. I spoke in to the silence that followed. "Polly, I'm sorry. I should never have let this happen."

Her neck stiffened, and she looked at me with a face of surprised admonishment. "Luke Bradford, that's the silliest thing I've ever heard you or any other human being say. You're a doctor, not a mind reader. I told you a bunch of half-truths and you acted accordingly. How could this possibly be your fault?"

"I should have listened more, Polly." I looked away for a moment, searching for the words. "I should have cared more."

Polly chuckled lightly. "Oh, piddle, Luke. Based on the words coming out of your mouth I can envision a whole new use for duct tape."

I was taken aback by her uncharacteristic frankness. "Polly Shropshire. I think I'm seeing a new you."

"Well," she said, shuffling slightly and straightening her back. "There needs to be a new me. And you need to put away any notions

432

about blaming yourself. You're an exceptional small-town doctor, Luke Bradford. I'm sure you'll be the same at medical research."

Despite her offer of absolution, I was unconvinced. Part of me even wanted to tell her about my misgivings regarding the decision, to hint at the probability of staying. But before I could speak, Polly squeezed my hand.

"Just promise me you will call every once in a while, to tell me how it's going. I need to change some things and be a better person." She paused, looked to the side, then leaned in closer. "But I still want the inside skinny on Watervalley's most celebrated newlyweds." With this she chortled lightly, once again poking fun at herself.

I smiled and spoke warmly. "Not a problem."

Soon after, I bid my goodbyes and departed. Several people from town were in the waiting area and upon seeing me leave, headed her way. My feelings were mixed, but I felt assured that Polly would be alright.

I called Christine on the way home and gave her an update. She asked me how I was feeling, which I knew was a veiled inquiry into the larger question of staying or leaving. My response was ambivalent. Christine responded tenderly.

"Luke, I hope it's okay. But I spoke to Connie earlier today. I told her how you were feeling. She wants to talk to you."

Initially, I wanted to respond back sharply, to admonish what I saw as a breach of my privacy. But I thought better of it. These were two women who loved me, and I was pretty lousy at expressing my emotions. I exhaled a long, slow breath. "Probably not a bad idea."

We talked a minute or so longer and said goodbye.

Connie's car was in my driveway when I arrived home.

Chapter 48

FOR THE LOVE OF CONNIE

A s I gathered my things to go inside, it occurred to me how my life with Connie had so dramatically changed. In the first few months of knowing her, I would have rather eaten a green bug than have been anywhere near her. But now her presence always lifted my mood and brought a sense of strength and comfort. I found her in the kitchen, preparing dinner and singing in her rich soprano voice. Yet instead of the usual hymn or gospel song, she was serenading Rhett and Casper with "Night and Day," a Cole Porter standard.

"Well, sounds like somebody's channeling their grandmother's incredible vocal prowess."

Connie responded with a modest grin. "Yeah, I've been thinking about her quite a bit lately. Getting pregnant out of wedlock probably wasn't her finest moment, but it must have taken a lot of courage to go off to Chicago by herself to start a singing career."

"Maybe you should go to Chicago and do the same."

"Maybe you should get washed up and ready for dinner before it gets cold."

"Gee, look who has her sassy pants on today."

Connie ignored me and continued to set the table. I washed my hands at the kitchen sink and we sat down to eat, filling glasses and passing dishes in the silent choreography of two people who knew each other's movements and habits intimately. There was an abiding ease and satisfaction in this reality that diffused my larger worries. In the moment, I felt lighthearted.

"So, I noticed you and Estelle sitting with the House family on Sunday. That transpired quickly."

Connie nodded her head. "Oh my. After I left you, I went home and told Estelle the whole story. Sweet Jesus, that girl's eyes were out on stems. She was so excited I thought she might just lie on the floor and vibrate. She insisted we call Matthew immediately and have a pow-wow. He and the children came over for dinner that night and I just have to tell you, we instantly fell in love with them. He brought the old phonograph and records, so Estelle could hear them and we all had a grand time together. Sunday morning, she and I were sitting on the pew waiting for the service to start. Next thing I know, Adelyn and Andrew came darting along and slid in next to us. Matthew caught up and, bless his heart, half apologized and asked if they could join us. Of course, we were delighted."

"I think it's a grand thing. I'm happy for all of you."

A secretive smile crept across Connie's face. "Actually, Matthew and I met again on Monday. I think he and I may form a little partnership."

"Doing what?"

"Re-opening Society Hill as a bed and breakfast."

"Really?"

"Yeah, I think so. Estelle doesn't need me at the bakery anymore, you're about to be raptured off to married people heaven, and Matthew thinks that the old mansion should be brought back to its former days of grand entertaining. He's planning on putting quite a bit of money into it, giving the place an elegance it hasn't know for decades. You have to agree; Society Hill has an incredible story. The whole secret tunnel-Al Capone-bootlegging thing will draw a lot of interest, not to mention my grandmother's records and her story. I think the bed and breakfast can be elevated to a national level and become a destination stay."

"Wow! That's an incredible idea. So, how will this partnership work?"

Connie offered a tempered smile. "Essentially, I'll be running the whole thing, which is fine by me."

Connie's gaze tightened into a rather uncanny and mirthful framing. "Oh, he'll be helping out, among other things." Having said this, she grabbed her tea glass and drank a large swallow. It was almost as if she didn't want to answer the question. I let it pass, absorbed by the extraordinary venture that she and Matthew were planning.

"By the way, Matthew called me today."

"Oh?"

"It was about the bachelor party. I think word must have gotten out that nothing has been planned. Matthew invited me to come up to his place Friday night after the rehearsal dinner. He's got a fire pit out back. Said we'd get a fire going and hang out."

Connie stirred her fork casually. "That sounds rather tame."

"Well, you never know. We may end up singing a few rousing campfire songs." I paused and drank a sip of tea. "Hey, you should join us."

Connie stared at me deadpan. "Tempting. Think I'll pass."

"Your loss."

She crossed her arms and frowned at me. "I don't get it. Grown men sitting in the dark around a fire. What's the appeal?"

I rubbed my chin and thought for a moment. "It's kind of hard to describe. There's just something about poor lighting and the opportunity for crude behavior. If you're a guy, you love it. You get to spit a lot and talk about hockey."

She shook her head and spoke with a breezy disdain. "Sounds cosmic."

"Well, he also mentioned having a bottle of twenty-year-old Scotch. So, it's possible we might drink a toast or two. Maybe even one to you."

Connie stared at me stone-faced. "Be still my beating heart." With her arms still crossed, she looked up at the ceiling and lamented. "What is it about men? If it flows downhill, they'll put ice in it and try to drink it."

"Subtlety isn't one of your charms, is it, Connie?"

After responding with an unamused scowl, she shook her head, gathered her fork, and resumed eating her dinner.

"Speaking of Lucky Charms, Christine told me you've been acting like you're fresh out of them."

"Meaning?"

"Meaning that you're in a blue funk over this whole Polly situation. Saying that you blame yourself."

I drank a final swallow of tea, pushed away from the table, and stared reflectively at Connie's guileless face. "Yeah. Yeah, I do. And I'm starting to think that my leaving might be a mistake."

Her response was unvarnished and direct. "Hmm, that bit of foolishness came on rather sudden. Usually there are some warning signs."

I shrugged. "It's just not that simple, Connie. Despite what anybody believes or says, to my thinking, I failed Polly."

"Sweetie, we all failed Polly. Any one of dozens of people could have spoken a kind word to her and made things different. What she did was a cry for help and the good news for her is that the kind folks of this community are more than willing to give it. But Polly failed herself, too. Heavens, she made gossip a deity and it got to the point where you had to take a hit of nitrous oxide just to be around her for a few minutes."

I spoke pensively. "I think she's well aware of that now. She said as much this afternoon."

"Then you shouldn't be feeling any guilt over this."

I scratched the back of my head and exhaled a long, brooding breath. "I suspect guilt may be a factor, but it's really more than that. It just boils down to a matter of practicality. I've burdened this whole decision process by placing everything on some ethereal plane; conjuring a lot of lofty thoughts about destiny and higher purpose and what my place is in the world. But it's not about me and the simple reality is this. I'm needed here. Despite all the well wishes I see it in their eyes. Nancy Orman talked to the mayor yesterday and there has been zero response to the opening. Who knows when another physician can be brought on board."

"Sweetie, I admire your concern. But there's a hole in your logic large enough for barge traffic."

I crossed my arms, mildly indignant at Connie's assertion. "Well, I'm not sure I agree with that little truth bomb."

My tone wasn't lost on her. She thought for a moment, her eyes vacantly searching the room as if she were deliberating on her next words. Her voice held a calm assurance.

"I've been thinking a lot lately about that Bible Grandfather Rayford gave to Hiram." She paused and looked at me for a sign of acknowledgement. I sharpened my gaze, a little dumbfounded at this change of subject.

"Okay."

"When I was a little girl Grandfather Rayford gave me a Bible on my tenth birthday. We were at church. He had just finished preaching the Sunday service and everyone had left the sanctuary except for my parents and me. Mama was pregnant with Estelle at the time. Grandfather Rayford asked me to come up to the pulpit with him. I wasn't sure what was going on and I remember being a little timid. But when I got there, he bent down and gave it to me. That Bible had my name embossed on the outside in gold letters. It made me so proud. It was a beautiful thing and I loved it instantly."

I silently nodded. Connie continued.

"Then, as we were leaving, a thunderstorm came out of nowhere and the rain fell in sheets. I made a run for it to the car and when I did my precious new Bible slipped from my hands and fell in the mud." Connie paused, shaking her head. "I was so upset. I just stood there and cried because I had always been taught to have a high view of scripture and dropping my new bible in the mud seemed like I had ruined something holy."

"But my grandfather quietly came and stood there with me in the rain, holding his umbrella over the two of us. He bent over and picked up my Bible, wiped it off with his handkerchief, and gave it back to me. I remember sobbing and heaving and doing my best to tell him I was sorry and that I had tried to catch it. But my grandfather looked at me with all the peace in world. He brushed his thumbs under my eyes to wipe away my tears and held my face in his hand. Then he told me something I've never forgotten.

"And what was that?"

"That I should never worry about the Bible hitting the ground. The Bible is God's word and it would endure. He said that it was much more important to catch God's needy before they hit the ground. You know, in most churches, we observe communion all the time even though there's only one time in scripture that the Lord told us that he would be present in the bread and wine. But he continually tells us in the gospels that he is always present in the poor and suffering."

I understood her words but was still at a loss. I spoke pensively. "Connie, I'm not sure I understand the connection here."

"You've learned that, Luke. That's why your heart troubles you. In your own way you love the people of Watervalley. Time and time again you've caught them before they hit the ground and they know it. That's why they're acting like they are. They're scared. Scared that you won't be there when their husband has a heart attack, or their child breaks an arm, or their baby has a fever and they can't get it down. But your passion is to do research, Luke. It's been that since the first day you showed up here. Now, I haven't had a direct interview with Him, but I believe God put that passion in your heart. That's why you can't let it go. So, I think you were perfectly right to deliberate all of this the way you have. That's what I meant a moment ago about a flaw in your logic."

My hard outlook had melted under Connie's affectionate words. I shrugged and spoke acquiescently. "Everything you say makes sense, Connie. But I don't seem to have your resolve."

"I think if you consult Abraham you'll find that uncertainty, dissent, and disagreement are part of a healthy theology." Having said this, she lowered her head and glared at me over the top of her gold inlay glasses, speaking in a slightly reproving monotone. "Not that you will."

I could do little more than grin at her insight but was nevertheless warmed by the quiet certainty of all that she had said. I slid back in my chair, extended my legs, and laced my fingers behind my head. I looked at her for the longest time; my eyes soft and my face framed in a warm and irrepressible smile. I felt in want of saying so many things. But in the end, I simply tilted my head slightly and proudly declared, "I love you, Connie Thompson."

At first, my pronouncement was met with zero impact. Connie regarded me unflinchingly. But in time the faintly upturned corners of her mouth betrayed her. She lifted her chin and pronounced with dry detachment. "Doesn't everybody?"

With that, we both erupted into an unexplainable, explosive laughter; a mirthful outpouring of two souls who shared a bond of understanding that words could not capture. In time, Connie reached over and took my hand. She spoke with the full measure of her heart.

"The truth is, Luke, life here will continue. The fortunate and the unfortunate will still be a part of every day. This world is old in sin and it will take more than the little light that you and I hold to make all the difference that's needed. Go to Nashville. Use that incredible brain that God has given you to bring hope to this world. But when you're done, come back here and use that incredible heart of yours to bring a little courage to the plain and simple people of this valley. In the fullness of time, God has seen fit to unite my family. The people of this valley are your family, Luke. You will always be loved, and you will always be needed. When the time is right, come back home to them."

Connie was right. I smiled and hummed a low sound of acknowledgement and we shared a moment of pure contentment.

Then, oddly, she inclined her head marginally to one side. By the smallest degrees, her expression sharpened, assuming a faintly wily air. "And you never know. In my experience, the good Lord always seems to have a trick up his sleeve."

"You say that like you know something."

Connie feigned ignorance. "I don't. And if I did, do you really think I'd tell?"

"So noted."

The assertion was in keeping with Connie's abiding faith and outlook, despite her rather curious delivery. We cleaned the dishes and she departed for home. I stood on my front porch and watched her drive away, consoled by all that she had said, and reluctantly resolved that I was making the right choice.

But I also knew that for the next several days and culminating in the wedding and reception, I would be looking into the eyes of those

I cared for and see the trace misgivings and uncertainty. They would wish me well, but the bittersweet element would be ever-present. I exhaled a deep sigh and took one last look upward into the far reaches of the oncoming twilight.

Even in Watervalley, it was not a perfect world.

Chapter 49

MATTHEW

Fortunately, the next couple of days were uneventful. Unfortunately for the Mayor, this included the town's business expo that he had so meticulously planned. The event was hosted Thursday morning at the Memorial Building. Despite a healthy advertising budget, along with several hundred invitations to businesses and corporations around the state and beyond, no one showed. That is, with one exception.

Around eleven o'clock, a handsome woman, professionally clothed in a business dress and heels, appeared through the double doors of the large Memorial Hall. A warm brunette, she was tall and slender and carried herself with a definitive poise and confidence. Despite wearing black rim eyeglasses that were plain and unremarkable, her tailored presentation had an intimidating air. But it took little imagination to see that the glasses served as an unintended mask. Hidden beneath them was a more accessible beauty; deep brown eyes that were inquisitive and full of slow surprise along with a lovely face that was fresh and striking. Her professional attire biased her age, offering an impression of being in her early forties. But something in her allure and bearing hinted that she was likely younger.

Upon entering the room, she stopped, and for a moment absorbed the mixed signals of elaborate preparations amidst complete vacancy. Walt was at the far end of the room, planted in a chair with his feet on a nearby display table and blubbering despondently to Matthew, who had dropped by to talk briefly about his plans for the bed and breakfast.

Upon seeing the woman, Walt leaped to his feet like someone caught in the act and made an immediate waddling beeline toward her. Carrying a leather briefcase, she walked to meet him with a steady, assured stride that was both deliberate and graceful.

As Matthew would later relate the story to me, Walt did his best to exude a charming welcome. But something about the polish and poetry of the woman had him tongue-tied. When he wasn't blurting his words, he was choking on them. To her credit, she negotiated past his awkwardness with politeness and an engagement that was tempered with unmistakable urban reserve. No longer able to stomach Walt's floundering, Matthew finally intervened and introduced himself, serving as something of an ad-hoc interpreter for the discussion. Fortified by his new wingman, Walt began to speak in coherent sentences. His bubbly enthusiasm returned.

But his gusto waned after asking her what her interest in Watervalley was. Her name was Evelyn Southall. She was from Nashville and was thinking about moving to Watervalley to open a bookstore.

Walt did his best to hide his disappointment, but per Matthew, she was too intelligent not to miss it and too polite to acknowledgment it. Matthew told me all of this late Thursday afternoon. He came by my office to talk about our two-guy bachelor party and to tell me about a small discovery he had made. But he dwelt on the story about the woman in a rather telling way.

"So, Professor House. I'm getting the impression you were a little taken with this well-coiffed bibliophile. Sounds like she was rather pretty."

He shrugged and spoke vacantly. "Pretty enough, I guess. But," he said reflectively. "You're the brunette guy. I tend to fall more into the blonde category."

"I'm pretty sure hair color is not a make or break factor in the chemistry of attraction."

Matthew was dismissive. "It doesn't matter. I think Walt did a pretty good job of scaring her off."

I let the matter drop. "So, in other news, I hear you've knuckled under the heavy-handed lobby of the Society Hill Book Club and are letting them meet up at the mansion again."

"Yeah," Matthew responded, his mouth set in a fixed grin. "It's all the easy money, fast cars, and loose women they throw at you. Besides, it's pretty much in keeping with the new plans for the place."

"Connie told me. Sounds great, although…seems like it all happened rather quickly."

"I would have to agree. But, what can I say?" He said with a wide-eyed expression of resolve. "It all just feels right."

"Hey, again. It sounds great. You'll get a kick out of Connie Thompson."

Matthew grinned slyly. "Get a kick or be kicked?"

"Probably both."

"She can be quite persuasive."

"This, we know."

447

"Anyway, I came by to talk to you about a couple of things. Remember the land behind the mansion, the 928 acres owned by the Frontenac Company?"

"Sure."

"I flew to Charleston Tuesday and met with the law firm who has been paying the taxes."

"Wow. You flew there?"

"I figured it was the only way to get them to talk with me."

"And?"

"It took a little doing to prove my relationship to Hiram. But once we got that worked out, what they told me was amazing."

I sat up in my chair, deftly focused. "Let's hear it."

"We know from the letters between Hiram and Rayford Coleman that Hiram agreed to leave town and not interfere in the life of his daughter, Maylene. But, according to the lawyers in Charleston, when Maylene turned eighteen in 1945, Hiram desperately wanted to give something to her. But if he did, then the story would come out. So, he did the next best thing he could think of. He set up a trust fund that would give ownership of the Frontenac land to Maylene's heirs per stirpes. The only caveat was that the transfer was to take place in seventy-five years. By that time, he knew that Maylene would likely be gone, and the chips could fall where they may. I guess this was Hiram's way of trying to vindicate himself to his eventual grandchildren."

"Then that means in about a year, Connie and Estelle will be the owners of the 928 acres."

"Correct."

"Why didn't the lawyers contact Connie and Estelle before now?"

"They were following Hiram's instructions. But when I showed up and provided all the proof about Emily being Hiram's great-granddaughter and us having owned the King's Street house, along with me now owning Society Hill, I guess they figured what the heck. The story was going to surface within a year anyway. To be honest, I think they were just as curious as I was. The guys I talked to were not part of the original deal. Hiram set this up with their grandfathers, and subsequently, I was able to fill in some blanks for them as well."

I nodded, absorbing all that Matthew had said. "Amazing."

"I also learned this. As a cover, Hiram was logging all of the timber on that land back in the twenties. It was probably so no one would think twice about seeing or hearing trucks making deliveries to the old spring house. In keeping with the syrup company façade, he had it replanted with nothing but sugar maples. That's why we saw so many of them."

"Have you told Connie and Estelle about all this?"

"I flew back in yesterday and met with both of them last night."

"How'd that go?"

"Good. As you know, they're already well off financially. So, Connie pretty much took it in stride. Estelle, however, got on a tangent about wanting to turn the spring house into a boutique dress shop."

"Out there?"

"Remember, this is Estelle we're talking about."

"Never mind."

Matthew smiled thinly and fell silent as if he were unsure of his next words. "Um, about tomorrow night. The rehearsal dinner will be over when? Nine-ish?"

"Sounds about right."

"Well, why don't you just bring a change of clothes and spend the night."

I pondered this a moment. "Okay, you sure?"

"I've got eight bedrooms for you to choose from."

"Fair enough. I don't plan on getting snockered, but then again, it might be a long way back to Fleming Street on hands and knees."

"Good," he said. "That's settled."

I thought this would bring the meeting to a close but once again Matthew seemed distant, preoccupied. He leaned forward in his chair and was about to speak but hesitated, his face framed in an expression of strained uncertainty.

"Matthew? You okay?"

He looked at me and smiled briefly, seemingly caught in a generous fog. When he finally did speak, it was in a voice that was methodic and calculated.

"Luke, I have one other thing I'd like to talk about."

"Sure." Despite what I thought was now a second nature friendship, Matthew was treating me with polite caution. I began to feel a stir of trepidation in the pit of my stomach. Finally, he exhaled a deep sigh and began.

"I haven't been completely forthcoming about my past."

"Not sure that's required."

"Fair enough. But there's one detail, in particular, that might have some relevance. It's about what I did in the Navy."

"Whoa," I injected. "I knew it. You were special ops, weren't you? I bet you've killed people with your bare hands." My question momentarily threw him, and he looked at me blankly.

"No, no. Nothing like that. It was quite the opposite. I worked in the infirmary of an aircraft carrier. I was an Advance Practice RN."

"Seriously?"

"Yeah, I started as a Corpsmen and worked my way up to Lieutenant. I did some civilian work after I got out but, with Emily being a doctor, we decided that one medical professional in the family was enough. I loved languages, so I went back to school and eventually got my doctorate in classical studies."

I was genuinely impressed, if not a little stunned. How had I missed this? I was retracing moments from the past, things Matthew had said, and the expert bandaging of his burned hand. His admission made perfect sense.

"Well, dang," I exclaimed lightheartedly. "Can't say I saw that one coming." I leaned forward in my chair. "So, an APRN and a doctorate. That's quite impressive." I paused again, contemplating for a few seconds. "But why are you telling me this?"

"Because here's the thing. A moment ago, we both agreed that Connie can be pretty persuasive."

"That, we did."

"Well, somehow, Connie found out about my medical experience in the Navy."

"God probably told her."

Matthew shrugged. "Certainly a possibility. Anyway, she mentioned last night that you were pretty shaken up by the whole Polly Shropshire affair."

I pressed my lips together and nodded. "It brought home the fact that any way you slice it, I'm leaving my patients in the lurch."

"Well, what if you didn't have to?"

"I don't understand."

"What if I took over the day to day running of the clinic? I'm an Advance Practice RN with a Family Nurse Practitioner certification. I know how to do assessments, I've handled plenty of burns, broken bones, trauma, and even delivered a baby or two. In Tennessee, I can write prescriptions as long as I have physician oversight."

"That would be great. But who would be the physician?"

"You would."

"But I won't be here."

"Doesn't matter. I could send you a daily e-mail, or we could talk on the phone once or twice a week. You already know all the patients, and I've got your medical records to go by. I think we could make it work...at least for a year or so while you're on the research grant."

I'm quite sure that by now I was staring at Matthew with my mouth completely unlatched. The idea seemed impractical at first brush. But with each passing second, it gained and and more plausibility. "Matthew, I don't know what to say. I mean, I guess this could work. How in the world did you come up with the idea?"

"In truth, I didn't. Connie did. Like I said, somehow, she found out about my medical past. The more I've thought about it, the more I like the idea. But in the end, it's up to you."

I recalled my conversation with Connie on the night of the party. She had mentioned that Matthew was a man of many secrets, but naturally, I thought she was talking about the bootlegging and Al Capone connections. I was dumbfounded and ecstatic all in the same breath. Then, a hard realization hit me.

"Matthew, I think this would be incredible. But I'm not so sure Dr. Bray will get on board. He's a good man, but this may be a stretch."

"Actually, I think that matter has already been handled."

"Handled? How?"

"Turns out, Estelle can be pretty persuasive as well. Apparently, she and Dr. Bray are old chums. My understanding is that she called him today and he agreed.

"You're joking."

"Nope. Estelle Pillow worked her mojo on your old professor. He's on board."

I collapsed back in my chair and tucked my hands under my arms, stunned. "It can't be this simple."

"Well, you do realize that you're the one taking the risk here."

"How is that?"

"I'll be working under your license."

I almost laughed outright. "Matthew, you may be the most detailed and meticulous person I know. I can't imagine you being anything short of thorough and dogmatic regarding patient care. Besides, an aircraft carrier holds what? About six thousand people?"

"Pretty close."

"That's more than the town's population."

"And, for what it's worth. Walt is good with this idea as well. I ran it by him earlier today at the Memorial Building."

I slumped in my chair. "Oh, great. Now, half the town already knows about it.'

Matthew was casually looking out the window and spoke with quiet authority. "Mmm, I doubt it."

"What makes you so sure?"

He squared his shoulders and absently rubbed his chin. The self-assured, military side of him was sieving through. "Because I have a carry permit. Just so happens that I was showing Walt my Glock while we were talking. I mentioned to him how disappointed I would be if he even told his shadow about our conversation." Having said this, Matthew leaned forward in his chair, winked at me, and spoke in an amused whisper. "Walt's an easy read. He's still a little intimidated by me, and according to the rumors, he still thinks I might have killed my wife. I figured I'd keep him guessing."

We both laughed spontaneously, wrapped in the jubilant, conspiratorial air of thick comradery. "Matthew, this is...well, this is incredible. Are you sure?"

"Yeah, I am. Watervalley is my town, now. I've got medical training, and I can help out. It's a good fit." He pressed his lips together in a gesture of quiet assurance. Then he added, "besides, remember when you came to my rescue on Christmas Eve? I told you that night that I'd like to return the favor. I know it's not quite the same, but maybe this can rescue your peace of mind."

I nodded thoughtfully. "More than you know."

Matthew fell back in his chair, clearly happier than I had ever seen him. Filled with an irrepressible smile, he lifted his chin and looked at me appraisingly. "Well, Luke. Looks like the ball's in your court. What do you think?"

I stared at him for a moment, puzzled that he would even ask the question. "I think we need to go tell the staff!"

Chapter 50

BACHELOR PARTY

My plan on Friday was to work until noon and take the balance of the day off. The wedding rehearsal was at four that afternoon. But the day was one of continuous and delightful interruptions. Throughout the morning a stream of well-wishers stopped by to congratulate, tease, and offer advice. More than I realized, the people I served…especially the elderly, had taken a certain custodial ownership of me and felt compelled to connect, to counsel, and perhaps to seek closure. Despite the smiles, I could see a sense of loss in their eyes. I had sworn the staff to secrecy about the pending arrangement with Matthew until all the details were finalized; practically making them spit in their hand and shake on the matter.

At three o'clock I was still seeing patients, but it mattered little. All I had to do was stop by the house to shower and change clothes before driving the seven blocks to First Presbyterian.

I arrived at the church with time to spare.

The next hour was a comical blend of attempted order and instruction against a backdrop of spontaneous mischief and laughter. Charged with instinctive and contagious happiness, everyone easily slid into moments of joking and folly despite Joe Dawson's patient and smiling efforts to guide us through the steps of the ceremony. Curiously, no one seemed more caught on the wave of celebration than John Harris. It seemed that for this evening, he had cast off his usual cloak of cynical commentary. He exuded an almost explosive friendliness, engaging everyone with openness and enthusiasm.

Combined with his well-timed and insightful wit, his normal command presence loomed large over the gathering, filling everyone with an infectious, festive mood.

The rehearsal dinner was held at the Depot Diner and jointly catered by its owner, Lida Wilkins and Estelle and her Sweet Life Bakery. Lida had graciously allowed me to book the entire restaurant for the event and the two of them together had magically decorated the place and prepared an incredible meal. The entire evening was a triumph of food, toasts, and speeches; a perfect prelude to the grand day that was to follow.

Despite the cacophonous laughter and all the excitement and euphoria that surrounded me that evening, it seemed I only had eyes for Christine. Often, words and sounds fell away as I watched her, caught in the entrancing web of her smile. Something in the splendor of her dark hair, her deep brown eyes, and her full and luxurious red lips went drunkenly to my brain. With her buoyant health, quick intellect, and spirited character, she was radiant and beautiful; at the flawless summit of her mortal enchantment. I heard the voices around me, but I was lost to her every gesture and movement; alluring, sensual, full of seductive grace.

The dinner came to a close, and I stood and offered a final thank-you to everyone. Just as I had suspected, my groomsmen, all of whom were older and married, gathered their wives and made a beeline for the door as if a fire alarm had gone off. John lingered a minute longer, but soon enough, he kissed his niece on the cheek, shook my hand in congratulations and left with Ann. Christine and I looked at each other and laughed.

"Well," she said. "You and Matthew go have fun. Behave and try not to talk shop too much."

"I imagine it will be pretty tame. The twins are having a sleepover at Connie's. Matthew and I will probably drink a couple of beers and be snoring before the news comes on."

After giving me a kiss, Christine and several of her bridesmaids left for her place to engage in whatever frivolities they had planned. I found Lida and Estelle in the kitchen, chatting nonstop and putting away the last of the pots and pans. I thanked them, gave them both a hug, then walked to the Austin-Healey and headed for home. Will Fox had agreed to keep Rhett and Casper for the night. So, after a quick change into some jeans, I grabbed my overnight bag and headed up to Matthew's. The day had been good; great even. Closing it out with a beer, a few laughs with a friend around a fire, and a long night's sleep seemed like a perfect end.

When I arrived at Matthew's front entry, the porch light was on. He met me at the door with a grand handshake and a cold beer. "Come in, bachelor boy. Let's get this two-man party started."

I chuckled lightly. "Well, we'll try to make up in enthusiasm what we lack in numbers."

I followed Matthew into the massive living room where from high above, the melodic, sultry voice of Violet Jamison was wafting down the broad staircase. "Matthew, tell me that's a recording. Because if it isn't, I'm getting in my car and leaving. Good chance I may never come back up here, ever."

He laughed as we passed through and into the kitchen. "I had a studio in Nashville remaster the vinyl records to a digital format. Pretty sweet, huh?"

"Just checking. Whether out front, in the basement, or up in the attic, every time I come to this place, there seems to be a little something--something that frightens the crap out of me."

Matthew took my bag and smiled. "I guess that makes the backyard new territory. But, for what it's worth, I got a fire going in the pit just before you came. Didn't see a single ghost...not that I was checking too closely."

"Comforting."

"Here, let me put your bag in a room. Head on out back, and I'll grab a beer and join you shortly."

"Sure. Deal."

I exited the rear door of the mansion and walked to the stone fire pit some fifty feet away. None of the back porch or outside lights were on, but the blaze was several feet high, illuminating two Adirondack chairs that Matthew had placed nearby. I took a seat, drank a swallow of the beer, and peered into the long lawn behind the house. Despite its robustness, the light of the fire faded after twenty feet or so, leaving everything beyond in a swallowing darkness. As I waited for Matthew, my eyes began to acclimate, and I stared into the dim night of the rear yard.

That's when I noticed the movement.

At first, it seemed like a play of shadows created by the flames, but I was beginning to catch glimpses of images moving toward me from the deep, black well of the backyard. It struck me as no small coincidence that the forms were coming from the direction of the small cemetery that lay in the gloom only a few hundred feet beyond. The irregular flicker of the fire made the images appear and disappear. Instinctively, I rose and strained into the darkness. My worst apprehensions were confirmed. Without question, there was a silent moving mass heading straight toward me. The primal, autonomic system took over, and my pulse quickened. In my rattled state of mind, the closer they came, I imagined the specters of a dozen or so men. I was about to call out when a massive hand grabbed my shoulder, and its owner bellowed a hearty "Boo!"

I jerked reflexively, recoiling away and turning toward the intruder.

It was John Harris.

By the time I had regained my composure, the group of men approaching from the rear yard had arrived, and I recognized many of my groomsmen and a few other close friends. I turned back to John who was now staring at me impassively. He reached out, clinked my beer bottle with his, and spoke in a low, deadpan voice. "Surprise."

I gushed a half-laugh of relief. "Holy crap. That was just cold. You could have told me everyone was going to be here."

"Eh, what's the fun in that? Besides, sport. I'm lousy at lying and probably blunter than I should be when telling the truth. The best thing for me to do was say nothing." He took an appeasing swig of his beer and continued. "I knew you were too polite to ask me directly. So, looks like my plan worked."

"What's with the ghost riders coming up from the back forty?"

"That's where everybody parked to stay out of sight. But then some of the guys wanted to check out the old cemetery. So, they all went. The appearance of the walking dead wasn't intentional. But, from my viewpoint, it worked out perfectly." John grinned and took another drink of his beer, clearly quite pleased with himself.

By now Matthew had joined the group, and all the men had gathered and focused in my direction. John held up his hand to collect their attention. "Gentlemen, we are here this evening to celebrate and offer some friendly marital advice to our friend and town physician, Dr. Luke Bradford. We do this time-honored tradition because a man should be allowed to make his own mistakes. And, he should have the company of good friends while he does it. Our host, Matthew House has an array of munchies available, and there's plenty of beer. So, enjoy yourselves and don't track dirt into the house."

As if on cue, John's short speech was followed by a chorus of "here-here," and a raising of beer bottles. An explosion of laughter and conversation followed. Despite the ready humor that permeated the group, I doubted that a more dissimilar congress of personalities had ever been gathered together in the history of Watervalley.

Maylen Cook, Hoot Wilson, Toy McAnders, Gene Alley, and even the surly Luther Whitmore along with numerous others were in the mix. One by one they found a moment to shake my hand and congratulate me. Some readily imparted some marital wisdom; others …not so much.

Holding both a chicken wing and a beer, Hoot Wilson gave me a massive bear hug. "Doc, I gotta let you in on a little secret. I got engaged today."

"That's great, Hoot. Congratulations."

"Yeah," he proclaimed with stoic authority. "Karen and I decided we didn't want to steal your thunder. So, she didn't wear the ring tonight."

I did my best to muster an accommodating, complimentary tone. "Well, that was certainly thoughtful."

Hoot continued, speaking with philosophic reserve. "Yeah, I've been carrying the ring around for several days. I was going to propose tomorrow morning at the annual Bass Fishing Tournament down at the lake. I figured the two of us out on my flat bottom boat, doing what we both love would be the perfect time. But, turns out, she had to come out to the farm this morning because one of the milk cows had mastitis."

I nodded, doing my best to show great facial interest. "Well, nothing brings out true love better than a bacterial toxin."

Hoot gave me a glance of uncertainty but nodded nevertheless. "The moment just felt right, you know. So, I popped the question, and she gave me a big high-five yes." Having said this, he pantomimed the flinging of a rod and reel. "Yup, I can still reel them in, doc. Hoot Wilson, master caster." He grinned proudly and proceeded to suck the meat off of the chicken wing.

"All good stuff, Hoot. I'm happy for you."

"And I'm happy for you too, doc…although I hate to see you go. Hey, while you're doing research, think you could come up with a cure for brain freeze?" I smiled, nodded and said nothing. By now Matthew had joined us. Hoot turned to him.

462

"Great job with the eats, Matthew. It's nice to come to a gathering where there's real man food and no celery stalks stuffed with pimento cheese."

"Good to know," replied Matthew. "There's plenty more. Help yourself."

Hoot nodded and headed off. I turned to Matthew and spoke confidentially.

"I think the first rule of Hoot's diet is that bacon goes with everything."

Moments later Gene Alley approached me, and in his weird and wacky way, he detailed an elaborate assertion of how women are descended from centipedes. He ultimately took a conspiratorial glance from side to side and leaned in, speaking in a whisper. "You'll understand this when she moves her shoes into your closet. Just be prepared."

"Thanks, Gene," I said cautiously. "Good tip."

The conversations were nonstop; filled with a pungent brew of wit and humor. In time the men migrated into small groups, their faces illuminated by the faint glow of the fire. Despite the dissimilar mix of those present, exchanges were easy and effortless. Matthew threw more wood on the coals, and the laughter and robust voices continued, absorbed into the great vat of darkness that surrounded us.

After an hour or so I headed inside to take a quick bathroom break. Upon my return, I found John Harris in the kitchen. He was waiting for me.

"Well, Professor Harris. I didn't take you for a wallflower at your own gathering."

463

John responded with a slightly cynical lift of his eyebrow. "Hoot's telling an extended story about one of his cows. I hate missing it because I'm sure it's gripping stuff, but I wanted to talk with you offline for a minute."

"Sure. By the way, nice speech and toast at the dinner tonight. Normally people are offended when you're talking and terrified when you're done. But everybody seemed to love it."

John twisted his mouth to one side, assessing me coolly. "I'm going to let that one go, given how it's your big night and everything."

I grinned. "So, what's on your mind?"

"You're gone for two weeks, right?"

"Correct."

"Well, I wanted you to know that by the time you get back, Ann and I will be married."

"Wow! That's big. Congratulations."

Spontaneously, I shook his hand, and John's mood eased to mellow humor. "Yeah, I umm, I'm very happy about it. She's a great gal."

"That, she is."

John folded his arms and looked down for a moment, gathering his thoughts. "I want to thank you, Luke, for all the conversations along the way. For helping me negotiate my way out of the past. Molly will always be part of my life. For the longest time, the only thought I had of her was her loss, and that overshadowed the present, making every day a misery. But now, when I think of her, I think of her life and not her loss. I think of the many wonderful years we had together, and I'm grateful. You helped me see that. And you helped me see that there are new chapters to be written with Ann."

John finished, and a contented silence fell between us.

"So, you're happy?"

"Very happy."

"Good." I paused and moment, shaking my head. "It's been quite the night for matrimony. Hoot told me earlier that he and Karen are engaged."

"Really? Huh, good for Hoot. He's getting both a wife and a veterinarian in one package. I didn't realize they were that serious."

"Yeah, Hoot came and talked to me several months ago. Said that something was missing in his life."

"You mean other than a reliable deodorant?"

"Something like that."

Somewhere approaching midnight, one by one the men began to congratulate me once again and depart for home. I had spoken to most all of them except for my reserved, reticent barber, Maylen Cook. In his quiet, observant way, he simply wasn't one to initiate conversation. So, as he left, I shook his hand and asked him, "Maylen, any words of wisdom for a happy marriage?"

For the longest time, he stood there as if cut from stone. Then slowly, he lifted his hand to scratch his head, and in his immovable hang-dog manner, he spoke in a dispassionate monotone. "Become a mind reader."

By midnight, everyone had left except for John. Matthew pulled a third chair around the fire, and the three of us talked about Matthew's new role at the clinic.

"I'm glad that's working out," said John.

"Me, too. The whole Polly business was giving me second thoughts."

John stared reflectively into the fire. "Yeah, I figured the idiot fairy would pay you one last visit before you got out of town."

From the glow of the flames, I could discern Matthew quietly grinning. I replied appreciatively. "Thanks for the sentiment, John. Delicately couched as always."

Ignoring me, he stood and spoke briskly.

"Hey, I just realized. We're missing something here."

"You mean besides sleep."

John shot me an acerbic grin. "No, smartass. Hang tight, and I'll be right back."

"So," said Matthew. "The wedding's tomorrow at four and the reception is afterward out at Christine's farmhouse."

"Correct. We thought about having it at the bandstand over at the lake, but as you heard earlier, they're hosting the annual Watervalley Bass Fishing Tournament there in the morning. By the way, being in the Navy and everything. Are you a fishing kind of guy?"

"Not unless I can forego the whole 'baiting the hook' thing and shoot them with guns."

"I don't think the tournament has a category for that."

By now John had returned with a Scotch bottle and three glasses he had retrieved from the kitchen. "Boys," he said. "This is the last of the old Scotch bottles from the cave of Knox McAnders. Seems like an appropriate time to crack it open and have a toast."

Matthew regarded me curiously. "Knox was my first patient in Watervalley... a grand, old gentleman. He was a teenager when Hiram was here, and his family made Scotch. I'm sure they all knew each other."

Matthew smiled broadly. "Sounds fitting."

We toasted my marriage, John's imminent betrothal, and Matthew's grand new venture with the B&B as well as his new role at the clinic. Soon afterward, John departed. I knew he wasn't much for hugging a man unless it involved the Heimlich maneuver, but I gave him one anyway. I thanked him several times, and he departed for his car.

Oddly, despite my weariness, I didn't want the evening to end just yet. Matthew and I remained by the fire and talked more. Perhaps it was the Scotch, or merely the satisfaction at being so soundly immersed in the life of Watervalley, but Matthew began to open up and talk about his life; about being a missionary kid and about his experiences in high school and college before the Navy.

"So, what was your first real job?"

"I turned eighteen during my Freshman year of college. That next summer was my first real job. I was a youth counselor at a camp for troubled inner-city kids, most of them between twelve and fifteen."

"Hmm, interesting. What kind of stuff did you do?"

"One of my big responsibilities as a counselor was to get the kids to talk; to let them know it was safe to open up."

I shrugged and poked the coals, sending sparks skyward. "Makes sense. Anything come of that?"

"Oh, yeah. One night around the campfire these 14-year old boys from the inner city started talking about sex."

"How'd that go?"

Matthew's expression grew wide-eyed. "It was pretty graphic. I mostly just listened. And, being the mature adult figure in the group, I would occasionally inject thoughtful comments to help guide the conversation."

"Oh, yeah?

"Yeah. You know, comments like, 'It that right?' and, 'No way, are you for real?' and 'Explain that to me again.'"

I laughed almost to the point of tears. "Quite the education, huh?"

"Unbelievable."

We talked on until the fire was exhausted down to a few smoldering coals. Well past midnight, we returned inside, and I quite blissfully crawled into bed. But as I drifted off to sleep, one last delightful thought occurred to me.

It was already my wedding day.

Chapter 51

WEDDING

I woke early the next morning; pre-dawn early. Even though I had only slept a few hours, I was firmly awake, keen for the day before me. For some length of time I was content to quietly stare into the dark pale of my bedroom, listening, anticipating. The grand old house was serenely silent. By infinitely small degrees, the leisurely splendor of morning light began to emerge around the edges of the curtained windows. I dressed, gathered my things, and left Matthew a note of thanks on the kitchen counter.

After tossing my bag into the passenger seat of the Austin Healey, I stood for a moment and breathed in a deep draft of the crisp and glorious morning air. I was held spellbound by the broad and gallant light spreading across the far rim of eastern hills. The moment overflowed with hope, joy, expectation. The sound of morning birds; the wafting, living fragrance of the flowers and honeysuckle; and the whispering call of the distant woods and open countryside pulled at all my senses. I started my car and drove.

In the past year I had come to understand and accept my reluctant love affair with the people of Watervalley. But as I traveled the random backroads, I realized that an abiding affection for the streams, fields, and rolling meadows of this wide plane had also become part of me. The land of Watervalley, with all of its rough sawn pageantry, its raw and powerful geography, had permeated my bones. The valley had been an enduring friend and I felt drawn to spend some solitary time together before my departure.

My mind drifted as I passed into the sweeps and curves of the higher hills. Soon enough, however, my thoughts centered on Matthew and his new role at the clinic. I was grateful. I knew that an incredible burden had lifted from me. But I also knew that in Watervalley, being welcomed was one thing. Being accepted was another. And yet, Matthew seemed to have effortlessly traversed that boundary.

As I had noticed before at church and had observed the previous evening, despite Matthew's clipped reserve, it occurred to me that he was the unqualified owner of the common touch. He easily accepted and admired people who, however plain or peculiar, were nobody but themselves. And yet with the blue bloods of the valley, he had the confidence and social ease of one who had emancipated himself from the need to curry favor or drop names. With his amiable, completely inoffensive nature, his response to everyone was warm and natural. He was at ease with everyone.

I realized that my simplified assessment of him on Christmas Eve had been completely incorrect and there was still much about him I did not know. He could be pragmatic yet preoccupied, shy yet fearless. No doubt, he had a powerful intellect. But it was coupled with a kind of wise humility. And he was blessed with the pedestrian old-school virtues of loyalty, respect, and a distaste for flaunted wealth, for gossip, for bragging. As much as I thought I knew him, I could rarely own that I knew what he was thinking at a given moment. And yet, without any knowledge of his medical skills, I knew that I was leaving the town in good hands.

In time my drive into the high hills brought me to the Watervalley Overlook about a mile from the County Line Market. It was the same place where nearly two years ago I had stopped on my first day in Watervalley to catch an initial glimpse of my new life. Moments before on that same day, I had had a thorny encounter with the man who would eventually become my best friend, John Harris.

After pulling to a stop, I emerged and leaned against the car, taking in the grand panorama below. The landscape was brilliantly illuminated with the fresh and clean austerity of sunrise; the world before me was unchanged, pristine, timeless.

I could only laugh at my own foolishness. I had arrived in Watervalley thinking that I would live out the seasons in obscurity; that cruel chance had stuck me here to wither while a better life eluded me. On reflection, I had been wrong. Watervalley had been kind to me. I had found friends who were lasting, a love who was virtuous and beautiful, and truths that were eternal. I now understood that such things were foundational to a good and happy life. All else was glitter, sound, and fury.

Conversely, even though my time here had gone well, my coming to Watervalley was not just a fortuitous accident. Standing there, I realized that on the day of my arrival, when I had stopped the car on the high overlook and gained my first view of the town far below, that the gust of wind rustling the leaves of the nearby trees had also wafted open a magic door to a splendid and more abundant life. In Watervalley I had found the broad land of a richer world. Here there was an order to life that permeated the day; a clarity that didn't exist in the tangled and untamed chapters of the life I had known before. The simple elements of the rural life; love, faith, work, the sun, the seasons, and the soil all came together here and taught one how to be wise by easier means, to hold tight to those things that were good and true and enduring.

The morning sun continued to expand across the wide floor of the valley and the warm breath of June began to replace the remnant nighttime air. I took one last look. I knew that this would be a day of moments; captured images that would be kept a lifetime. This one held its own perfection. I started the car and headed back to town.

The balance of the day became a blur, as all such days do.

It seemed that the next few hours of my life were fast-forwarded. I remember eating breakfast at the diner and being constantly greeted and lauded like a Hollywood celebrity. Last minute phone calls and coordination tasks filled the day. Dogs, dry cleaning, gifts, airline tickets, luggage, passports, keys, tuxedos, rings, laughter, excitement, and arrival times were discussed and re-discussed, all hurling together at a surreal and blinding pace.

Driving his new AMG S 63 Mercedes sedan, John arrived at my house in the early afternoon and followed me to Christine's. I left my car near the road at the end of the long drive for our getaway after the reception. I climbed into the passenger seat of John's car and we headed back to town.

"Nice wheels. How much did this set you back?"

He spoke with seasoned indifference. "About a buck and a half. Not that it's any of your business."

"Pace yourself now, big fellow. I realize that the strain of being on your best behavior for so many hours is going to be hard to sustain. But try to play nice for as long as possible." As was normal, John ignored me.

"So, any last-minute regrets?"

"Given your general personality, John, are you sure that's a question you should be asking?"

"Knock it off, smartass. I'm serious."

I laughed and gazed at the countryside gliding by. "Oh, not really. I haven't talked about it much. But it would have been nice if my parents could have been part of this day. I'm sure Christine feels that way about her father."

John nodded reflectively. "Well, I'm sure they would have been damn proud of you, sport."

"I'd like to think so," I said thoughtfully. "But hey, I'll have you and Connie as my surrogate parents. I'll just pretend I'm your two's imaginary love child."

John turned to me, his face twisted in a hard, scrutinizing frown. He was thinking. I returned his gaze with a tightened, studied grimace. After another moment's consideration, we both spoke simultaneously.

"Naaaaah…"

John refocused on the road ahead, now wearing a scowling smirk. He addressed me in a low, instructive voice. "Don't ever go there again."

"Understood."

We passed the remainder of the trip to my house in a silent but mirthful comradery. As had been planned, John had brought his tux. We both changed, went over last-minute details, and arrived at the church as instructed at two o'clock, a full two hours early.

So now, we waited.

There was a sizable conference room adjacent to Pastor Dawson's office where Christine and I had undergone our marital counseling. This was to be my temporary purgatory until making an appearance through a sanctuary side door a few minutes before the ceremony. In time all of the groomsmen arrived. To a man they were neatly tailored and focused but stiffer than a fence post. All of them, that is, except John. With his imposing presence and swagger, he had them laughing and light-hearted within a matter of minutes. Moments later, Joe Dawson appeared at the door and in his unfailing, cheerful manner, announced that guests were beginning to arrive. John and all the groomsmen departed, leaving me with my thoughts and my watch that, over the next hour and a half, I would glance at some three million times.

In contrast to the light-speed pace of the earlier hours, time now stopped. I did my best to occupy my thoughts, but with little success. I was jittery, edgy, uncertain as to what I should do with this pre-nuptial gap. The room also served as Joe's library. But this wasn't a time to start a book, or check e-mails, or catch up on baseball scores. So, I sat, occasionally checked my watch, and waited.

Long minutes later, however, I heard the footfalls and rustling of very animated female voices in the hallway. I couldn't catch Christine's in the mix, but I was certain that she and the bridesmaids had made their arrival. An amazing insight occurred to me. Of the endless details that I had dealt with throughout the day, there was one thing I hadn't thought about: her.

It was a rush of blood to the head; a flushing, intoxicating, realization. That spirited, gorgeous woman I had so awkwardly met on that August morning was to be the one. Her presence had changed the arc of my life's trajectory for all the days that would follow. I had captured her heart and she, mine. A grand, pleased smile inched across my face.

Yet admittedly, my thoughts then moved to a more primitive plane.

Perhaps like all men, somewhere deep within me was the awestruck schoolboy who awakens one morning to realize that all of his thoughts are consumed with the opposite sex. His entire world is dominated by that first obsessive primal awareness of curves, lips, hair, eyes. I was far from being an adolescent. But it seemed that the voice of that long-ago schoolboy was now murmuring in my ear, full of red-blooded anticipation of the fruit that soon would no longer be forbidden. He was shamelessly whispering, "You are about to be so lucky." My smile sharpened to a proud, puckish grin. Indulging in the moment, I couldn't have agreed more.

I glanced at my watch. The ceremony was still an hour away. Leaning back in the chair, I closed my eyes, blissfully unaware of the drama unfolding in the sanctuary.

As it turns out, in regard to my leaving town, the people of Watervalley didn't necessarily hold a grudge. But they did hold an opinion. I had made a unilateral decision that affected their lives, yet they had been offered no opportunity to vote their point of view. Amazingly, the news of Matthew's new role at the clinic was still largely unknown. Thus, the wedding ceremony served as a passive ballot box, a way to express a small note of resentment.

As the first guest arrived, they declared themselves as friends of the bride and were appropriately seated on the left side of the church. But quickly, a pattern emerged. Within twenty minutes, the entire left side of the church was full while the right side had only a dozen or so, including Mathew and his son Andrew along with the wives of the groomsmen. Later arrivals refused to be escorted to the right side and chose to simply stand along the outer left side wall. Eventually, people were backed up into the Narthex and the whole affair was about to reach a point of crisis.

That was, until Connie arrived.

Quickly assessing the situation, she walked to the front of the church, climbed two steps to the pulpit level, and turned toward the crowd with a look that would pulverize concrete.

"Listen up, folks. I know you're all trying to prove a point here, but this is not the time or place. This is the wedding of two fine young people; not an opportunity to air your hurt feelings. So, if over the last two years, you or one of your loved ones have been affected in a positive way by Luke Bradford, then you need to get up and move to the other side. But, if by some miracle of the good Lord you don't think that counts for anything, then by all means, keep your self-righteous fanny right where it is. Alright, people. I've said my piece. Now, what's it going to be?"

I wasn't there, but I was later given several accounts by friends who swore that upon finishing, Connie's eyes exuded a strange orange heat. What followed was a near stampede as an entire block of people shifted to the right side of the church, causing the old building to moan under the burden. The narthex crowd backfilled the left side. But the transfer had been so absolute, Connie nearly had to redirect some of the migrants back across to the left side. Eventually, all the pew seats were filled and both outer walls were lined shoulder to shoulder. At the time, Christine and I were none the wiser. At four, Joe came and for me.

We entered from a side door near the front. From there I went and stood on the small X that had been taped to the floor. I was wearing an irrepressible smile and looking a lot more confident than I felt. Christine's mother and grandmother were escorted in and seated. The groomsmen moved to their appointed "X" on the floor and then, as the organ played, the bridesmaids each made a slow processional down the aisle and took their place...all nine of them. It was an eternity. I thought I might need to shave again by the time they finished.

What followed was an unexpected surprise. A bagpipe player, dressed in full regalia, made his way forward playing a distantly familiar tune. He stopped at the front to finish and while doing so, Adelyn House came with a basket of rose petals, carefully scattering them along the way. In her lacy white dress and with a light blue ribbon in her blonde hair, she looked absolutely angelic. She walked with a steady gait but was delightedly looking up at all the smiles around her. After reaching the front of the church, she threw out the last petal. Then, curiously, she winked at me in that overly accentuated manner of young children whose motor skills lacked subtlety. A moment later, the wedding march began.

Escorted by John, Christine appeared at the open Narthex doors and proceeded forward. She came proudly, her warm curves molded into her pristine wedding dress. Her every movement was fluid, full of effortless grace. As she grew closer, her smile was tender and melted.

There was liquid stealth in her deep and adoring eyes, as if she were searching every nuance, every gesture of my affectionate gaze.

To my delight, I was stunned. Before me was a woman at the flawless pinnacle of her natural beauty, a rose that was yet to lose a single petal. But there was something more, something profound in her presence that I was yet to grasp. Except for the thin canopy of her veil, Christine's shoulders and slender arms were fully exposed, revealing a tempting measure of her tanned and sumptuous skin. Against the crisp white of her dress, the combination was transcendent, a divine blend of regal and seductive. This seamless fusion of the virtuous and the sensuous was unforeseen, provocative, bewitching. Instantly, she went drunkenly to my head; an opiate that crowded out all else save for a burning escalation of both reverence and desire in equal measure. I was speechless, and my astonished face did little to hide it. If her intention was to astound me, she had overwhelmingly succeeded.

Joe began the ceremony, but his words fell away. All the candles, and the sounds, and the people, vanished. There was only Christine, looking at me with perfect brown eyes that were sweet, and affectionate, and yielding. I said the vows, knelt for the prayers, and heard the music. But my gaze was transfixed.

Spellbound into the deep well of her eyes, I was reminded of my previous revelation about this small place on earth. Christine and the incredible beauty of the valley were natural companions. There was something intrinsic and inseparable shared between them. In the warmth of her loving gaze, in the fresh and wholesome light of her face, there was something of the rolling fields, the wind and sky; the billowing grasses of the high meadows --earthy, sensuous, bursting with health. I knew that one day I would return, if for no other reason than to witness the animated splendor in Christine's eyes as she breathed in the unvanquished air of this tucked-away valley, this small Eden.

It seemed that the ceremony had scarcely begun when I heard Joe pronounce the words, "Man and Wife," and "You may kiss the bride." I did so with gusto.

The explosive sound of the organ filled the church and we ecstatically made our way along the aisle and down the front steps before retreating along the side back to Joe's office. The crowd departed for the reception while and pictures were taken in the sanctuary. Soon enough, we were in the back seat of John's car and headed to Christine's farmhouse where the grand gathering would soon begin. Christine and I looked at each other with bursting smiles and yet with an easily acknowledged awkwardness. Everything up to this moment had been scripted. But now was different. Now was live. I spoke first.

"So, how do you feel Mrs. Bradford?"

She laughed, an open affirmation of the previous moment's clumsiness. "I feel perfectly happy, Dr. Bradford. And you?"

"Never better."

"You did just fine with the ceremony."

"Thanks. By the way, I did say yes, didn't I?"

"Pretty sure."

"Good. That part was a little tricky."

"I noticed that you seemed a little pre-occupied."

"Well, Mrs. Incredible, Knock-Out, Gorgeous. Can't imagine what in the world I might have been thinking about."

Christine smiled demurely. "Are you saying you like my dress?"

"Yes. And I like what's in it, too."

Having heard this, John spoke abruptly from the front seat. "Okay, you two. Let's try to maintain our PG rating for the balance of this little excursion."

"My," I said jovially. "Would you listen to Professor Prude up there." I leaned forward and addressed him in a confidential voice. "It's okay, John. The lady and I are married."

John grunted. "Like hell. Legal does not equate to allowed."

Christine and I giggled. "Not to worry," I said. "I'm pretty sure no one in the aft compartment has any issues with impulse control."

Christine immediately nudged me, offered a taunting grin, and spoke in an enticing whisper. "Speak for yourself."

Chapter 52

BEAUTIFUL IN ITS TIME

The reception was every bit the grand affair that I had surreptitiously gathered it would be. Despite her normal reserve, Madeline Chambers had apparently decided to reaffirm to Watervalley that she was still a banker's daughter. The channeling of her Cavanaugh roots undoubtedly found a kindred spirit in her mother-in-law, Mattie Chambers, whose perpetual saucy nature had no qualms with exacting a little one-upmanship to any of the valley's blue-bloods, self-proclaimed or otherwise. This wedding and reception wasn't just going to be the event of the season. It was going to be the event of a lifetime; a demarcation in the town's social history. Additionally, it occurred to me that my being a doctor probably fit the script rather nicely.

There was not just one, but two bands. They took turns alternating between sessions of rock and country followed by jazz and big band music. The tables of food went on forever, containing a selection that would make a cruise ship Captain envious. And as would be expected, Bacchus made a grand appearance. Wine and beer were in plentiful supply, and mixed drinks were available provided one had patience and determination. There was an intentional funneling of access to the hard stuff…not so much in an effort to be penny-pinching, but more to provide a governor to those who had a propensity to go full throttle when it was free.

As was planned, a large drone circled high above, videoing all that was below and occasionally making a swooping dive for a close-up. Some of the more rough-hewn farmers saw this as a suspicious intrusion. One or two of them shouldered up to me with beer in hand and let it be known that their truck had a rifle rack and that they would be glad to take care of the annoyance. I convinced them to ease off of that idea for a while and then immediately found the drone operator, advising him to keep it high and wide.

Christine and I were constantly pulled away from each other for it seemed that everyone wanted their moment with us. I guess it was understandable. We were the reason they had come. At one point, John slid in beside me. He put his hand on my shoulder, never breaking his focus at the large crowd. "How are you holding up, sport?"

"I'm grand. Just taking it all in. Looks like our in-laws know how to throw a rather grand shindig."

"You noticed, huh?"

"Yeah, the only thing missing is you being tucked away in a dark paneled room with a bunch of Mafioso types, granting wishes to the little people."

"That sounds more like Connie's department. She's the one that parted the waters over at the church."

"So, I heard."

"I saw it unfolding. But Constance Grace was the one who knew how to fix it. She's always had that knack of finding the right words. God knows that's why I love her."

I grinned and briefly glanced at John in a gesture of acknowledgment. "Don't we all."

He exhaled a long, slow sigh. "Meanwhile, here we are in Watervalley. And that little stunt at the church is just a reminder that stupidity is never lacking."

I shrugged and smiled. "They're just people, John. Just folks of average destinies who struggle to understand why I feel so compelled to pursue work in the stiff, ivory-towered world of academia."

"Eh, maybe you're right. Anyway, looks like you'll still have a toe back in this world."

"That's the plan. It's worked out wonderfully. I think Matthew will do an excellent job."

"Yeah, what about him anyway?"

"What do you mean?"

"I can't quite figure him out. I mean, it's impossible not to like the guy. But I never feel like I know what he's thinking. He scares me."

I turned and faced John, dumbfounded. "He scares you?"

He was dismissive. "I'm not saying he frightens me. I'm just saying I can't get a consistent read on him. He may be smarter than all of us."

"Well," I said, returning my gaze to the crowd. "That may very well be the case. And for the town's sake, let's hope so."

John nodded. Spontaneously, it seemed our eyes were drawn to Christine who was in an animated conversation a short distance away. His eyes softened and spoke with muted pride. "You've won the grand prize with that one, Bradford."

My response was low and breezy. "Oh, don't I know it."

"Her dad would have liked you."

"Because I'm a doctor?"

He glanced at me sourly. "No. Albert Chambers wouldn't give a rat's ass about that. He would have liked you because you're a good man. You've got a generous heart. You don't give up on people. Christine got her poise and style from her mom. Madeline is a wholesome soul and a class act. But Christine got her grit and love of the soil from her dad. He was a noble man and an enduring friend."

"Well, on that subject. Don't you have a father-daughter dance coming up here shortly?"

"True enough. Not that I'm comfortable with it."

"It's a slow dance, John. Just let Christine lead."

"That's not what I meant, smartass."

I laughed. "I know what you meant, John. But you're a better man than you think. Life's given you some tough chapters. But this is one day, one page that's a good one. Christine adores you. She knows you're not her dad. But she definitely has some of your fire. This is her day and you're her surrogate father. Enjoy every second of it." I paused a moment and looked him in the eye. "And John, thanks for everything."

He shook my hand and said nothing more. For some time, we stood with each other and watched the roar and conversation of the crowd. He seemed grandly content to stay close, to keep in my company. I would miss him, and I got the sense that he was realizing the same.

Dozens more came by to congratulate me and shake my hand. By now word had spread about Matthew's new role and that I would still have an arms-length involvement with the clinic. One by one, I could see a change in the eyes of these hearty, rugged men and women.

The previous doubt was now replaced with an unspoken gratefulness. It seemed that the last vestige of any shadowy issues had been cleansed away. The day had attained an unforeseen perfection.

Soon afterward, while everybody watched, Christine and I performed the opening dance. It was delightful and slow. For some reason, we were beyond words and fully comfortable to simply smile adoringly at each other. A dance between John and Christine followed. As soon as it began, I went and found Connie. She was seated and resistant to the idea. But I insisted and grabbed her hand.

"Come on, woman. You're dancing with me." Reluctantly, she agreed, and I led her to the dance floor. Our arrival brought out a low roar and applause from the crowd. Even Christine and John stopped and clapped. Connie draped her arm over my shoulder and I spoke in a low voice. "I understand you had to direct traffic a little back at the church."

"Oh, it was nothing. Just a little teachable moment for a few of the neighbors."

"Sorry I missed it. Are you enjoying yourself?"

"Tremendously, up until about four minutes ago when some fool asked me to dance."

"And I love you, too, Connie."

"Oh, stop it. I'm just afraid I'll get all blubbery with everybody watching."

"I think that would be fine, Connie. In fact, it might prove a point. Most of them think you don't have a drop of water in you."

"My, my. You are the charmer, aren't you?"

I ignored her. "Connie, have I ever told you thank you?"

"For what?"

"For everything. For always being there. For taking care of me. For just being you."

"It's not necessary."

"Okay. Fine, then. I won't."

"Don't push your luck, doctor boy. 'It's not necessary,' is only an expression."

I cut my eyes at her and grinned. She looked up and met my stern gaze with an equal measure of glaring disdain. But I could see the corners of her mouth begin to crumble, and soon a broad grin erupted. I leaned in close to her ear and whispered.

"I love you, Constance Grace. And I always will."

In that moment, Connie seemed to have lost all of her defensive measures. "I love you, too, Luke." She pressed her lips together firmly, and large tears began to emerge in her eyes. We continued our slow, shuffling dance until eventually, she did her best to smooth away the tears streaming down her face. Gathering herself, she spoke in a kind but resolute voice.

"Thanks for the dance, Luke. But I want you to know that as soon as we're done, I plan on smacking you for making me cry in front of everybody."

"Not a problem."

The band kicked up a lively tune, and the dance floor filled immediately. For the next couple of hours, everyone celebrated. The laughter, the merriment, and the smiles were endless. At some point, Christine did the traditional toss of her bouquet to a rather sizeable crowd of anxious and surprisingly aggressive singles. Apparently, in the business of matrimony, all possible good omens were given full credence. Along the way I enjoyed a delightful slow dance with Madeline Chambers who was more talkative and animated than I had ever seen her. I was reminded of how much I truly liked her, and I knew that in the category of mother-in-law, I was fortunate.

It was near time to go inside and change when I felt a small hand tug on my coat sleeve. It was Adelyn House. Almost instinctively, I smiled and picked her up, balancing her on my hip.

"Adelyn, you did a wonderful job as the flower girl. You were beautiful."

She spoke with a polite and careful pronunciation of her words.

"You're welcome. I have to leave now because Andrew and I have to go home. It's almost our bedtime."

"I understand. Thank you for coming and telling me."

"I also want to congratulate you. Daddy said that's what people are supposed to do."

"That's right. And thank you for that, too. But that wink you gave me at the church was congratulations enough."

With her grandly expressive face, Adelyn stiffened her neck and gave me a puzzling look. "That wasn't a congratulation. That was about the angels."

It took me a moment to assimilate what she was saying. Then, I remembered. I spoke in an accommodating voice, endeavoring to humor her. "Oh, I see. And were there many angels there?"

She nodded her head up and down emphatically. "A lot. And three of them were your friends."

I looked at her curiously. "My friends?"

"Umm-hmm. The three people in the picture at your house. The one with you as a little boy. They were there."

Forgetting all manner of etiquette, I could do little more than stare at her blankly. I was speechless. She was referring to the picture of my parents and my Aunt Grace. Adelyn was a gifted child, yet it seemed unlikely she would have concocted such a tale out of the blue, much less have the planning and forethought to wink at me as a staging for a later story. Part of me was doubtful. And yet, from deep within was a voice that cautiously hoped that perhaps it was true. I simply couldn't know for sure. Regaining myself, I smiled and thanked her once again. I set her down and watched her walk to her waiting brother. The day held fascinations that were larger than I knew.

Soon it was time to change and make our getaway. As planned, I was changed, ready, and waiting in the front entry hall shortly after eight. As was not planned, Christine arrive some twenty minutes later. I sat patiently and chatted with the photographer, knowing that this might be a harbinger of married life. But when she did appear down the steps, the wait was all but forgotten. She was gorgeous. Wearing a light blue sundress, she looked incredible. She hugged her mother and turned to me.

I took her hand. "You ready for this?"

Under a virtual downpour of rice and a continuous roar of cheers, we dashed our way to Mr. Clancy's carriage. After we climbed aboard, I held my breath to see if the old horse could exert the necessary inertia to get the wheels moving. To my delight, she took off abruptly; so much so that Mr. Clancy had to reign her in.

The long driveway was lined with people shouting and clapping and waving goodbye. Oil lamps had been placed along both sides, providing an enchanting illumination against the waning twilight. The moment seemed incredible, dreamlike, surreal. I was leaving Watervalley.

To my amazement, that reality threw me, and there was an unexpected moment of genuine apprehension. But it passed quickly. With my new bride, I was about to embark on an extraordinary adventure, a new and different episode on my life. When it was done, Watervalley would be here. The farmers would still plow their fields, Maylen would still cut hair, and Mayor Hickman would continue to dream up idiotic ideas that would prove that the space between his ears housed a perpetual vacancy. The seasons would roll forward, life would continue, the earth would endure. Watervalley would grow and change, but not so much as to lose its identity. For me, there was a deep and abiding comfort in that knowledge.

Christine roused me from my temporary trance. "Sweetheart, it's time to keep your promise."

"My promise?"

"Yes, Luke. The honeymoon."

"Oh, right. The honeymoon. Well, tonight is Nashville, the Presidential Suite of the Hermitage Hotel. Tomorrow afternoon we catch a plane to Rome, first class, mind you. We spend the night there and then take the train to a place called Poggio Ai Santi. It's in Tuscany and overlooks the Mediterranean. A week later we take the Eurail up through Provence to a place called Chateau De Rochecotte. We stay there for a few days and then to Paris for a few more. From Paris, we fly home."

For the first time in memory, Christine was speechless. She flatly stared at me in a blend of excited disbelief. "Wow. That was too detailed. You couldn't have just made it up."

"Of course not. That's it. That's our honeymoon."

"I was thinking something at the beach in Florida or maybe a place in the Caribbean. But Italy and France?"

"Italy and France."

"How are you affording this?"

I laughed and shrugged lightly. "I'm not."

"I don't understand."

"Your Uncle John. He's paying for all of it."

"Uncle John is paying for it?"

"Yup. I fought him tooth and nail but, in the end, he insisted. His only requirement was that I not tell anyone. Because, if where we were going got out, you would know something was up. He didn't want to have to deal with any discussions on the subject."

"So that's why all the silence on the honeymoon?"

"That's why."

"Wow," she said again in disbelief. "My sweet Uncle John."

"You may be the only person alive who would put those words in the same sentence. But at any rate, I think he loves you more than you know."

Christine looked at me artfully. "I think he loves *you* more you know."

I gazed downward and smiled. "Could be."

After a moment, I took Christine's hand. "All I know is that for the next two weeks, we are in for an incredible time."

By now we had reached the end of the drive and Mr. Clancy pulled the old horse to a stop. The sides of Summerfield Road were lined with parked cars. A number of the guests were already there waiting, primarily to see my reaction at the state of my Austin Healey. As I helped Christine down from the carriage, she put her hand to her mouth in dismay. "Oh, Luke. Look what they did."

My car was covered in shaving cream and glitter. There was soap writing on the windshield along with several long strands of rope adorned with cans and bells. It was a disaster. I was unaffected.

As we walked toward it, I spoke with great amusement. "Looks like they did a masterful job of trashing the blue baby."

Christine looked at me curiously. "What are we going to do?"

Never breaking stride, I smiled and grabbed her hand. "Come with me."

We went hurriedly past my car and then three cars beyond. I reached in my pocket and grabbed the keyless remote. The lights of the next car ahead blinked. I released Christine's hand and nodded toward the passenger side. "Hop in."

She did so. Seconds later, we were pulling away before any of the pranksters had a chance to catch up or realize what we had done. We were in John's new AMG Mercedes.

"Luke. This car is incredible."

"Yeah, John bought it two days ago. We're just borrowing it, though."

"Where's all our stuff?"

"In the trunk. That's why I had you leave your luggage at my house."

"So, you and John had this all planned out?"

"Absolutely, this was your day, sweetheart. I wanted it to be perfect."

Christine turned and stared ahead in a mixture of astonishment and adoration. I remained focused on the road but occasionally looked her way with a quiet, contented smile. In time her eyes softened, and she turned toward me, searching my face. She was incandescently happy.

"Something on your mind, brown eyes?"

She leaned back against her seat absorbing the moment.. "Yes," she said with quiet confidence. "I have something I want to tell you."

I looked her cautiously. "Okay."

"I love you, Luke Bradford. I look at you and I see the answer to a lifetime of searching, of wondering, of prayers. Being with you has been a dream that I thought would never happen. So, this may sound a little silly, but thank-you. Thank-you for pursuing me even though I kept turning you down. Thank you for being willing to stay in Watervalley because you thought that would make me happy. Thank you for loving me even though we may never be able to have children of our own. And thank you for making this day perfect, more so than I had ever imagined."

I smiled warmly. "I've been in love with you from day one, Christine. So, all those things were easy." I let a long moment pass and then added. "Now, on the other hand, dealing with your grandmother…"

"Stop," she blurted teasingly, shaking her head. "Is there a serious bone in your body?"

"Does there need to be?"

"I guess you have a point."

We rode along in silence. But after a short while, she leaned toward me and spoke in a sultry whisper. "So, all that is to say that I want everything to be the perfect for you, too." She paused, moving closer to my ear. "And this day isn't over yet."

I spoke quietly and emphatically. "Sweetheart, I have no doubts on that subject."

A pleased, impish grin emerged, and she tucked a loose strand of her long hair away.

"Luke, can I ask you a question?"

"Sure."

"During the ceremony, you seemed distracted. You were looking at me the entire time, but you seemed elsewhere. Am I getting that wrong?"

"Oh, I was there the whole time. I was just looking into your eyes."

She seemed unconvinced and lifted an amused but wary eyebrow, no doubt, somewhat skeptical of my response. "I see. And tell me, Luke Bradford," she said playfully. "What do you see when you look in my eyes."

I didn't speak immediately. I doubted I would ever be able to put into words the depth of love I had for her; of how when I looked into the well of her eyes, I saw all the possibilities for happiness that one lifetime could hold. It seemed that so many things about her would always fascinate me, would always amaze me, would always be a mystery to me. And oddly, I knew that I wouldn't want it any other way.

In time, I turned to her, smiled, and answered with a single word.

"Forever."

POSTLUDE

Eight Months Later

Luke smiled at the receptionist but never broke stride. He was late; shamefully late. He knew the white coat and the physician's medical ID gave him a license to bluff his way past without checking in. But once he slipped through the door to the clinic hall, he was lost. Christine had texted him the exam room number, but Vanderbilt Women's Health was a large enterprise. A passing nurse read his apprehension. Before she could speak, he blurted, "Exam room seventeen?"

"Down the hall and to the right?"

"Thanks!"

He stepped quickly. By all calculations, this was week eighteen and missing the first ultrasound was punishable by public flogging. Acts of contrition performed in the name of marriage maintenance would be required. Rounding the corner of the long hall, the thought occurred to him; flogging might be preferable.

He shoved opened the exam room door and began a litany of apologies.

"Sorry, sorry. I got caught up in a phone call with Matthew. Big happenings on the home front. But, it can wait. So, where are we? Are we done? Did I miss it?"

Dr. Tian, the OB-GYN was stretched out in the chair next to the exam table, conversing lightly with Christine. Despite her full-blooded Chinese heritage, she spoke with a thick southern drawl, having been born and raised in the town of Cullman, Alabama.

"Well, Luke. You got here on the right day. There might be a few style points for that."

"I can lie on the floor and let you kick me for a while."

Dr. Tian smiled at Christine, offering her a conspiratorial wink. "Hold that thought," she said to Luke as she rose from her chair. "We did take a preliminary peek while we were waiting."

He turned to Christine. "So, what's the news?" She looked at Dr. Tian, the two of them exchanging a silent, mischievous glance.

Dr. Tian filled the void. "Why don't we show you?"

Luke sharpened his gaze, searching back and forth between the two of them. As Dr. Tian began to slowly glide the probe across Christine's swollen abdomen, Luke studied the monitor intensely. The confusion on his face was easily read.

"Okay, I know I have a medical degree and a nifty monogramed white coat to prove it....but, I'm clueless. What am I looking at here?"

Finally breaking her silence, Christine gazed at him tenderly.

"Triplets."

ACKNOWLEDGEMENTS

Many thanks to my devoted readers who have waited so patiently for this story. Seriously. I mean it. I'll try not to be so long with the next one.

As always, thanks to my family and friends for their continued love and support.

Thanks to Lisa Strong for her wonderful artwork for the cover. Pay her a visit at https://lisastrongart.com/.

And special thanks to Bill and Teresa for their fabulous assistance with editing.

Jeff High is the award winning and bestselling author of the Watervalley Series. After growing up on a farm in rural Tennessee, he attained degrees in literature and nursing. He worked for many years at Vanderbilt University Medical Center and as a travel nurse in open-heart surgery. When not at the keyboard, he divides his time between his farm in Tennessee and working as an RN in Augusta, Georgia.

For stories, gossip, and anecdotes from your favorite Watervalley characters, visit

watervalleybooks.com

Because…there may not be a lot to see in Watervalley, but what you hear makes up for it!

And hey, like us on Facebook!

www.facebook.com/JeffHighWriter/

We'll love you for doing it!

37411212R00302

Made in the USA
Middletown, DE
26 February 2019